# The Unaccomplished
# Lady Eleanor

# The Unaccomplished Lady Eleanor

*Wendy Burdess*

ROBERT HALE · LONDON

© Wendy Burdess 2007
First published in Great Britain 2007

ISBN 978-0-7090-8414-3

Robert Hale Limited
Clerkenwell House
Clerkenwell Green
London EC1R 0HT

The right of Wendy Burdess to be identified as
author of this work has been asserted by her
in accordance with the Copyright, Designs and
Patents Act 1988

2 4 6 8 10 9 7 5 3 1

Typeset in 10/13½pt Goudy
by Derek Doyle & Associates, Shaw Heath
Printed and bound in Great Britain
by Biddles Limited, King's Lynn

# CHAPTER 1

Nottingham, England – May 1815

ELEANOR Myers was miserable. In fact, in all her nineteen years and five months, she could rarely recall ever feeling more miserable. The wretched interminable carriage journey was merely adding to her despondency: the lumbering and jolting of the conveyance, mirroring perfectly the combination of emotions roiling and jostling in her stomach. The weather too was doing little to alleviate her sombre mood, foregoing all the meteorological characteristics normally associated with the first week of May in favour of those more attuned to a typical day in autumn. The sky, a menacing shade of grey, had been blithely dispensing a series of heavy downpours throughout the day and, by the sound of fresh plump drops clattering loudly on the roof of the carriage, was on the verge of providing yet another unwelcome torrent.

Sighing heavily, Eleanor closed her eyes and leaned her head against the plush blue velvet squabs, pondering her dire predicament. The anger and resentment which had been coursing furiously through her veins since the previous evening, when her stepmother and her father had elected to make their 'announcement', had now melted away to be replaced by a deep sense of dread.

Of course, she had known from the moment her father had brought his new wife into their home that things would never be the same: that the woman was more than likely to implement some changes to the running of the household at Merryoaks despite Eleanor having done an admirable job of managing the domestic side of the estate herself for the last six years. Perhaps,

she had naïvely thought, the new Lady Myers would wish to change the laun-
dry day, or take in hand the rather volatile behaviour of their long-standing
cook, whose erratic moods produced a variety of culinary results ranging from
absolutely outstanding to disastrously diabolical depending on her tempera-
ment and the alleged shape of the moon, on any particular day. To her chagrin
however, it was not cook who had borne the wrath of the newest addition to
the household but, rather unexpectedly, Eleanor herself.

Recalling her rather inauspicious first meeting with the woman, perhaps
she should not be so surprised at the way matters had turned out. Her father
had invited the then Hester Scones to dinner in order that his fiancée and his
only child could make one another's acquaintance. Despite her well-planned
intentions for the day Eleanor had found herself embroiled in a mission of
mercy with Zach, the local farmer, aiding his rescue of a stray lamb, which
had, by seemingly miraculous means, ended up on the opposite side of the
river to the rest of the flock. Far from being distressed by its lonely predicament, the lamb had appeared completely content, demonstrating no inclination whatsoever, despite their energetic attempts, to return to its fold. The
rather messy, but hilariously funny task had lasted most of the day and had
resulted, finally, in one rather indignant lamb being returned to its rightful
place and a rather dishevelled Eleanor arriving home much later than
planned. Placing more importance on welcoming the woman her father had
fallen in love with than wasting time first changing her attire, she had
bowled, somewhat effusively, into the drawing-room eager to meet her future
stepmama. It had been clear, however, from the cool, disparaging look with
which Hester Scones had first greeted her, that Eleanor's enthusiasm was
entirely one-sided.

'Really, my girl,' the future Lady Myers had sniffed, as she'd examined
Eleanor balefully through ice-cold blue eyes, 'I would have expected you to
have made a little more effort given the significance of the occasion.'

Eleanor had thought at first that the older woman had been joking, but
one did not need to be long acquainted with Hester Scones to realize that
the woman never joked. In fact, Eleanor had wondered, on more than one
humourless occasion, if Hester actually knew what a joke was. Quite unaccustomed to such rudeness, Eleanor had attempted to maintain her welcoming smile whilst explaining the comical adventure which had resulted in her
tardiness. She had a particular gift for relating an entertaining tale – so
much so that her hilarious recounting of some of the pickles in which she
had found herself had often reduced her father to tears of laughter. But that

evening, it had soon become clear that all attempts at humour were completely futile as even her normally ebullient papa appeared to have discarded his ready sense of humour under the spell of the poker-faced widow he was soon to make his wife.

The recounting of humorous tales though was just one of many of Eleanor's attributes upon which the new Lady Myers thought fit to pour scorn. After only a few weeks in her new home, the woman had pronounced on what she perceived as her stepdaughter's many failings and readily aired her views to anyone who cared to listen and, indeed, to those – such as Eleanor – who did not. Eleanor's wardrobe, for example, she had described as 'not fit to dress a servant'; her behaviour as 'that of an outspoken tomboy' and her accomplishments as a young lady, 'positively shocking'. Whilst not using quite the same extreme descriptions as her stepmama, Eleanor did acknowledge that having been without the influence of a female for almost half her life, her wardrobe could most definitely be described as out-dated; her manner, given the fact that she had no interest in the inane chit-chat indulged in by the rest of her class, could, most probably, be viewed as outspoken; her embroidery skills did indeed leave much to be desired and her pianoforte playing was, without a doubt, verging on the excruciatingly painful. During her upbringing however, both she and her father had placed little importance on such matters and her father had focused instead on providing a happy, intellectually stimulating environment for his energetic, inquisitive young daughter. The two of them had read poetry together, mastered their horse-riding skills, and regularly enjoyed more than a few heated discussions regarding their favourite topic of politics. Eleanor's upbringing, with the sad exception of her dear mother's death, had been fun, carefree and interesting – a highly enjoyable period for both her and her father.

With the arrival of the new Lady Myers, not only had the easy-going atmosphere in the house dissipated, but her father's priorities also appeared to have altered.

'Perhaps Hester does have a point,' he'd murmured, sheepishly, when he'd commented on the fact that Eleanor had been wearing the same gown for several days, leaving her with little choice but to inform him that his new wife, with neither Eleanor's knowledge nor consent, had given away most of her other dresses to the local seminary, viewing them as 'shoddy'.

'I blame myself,' he had continued morosely, much to Eleanor's dismay. 'I should have been aware that young ladies require instruction in fashion. I should not have left it so long before marrying again.'

Eleanor had resisted the urge to tell him that she wished he had not married at all; that she had been perfectly content with her 'shoddy' gowns and with their life pre-Hester. Instead she had attempted to reassure him that, in her eyes, he had no failings whatsoever as a father – except one which she did not dare to point out – that he appeared to be completely besotted with his dour new wife, freely giving in to her every frivolous whim. Some of these whims Eleanor had almost understood, such as ridding the drawing-room of its previous shabby pale-green décor and replacing it with more fashionable – albeit rather garish – shades of yellow. Other 'whims' though, she could not help but feel had been acted on from pure malice, such as instructing the gardeners to rip out the herbaceous borders Eleanor had lovingly tended over the years, and replace them with a rather uninspiring arrangement of roses; relegating her mother's cherished collection of china teapots to a box in the cellar and substituting it with a very dubious display of thimbles, and forbidding Eleanor to continue her voluntary work at the local orphanage for fear she might carry home some dreadful disease. Despite the hurt and anger these actions had caused Eleanor, she had stoically bitten her tongue, not wishing to spoil her father's newfound happiness. However, when Hester had invited over her old Uncle Arthur for dinner the previous week, and the ancient specimen had freely groped her leg under the table, Eleanor had found herself devoid of all tongue-biting skills.

'I beg your pardon, sir,' she had declared indignantly, holding up the wrinkled, liver-spotted hand and placing it firmly on the table, 'but I appear to have found something of yours – on my knee!'

In a histrionic outburst, Hester had gasped loudly and dramatically fled from the room in a torrent of mortified tears. Eleanor's father, apparently glued to his seat, had appeared somewhat aghast, staring at his daughter with wide eyes and a gaping mouth. Uncle Arthur meanwhile, the only member of the party completely unperturbed by the incident, had merely giggled boyishly and summoned over one of the footmen to enquire if there were any more sprouts.

When Eleanor had been informed the next morning that Lady Hester was suffering from an attack of the vapours and had taken to her bed, she had strongly – and, as it had turned out, quite correctly – suspected that the woman was utilizing the time to plot her retribution. What she had most definitely not expected, however, was the extreme to which even Hester would go to achieve her goal of having her husband all to herself and Eleanor well and truly out of the house.

8

Yesterday evening, Eleanor, her father and Hester, had taken their seats around the supper table, Hester having apparently recovered enough from her vapour attack, to make her way down the stairs leaning, rather pathetically, on her husband's arm. They had just received their first course of ham and pea soup, when the revenge – in all its spiteful glory – was revealed. The announcement was preceded, Eleanor couldn't help but notice, by Hester giving her father a rather indiscreet kick under the table. The loud yelping sound that resulted had been hastily converted into an unconvincing cough.

Without meeting her eyes, her father had begun to break the news. 'Er – Eleanor dear, Hester – *ouch* – I mean – er – we – er – have had a rather marvellous idea, my darling,' he had declared, his tone overflowing with a strained enthusiasm, which immediately alerted Eleanor to the fact that the idea was to be the very antithesis of marvellous. 'Why, we have – er – arranged for you to spend some – um – time with your godmother, Lady Ormiston, in London. Now won't that be splendid?'

Eleanor's heart had stopped for a second, knowing instinctively that by 'time' he was not referring to a short holiday. She'd slanted a glance at her stepmother and could not fail to notice the look of victory spreading triumphantly across the older woman's face.

Determining not to allow her so much as a glimpse of her feelings, Eleanor had used every inch of her resolve to keep both her countenance and her tone as neutral as possible as she'd raised a spoonful of soup to her lips. 'I see,' she had replied evenly, feeling prickly tendrils of panic slowly winding themselves around her slender body. 'And may I ask why, Father?'

'Of course, my dear,' her father had replied, the lines of concern etched deeply upon his forehead, completely belying the forced lightness of his tone. 'We – er – thought that it was about time that you found yourself a – um – husband. After all, my darling, as Hester has correctly pointed out, you are not getting any younger.'

Eleanor had recoiled inwardly but managed to maintain her calm composure. 'I am well aware of that fact, Father,' she had replied, coolly, retrieving her napkin from her lap and dabbing at the corner of her mouth. 'However, I have no wish to marry. I am quite content with my life as it is.'

'That's as may be, Eleanor dear,' Hester had pointed out, her voice dripping with ice, 'but you cannot stay here with us forever and, at your age, it is high time you had a husband and a home of your own. I took the liberty of writing to your godmother, Lady Ormiston, several days ago, after your . . .

9

shall we say . . . *shocking* performance in front of Uncle Arthur. Why, at the mere thought of it I feel quite faint,' she declared, closing her eyes and placing the back of her hand to her forehead in a performance which Eleanor thought would not have looked out of place in a theatre. Inhaling deeply, the older woman lowered her hand and made to continue her speech. 'I have notified Lady Ormiston of your . . . *predicament* and received a reply this very morning informing me that she is only too happy to receive you. Indeed, given the fact that she has recently been widowed, I believe she will be more than grateful for a little project with which to amuse herself. She is to arrange instruction for you in all the skills necessary to becoming an accomplished young lady, which will, of course, help us in finding you a husband. Lord only knows,' she continued, casting her husband an affected look of concern, 'we have little hope at the moment. You will leave for London the morning of the morrow.'

Eleanor had opened her mouth to reply: to say that she was unaware she had a *predicament*; that she did not take kindly to being referred to as a *project*; and that it was not *her* behaviour which had been shocking at the leg-feeling dinner party, but that of Uncle Arthur. Her eyes had met those of her father however and she had instinctively known, by the pleading look he cast her, that all protestations were pointless. Hester had, as usual, done a first-class job in wearing down her new husband. Feeling tears burning her eyes, she had fought back the urge to pick up her bowl of soup and pour it right over Hester's head. Instead, she had calmly put down her spoon, placed her napkin on the table, stood up gracefully and walked, head held high, out of the dining-room. Once the door had clicked shut behind her, her resolve quickly disappeared and she had raced up the stairs to her bedchamber, flung herself furiously on to the bed and cried solidly for several miserable hours.

This morning, after a rather fitful night's sleep, she had, in an almost dream-like state, thrown a few of her belongings into a valise and waited upstairs until she'd heard the carriage drawing up at the front of the house. Her father had been waiting for her alone in the reception hall as she'd descended the marble staircase.

'Please do not be upset, my dear,' he'd pleaded, embracing her tightly. 'Hester only wants what is best for you, as, of course, do I.'

Eleanor had fought back the urge to tell her father exactly what a manipulative piece his new wife was turning out to be, but she realized it would be futile. Hester, no doubt heady with her victory, would merely dismiss any such comments as sour grapes.

Instead, she had hugged him tightly, told him she loved him and walked out of the door bearing two powerful emotions: an overwhelmingly intuitive feeling that when she next returned to Merryoaks, it would be under very different circumstances indeed; coupled with a deep sense of regret that she had missed what would have been an ideal opportunity to drench Hester in ham and pea soup.

The chaise veered sharply around a corner, slamming Eleanor's head against the window and rudely awakening her from a restless doze. She had no idea how long she had slept, or indeed how long she had been in the wretched carriage. What she was immediately aware of was that, rather than the sleep restoring her spirits, it had left her with a newly bruised, groggy head and a very sore, aching neck. Wincing as she brushed a stray lock of hair from her face, she realized that it wasn't just her neck that was aching, but rather every part of her body. She linked her hands and raised her arms above her head, arching her weary back as she stretched. As she lowered her arms again, her stomach emitted a ludicrously loud rumble, alerting her to the fact that she was also starving hungry. It did, she realized, seem an interminable age since they had stopped at the last posting-house to change the team and partake of some refreshment and even then she had only nibbled on a hunk of rather stale bread, opting to forego the mouldy cheese which had accompanied it.

In an endeavour to distract her thoughts from her aching bones and empty stomach, she leaned forward and rubbed a patch of condensation from the steamed-up window. Peering outside, she hoped to spot some landmark, which would provide a clue as to their whereabouts but, what little light there had been during the day was on the verge of disappearing completely and the gloomy combination of drizzle and swirling mist conspired to make visibility all but impossible. Just as she was about to relinquish her search and lean back once again in her increasingly uncomfortable seat, the carriage made another – thankfully much more controlled – turn and a shiver of apprehension flashed through her as she found herself gazing straight at an enormous, illuminated building, rising out of the mist like a proud, indomitable beast: her destination – the unmistakable Whitlock Castle.

It was six years since Eleanor had last set eyes on Whitlock, the imposing ancestral seat of the Ormiston family. Situated some five miles outside London, in its own sweeping grounds, the building had been much altered, extended and modernized over the centuries and now sported an eclectic mix of towers, turrets and wings, all paying architectural tribute to the particular period in which they had been constructed whilst, at the same time, blending together perfectly to create one of the most impressive buildings in the area. Rumour had it that the corridors of the castle were haunted by the Wailing Whitlock Widow – the forlorn spirit of a young woman who, having lost her husband in battle the day following their wedding, had been so devastated that she had thrown herself to her own death from the highest tower. With its rows and rows of candle-lit mullioned windows, the castle appeared even larger than Eleanor remembered and, outlined against the gloomy grey background and eerie mist, it took very little imagination indeed to envisage the spirit floating mournfully around the formidable building.

As the carriage lumbered its way up the gravelled drive, Eleanor's sense of dread increased as her thoughts turned to more corporeal matters and the increasingly imminent reunion with her godmother. The formidableness of the castle was nothing compared to that of its matriarch, her mother's cousin, Lady Ormiston. Ever since childhood, Eleanor had lived in terrified awe of her godmother – a fear that, if the jumble of nerves now welling in her stomach was any indication – had obviously not dissipated with adulthood.

Her godmother did, she know, hold her in very low regard, an opinion that had remained unaltered during Eleanor's last visit to the castle all those years ago. Her father had taken her to visit Lady Ormiston, two years after her mother's death. The visit had been what could only be termed as a complete disaster, culminating dramatically with a 13-year-old Eleanor dangling very precariously from an apple tree in the orchard. The result of her energetic exploits had been one broken ankle and one very annoyed and exasperated Lady Ormiston.

'Really, Edwin,' she had tutted despairingly at her cousin's widow, surveying Eleanor through her lorgnette, 'you really must learn to control the child. Why she is far too rambunctious by half. Such behaviour is most unbecoming in young ladies. They should not be running around climbing trees: they should be engaging in much more genteel activities. If you do not take her in hand immediately I dare not think of her prospects as a young woman.'

Thankfully, her father had seen the funny side of the incident and they had had, much to Eleanor's relief, very little contact with the woman since. A situation that, undoubtedly, would not have changed, had not the interfering Hester appeared on the scene.

As the chaise drew to a halt in front of the imposing, studded oak entrance and the door of the carriage was thrust open, Eleanor felt a wave of nervous nausea wash over her. For goodness' sake, she chided herself, she was not a child now: she was a grown woman – one who knew her own mind and could stand up for herself in any situation. She would not, she resolved, act like a frightened ninny. Taking in a deep, calming breath, she hesitantly negotiated the steps of the carriage then proceeded to climb the wide stone steps to the enormous door, being held open by a very elaborately dressed butler.

The man inclined his head of thick grey hair. 'Good evening, my lady,' he said gravely, as Eleanor made her way into the impressive wood-panelled entrance hall. 'My name is Giles. Welcome to Whitlock Castle.'

Eleanor offered him a weary smile. 'Good evening, Giles,' she said. 'I believe my godmother is expecting me.'

The man's ruddy face and voice remained completely expressionless. 'Indeed she is, ma'am. I am to show you to your chambers then you are to meet her grace in the drawing-room in half an hour. If you would follow me,' he continued solemnly, 'I will show you to your rooms.'

Eleanor nodded her compliance, grateful for the chance to stretch her legs. As she followed his stout frame through the maze of dimly lit corridors, steps and stairs, she temporarily forgot her nerves and found herself gazing in awe at the ancient wall hangings, antique furniture, suits of armour and imposing family portraits lining the grey stone walls. Items which, as a 13-year-old, she had no memory of, but now, old enough to appreciate their beauty, gave her the feeling of being immersed in a deep sense of aristocratic history. How many people, she couldn't help but wonder, had lived in this castle over the years; and what tales would the walls be able to tell of the dramas which had unfolded here?

Lost in her musings, she started slightly as she realized Giles had come to a stop and was in mid-flow, issuing a stream of instructions.

'. . . and left again to the drawing-room, my lady,' he was saying. 'I will leave you now to acquaint yourself with your chambers.' He pushed open an ancient oak door, which creaked loudly. 'Her grace will expect you in half an hour,' he concluded, inclining his head before turning his back to her and marching back briskly from whence they had come.

'Er . . . thank you, Giles,' muttered Eleanor to the departing figure.

Moving to the threshold she peered inside the room and felt her eyes widening in amazement as she absorbed the welcoming sight before her. Her last memories of the rooms at Whitlock had been shabby, old-fashioned and draughty. From what she saw of this room, however, it was clear that the building had undergone some major refurbishment. The first thing that astounded her was the sheer size of the room: her chamber at home was considered large, but this room was enormous. On the wall to her left, a huge fire burned in the grate, and she felt its hospitable warmth envelop her body instantly as she stepped inside and closed the door behind her. In addition to the glow of the fire, there were three large silver candelabras placed around the room, creating a cosy, warm ambience, which immediately lifted her spirits. The wall immediately facing her contained a row of three windows. Their wooden shutters had been closed, blocking out all evidence of the miserable weather outside. In front of the windows, was a mahogany writing desk and chair and in the corner a high-backed armchair covered in cream damask. By far the most imposing piece of furniture in the room, however, was the ancient, carved-oak four-poster bed, draped with heavy brocade curtains in deep rose, with a matching coverlet. Unlike the walls and ceilings of the corridors of the castle, those of her bedchamber had been elaborately plastered with fashionable panelling and intricate coving, the detail of which was shown off to perfection by the warm shades of cream in which the room had been painted. On the walls hung an assortment of landscape paintings each encased in a heavy gold frame while an Aubusson carpet in subtle shades of pink covered the floor. A modern white-panelled door to the right of the ornate Palladian marble fireplace, led into a large dressing-room complete with a small blue velvet sofa, a three-drawer dressing table and a very large, unavoidable free-standing mirror. Eleanor groaned loudly as she caught sight of her reflection. She looked exactly as she felt – tired, dirty and dishevelled. Her dark-green travelling gown and pelisse were creased and dusty, her thick, deep auburn hair, unruly at the best of times, now wild and disorderly as it succeeded in its obvious mission to escape the confines of her bonnet. Not at all the impression of the grown-up, independent young woman she wished to portray to her godmother. She should really repair her toilette and change her attire but in the absence of her valise, she would have to make do. She removed her pelisse and bonnet, splashed her face with water from the washstand, re-pinned her loose strands of hair and smoothed down her skirts. Then, feeling slightly more refreshed, she perched on the edge of the bed and attempted to prepare herself mentally for the meeting she had been dreading for the past four-and-twenty hours. Being normally of a sanguine disposition, she brusquely set aside all negative thoughts regarding the scheming Hester, and turned her attention to the positives of her situation. Taking in the beautiful décor and exquisite furnishings of her chambers, she decided that perhaps it wouldn't be so bad at Whitlock after all. Having seen fit to provide her with extremely comfortable quarters, perhaps the old lady was actually looking forward to her company. In fact, she pondered, perhaps Hester had actually done her a favour: perhaps it *was* time she left home – experienced new things; saw a little of life. She certainly had no wish to marry, but she could make the most of her circumstances. She would, she resolved, greet her godmother as an equal, on a level footing and she would, under no circumstances at all, let the old woman intimidate her.

Feeling relatively cheerful, she cracked open the creaking wooden door and marched assertively out into the corridor. No sooner had the door swung shut behind her however, than a frisson of apprehension slid down her spine. Compared to the cosy warmth of the rooms she had just vacated, the cold stone corridor, lit only by a few sparsely placed old-fashioned wall lanterns, emitted a sinister, alien air. The *objets d'art* which she had admired only a few minutes before, now appeared threatening and ghostly in the faint flickering light. A sudden vision of the Wailing Whitlock Widow, futilely searching the corridors for the ghost of her beloved dead husband, flashed through Eleanor's mind. She shivered involuntarily as she felt several sets of dark, painted eyes boring into her menacingly. For goodness' sake, she chided herself, shrugging away her apprehension as pure foolishness, they were only paintings and there was no such thing as ghosts. Desperately, she tried to recall some snippet of the directions Giles had given her, or at least something of the route they had taken from the main entrance hall. Well, it could only be left or right, she determined, so she would try left first which was the direction in which Giles had disappeared earlier.

Her kid leather boots scuffing against the grey stone floor was the only sound she could hear as she made her away along the corridor, the heavy silence adding to her sense of unease. She breathed a loud sigh of relief when, at the end of the passageway, she located a narrow stone staircase and scampered quickly down the steps hoping to find something she recognized and some sign of life on the floor below, but the corridor in which she found herself was not at all familiar, containing an array of stags' heads, which undoubtedly she would have remembered. At a complete loss as to which way to go now, she opted to turn right, but this, as she found out only a few short minutes later, turned out to be a dead end. Sighing she retraced her steps back the way she had just come. Overcome with fatigue and hunger, she felt her optimism rapidly dissolving as frustrated tears pooled in her eyes. Quickly however, she pulled herself together and, taking in a deep, calming breath, blinked back the tears. With her head held high she continued to the end of the corridor, ignoring the two other, equally sized passages leading from it. Suddenly, just as she was passing one of the ancient oak-studded doors, it burst open dramatically and before she knew what was happening, something very large and solid barged into her with an almighty force. She felt herself tumbling and landed with a hard thud on the cold flagstones.

'For goodness' sake, woman! Don't you look where you are going?'

Completely taken aback, a stunned Eleanor tilted her head upwards and found herself gazing directly into the face of a clean-shaven young man, with a mop of tousled, jet-black hair and a decidedly angry countenance.

'Well?' he demanded, glaring down at her disdainfully. 'What have you to say for yourself?'

Opening her mouth to reply, Eleanor found herself devoid of speech. 'I – er—' she stammered pathetically, feeling a wave of emotion suddenly wash over her. The man, hands on his hips, continued staring down at her balefully, making Eleanor wish she were anywhere in the world other than lying in a crumpled heap at his feet in this enormous, menacing castle. Covering her face with her hands, she felt herself unable to hold back the tears she had been fighting most of the day and they began silently streaming down her face.

'Now then, now then, what's going on here?' boomed a stentorian voice. Startled, Eleanor raised her head again and was this time met by a much more familiar sight: that of her godmother, Lady Ormiston. Her memory of the woman had not diminished at all. She was as loud and as fearsome as Eleanor remembered: her large form dwarfing everything around her; her grey hair pulled back from her round face in a tight, severe bun, topped off with a lace cap. Dressed head-to-toe in mourning black, she bustled towards them, her wide, old-fashioned panniers swaying violently from side-to-side, almost knocking over the ancient artefacts lining either side of the corridor. Eleanor cringed inwardly at the irony of the situation. Only minutes ago she had resolved to greet her godmother as an equal, on a level footing, and here she was crying in a heap on the floor, but before she had time to gather her thoughts, the dowager came to an abrupt halt in front of them.

'This woman walked right into me, Aunt,' announced the young man, glaring accusingly at Eleanor. 'I have had no apology and now she is snivel-ling like a child.'

All at once, the blatant arrogance of his tone, caused a wave of red-hot, indignant rage to pulse through Eleanor: she had done absolutely nothing wrong; she was tired; her entire body ached; the bruise on her head which had now developed into rather a large lump, was throbbing terribly; she was hungry and grimy and, most of all, she was in absolutely no mood to be treated as though she were nothing more than a piece of unwelcome dirt.

With as much dignity as she could muster, she pulled herself up from the floor and, tilting up her chin defiantly to face, what she now realized was rather a tall, broad-shouldered young man, she inhaled deeply.

'I beg your pardon, sir,' she countered frostily, looking directly into a pair of large dark-brown eyes, 'but it was *you* who knocked *me* over. If you had but looked into the corridor before barging out like a wild animal, you would have seen me immediately and the entire incident would have been avoided.'

The young man glowered at Eleanor, dark fury now colouring his features, but before he could reply, the dowager interjected.

'Well, Eleanor,' she declared authoritatively, crossing her arms over her ample bosom, 'Giles informed me you had arrived. By George, I knew that I was going to have my work cut out with you, but I must say I didn't expect you to be causing trouble within your first half-hour of being here. Now, let me have a proper look at you,' she instructed, taking a step back and raising her lorgnette to her small, black eyes, in exactly the same way she had done six years previously. Eleanor felt all her earlier resolve shrivel up and disappear in a puff of smoke as she instantly reverted back to a gawky, self-conscious young girl, at a complete loss as to what to do with her arms. Awkwardly, and in the absence of any better idea, she let them hang loosely by her sides.

The dowager pursed her lips as she surveyed her goddaughter's stunning crown of glossy auburn hair; her large oval, emerald-green eyes and her flaw-less, peachy skin. After what seemed to Eleanor like an eternity, she lowered her lorgnette and placed her hands on her expansive hips. 'Well,' she declared matter-of-factly, 'I suppose we should be thankful that you have at least inher-ited your mother's looks. You could do with a little more meat on your bones, but at least you have a decent bosom and I've never known a man turn up his nose at one of those.'

Eleanor's eyes widened and she felt a deep blush rush from the tips of her toes and flood her cheeks. She had never before been talked to in such a frank and open manner and, worse still, in front of a gentleman. As the gentleman in question emitted a snort of undisguised laughter, Eleanor flashed him a reproving glare and noticed that his anger appeared to have completely dissolved as he now leaned nonchalantly against the wall with one leg propped up behind him and his arms crossed over his broad chest. The annoying smirk playing at his lips, showed that he was obviously, much to her disgust, finding the whole spectacle completely hilarious.

She cringed again as she realized that her humiliation was not yet over – Lady Ormiston was unreservedly continuing her speech: '. . . but as to your behaviour, my girl,' she said, shaking her head despairingly, 'why your stepmama informs me it is reprehensibly unbecoming and that your accomplishments are gravely lacking. If I recall, I believe I warned your father, what would happen if you were not taken in hand and, although I am not one to boast, I am very rarely wrong in such matters. One only has to look at the results of his attempt at child-rearing to see how right I was.'

Criticism of herself Eleanor could suffer stoically, but criticism of her father was something she would not endure. She opened her mouth to protest, but her godmother raised an admonishing hand.

'I have neither the time nor the inclination to discuss the matter further, Eleanor,' she boomed authoritatively. 'Now, return to your chambers and dress for dinner. We will eat at eight of the clock sharp.'

With her closing instructions, the old woman turned on her heel and marched briskly back down the corridor, her skirts rustling noisily. Desperate not to be left alone with the repulsive young man, Eleanor, holding her head high, turned around and made to return to her chambers. Why the very nerve of him sniggering at her like that. Call himself a gentleman? Eleanor, thanks to her time spent with Zach, the farmer, could think of a great many words to call him, but 'gentleman' was certainly not one of them. She had no idea who he was – obviously some annoying nephew of Lady Ormiston's. Well hopefully he wouldn't be staying long. Indeed, she hoped she wouldn't have to have anything else to do with—

The sound of Lady Ormiston's voice booming at her from the opposite end of the corridor suddenly interrupted her thoughts.

'Oh, and Eleanor. . . .' she called.

With some effort, Eleanor affected a pleasant expression as she stopped and swung around to face her godmother.

'. . . do watch where you're going in future, my girl. The last thing I require is to hear of any of my servants being discomposed as a result of your boisterous antics.'

Another irritating snort of laughter came from the direction of the young man who had not moved from his position against the wall. Eleanor whisked around quickly again before he could see the colour returning to her cheeks with renewed heat. With the exception of Hester Scones, she did believe she had never disliked anyone more in her entire life.

# CHAPTER 2

THE expedition to the dining-room a half hour later was relatively uneventful with only two wrong turns and, thankfully, no humiliating collisions. Congratulating herself on locating her evening's destination well ahead of time and any other guests, Eleanor was directed by a footman into a perfectly square, pale-green saloon, adjacent to the dining-room, which had also, judging by its modern, elegant décor, undergone a recent redecoration. Against the back wall of the room stood a long mahogany sideboard with two silver chandeliers, a number of crystal decanters and a vase containing an enormous bunch of fresh pink lilies. In front of the blazing fire stood a round ormolu table together with a sofa and several chairs all upholstered in invisible green silk. With a most unladylike flounce, Eleanor slumped down into one of the high-backed armchairs and accepted a glass of ratafia from the footman. Feeling positively weak with the combination of tiredness and hunger, she would have liked nothing more than to have taken dinner alone in her room before retiring early. She had briefly contemplated proposing such an idea but, given the unfortunate incident earlier, had concluded that she had best cause as little fuss as possible. Using every last scrap of energy, she had therefore changed into her only evening gown – a very tired-looking, creased garment in faded blue silk – and made her weary way back through the maze of corridors to the ground floor.

Now sipping at the sweet almond-flavoured liquid in the comfort of the chair, with the soothing sound and warmth of the crackling fire, she was aware of her body unwinding and her eyelids, weighted down with sleep, very slowly closing. All at once, however, the door burst open dramatically and her godmother's vociferous voice signalled the end of her peace.

'Now, Eleanor,' she boomed, 'allow me to introduce you to our guests for this evening: Lady Carmichael and her daughters Felicity and Gertru—'

Rudely startled from her light doze, Eleanor leapt from her seat and spun around to face her godmother and her three guests. In the process the glass of ratafia slipped from her hand, the tumbler promptly dispensing its contents over the front of her skirts, before landing with a small thud on the faded-green Persian rug below her. Gasping in dismay as she watched the glass bounce and scatter its few remaining sticky drops over the carpet, Eleanor raised an appalled hand to her mouth.

'Oh,' she stammered, feeling a rush of pink stain her cheeks, 'I am so sorry. I do believe I nodded off slightly and I—'

Shifting her gaze from the glass to her godmother, she cringed inwardly as she noticed an expression of pure horror intermingled with disbelief spread across Lady Ormiston's rounded countenance. The old lady had come to an abrupt halt, just inside the doorway, her three plump guests bouncing off one another as they failed to stop quite so rapidly.

'Hmph,' sniffed the dowager, through pursed lips. 'I thought it would be too much to ask that we have no more disasters before dinner. I do declare, Eleanor, that I have never met such a clumsy, unrefined young woman in all my life. Why, I dare not think what your poor mother, my cousin, would have thought of your behaviour,' she said, shaking her head so vehemently that the ribbons on her lace cap danced in exasperation. In sympathy with their hostess, the ugly trio behind her, all of a similar shape and height, and all dressed in extremely unflattering frilly, pastel gowns, all shook their heads too.

'Stevens!' roared the dowager suddenly, causing the trio, Eleanor and indeed the summoned footman, to jump. 'Clear up this mess right away,' she ordered, pointing toward the glass.

'Of course, your grace,' simpered the tall, thin young man, immediately scurrying over to the scene of the incident. Picking up the empty glass, he began dabbing furiously at the stain with a white serving cloth.

'And as for you, Eleanor,' continued the dowager, turning her dark eyes to the rather large wet patch decorating her goddaughter's dress, 'I suggest you go upstairs and change your gown immediately.'

'Oh,' muttered Eleanor, biting her lip. 'I'm – er – I'm afraid I cannot.'

'Cannot?' repeated Lady Ormiston, furrowing her lined brow. 'Why on earth not?'

'Well,' replied Eleanor hesitantly, knowing instinctively that her reply was going to cause a stir, 'because this is the – er – only evening gown I have.'

An incredulous snort of laughter escaped the older of the two girls standing behind her godmother.

Lady Ormiston's brows knitted together in confusion as she tried to make sense of Eleanor's confession. 'Are you telling me, Eleanor,' she puzzled, in the same deliberate tone one uses when talking to a child, 'that you – the daughter of an earl – have only one evening gown to your name?'

Desperate not to make a cake of herself yet again in front of her new guardian, Eleanor attempted to offer, what to her, was a perfectly logical explanation for the state of her wardrobe. 'I'm afraid I am, your grace,' she explained, before adding quickly, 'but it's not that my father refused to buy me gowns; it's rather that I never wished for any.'

Unfortunately, her truthful clarification of the situation only served to make matters worse, as the collective gasp which followed her confession could not have been louder had she announced something positively scandalous such as she wished to remove all her clothes and take a stroll around the grounds, or she was about to run off to Gretna Green and marry one of the stable boys.

'*Never wished for any gowns*,' repeated Lady Ormiston, walking slowly over to the armchair opposite that of Eleanor's and easing her large frame into it. 'Why, I do believe I have never heard anything like it in my entire life.'

Taking their cue to be seated from their hostess, the three stout guests bustled across the room and took their places on the green sofa directly in front of the fire: Lady Carmichael in the centre with one mousy, ringleted-haired daughter either side of her. Eleanor gingerly resumed her seat and stared dolefully at the damp patch on the front of her dress as she felt four sets of eyes examining her curiously.

At length, a high-pitched whine broke the uncomfortable silence. 'I must confess,' announced Lady Carmichael, smoothing an imaginary crease from the skirt of her fussy, high-waisted yellow gown adorned with far too many ribbons, 'that I have never before met a young lady who has no interest in gowns. We have done little else over the past few months than prepare a collection for Felicity for her come out which, as you know, Lady Ormiston, is to take place in a little under three weeks.'

'How could I possibly forget,' replied Lady Ormiston prosaically, accepting a glass of brandy from a second footman who was proffering an assortment of drinks on a silver tray. 'I do believe, Cynthia, that you must have told me the date in excess of one hundred times.'

'Oh dear, have I really?' tittered Lady Carmichael, as she reached for a glass of ratafia from the tray. 'It's just that we are all so dreadfully excited about it, are we not, Felicity?'

Felicity smiled superciliously. 'Indeed we are, Mama,' she replied, in a whine identical to that of her mother's.

'Of course, we are hoping for a very good offer following her come out,' enthused Lady Carmichael, taking a sip of her drink, 'which shouldn't be too difficult, given that Felicity will be the belle of all the balls this Season.'

Eleanor sneaked a peep at the girl in question, taking in Felicity's dumpy frame and square-shaped head, which, in the absence of any kind of neck, seemed to sit directly on her shoulders. She couldn't help but feel that Lady Carmichael's expectations were rather optimistic.

Undeterred by the pitying, disbelieving looks cast her by both Eleanor and her hostess, Lady Carmichael continued her speech. 'Do you know, Lady Ormiston, that we have been planning Felicity's come out for almost two years now?'

The dowager raised her brows in mock surprise. 'Really?' she replied. 'It seems so *very* much longer.'

Detecting the lilt of sarcasm in her godmother's tone, Eleanor bit back a smile.

'Exactly what I said this very morning,' carried on Lady Carmichael, obliviously. 'I shall feel myself quite bereft once the event is over. Although, of course, we will then move on to planning a wedding,' she added, flashing Felicity a knowing smile.

'Good Lord,' muttered the dowager drily, staring into her brandy glass as she swirled around the amber liquid. 'Is there to be no end to it?'

At her godmother's blatant rudeness and Lady Carmichael's blatant disregard of it, Eleanor tried desperately to control her lips, now twitching furiously with uncontrolled laughter. Her amusement, however, had not gone unnoticed by the entire party, as she caught Felicity studying her maliciously through narrowed porcine eyes.

'May I ask if you are yet betrothed, Lady Eleanor?' enquired the girl, coldly.

Eleanor opened her mouth to reply, but before a word was forthcoming, Lady Ormiston intervened.

'Not yet,' she replied matter-of-factly. 'Her stepmama has tasked me with finding her a suitable husband and I can therefore assure you that Eleanor will most definitely be married off by the end of the Season.'

Eleanor gasped loudly, completely taken aback at the old woman's frankness. 'I'm afraid that will not be possible, Godmother,' she protested. 'You see, I have absolutely no wish to marry.'

'*No wish to marry?*' repeated Gertrude, wrinkling her rather large nose, with a very angry-looking pimple perched on the end of it. 'But if you do not marry then what on *earth* will you do?'

'I shall return to the country and carry on exactly as I was,' replied Eleanor obdurately.

Felicity tossed back her ringlets. 'Good Lord,' she declared haughtily, 'how very tedious. Why on earth one would wish to remain a spinster and bury themselves in the country when there are so many balls and parties to attend is quite beyond me. Personally I can think of nothing more boring,' she continued, placing her glass of ratafia on the ormolu table in front of her. 'I cannot wait to be married and to have a home of my own – a very large one, of course.'

'Oh yes,' piped up Gertrude innocently. 'Felicity was saying only yesterday that Whitlock would suit her very well indeed, weren't you, Felicity?'

Eleanor turned her head towards the trio just in time to see Lady Carmichael giving her youngest daughter an admonishing nudge in the ribs, while her older sister flashed her a censorious glare.

'What I *actually* said, Gertrude,' corrected Felicity, flushing slightly, 'is that something about the *size* of Whitlock would be ideal. I didn't, of course, mean Whitlock itself, Lady Ormiston,' she clarified with a decidedly affected laugh.

The dowager regarded her with a look of intense incredulity. 'I should think not,' she replied tartly. 'For that would mean you would have to marry—'

She broke off abruptly as, at that very moment, the door was thrust open and all four heads swung in unison to see the young man Eleanor had 'met' earlier, strutting confidently towards them. Eleanor immediately averted her eyes as she felt her heart sink right to her feet: as if the wretched evening wasn't bad enough. The man came to stand in front of the fire, facing the small party.

'Good evening, ladies,' he said, completely ignoring Eleanor and bowing deeply to Lady Carmichael and her daughters. 'And may I say how very beautiful you are all looking this evening.'

Eleanor rolled her eyes and began studying her fingernails, which seemed infinitely more interesting than the man. Obviously not of the same opinion, Gertrude and Lady Carmichael both flushed a rather unattractive shade of pink and giggled girlishly.

'Good evening, Lord Prestonville,' cooed a flustered Lady Carmichael. 'I see you are looking as dashing as ever.'

Clasping his hands behind his back, James inclined his head towards the woman in acknowledgement of the compliment. 'How very good of you to say so, my lady,' he replied – somewhat pompously, thought Eleanor. 'And may I say how well that delightful shade of lemon suits you.'

Gertrude and Lady Carmichael giggled again. Amazed at their simpering behaviour in front of the affected specimen, Eleanor raised her eyes in order to examine him properly. He looked well enough, she thought, taking in his shiny black hair; deep-brown eyes framed by long lashes and immaculate, fashionable evening dress, of a coat of blue superfine, tight-fitting black breeches and crisp white shirt topped off with a very elaborately set neck-cloth. However, quite how any woman could find someone so conceited and arrogant in the least bit charming, was positively beyond her.

The man turned his attention to Lady Ormiston. 'Please do forgive the interruption, my dear Aunt,' he drawled, in his deep, well-modulated voice, 'however my plans for this evening have been changed rather abruptly and I wondered if I might have the pleasure of joining you lovely ladies for dinner this evening?'

'Why, of course, James,' replied Lady Ormiston, clearly delighted to have her nephew's company. 'Stevens!' she roared, causing the entire party to jump again and Stevens to visibly quake in his buckled shoes. 'Set another place for my nephew immediately.'

'So, James,' twittered Lady Carmichael, whipping open her fan and fluttering it furiously, 'to what do we owe this unforeseen but most welcome pleasure? Don't tell me you are already bored with the Season? I should have thought there were any number of young ladies at functions across London this evening positively desperate to set eyes on the Marquis of Rothwell.'

A knowing smile spread across James's face, as he raised his brows in mock innocence. 'I do declare, Lady Carmichael,' he replied, tugging down the ends of his cravat, 'that I have absolutely no idea from where this ridiculous assumption of my popularity with the fairer sex emanates.'

Lady Ormiston took a large gulp of brandy. 'I would think, dear Nephew,' she cut in abruptly, 'that it emanates from the fact that you are one of the most eligible, handsome bachelors in all of England and that there has already been a mountain of caps set at you this Season. Not just by the young chits either, but by their prowling, ambitious mothers who are desperately hoping you'll be casting your eye in the direction of their simpering daughters. Am I correct, or am I not, Cynthia?'

Lady Carmichael flushed slightly. 'Oh, I'm – er – sure you are, Lady Ormiston,' she floundered, with a small embarrassed cough.

'And let's not forget, James,' continued Lady Ormiston matter-of-factly, 'once this dreadful "title" business is sorted out, you will also be one of the *richest* bachelors in England.'

Lady Carmichael cleared her throat. 'Ah-hem,' she interrupted hesitantly, 'may I ask what the latest situation is regarding the – er "*title*" business, Lady Ormiston?'

'Indeed you may not, Cynthia,' replied the dowager stoutly. 'Our solicitors have recommended we do not speak of the matter until it is concluded and I wholeheartedly agree with them. After all, we all know only too well how much the gossips would love to find out all the intimate details and then twist and turn them for their own entertainment. Am I correct, or am I not, Cynthia?'

The flush in Lady Carmichael's cheeks deepened. 'Well – er I have no doubt you – er are, Lady Ormiston,' she muttered, shifting awkwardly in her seat.

'Anyway,' cut in James, lightening the tone, 'enough of boring legal matters. Now tell me, what were you charming ladies discussing before I interrupted you so rudely?'

'Oh,' rasped Felicity, 'we were discussing marriage, my lord, and Lady Eleanor was just telling us how she has no wish to marry.'

James lifted his brows as he turned to Eleanor. 'Was she indeed?' he replied, with a sardonic glint in his eyes. 'Then may I recommend we keep such devastating news to ourselves? After all,' he continued, deliberately moving his dark gaze to the stains on the front of her gown, from which, thanks to the heat of the fire, a little steam was now rising, 'we would not wish to disappoint the great number of gentlemen who have been eagerly awaiting the arrival of such a . . . *sophisticated* and . . . *highly accomplished* young lady.'

The hint of sarcasm in his tone was lost on neither Felicity nor Eleanor as Felicity released a rude snort of laughter and Eleanor threw him a contemptuous glare.

Lady Carmichael's fan fluttering increased in speed. 'And what of you, James, dear?' she simpered. 'How do you feel on the subject of marriage?'

James threw her a disarming smile. 'I feel that it is a most delightful institution, Lady Carmichael,' he replied smoothly.

'Oh,' she cooed, her small blue eyes shining brightly. 'So, does that mean that you yourself may be considering entering into such a delightful institution soon? After all, James, I would consider eight-and-twenty to be the ideal age for a gentleman to marry.'

James pulled a rueful face. 'Alas, my dear lady,' he replied wistfully, 'as ideal as my age may be, I can state most definitively that I have no plans to become shackled for the foreseeable future.'

'But perhaps,' added Lady Carmichael optimistically, 'should you meet the right young lady, then you may change—'

A sudden knock at the door caused her to break off as all attention was diverted towards Giles, entering the room bearing a silver salver upon which rested a single white envelope.

'Forgive the interruption, my lord,' said the butler, bowing his head, 'but an urgent note has just been delivered for you.'

A faint smile hovered about James's lips as he raised an expectant eyebrow. 'Has it indeed?' he declared, vacating his spot in front of the fire and walking towards the servant.

Retrieving the envelope from the tray, James dismissed Giles with a curt nod. Then, with his back to his rather over-attentive audience, he proceeded to rip open the seal and quickly scan the missive. His reading complete, he tucked the note into his jacket pocket and turned back to face the party. The faint smile that had been playing on his lips a moment earlier had now developed into one of unabashed smugness. 'I am afraid, dear ladies, that my plans for this evening have changed yet again,' he announced. 'Do please forgive me, but I shall not now be able to join you for dinner after all.'

A wave of blatant disappointment spread over Lady Carmichael's countenance.

'Oh dear,' she sighed mournfully, her fan fluttering coming to a deflated end. 'Felicity was so looking forward to your company, James. As indeed were we all, of course,' she added quickly as Felicity's foot rather sharply met her mother's shin.

Feeling almost nauseous with the pathetic adoration being poured upon such an obnoxious rake, Eleanor was unable to hold her tongue for a second longer. 'Indeed we were all *so* looking forward to it, my lord,' she added archly, 'that I do believe, upon hearing such devastating news, my appetite has quite deserted me.'

James turned to face her, the sarcastic glint once again present in his dark eyes. 'Deserted you has it, my lady?' he retorted adroitly. 'Then in that case, might I suggest you retrieve it immediately. After all, as my aunt has already pointed out, you could do with a little more meat on *some* of your bones.'

A sudden rush of pink stained Eleanor's cheeks as a surge of furious anger shot through her: of all the rude, intolerable, impudent, arrogant— She opened her mouth to reply but in a flash James turned on his heel and disappeared out through the door, leaving her seething.

*

Eleanor awoke the next morning feeling no more refreshed than when she had retired; every bit as furious as when she had retired; and even more despondent than when she had retired, which, in itself, was not insignificant given the evening she had endured with the unbearable Carmichaels. Not usually prone to melancholy, she attempted, as she lay in bed gazing at the delicate anthemions of the ceiling cornice, to find something positive in her situation. Other than the fact that she was in excellent health however, she failed to think of a single thing. She was immured in a labyrinth of a castle in which she had little hope of ever finding her way around; surrounded by domineering (her godmother), arrogant (James) people; she was being forced to spend her evenings in the presence of insufferable guests (the Carmichaels); her days engaging in ridiculously boring pursuits; she had no friends around her and, as if all that were not bad enough, in a matter of months – or even worse, *weeks* – she was to be married off to the first man who showed the slightest bit of interest in her. Feeling completely wretched she pulled the coverlet over her head wishing to postpone the start of the day for as long as possible.

Completely absorbed in her self-pitying musings she failed to hear the timid knock on her bedchamber door. Indeed, she was so immersed in her depressing thoughts that she wasn't even aware of the door being cracked open and a little head being put round it, followed shortly by a slim body. It was only the sound of a discreet, timid little cough, which alerted her to the fact that someone was in the room with her. Hesitantly, she pulled back the cover from her face and found herself looking at a pretty girl, two, possibly three, years younger than herself, with a head of strawberry blonde curls and a sweet, heart-shaped face jam-packed with golden freckles. She was wearing a plain, navy-blue dress, much too large for her and looking, in equal measures, both nervous and awkward. She bobbed a curtsy and blushed furiously before saying in a thick cockney accent, 'Begging your pardon, miss, but her ladyship sent me up to help you dress, and I did knock like, but there weren't no reply and I didn't know what to do, miss so I just came in like, and I'm not sure if I should have done, but that Lady Ormiston sent me up here and I don't want to create no trouble with her 'cos she can be a bit of a tyrant when the mood takes her and—'

'I – er see,' interjected Eleanor, sensing that if she did not do something to bring the explanation to a halt then the girl might carry on for some time yet. 'What is your name, girl?' she asked propping herself up on her pillows.

'Milly, miss,' she replied, obviously relieved that she was not to be scolded for her uninvited actions. 'I'm your new lady's-maid, miss. Come to help you get ready, I have,' she concluded, beaming proudly as she clasped her hands in front of her.

'Well, Milly, that's very good of you, I'm sure,' replied Eleanor kindly, taking an instant liking to the young woman, 'but I'm afraid I'm quite capable of dressing myself and I really have no need of a lady's-maid.'

A wave of disappointment spread over Milly's face as she assimilated this unwelcome piece of information. 'Oh,' she said despondently, gazing at her feet for a moment and nervously nibbling her bottom lip. Then, obviously having had a rather inspiring thought, she suddenly raised her head again and fixed Eleanor with her sparkling blue eyes. 'Well, that's all well and good, miss,' she declared brightly, beaming once again, 'but her ladyship says I'm to look after you so that's what I'll have to do, like.'

Eleanor bit back a smile at the girl's obvious enthusiasm. 'I'm afraid, Milly,' she said gently, 'that whatever her ladyship says is of no consequence. I have never had a lady's-maid in my life and I . . . well, to be honest, I really wouldn't know what to do with one.'

'Oh,' said Milly, once again dropping her gaze to the floor and nibbling her lip. 'But that means, miss,' she said after a few more seconds contemplation, 'that I'll be sent back to them there kitchens. Not that I don't like them there kitchens, mind,' she added quickly, 'but her ladyship had said that if I did a good job, then if anything else came up like, then she'd think about giving it to me. And I have done a good job, miss, honest I have. You can ask cook and everyone down there. Been working there nigh on two years now and this post came up and her ladyship said I could have a go at it like and my ma were really proud and pleased, 'cos it's a whole tanner a week more and now I'll have to go back and tell her ladyship that you ain't wanting no lady's-maid and my ma'll be disappointed 'cos our Tommy's needing new shoes and Theresa ain't got no coat and— Oh, I'm sorry, miss,' she gulped, as two large, plump tears rolled down her pretty face. 'None of this ain't any of your business. If you're not wanting a lady's-maid then that's up to you and you've every right to say so, I'm sure. Now if you'll excuse me, miss, I'll be on my way and begging your pardon for disturbing you so.' And with that, she pulled a large white handkerchief from her sleeve, turned round and made to leave the room.

Eleanor, completely taken aback by the devastating effect her news had had and the brief insight into the consequences of her refusal to accept Milly as her maid, suddenly leapt out of bed and blocked her path to the door.

'Wait, Milly,' she said, taking hold of the girl's slim shoulders. 'I'm sorry. I didn't realize the job was so important to you. If you don't mind staying, then I would like very much if you would be my maid.'

Milly fixed her with her clear blue eyes, brimming with tears. 'I don't want to be no trouble, miss,' she said, twisting the handkerchief between her hands. 'If you're just saying that 'cos you're feeling sorry for me, then I'd rather go back to them there kitchens. I don't want no pity, miss, really I don't, and I shouldn't have gone telling you all them things about my family and the like. No, if you're not wanting no lady's-maid miss, then them there kitchens it is for me and I'll be glad of it.'

'I'm sure you would,' said Eleanor, smiling warmly at the girl. 'But, come to think of it, I am pretty dreadful at dressing myself and I haven't the first idea about how to style my hair or any of those things that I'm supposed to do. So . . . if you could help me, Milly, and not go back to the kitchens, then I'd be mighty glad of it.'

'Oh, do you really mean it, miss?' said Milly, her lips curving into a watery smile. 'I mean I haven't had much practice, not with being stuck down in them there kitchens, but I do have lots of sisters, miss, and we're always larking about like, pretending we're ladies and all. And I'll do the best job I can, miss, to make you look grand and all. Which shouldn't be too hard, given how pretty you is and everything.'

'Now, Milly, you don't have to resort to flattery,' chuckled Eleanor. 'But I do believe, between the two of us, we can keep you occupied. What do you think?'

'What do I think?' repeated Milly. 'Why, I think, miss, we two are going to rub along just grand.' Then, in an endearing gesture, which completely caught Eleanor off guard, Milly flung her arms around her new mistress and hugged her tightly.

Despite the weather, which was steadfastly continuing the dismal, gloomy theme it had established the previous day, Eleanor found herself in much brighter spirits in Milly's effervescent, chattering presence. She was also delighted with the view from her room which had been unveiled in all its magnificently lush splendour the moment Milly had flung open the wooden shutters covering the windows. Completely devoid of any bearings within the castle, Eleanor was surprised to discover that her rooms were located in the original part of the building looking directly out on to the wide expanse of lawn at the front, which was cut perfectly in half by the gravelled drive along which she had travelled only a few short hours earlier.

The location of her rooms, however, was not the only thing to surprise her. Milly, much to her amazement, had set about attempting to tame Eleanor's abundance of thick hair which, in the shameful absence of either brush or comb the previous day, combined with a fitful night of tossing and turning, had resulted in an extremely daunting tangle. In no time at all, the girl had brushed, twisted, curled and pinned her shiny mane into a sophisticated and fashionable chignon, at which even Eleanor, having normally not the slightest interest in such things, was both amazed and delighted.

Her high spirits did not last long though as she located the light, pale-gold stylish breakfast-room – courtesy of Milly's excellent directions – to find her godmother awaiting her. The old woman was seated in front of the row of leaded windows at a circular table, around which were eight Hepplewhite chairs. The table was overlaid with a dazzling white cloth and set with white china and gleaming silver cutlery. A splash of colour was provided by a huge arrangement of fresh spring flowers crammed into a round vase. Another mahogany sideboard stood alongside the wall to the right of the room on which were laid out a number of hot and cold dishes, some covered with shining silver domes.

'Ah, Eleanor,' said the dowager, putting down the newspaper she had been reading and removing her eye-glass. 'At last. I've been waiting to have a word with you, my girl.'

Eleanor quailed inwardly at the older woman's ominous tone. 'Good – er morning, Godmother,' she stammered, as she approached the table. 'May I – er – ask what it is you wish to speak to me about?'

'Indeed you may,' replied the dowager, as Eleanor lowered herself into the chair held out by Stevens. 'I wish to speak to you about your plans. Given that we are already well into the Season, we have frighteningly little time in which to find a man to take you. At the end of June anyone of any consequence will have fled London in search of a much healthier climate. It is therefore imperative that we waste not a moment in our search for a husband.'

Eleanor felt a wave of dread wash over her as she shook out her napkin. 'But, Godmother, I really must insist that I do not—'

'And I will hear no more ridiculous protestations about marriage,' interjected Lady Ormiston briskly, motioning to Stevens to refill her coffee cup. 'It is simply the done thing, Eleanor and, whether you wish to or not, one has to abide by the done thing. Granted, there are some *departments* of the institution which are . . . shall we say . . . a little *messy* and . . . well . . . damned *tiresome* at times. . . .'

Whilst she knew very little of such matters, there was no doubt to which *departments* the dowager was referring and Eleanor felt a deep flush darkening her cheeks while Stevens shook visibly and splashed a little coffee on to the saucer of the dowager's cup.

Lady Ormiston flashed him a reprimanding glare. 'However,' she continued drily, turning her attention back to Eleanor without even a hint of embarrassment, 'as women we simply have to put on a brave face and bear such minor inconveniences. But before you have to face any of that nonsense we have the rather daunting task of finding the man. Now what I have arranged to help us in our quest is this: you will begin your dancing lessons today – I have arranged for a dancing master who will be here in precisely one hour. This afternoon I will supervise your embroidery and your pianoforte. Tomorrow morning you shall have another dancing lesson and then in the afternoon. . . .'

As her godmother continued to reel off the list of exceedingly tedious activities, Eleanor felt her appetite dwindling and her spirits slowly sinking through the floor and beyond. If only she were at home now: in a house where she had no problem locating rooms; in a house where she was free and not forced to partake in a daily round of frivolous, time-wasting pursuits. All of this was Hester Scones's fault, she couldn't help but reflect, as her regretful thoughts turned once again to ham and pea soup.

# CHAPTER 3

WITH the exception of being swung around the drawing-room by her father when she was six years old accompanied by her mother playing a jaunty tune on the pianoforte, Eleanor had no experience at all of dancing, a fact that became blatantly obvious the instant the dancing master, Monsieur Aminieux arrived at the castle. M. Aminieux was a French gentleman of some middle fifty years with a head of tight silver pomaded curls, a theatrical manner and an obvious penchant for strong cologne and bold, fop-like apparel. This particular day, his attire included voluminous bright pink breeches, a frilled lilac shirt and a bright yellow waistcoat copiously embroidered with plump piglets in a variety of sitting, walking and reclining positions. Eleanor had never seen such a flamboyant sight and had had to stifle a giggle upon being introduced to the man.

For all his frivolous exterior though, it soon became obvious that M. Aminieux was something of a stringent task-master.

'*Non! Non! Non!*' he cried, for what seemed like the hundredth time, shaking his head of curls so frantically that yet another small cloud of powder landed over Eleanor's face. 'It is not like that. It is like this.' He released his hold of Eleanor and, positioning his arms as though he were holding a much more able partner, began waltzing around the ballroom on his own. 'You must be *elegante*. You must be light on the feet. See how I am floating here.'

Eleanor sighed deeply as she watched his rotund, multi-coloured form, waddling around the polished wooden boards of the room. In fact, had she not been so exhausted, she had no doubt she would have found the ridiculous sight quite amusing. But she was both exhausted and a little nauseous – the latter which she attributed to the overpowering smell of M. Aminieux's cologne. She seemed to have been dancing for hours, although in reality it was only a little over fifty minutes. There were so many wretched things to think about: where to put one's arms, what to do with one's feet, how to hold one's head. How anything that was designed for pleasure could be so dreadfully taxing, was quite beyond her. To make matters worse, the entire lesson was being supervised by Lady Ormiston whose booming voice, at irregular but frequent intervals, insisted on adding to Eleanor's already lengthy list of instructions.

Monsieur Aminieux waltzed back around to his pupil and took hold of her once again. Eleanor placed her arms in what she optimistically hoped to be the appropriate positions, only to have them immediately readjusted once again by her disapproving instructor.

'*Alors*,' he announced brusquely, unable to hide the lilt of impatience in his voice, 'now we will try again. And . . . one, two, three. One, two, three. . . .' he counted, as he began swinging Eleanor vigorously around the floor.

'Hands, Eleanor! Hands!' boomed the dowager.

'Feet! Feet!' commanded M. Aminieux.

'Head, girl! Head!' shrieked the dowager.

Eleanor's concentration vacillated frantically between the nominated body parts. After only a few minutes, M. Aminieux called a halt.

'*Non! Non! Non!*' he cried again, almost casting Eleanor aside in disgust. 'It is all wrong. She is too clumsy. She is like the rhinoceros, this girl. I have never had such a pupil. Never *dans ma vie!*'

'That I can quite believe, sir,' remarked a deep voice from the direction of the doorway. Eleanor turned abruptly to see James observing the scene with undisguised amusement. 'Although I think perhaps you meant a *hippopotamus*, M. Aminieux. That rather large, ungainly African animal that spends much of its time wallowing in mud.'

Completely taken aback by yet another demonstration of such blatant rudeness, Eleanor placed her hands indignantly on her hips. Never had she encountered such an amount of insulting behaviour as she had been forced to endure in less than a day at Whitlock. To make matters worse, no one, she quickly realized, was showing her the slightest bit of interest as all attention was, yet again, focused on James – the dowager and M. Aminieux both equally, for some unfathomable reason, apparently delighted to see him. James strode confidently across the wooden floor towards the dancing master, whose whole mood appeared to have changed in an instant and was now beaming broadly. James was followed by a second young man whose pale-red hair, wiry build and elongated face put Eleanor rather in mind of a weasel.

Her anger at the manner of the interruption however, was offset greatly by the welcome opportunity to take a much-desired rest. Unobserved, she therefore pushed aside her annoyance and slipped over to the side of the room

34

where she sank gratefully into one of the blue velvet gilt chairs, removed her slippers and leaned over to massage her aching feet.

'Ah, M. James,' exclaimed M. Aminieux, inclining his head to the younger man. 'How delightful to see you, my lord.'

'Indeed it is a pleasure to see you too, *monsieur*,' replied James, stopping in front of the dancing master and returning the gesture. 'Please do forgive me for interrupting, sir, and you, too, Aunt,' he continued, bowing to the dowager, 'but I wished to introduce an old friend of mine from university, whom I have not seen for quite some time, Mr Derek Lovell.'

The young man, who had been hanging back behind James, stepped forward and bowed to both the dowager and the dancing master. 'Delighted to make your acquaintance,' he gushed, in an unpleasant nasally voice which, Eleanor considered, matched his unappealing physical appearance perfectly.

'Mr Lovell has just returned from overseas and wishes to spend the Season in London. I have invited him to stay with us here at Whitlock.'

'But of course,' replied the dowager, smiling graciously. 'You must stay with us, Mr Lovell. I will have a room prepared for you at once. Stevens!' she bellowed, causing the name to bounce vigorously from all four walls of the vast ballroom and everyone in it to quake.

As if by magic, a quivering Stevens appeared in the doorway. 'Yes, your grace?' he mumbled.

'Mr Lovell is to be staying with us for a while, Stevens. Have a room made up for him immediately. The blue room next to James should suit very nicely.'

As Stevens scuttled away to fulfil the order, the dowager turned her attention back to her nephew. 'Now, James, will we have the pleasure of your company at luncheon today?'

'Indeed you will, Aunt,' replied James, smiling serenely. 'Derek and I have only just returned from the city after something of a – er – heavy night.' He gave Mr Lovell a knowing wink, which was returned with a rather unpleasant sneer.

Monsieur Aminieux chuckled conspiratorially. 'Ah, the young men. They like to be having the fun.'

The dowager tutted and shook her head in mock despair. 'Really, James, I think the less I know about your nocturnal exploits the better.'

James chuckled and planted a kiss on his aunt's lined cheek. 'I fear, dear Aunt, that in that assumption, you are quite correct.'

Listening to the jovial banter as she massaged her feet, Eleanor carelessly sounded her own, less favourable opinion. 'Hmph,' she snorted, as she pondered the unfairness of it all. How much easier – and undoubtedly much more fun – life would be, if only she'd be born a male.

By the sudden silence that ensued, it took only seconds for her to realize that her note of disapproval had been somewhat louder than she had intended. Cursing herself silently, she slowly raised her head to find four sets of questioning eyes regarding her intently and an expression of incredulity visibly sweeping over the dowager's face as she observed her shoe-less goddaughter with her dress scrunched up around her knees.

'Ecod! Cover yourself up, girl!' she suddenly roared, so loudly that Eleanor almost jumped out of the seat.

Hastily she tugged down her dress and pulled on her slippers. 'Sorry, Godmother,' she sighed contritely, realizing she had once again failed to behave in the expected decorous manner. Would she ever get the hang of this so-called 'proper' way to behave, she wondered. Especially when the proper way to behave seemed to go completely against her natural behaviour.

James, she noticed, was regarding her deprecatingly, one corner of his mouth tugging upwards. 'Well, Aunt, *monsieur*,' he declared, 'I think it best that we leave you now. You obviously have an *enormous* amount of work to do.'

'*Enormous?* That is not the word for it,' replied M. Aminieux despairingly, throwing his hands dramatically to his head. 'I think it would be easier to fly than to teach this girl to dance.'

By the time luncheon came around, Eleanor's feet were throbbing terribly. Having given up on the waltz, the dancing master had then attempted to teach her the quadrille. Its complicated routines of figures and changes had unfortunately met with even less success and a great deal more furious curl shaking.

'I am having the headache,' he had declared when the dowager had invited him to eat with them. 'I cannot eat when I am having the headache.'

If Eleanor had not felt ravenously hungry herself, then she, too, would willingly have foregone luncheon. She had no desire at all to spend a minute longer than necessary in the presence of the ghastly, insulting James. But the combination of a light breakfast and several hours' dancing had worked up something of a rather large appetite. She entered the dining-room to find James and Mr Lovell already seated at the table. There was no sign of the dowager.

'Ah. Make way for the hippopotamus,' James announced jokingly, as Eleanor crossed the room to the table.

Mr Lovell sniggered, which only added to the sense of irritation, Eleanor was now accustomed to feeling in James's presence.

'My, my,' she replied acerbically, 'such a mature sense of humour, I see. Why, I am sure any group of six year olds could not fail to find you amusing, *sir.*'

A bemused expression spread across James's face. He lifted his brows at her. 'Are you aware, Lady Eleanor, that such a cutting tongue is most unbecoming in a young lady?'

Eleanor fixed him with a hard gaze. 'And are *you* aware, my lord, that such childish, insulting behaviour is most unbecoming in a gentleman?'

James's eyes narrowed balefully. Before he could reply, however, the dowager bustled busily into the room and claimed her seat at the head of the table.

'Really, Eleanor,' she exclaimed, immediately sensing the tense atmosphere between the pair, 'I do hope you are not irritating James yet again. You really must learn to hold your tongue, my girl. It really does not do for young ladies to voice their opinions on all and sundry. Indeed it is positively unbecoming.'

Eleanor's mouth fell open in astonishment. Why on earth was it that the dowager thought she was always in the wrong whereas James—?

Her train of thought was interrupted by Giles who suddenly appeared in the doorway. 'Lady and Miss Felicity Carmichael to see you, your grace,' he announced, his tone reverberating with disapproval. 'I have informed her ladyship that you are at luncheon, ma'am, but she insists it is a matter of some import.'

Lady Ormiston emitted a loud groan. 'Good Lord, as if it wasn't enough that they invited their ghastly selves to dinner yesterday evening under the pretext of discussing some charity event with me. What on earth can they be wanting now? Oh well, the sooner we get it over with the better, I suppose. Show them in, Giles,' she gestured impatiently.

The butler bowed before vacating his spot and returning several seconds later with the unexpected guests.

'My dear Lady Ormiston,' gushed Lady Carmichael. 'Oh and you too, James. We did so hope that you would be – er—' she broke off as Felicity nudged her sharply. 'Anyway,' she blustered, 'please do forgive the intrusion, particularly as you are about to take luncheon, however we needed to see you on a most urgent matter.'

The dowager's eyes narrowed as she surveyed the visitors suspiciously. 'Did you indeed, Cynthia?' she sniffed. 'And what, may I ask is this urgent matter?'

Lady Carmichael flushed slightly. 'Well, we do believe that – er – Felicity may have left her shawl here yesterday evening.'

The dowager snorted in disbelief. 'That is indeed pressing, Cynthia. Why, if I didn't know you better, I would assume you were simply looking for an excuse to visit me again. Although, perhaps, it is not myself that you wished to see.'

Lady Carmichael flushed guiltily while Felicity cast her mother an accusing glare. 'I am sure, Lady Ormiston,' flustered the older woman, 'that I have not the faintest idea what you mean. Felicity and I were simply on our way to Richmond this morning and, as we were to pass by Whitlock, then it made perfect sense for us to call in. However, I can see you are busy and . . . come, Felicity,' she continued, cupping Felicity by the elbow. 'Let us leave these good people to their luncheon.'

James leant over to his friend and whispered something to him that Eleanor didn't quite hear, but which resulted in Lovell's obnoxious sneer spreading across his countenance and James's eyes sparkling with mischief. 'Come now, my dear Lady Carmichael,' he announced. 'Now that you are here would you not do us the pleasure of joining us for luncheon?'

Felicity, Eleanor noticed with a stab of surprise, shot James a look overflowing with contempt. Lady Carmichael, on the other hand, seemed quite at sixes and sevens that her plan had obviously been rumbled. 'Well,' she stuttered, shuffling her feet awkwardly, 'I really do think perhaps that we should be on our way. After all, it was very improper of us to call so unexpec—'

'Oh do stop twittering and sit down, Cynthia,' boomed Lady Ormiston. 'Can't abide dithering.'

Lady Carmichael, visibly delighted she had finally achieved her desired result, produced a tremulous smile. 'Well, if you insist,' she simpered. 'We would be delighted to join you. Particularly as we missed the pleasure of James's company yesterday evening.'

'Now you shall have the pleasure not only of my company but also that of an old friend of mine from university,' announced James with a winsome smile. 'This, my dear Lady Carmichael, is Derek Lovell.'

Mr Lovell nodded graciously.

'Oh, how delightful,' twittered Lady Carmichael, as she unbuttoned her pelisse. 'Is that not delightful, Felicity dear?'

Felicity handed her bonnet over to a waiting Stevens and smoothed down her hair. 'If you say so, Mama,' she replied coolly, evidently unimpressed with her mother's scheming.

Lady Carmichael, oblivious to her daughter's indifferent response, continued unabashed. 'And may I ask if you are here for the Season, Mr Lovell?' she enquired enthusiastically, relinquishing her bonnet to the footman and sashaying over to the table.

'Indeed I am, madam,' replied Mr Lovell soberly.

'Oh, how absolutely splendid,' trilled Lady Carmichael, slipping into the chair next to Eleanor. 'In that case we must extend an invitation to you to Felicity's come out. We are most excited about it.'

'And rightly so, Lady Carmichael,' affirmed James archly. 'I have no doubt the event will be the great success of the Season.'

Mr Lovell, holding his napkin to his mouth, gave another sly snigger.

'Oh, do you really think so, James?' enthused Lady Carmichael, unaware of the pair's amusement. 'We do so hope that you will be able to attend. Without you it would not be the thing at all.'

James smiled reassuringly. 'My dear Lady Carmichael,' he said silkily, 'I can assure you that wild horses would not keep me from the event.'

Lady Carmichael sighed satisfactorily, evidently delighted with the man's answer. Eleanor, however, in her usual percipient way, had not failed to miss the thread of sarcasm running through his tone and, judging by the menacing look Felicity shot him, she was most certainly not the only one.

Eleanor arrived back in her chambers a little after six o'clock having spent the entire day under her godmother's watchful eye.

'Ooh, miss,' exclaimed Milly, who had just finished supervising the filling of Eleanor's bath, 'you look fit to drop.'

Eleanor made her weary way over to the bed and flopped down on to her back. 'That, Milly,' she sighed, gazing dolefully at the ceiling, 'sums up *exactly* how I am feeling. Not, I hasten to add, that I have been doing anything *remotely* useful. Unless, of course, you are of the same opinion as my godmother that it is absolutely essential I learn how to embroider hideous pearl daisies on to a ridiculously useless reticule, or that I am fully instructed in all the complicated steps of several, quite torturous dances.'

Milly's eyes lit up. 'Dancing, miss? Oh, I do love dancing, I do,' she sighed dreamily, hugging a towel she was carrying tightly to her chest. 'We're always dancing in my house.'

'Really?' asked Eleanor, propping herself up on her elbows. 'What kind of dancing, Milly?'

'Oh, all kinds, miss. That there quadrille is good fun but my favourite is the waltz. Even though I've heard that some of them grand ladies are refusing to do it, on account of it being a bit daring and all.'

'But . . . how on earth did you learn all those dances, Milly?' asked Eleanor, furrowing her brow. 'I do declare my head was fit to burst having to concentrate on only one of them today.'

'My brother, Herbert, miss. He's worked in some grand houses. And he don't miss much does our Herb. Picks up all the steps while he's standing around. Then comes home and learns them all to us.'

'Really?' asked Eleanor, beaming broadly as an idea just occurred to her. 'Do you think you could teach me, Milly?'

Milly seemed completely unperturbed by the idea. 'Of course, miss,' she said, dipping her elbow into the bath water to check its temperature. 'Ain't much to it really.'

'Can we start now?'

'But what about your bath, miss?'

'Oh, don't worry,' said Eleanor, leaping off the bed, 'I can have a cold one later.'

Eleanor's second dancing lesson of the day turned out to be much more enjoyable than the first. Indeed, with Milly's no-nonsense approach and overriding sense of fun, Eleanor declared that she had not laughed so much in what felt like a very long time.

As delighted as Milly so obviously was with both her new post and her new mistress, however, the girl was unable to conceal her disappointment at the state of Eleanor's wardrobe.

'I've cleaned your frock as best I could, miss,' she said, holding up the old blue evening gown for Eleanor to inspect before she went down for dinner that evening. 'There's still a few marks, but I've scrubbed and scrubbed and there ain't no shifting them.'

Eleanor took the gown from the younger girl. 'Oh, don't worry, Milly. You've done an excellent job. Thank you for trying so hard. It looks just fine.'

Milly flushed slightly at the praise and began helping Eleanor into the garment. 'I hope you don't think I'm speaking out of turn or anything, miss,' she ventured shyly, as she did up the buttons at the back, 'but I did think a grand lady like you would be having some fine gowns.'

Eleanor, standing in front of the full-length mirror, regarded Milly's face in the glass. 'Oh, Milly,' she chuckled, 'I'm afraid fine gowns don't interest me in the slightest and besides, I'm no grand lady – I'm just me.'

Milly stopped buttoning and stared at her mistress's reflection. 'Well, miss,' she exclaimed, 'there's all them out there pretending they're grand and titled like when they're not, and then there's you who is grand and titled who's pretending you isn't. I ain't never heard the likes of it.'

Eleanor chuckled. 'Talking of titles, Milly,' she then said pensively, as the maid resumed her buttoning, 'do you know anything about this so-called "title" business' with Lord James?'

'Oh, yes, miss,' declared the girl matter-of-factly. 'It's been the talk of the place for ages. Ever since the old master died, and that's nigh on nine months now. There we all was expecting Master James to inherit the title and all, and glad of it we were too, him being so kind and clever. I don't mind telling you, miss, the place was in a right state 'til he came along. Sorted it all out good and proper so he has.'

'So the refurbishment was all sorted out by James then?' asked Eleanor.

Milly nodded her head and carried on. 'Aye, miss, he's done a grand job, and we were all just waiting for him to take over the title, but then we learn that some other blighter has put their claim in for it and no one knows who they are or nothing. And so poor Master James, miss, he can't be calling himself the duke 'til the whole thing is cleared up. Dragging on and on it is, and them there solicitors are forever here trying to sort it out. Here for about three hours yesterday, they were. And you can always tell when they've been, miss, 'cos the Master, well, it puts him in a right bad humour.'

'Hmm,' said Eleanor, recalling the obvious bad temper James had been in at their first encounter yesterday. 'I suppose if it's been going on for as long as you say, it's hardly surprising he's finding it all a little wearing. I suppose he feels like he is just kicking his heels until it's all sorted out.'

Milly stopped buttoning and regarded Eleanor in the mirror with a cheeky grin. 'Oh no, miss,' she said. 'He's doing much more than kicking his heels, if you gets my meaning.'

Eleanor wrinkled her brow. 'I'm . . . not sure I do actually, Milly.'

'Oh, miss, you are such an innocent,' chided the girl playfully, tapping Eleanor's arm. Then, lowering her voice, 'We-ll, not that I'm one to gossip nor nothing, miss, but rumour has it that Master James is having one of them there *relationships* with the Duchess of Swinton.'

'Really?' said Eleanor, her eyes widening. 'And do you think that he will seek to marry her once this business is sorted out?'

Milly collapsed into a fit of giggles. 'Oh I wouldn't be thinking so, miss. You see she's already married.'

*

'So, Mr Lovell,' said the dowager at dinner that evening. 'James has told us you were friends at Oxford.'

'That is correct, ma'am,' replied Lovell graciously.

'And what may I ask have you been doing since you left university?' enquired the dowager, cutting into a large slice of game pie.

'Mostly travelling, my lady,' informed Lovell, helping himself to the dish of boiled potatoes. 'I have spent several years in Europe.'

'Have you indeed? And what are your intentions now that you have returned to England, Mr Lovell?'

'I am not yet sure, ma'am,' replied the man, replacing the dish of potatoes in the centre of the table. 'However, I am toying with the idea of entering into politics.'

'Oh, really,' sniffed the dowager with a slight hint of disapproval. 'May I ask which party you are inclined towards, Mr Lovell?

'You may indeed, ma'am. I feel a particular affinity with the Tory party. I am extremely interested in the measures they are taking to control the wretched Luddites.'

Eleanor almost dropped her knife and fork in horror. 'You do not mean to say, sir, that you actually agree with the bill declaring machine-breaking a capital offence? Surely one cannot equate the value of a machine to the value of a man's life?'

'On the contrary, ma'am,' said Lovell superciliously, not looking at her but concentrating on his plate of food. 'These men have no right to stand in the way of progress and they should therefore be made to suffer for their ac—'

'Oh, I think these men are suffering enough already, Mr Lovell,' countered Eleanor zealously. 'Can you tell me how you would like to provide for a wife and family on only milk and potatoes? I cannot even begin to think how those poor people—'

'That is enough, Eleanor,' interjected the dowager firmly, putting down her own knife and fork. 'I am sure Mr Lovell will agree with me when I say that gentlemen find it most unbecoming when a young lady engages in conversation regarding politics.'

'I must confess, ma'am,' declared Lovell, throwing Eleanor a desultory glance, 'that I wholeheartedly concur with your opinion. There are some topics which are quite beyond the understanding of females, and politics is most definitely one of those.'

'Thank you, Mr Lovell,' pronounced the dowager, flashing the man an appreciative smile as she raised her glass of claret to her lips. 'My sentiments exactly.'

'Actually, Aunt,' piped up James, holding a forkful of pie before his mouth, 'I must disagree with you. I would be most interested to learn if Lady Eleanor has an opinion regarding the current war with the French.'

'Oh, indeed I do, sir,' admitted Eleanor enthusiastically, her passion for political discussion causing her cheeks to flush and her eyes to shine brightly. 'I believe that the Emperor Napoleon is an astonishingly clever man; however, the Duke of Wellington is far more—'

'Good gracious, girl,' declared Lady Ormiston, visibly appalled. 'That is quite enough. And James, please do refrain from encouraging her. The next thing she will be telling us is that she is a blue stocking and I really cannot think of anything more unbecoming than *that*. Indeed, it is going to be difficult enough to find a man to take her without any added complications. Now, let us move on to much more genteel subjects: tell me, Mr Lovell, what do you think of the appalling weather we are having for this time of year?'

The baleful look that Lovell shot Eleanor before turning his attention to the dowager, was returned with one equally as defiant – an exchange which firmly established that there was to be no love lost between them.

# CHAPTER 4

DURING Eleanor's first two weeks at Whitlock, a routine began to establish itself, with the assorted residents of the castle involved in a quite diverse mix of activities – some more gratifying than others. Whilst Eleanor was forced to spend the majority of her days in the instruction of the boring accomplishments Lady Ormiston had deemed 'necessary' for her, Derek Lovell appeared to be having a much more pleasurable time. The man had settled into the habit of leaving the castle dressed to the nines every evening and not returning until after breakfast the following day when he would take to his bed and not be seen again until the following evening when the same sequence of events would be repeated. James, too, appeared to have quite a hectic social life, accompanying Lovell on several occasions or, just as he had done on Eleanor's first evening at the castle, flying out of the house at short notice, following the receipt of yet another mysterious note.

This particular evening, the two had obviously seen fit to adapt their routine somewhat and, to Eleanor's great chagrin, were both present in the dining-room when she entered. As if that unpleasant surprise wasn't bad enough, Giles then made an announcement that made her heart sink even further.

'Lady Ormiston will not be joining you for dinner this evening, my lord,' he informed brusquely. 'She is feeling somewhat . . . *drained* after . . . recent activities.' This last statement was followed by an accusing glare at Eleanor.

James gave a snort of laughter. 'Can't say I'm surprised,' he declared, regarding Eleanor with twinkling eyes, 'after all she's had to put up with of late.'

As Eleanor took her seat, Lovell gave another of his odious sneering sniggers. Although this filled her with an overwhelming urge to slap his smug face, she did her utmost to ignore him. Instead, furiously shaking out her white napkin, she addressed herself resentfully to James. 'And what, *sir*, do you mean by that precisely?' she demanded.

James regarded her with a rather superior smile. 'Only that I think anyone forced to spend a day in your company, Lady Eleanor, would find themselves a little . . . *sapped* of energy. Particularly as you seem to be devoid of the most basic accomplishments.'

Another disparaging snort from Mr Lovell caused a bubble of indignant rage to swell in her stomach. She speared him with a contemptuous glower before turning her eyes once more to James.

'Well, that would depend, sir, would it not,' she expostulated stoutly, 'on what one defines as an accomplishment?'

'Indeed it would, madam. And may I take it from that statement that you do not class the subjects in which you are currently undergoing instruction as accomplishments?'

'No, I do not, sir. I would class those subjects under the heading of "frivolous entertainment".'

James gave a languorous smile and tilted his head to one side. 'Would you indeed?' he asked, his voice lilting with amusement. 'Then pray do enlighten us, Lady Eleanor, as to *your* accomplishments.'

'Oh, I have a great many, sir,' replied Eleanor resolutely, reaching for a bread roll.

Lovell tittered lasciviously, raising a glass of claret to his pale, thin lips. 'None that would be of any interest to a gentleman though, I'd wager.'

James, ignoring his friend, raised a dubious eyebrow to Eleanor. 'Do you indeed?' he asked, the corners of his mouth tugging upwards. 'Then, name me one.'

'Very well then,' replied Eleanor coolly, breaking open her roll. 'Chess.'

Derek Lovell almost choked on his wine.

'Chess?' exclaimed James incredulously, wrinkling his brow. 'Forgive me, Lady Eleanor, but chess is a game of some intelligence; a game requiring much skill and concentration. It is certainly not a game for young ladies.'

Eleanor shrugged nonchalantly. 'While it is obvious from your *friend's* comments, sir,' – she flashed Lovell a disgusted glare – 'that chess is not the usual game in which you indulge with young ladies, I can assure you that it is quite within our capabilities.'

Another titter from Lovell caused her flesh to crawl. 'Oh I can assure you, Lady Eleanor,' he drawled condescendingly, 'that the games in which we indulge with young ladies, do most certainly not involve *chess*. But tell me, madam, how are you at something much more . . . *entertaining?*' His eyes roved over her, coming to rest on her bosom. 'How are you at, for example . . . Faro or . . . Hazard? Are such games also within your *capabilities?'*

Eleanor resisted the urge to cover her chest with her hands. 'Oh indeed they are, sir,' she replied with alacrity, refusing to allow the man to intimidate her, 'however I do not partake in such dissipating pursuits. Gambling is for fools.'

His eyes jerked up swiftly to meet hers. 'Are you calling me a fool, Lady Eleanor?' he enquired icily.

Eleanor met his gaze with equally coolness. 'I have no idea, sir,' she declared with mock innocence. 'Am I?'

'That's enough, Lovell,' cut in James, his eyes sparkling with amusement. 'What I am most interested in is for Lady Eleanor to prove her chess theory to me. Will you do me the pleasure in joining me in a game after dinner, Lady Eleanor?'

Eleanor began spreading her broken roll with butter. 'If you wish,' she replied prosaically.

'Oh, I do,' said James fervently. 'I wish very much indeed.'

James Prestonville, current Marquis of Rothwell scratched his head. He was flummoxed. How on earth had this chit of a girl managed to achieve checkmate in so few moves? It wasn't even that he was a bad chess player. Indeed he was one of the best at Brooks's, having beaten all of the members there at one time or another. But he himself had never been beaten quite so quickly. He scanned the board: with his queen surrendered long ago, and a bishop and a castle ready to pounce on his king whichever way he moved, he was well and truly beaten.

'Well, Lady Eleanor,' he declared, an amused smile playing about his lips 'I do declare that that is checkmate.'

'It would appear so, sir,' replied Eleanor sweetly. 'Does that mean that you would now like to retract your earlier statement regarding inferior female intelligence?'

James snorted laughter. 'It was one game, dear girl.'

'Then perhaps you would like me to demonstrate my point again, sir?'

'Perhaps I would. Set the board up again.'

There was nothing more pleasing, pondered Eleanor, as she positioned her queen in the final move of the game, than beating such an arrogant opponent as the Marquis of Rothwell.

'Blast,' he cursed, as he sized up his second checkmate position of the evening. 'I do believe we shall make it the best of five games, Lady Eleanor. Set the board up again.'

Derek Lovell, apparently bored with hanging around for his playmate, suddenly heaved his long wiry frame out of the leather wing chair where he had been lounging with the newspaper. 'Come on, old chap,' he intervened impatiently. 'Time to stop playing with little girls and go out and find ourselves some serious sport.'

Eleanor shot him with a revolted glare.

James, on the other hand, did not even look at the man, but instead concentrated on setting up the chess pieces on his side of the board. 'Hmm. I do believe I shall give it a miss tonight, Lovell. You go on without me. Ask Stevens to order the carriage for you.'

'Hmph,' snorted Lovell tetchily as he marched towards the door. 'As you wish, but there's – er – just one thing, old chap,' he said, pausing with his hand on the brass knob and turning back to James.

'What's that?' enquired James, still intent on the chess board.

'Well, I couldn't have a word in private, could I?'

'Oh, don't mind me, Mr Lovell,' said Eleanor archly. 'If I'm not mistaken, Lord Prestonville, I do believe Mr Lovell is about to ask you to loan him some money. Now what was it I said earlier about gambling?' She placed a finger on her lips and raised her eyes to the ceiling as if desperately trying to recall that particular piece of information.

While Lovell flashed her a glare that told her unequivocally that he could happily have strangled her, a bemused chortle escaped James.

'I do believe you are right, Lady Eleanor. How much do you want, Lovell?' he asked, digging a hand into his breeches pocket. 'Fifty enough?'

Still glaring at Eleanor, Lovell said, 'Couldn't make it a hundred could you, old chap?'

James raised his eyes to look at his friend and shook his head in mock despair. 'You don't change, do you, Lovell?' he said, drawing out a roll of bills and handing one out to the man. 'Just make sure you have a bit more luck than last night,' he said, as Lovell took the note from him, muttered some words of thanks and left the room, his face dark with fury.

'I believe you have quite upset the man, Lady Eleanor,' chuckled James.

'Yes,' mused Eleanor, as a momentary stab of foreboding pierced her stomach, 'I do believe I have.'

*

As she moved the last piece of the fifth game, Eleanor was so tired she could barely keep her eyes open.

'That is three out of five, sir, and I believe that means I have won your challenge which means that you *must* retract your earlier derogatory statement.'

James was regarding her with a rather strange look in his eyes – a look which even she, as perspicacious as she was, could not read at all. 'I don't know,' he said pensively.

'But that was the agreement, sir,' countered Eleanor indignantly.

'Actually, madam,' said James, his twinkling eyes fixed on hers, 'I confess I have no recollection of that being the agreement.'

Eleanor couldn't believe the arrogance of the man. How she could possibly have enjoyed playing chess with him for even a single second, was quite beyond her.

'Forgive me then,' she snapped, standing up suddenly from the table, 'I obviously mistook you for a gentleman who keeps his word.'

A smile hovered around James's lips as he continued to regard her strangely. 'Or perhaps you just mistook me for a gentleman, madam,' he remarked, as Eleanor stormed out the room, slamming the door behind her.

Four days later and the weather changed quite dramatically – the sky swapping its menacing, oppressive, steely grey for shades of brilliant deep blue broken only by the occasional wisp of a lonely cloud. And the weather wasn't the only thing that was showing an improvement. Thanks in no small part to Milly's secret daily tuition, Eleanor was now able to perform a passable waltz, much to M. Aminieux's delight.

He puffed out his rounded chest, clad in a hideous orange frilled shirt. 'Ah, I am not one to do the blowing of the trumpet, but see how she is coming along,' he boasted to the dowager.

'Indeed, M. Aminieux. I must congratulate you on such a good job. There is a little to do yet, but I believe we will have her dancing around the ballrooms of London very soon indeed.'

Milly had jumped up and down with excitement when Eleanor had informed her of the dancing master's praise.

Not coming along quite so well, however, were her musical accomplishments. As she attempted to practise a rather mournful sonata on the pianoforte that evening, she started suddenly as she became aware of a noise coming from a darkened corner of the room and an eerie feeling of being watched.

'Who's there?' she snapped, swivelling on the stool so that she faced the noise.

'Is that a hint of fear I detect in your voice, Lady Eleanor?' came the nasal reply.

A seed of apprehension took root as she recognized the voice. Instantly she brushed it away. She would not be bullied by the likes of Derek Lovell. 'I am sorry to disappoint you, sir,' she replied, turning back to the pianoforte, 'but there is very little of which I am afraid.'

'Is that so?' enquired Lovell, walking out of the shadows towards her. 'Not even being alone in a room with a man whom you know very little about?'

'Oh, I can assure you I am more than capable of looking after myself, sir,' she replied stoutly, turning over the pages of her music, which were propped up on the stand above the keyboard.

Lovell reached the pianoforte and, bending down, rested his elbows upon it so that his face was level with hers and much too close for Eleanor's comfort. Not giving him the satisfaction of appearing perturbed by his invasive proximity, however, she carried on leafing through the sheets nonchalantly.

'You play quite . . . *dreadfully*, my lady,' he remarked with his usual sneer.

Eleanor flashed him her most gracious smile. 'A fact of which I am well aware, sir,' she declared, turning her attention back to the music.

He did not reply, but Eleanor was aware of his eyes wandering over her body.

'Your pianoforte playing does not detract from your other charms however, Lady Eleanor. I wondered perhaps if you would be interested in adding another much more worthwhile accomplishment to your bow . . . one which involves pleasing a gentleman.'

Eleanor quailed inwardly as she was aware of his eyes resting once again on her bosom. Refusing to be intimidated though, she merely gave him a distracted 'Hmm', as if giving the matter a little consideration. Then she suddenly rose from her stool and, looking him directly in the eye, said, 'I am afraid I shall have to decline your *kind* invitation, Mr Lovell. Now if you will excuse me, I must—'

She made to leave the room, but Lovell was beside her in a flash. Grasping her tightly by her upper arms, he turned her toward him, his face now only inches from hers. She could smell whisky on his breath.

'I am quite unaccustomed to having my offers declined, Lady Eleanor,' he almost spat at her. 'Perhaps if I were to oblige you with a little demonstration of what I had in mind, you would not dismiss the notion quite so readily.' He pulled her closer to him, his eyes fixed on hers.

Eleanor did not flinch and met his gaze coolly. 'I feel I should inform you, Mr Lovell,' she said calmly, 'that if you do not remove your hands from me this instant, then I shall scream for all I am worth.'

Lovell sneered insidiously. 'I do believe that perhaps you are afraid of something after all, Lady Eleanor.'

'Not afraid, sir,' replied Eleanor, firmly. 'Merely repulsed.'

Lovell released his hold of her. 'Oh, don't flatter yourself, Lady Eleanor,' he said, digging his hands into his breeches pockets and sauntering over to the fireplace. 'I was merely seeking to amuse myself in this draughty old castle. Not much else for a chap to do stuck out here.'

Eleanor smoothed down her skirts and made to leave the room. She paused with her hand on the knob and turned back to Lovell. 'May I suggest, sir, that if the standard of accommodation is not to your liking, you consider making alternative arrangements.'

And with that, she flounced out of the room, recoiling at the irritating sound of Derek Lovell's laughter following her.

# CHAPTER 5

'ELEANOR, I am to take a trip into Richmond this afternoon and should prefer a little company. We will leave immediately after luncheon,' informed the dowager at breakfast that morning.

Giving no thought at all to their destination, Eleanor, with a mouthful of toast, had vigorously nodded her acquiescence, grateful only for the chance to escape yet another afternoon with her wretched embroidery tambour. Her enthusiasm increased dramatically however, as they approached the town which, to her great delight, was both interesting and enchanting, possessing all the charm and convivial atmosphere of a rather large village. The dowager, relishing the opportunity to provide her goddaughter with a history lesson, instructed the coachman to include on their route the famous Richmond Palace – an old favourite of Elizabeth I; Ham House – an outstanding example of Stuart architecture; the stunning parkland – favoured much by Charles I as a hunting ground; and Marble Hill House – the former residence of the late George II's mistress, Henrietta Howard.

Having alighted from the carriage in the town centre which contained a large number of stunning contemporary houses, the dowager made her purchases of shortbread and lace and then announced that she should like to take coffee. Leading Eleanor to a beautiful coffee house on the banks of the river along which were scattered a number of elegant white geese, they had just assumed their seats on the terrace when a familiar whining voice drifted over to them.

'Coo-ee, Lady Ormiston.'

They both turned their heads simultaneously to see Lady Cynthia Carmichael bustling toward them, followed by her equally bustling daughters, Felicity and Gertrude.

A look of blatant disbelief spread over the dowager's countenance. 'Good lord,' she muttered. 'Is nowhere safe?'

Eleanor bit back a smile.

'Oh my goodness,' flustered a beaming Lady Carmichael as she reached their table, 'I can scarce believe it. The girls and I so wanted to make the most of this beautiful day and where better than Richmond, I said to them this morning. It would appear that we were quite of the same mind, Lady Ormiston,' she gushed before adding, as she flopped down into one of the wrought-iron chairs, 'You don't mind if we join you, do you?'

The fact that the dowager did not reply, did not appear to affect Lady Carmichael's enthusings in the slightest as she gestured impatiently to her two daughters to sit down in the remaining seats.

'I cannot tell you, Lady Ormiston,' she continued, fiddling with the ribbons of her bonnet, 'how much we are looking forward to the garden party at the weekend. Felicity has scarce been able to contain her excitement. I take it that . . . James will be present?'

'Of course,' sniffed the dowager impatiently, attempting to catch the eye of a waitress.

Lady Carmichael beamed in satisfaction and flashed Felicity a knowing look. 'Oh how very delightful.'

By the end of the very long hour which they had spent in the coffee house, Eleanor considered herself quite well informed on the feeding habits of swans. Indeed she had been studying one of the birds quite intently for the duration of their stay. It had quickly proved markedly more interesting than listening to the twittering of the Carmichaels.

As Felicity and Gertrude ordered another cake, Eleanor and her godmother bade their farewells and were in the process of making a hasty retreat when the honking of the swan she had been observing caught Eleanor's attention. Hoping it wasn't anything threatening which was exciting the bird so, she turned her head in the direction of the river just as she reached the corner of the coffee house, which led on to the main street. What she did not foresee, however, was that someone else should be coming around the corner at exactly the same time.

'Oops!' said Eleanor apologetically, as she found herself face-to-face with a very beautiful woman with jet-black hair, dressed in a graceful gown of pure white and a shallow crowned white bonnet. Taking a step back, the woman looked disapprovingly down her button nose at Eleanor, before picking up her skirts and walking around her.

'Really, Eleanor,' tutted the dowager having observed the scene. 'You simply *must* learn to look where you are going. I dread to think what the

Duchess of Swinton would have said if she had landed on the grass in *that* gown.'

The following week the castle was a hive of activity, with the team of poor gardeners working all hours of night and day in their efforts to have the extensive grounds looking their very best. They had done an admirable job of the lawn at the front of the castle, which had been mowed and trimmed to such an extent that from a distance it resembled a piece of smooth green baize. Eleanor, desperate to discard the tedium of her 'accomplishments' and engage in an activity she both enjoyed and could see some purpose to, was positively itching to help. However, she dared not even propose such an idea, acutely aware that such unconventional behaviour would undoubtedly be classed as 'unbecoming' by her godmother.

Whilst the activity of the gardeners was of great interest to her, the forthcoming party was not. Indeed she would have gone as far as to say that her feelings towards the event were those of complete indifference. Milly, on the other hand, was positively bursting with excitement and did not even attempt to hide her disappointment at Eleanor's lack of enthusiasm – in particular her blatant admission that 'she really didn't mind at all what she wore to the event'.

'Do you not know, miss, her grace's garden party is one of the most top-lofty events of the Season? All them grand lords and ladies coming and you not giving so much as a by-your-leave about what to wear. I ain't never heard the likes of it.'

In the end, amidst much protesting from Eleanor, the girl had insisted on taking one of her old summer dresses so she could 'do it up a bit' and had obviously felt so strongly about it that Eleanor had not dared to resist.

The morning of the party dawned clear, bright and balmy, which resulted in a collective sigh of relief from all those in the castle.

As Milly dressed Eleanor's hair she was practically dancing with excitement.

'Oh, miss,' she gushed enthusiastically, 'what a rare treat me being able to see it all. We don't get to see nothing stuck down in them there kitchens.' With the last curl in place, she suddenly stepped back to admire her handiwork. 'Now if you ain't the prettiest one there, miss,' she declared, reaching over to pinch Eleanor's cheeks slightly, 'then my name's not Milly Maguire.'

Eleanor gazed at her reflection in the mirror. She had to admit that she did look quite . . . well . . . *pretty*. Milly had dressed her hair in the fashionable Grecian style with soft curls falling flatteringly around her face and through which she had threaded a green silk ribbon. Her old round sprig muslin gown had undergone something of a transformation with a new green tiffany sash and green trimming around the puff sleeves. The girl obviously had an excellent eye for colour as the shade of green she had chosen accentuated Eleanor's flashing emerald eyes and complimented her peachy skin tone perfectly.

'Milly, you've done a marvellous job,' declared Eleanor, smiling at her. Milly beamed proudly. 'Well, off you go then, miss,' she said, gesturing to the door.

'Erm, well actually,' said Eleanor, rising to her feet, 'let's just watch from the window for a while. I have no wish to stand around making hideous conversation for a moment longer than I have to.'

Milly rolled her eyes and shook her head. 'What I wouldn't give to go to such a fine affair and there's you doing all you can to stay up here with me.'

'Oh, believe me,' replied Eleanor giggling, 'it is *much* more fun up here with you, Milly.'

The girl shook her head in disbelief but did not protest. The two of them hung out of the bedchamber window, observing the proceedings. A steady stream of town coaches, barouches, landaus and phaetons made their way up to the gates of the castle where their exquisitely dressed occupants disembarked and made their leisurely way into the grounds, where an array of refreshments had been laid out on long trestle tables, covered with gleaming white cloths. A large number of immaculately dressed and obviously, from their puce faces, overheated footmen flitted about the rapidly increasing throng with trays of sparkling golden champagne.

The first person Eleanor recognized as she surveyed the crowd was Derek Lovell, chatting animatedly to a couple of very serious-looking gentlemen. She had seen very little of him since the incident in the music-room and was grateful for it. She really did find him a most odious creature. James was standing a little way from Lovell, dressed immaculately, as usual, in biscuit-coloured pantaloons, white shirt and stockings, gleaming Hessians and an exquisitely tailored dark-blue jacket. He was surrounded by a giggling group of blushing debutantes who were all obviously hanging, doe-eyed, on to his every word.

'Good lord,' exclaimed Eleanor, gesturing toward him. 'If you ever see me acting like that in front of a man, Milly, you have my permission to shoot me. What on earth is it about him, do you think, that seems to turn women into complete idiots?'

'Oh, miss,' enthused Milly, with a slight flush. 'He's awful handsome and very charming, don't you think?'

Eleanor flashed her a disbelieving look. 'Indeed I do not,' she replied indignantly. 'I think he is the most rude, arrogant, conceited, pompous man I have ever had the displeasure to meet.'

Milly giggled. 'Well, I have to say, Miss Eleanor, I'm thinking you'll be on your own with that opinion. Oh, look over there, miss, there's them Carmichaels. Could do with eating a few less macaroons if you're asking me.'

Eleanor looked over to where Milly had pointed and observed the plump forms of Lady Carmichael and Felicity alighting from their burgundy carriage. The older woman was dressed in a fussy turquoise gown, much too young for her advancing years. Felicity wore a similar creation in an unflattering shade of pink. They made their way to the crowds already gathered on the lawn.

'My,' exclaimed Milly, surveying the sight, 'ain't it all grand, miss? I ain't never seen such a sight in all my life.'

Although having not the slightest desire to partake in the affair, even Eleanor had to admit that it did indeed appear to be quite grand. From the crests on the carriages she had observed, it appeared that all of the nobility from London and the surrounding area had travelled to Whitlock for the party.

'Oh,' gasped Milly suddenly, grasping Eleanor's arm, 'did you ever seen such a fine gown, miss?'

Eleanor's gaze followed the younger girl's and came to rest on a tall, reed-slim woman, with jet-black hair exotically arranged, wearing a beautiful white silk gown adorned only by the simple white netting of the sleeves: a dress so plain and exquisite that it awarded its wearer an angelic air and made every other frock at the party appear brash and over-fussy. The woman was holding the arm of a much older but very distinguished-looking gentleman with silver-grey hair, dressed equally as stylishly. The two cut a most dashing pair.

Something was nagging at Eleanor that she knew the woman and then, in a flash, she suddenly realized from where. 'That, Milly,' she announced, 'is the Duchess of Swinton.'

Milly's eyes almost popped out of her pretty head.

The Duke and Duchess of Swinton threaded their way elegantly through the ever-increasing horde, making polite conversation as they encountered various acquaintances along the way. They were obviously heading towards their hostess, the dowager, who was chatting to a group of people near one of the trestle tables upon which huge crystal bowls of punch had been arranged packed with pieces of fresh fruit, alongside an assortment of pastries, savouries and sweetmeats. The dowager had shed her mourning black and was wearing an old-fashioned hooped gown in lilac which made her appear slightly less intimidating.

Upon making her aware of their presence, the dowager turned around to greet the duchess as did the man who was now standing alongside her – James Prestonville.

'Oh, my word,' exclaimed Milly nervously, her eyes now as wide as saucers.

The duchess sank into an elegant curtsy while the dowager and the gentle-men inclined their heads in greeting. A few pleasantries passed between the two couples before the duke and duchess smiled graciously and moved away from James and the dowager in order to circulate. Milly emitted a loud sigh of relief.

Just at that moment, a sharp knock on the door caused both girls to turn around abruptly.

'Her grace requests that you come downstairs immediately, ma'am,' announced a very serious-looking Giles. 'Indeed, she was quite insistent.'

Eleanor groaned loudly and pulled a rueful face. 'Oh, well, Milly, wish me luck.'

'You're not needing no luck, miss,' said Milly reassuringly. 'You're as good as any of them down there.'

The dowager made a beeline for Eleanor the moment she appeared in the garden. She was obviously in a state of some agitation.

'Where have you been, girl?' she chided despairingly, cupping her goddaughter firmly by the elbow and steering her towards a group of guests. 'How on earth I am expected to find a man to take you when you lock your-self away upstairs is quite beyond me.'

'Sorry, Godmother,' replied Eleanor dolefully.

'Nevertheless, you are here now and you look quite ... *presentable*, thank the Lord.'

Eleanor almost fell over at the reluctant compliment.

'Ah, Lady Ormiston,' came a high-pitched whine from behind them.

Lady Ormiston rolled her eyes impatiently and came to an abrupt halt. 'Cynthia,' she declared before affecting a more pleasant expression and turn-ing around to face Lady Carmichael and her daughter. 'Looking quite – er – *decorative*, I see.'

'Well, one must make an effort for such a grand event, must one not?' tittered Lady Carmichael. 'Felicity has spent days deliberating over which gown to wear.'

'Has she indeed?' sniffed the dowager, casting an incredulous eye over Felicity's hideous frilly pink creation dripping with lace and ribbons.

'This gown was purchased from Madam du Faut, one of the most celebrated *modistes* in Conduit Street,' informed Felicity haughtily. Her eyes roved superciliously over Eleanor's – in comparison, rather plain – dress. 'I don't suppose you will be acquainted with her, Lady Eleanor?'

Eleanor flashed her an ingenuous smile. '*Thankfully*, I am not, ma'am.'

Felicity's pale-blue eyes narrowed spitefully.

Before Eleanor had a chance to reply, however, James appeared at her side.

'Ah, the beautiful Carmichaels,' he said, bowing courteously. 'And dressed in the most exquisite gowns, I see.'

As her mother giggled girlishly, Felicity flashed Eleanor a look which she found extremely discomfiting. Thankfully, her godmother, keen to progress her search for a prospective husband, quickly whisked Eleanor away from the Carmichaels and proceeded to introduce her to what seemed like every single person in the south of England. Despite the large number of people present, Eleanor was amazed to discover that all their conversation consisted of only three extremely dull topics: the weather, the latest fashions and past or future social events – the success of the third obviously depending, in no small part, upon the first and the second. She stifled a yawn as a girl of around her own age with a dreadful stutter, by the name of Cecily or Celia – she could no longer remember – was trying to ascertain her opinion on the recent level of rainfall. Lady Ormiston had been commandeered by the girl's mother – a woman equally as formidable-looking as the dowager herself.

Never one to miss an opportunity, Eleanor chose her time well and, making an excuse to the girl that she had an instruction to pass to a member of the staff, she slipped away unnoticed by her guardian.

Filled with an overwhelming urge to escape the crowd and unable to bear one more prosaic conversation, she headed away from the manicured lawn, towards the wood which ran alongside one side of the grounds. As she did so, she noticed a small crowd of men gathered there and, as she got nearer, her spirits rose significantly as she saw that they had with them a number of bows and arrows and appeared to be in the throes of arranging an archery competition – something which she often engaged in at home with Zach, the farmer and his two sons. A short, stout man with a thick black beard appeared to be the organizer and he started slightly as he saw Eleanor approaching.

'We ain't doing nothing wrong, miss,' he explained. 'Just a bit of fun for the gamekeepers and us farmers, like. Lady Ormiston knows all about it.'

'I see,' said Eleanor. 'Well it looks a lot more fun than the wretched garden party. Would you allow me to join in?'

The man raised his eyebrows in astonishment. 'You her ladyship's goddaughter, miss?'

Eleanor nodded expectantly. 'That's right,' she said amiably. 'And you are?'

'Mickey Humphreys, miss. Local farmer.'

'Well, Mickey Humphreys local farmer, do you think I could take part in your competition?

Mickey removed his cloth cap and scratched his head, which, contrary to the profusion of hair on his chin, was surprisingly bald except for a smattering of long black strands. 'I don't know, miss. Archery ain't no sport for young ladies.'

Eleanor's eyes widened with pleading. 'Oh, please, Mickey,' she begged. 'I am going out of my mind with boredom.'

A wide, bemused grin spread across Mickey's face. 'Oh, all right then, miss, but just make sure you don't hurt yourself.'

Eleanor beamed back at him. 'Oh I won't, Mickey. I promise.'

Mickey introduced Eleanor to the rest of the men – four of whom were farmers and five of whom were the gamekeepers of the castle estate. They were all, in equal measures, both shocked and amused at the unconventional addition to their contest. Only three of the farmers and three of the game-keepers were to take part in the competition and straws were drawn to decide whom. Having selected the teams thus, Mickey, who had not been drawn as a participant, produced a knife from the waistband of his trousers and marked out a small round circle on the trunk of the tree. A line of twigs was then placed some way away from the tree, which marked the shooting line. The rules were that they were each allowed two shots and the nearest four partic-ipants to the target would then go through to the next round.

There was no denying that the men were expert shots all hitting extremely close to the target and a couple even hitting directly in the middle of it, which caused a round of applause from those watching. Eleanor was the last to go. She was used to being observed by Zach and his sons but under the scrutiny of ten strange men, all watching her in amused silence, she felt extremely self-conscious. Still, she resolved, she could not back down now. She must not make a cake of herself – for her own credibility. Taking in a deep reassuring breath she pulled back her bow and released the string. The arrow flew threw the air and landed with a thud right bang in the centre of the circle.

A collective gasp of surprise rose from her audience followed by a raucous round of applause and much head scratching.

'Well, miss,' announced an astounded Mickey. 'That's you good and proper through to the next round.'

Eleanor flashed him a relieved smile.

The next round was a man's handkerchief with a hole cut through the middle and the shooting line was moved back about a foot. This time only the best two would go through to the next and final round and they were only allowed one shot. Two of the men missed the handkerchief completely which resulted in much guffawing and name-calling from their audience, although Eleanor suspected the name-calling had been tempered somewhat due to her presence. Again she was the last to go. She took her time in lining up the target and held her breath as she released the string and watched the arrow on its course. She could scarce believe it when it found its target and another round of disbelieving but respectful applause rose from the men. Now there were only two of them left, a large stocky gamekeeper by the name of Will and Eleanor herself. For the final target, Mickey produced two apples, which had the men in fits of laughter. Tying both apples to the tree some twelve inches apart, Will gestured to Eleanor to go first. She had not felt so nervous in a very long time. Taking her time again, she released the arrow and to her complete and utter amazement it shot right through one of the apples slicing it clean in half. Turning around to look at her stunned audience, she couldn't help but giggle at their amazed expressions. Will went next, his arrow just clipping the side of the other apple. A large round of applause and a rather loud cheer came from the crowd followed by a lot of complimentary back slapping as they all agreed that Eleanor had won.

'Well, miss,' declared Mickey, removing his cap, 'the prize goes to you so it does. That's a couple of brace of rabbits. Caught fresh this morning.'

'Please do forgive me for interrupting, Mickey,' suddenly interjected a deep voice from directly behind her, 'but I require an urgent word with Lady Eleanor.'

A startled Eleanor gasped loudly as James grasped her upper arm and steered her away roughly from the bemused group.

Lowering his voice so as not to draw attention to them both, he said, as he led her back towards the lawned area, 'My aunt has been somewhat concerned over your whereabouts, Lady Eleanor. She asked that I come and find you.'

Eleanor flushed guiltily. 'I – er—'

'—have been demonstrating another of your alternative accomplishments, I see,' he interjected drily as they came to a halt on the edge of the manicured grass.

Eleanor felt the now familiar swell of indignant anger, which always seemed to fill her whenever she was in this man's presence. 'I was bored,' she protested, 'and I like archery and I—'

James cut her off abruptly. His eyes were sparkling with that thing that she couldn't identify. 'Save your excuses for my aunt, madam. I have no idea what she will say when she learns of your behaviour.'

Eleanor stuck out her chin defiantly. 'Oh, I have a very good idea, sir,' she said petulantly, 'but please, do not let that detract from your pleasure in telling her.'

Thankfully for Eleanor, just at that moment, a couple of gentlemen approached James and, after greeting him with much bowing and hand shaking, then began quizzing him about the fishing rights to the land.

Eleanor slipped away.

In no mood to return to the party, she wandered around to the stable block at the back of the house. Spotting an ideally located bale of hay in a quiet corner of the yard bathed in glorious sunshine, she climbed on to it and, sinking into the hay, made herself comfortable.

She must have dozed off slightly because when she awoke it was to the sound of voices coming from around the corner – one of a male and one of a female. It took but a moment for her to recognize them.

'Ah, what a surprise to see you here, my lord,' said Felicity Carmichael. 'I would have thought your admiring little group of debutantes would not have let you out of their sight for a moment.'

James Prestonville gave a polite chuckle. 'Oh, I can assure you, ma'am,' he replied sincerely, 'that any debutante's interest in me is purely fleeting. Now if you will excuse me, I was just – er – looking for someone.'

'Of course,' said Felicity graciously. 'However, I am grateful for the chance to have a word with you in private, my lord.'

'Oh?' he said, obviously surprised. 'And may I ask why, ma'am?'

'Of course. It is regarding my own come out which as you know is to take place next week.'

'So I have been informed, ma'am,' said James, his voice now tinged with amusement. 'On *several* occasions, I believe.'

'Yes,' replied Felicity coolly. 'My mama is somewhat excited about the event. A fact which seems to amuse you and your friend Mr Lovell greatly, does it not, my lord?'

James gave another chuckle. 'I think it is fair to say, ma'am, that your mother makes little disguise of her desire to have me as her son-in-law.'

'Hmm,' said Felicity, tartly. 'Well, perhaps you will find it not quite so amusing, sir, to note that I shall be expecting a proposal of marriage shortly after my come out.'

'That does not surprise me in the least, madam,' replied James affably. 'Is that not the usual way one goes about things?'

'Oh indeed it is, sir,' Felicity agreed at once. 'But what you are most likely not aware of, is that the offer I am expecting is from your good self.'

James emitted a snort of incredulous laughter. 'Forgive me, madam, but I think you must be all about in your head,' he exclaimed with a chortle.

Felicity gave a hollow laugh. 'Oh, I hold no illusions that it would be a love match, sir,' she pronounced calmly. 'Indeed, that does not interest me in the slightest. What does interest me, however, is becoming the next Duchess of Ormiston and mistress of Whitlock.'

'I see,' mused James blithely. 'Well, I am sorry to disappoint you, madam, but as you know, I have no plans to marry in the foreseeable future.'

Felicity's tone was deadly serious. 'Perhaps you did not, sir, but, as we all know, plans can quite easily be changed.'

'Oh, indeed,' agreed James brightly. 'However, only if one wishes to change them, madam, and I have no desire to marry you, or anyone else.'

'Hmm,' pondered Felicity aloud. 'Perhaps, sir, you would feel a little differently if you had a . . . reason to marry.'

'Perhaps I would, madam,' he said, a hint of impatience now evident in his tone, 'but I can assure you I have no such reason.'

'At the moment perhaps, sir,' remarked Felicity. 'However, you might change your mind if you discussed the advantages of marriage with someone who is already engaged in the institution. Someone like, perhaps . . . the Duke of Swinton.'

'The Duke of Swin— What on earth—' stammered James, obviously having been caught off guard.

Felicity's tone remained as calm as ever. 'Is the duke aware, I wonder, that his wife is playing him false?' she enquired innocently.

James quickly regained his composure. 'I have no idea what you are talking about, madam,' he replied ingenuously.

'Oh, but I think you do, sir,' countered Felicity. 'Does not the address 24

Wimpole Street mean anything to you?'

James gasped loudly. 'How on earth do you—'

Felicity gave a spiteful titter. 'Oh, I have my ways, sir. Indeed, one can glean a whole host of information from servants and drivers, should one be prepared to pay highly for it. Information such as what happens in your little love-nest in Wimpole Street whenever the duke takes it into his head to go to his club – which, I believe he does quite regularly and quite spontaneously. In which case a note is hastily delivered to yourself informing you of the duchess's . . . *availability*.'

'Why you little—'

'Oh, do not misunderstand me, sir,' she continued serenely. 'I would be quite happy for you to continue your *liaison*, should you comply with my wishes. However, should you see fit not to, then I think it is only fair that the duke is made aware of the – er – duplicitous nature of his spouse.'

James's voice now took on a dark edge. 'Are you telling me, madam, that unless I offer you marriage, you will inform the Duke of Swinton of my—'

'Indeed I am, sir and I hear the duke is a first-class shot. Why, I do believe he was awarded a medal for bravery in the battle of Vittoria.'

'Good Lord,' he exclaimed disbelievingly. 'I always knew that you were a cold fish but I never imagined you could be so . . . so—'

'I think *calculating* is the word you are looking for, sir.'

'That, I can assure you, is only one of many, madam.'

'Of course, there is no need to rush your decision,' informed Felicity brightly. 'Please do take a little time to consider my proposal.'

James's voice now reverberated with anger. 'I need not a second to consider it, madam,' he hissed. 'You may play your little games, but I wish to have no part in them. I would not marry you if you were the last woman on earth. And do not flatter yourself that you are the only one who has a calculating mind. If I wished to I could spread a rumour about you in a flash which would ruin you forever.'

'You wouldn't dare,' expostulated Felicity stoutly.

'Wouldn't I?' countered James icily. 'I think perhaps you underestimate me, madam.'

Eleanor heard his feet crunching against the gravel. He must have turned his back on Felicity and be walking away from her. She shivered as she heard Felicity hissing to his retreating back, her caustic tone dripping with loathing, 'And I think, perhaps, *you* underestimate *me*, sir,' she spat.

Eleanor could not quite believe what she had just heard. Felicity

Carmichael had attempted to blackmail James into marrying her. She had disliked the girl the instant she had made her acquaintance, but she never would have dreamed she was so—

Her musings were cut short as she became aware of footsteps walking around the corner towards her, muttering a series of rather shocking imprecations. Before she had a chance to move, however, Felicity was standing directly before her.

Desperately attempting to arrange her countenance from one of pure horror into something resembling normality, Eleanor tried to speak, but no words were forthcoming. It was too late anyway. Felicity's ugly features twisted into an expression which Eleanor could only describe as pure evil. Then she turned on her heel and marched back from whence she had come. Eleanor had never felt so frightened in her entire life.

# CHAPTER 6

'ARE you sickening for something, miss? You're not yourself and you're awful pale.' Eleanor glanced at her reflection as Milly pinned up her hair the following day. She had contemplated telling Milly about what she'd overheard yesterday, but decided against it. She had also contemplated talking to James, but didn't see how that could help anything and besides, he might have brushed the whole thing off after having sniggered about it with the odious Mr Lovell. Despite being unable to wipe the evil parting look Felicity had given her from her mind however, she tried convincing herself that she was reading too much into the whole thing. The best thing she could do, she had concluded, was to try and forget the entire incident. After all, the way James had so vehemently refused Felicity's request, should have put an end to the matter.

She smiled weakly at Milly's concerned face. 'No, I'm fine, Milly, honestly. I just didn't sleep very well, that's all.'

The dowager was at breakfast when Eleanor made her weary way downstairs. She merely glanced at Eleanor for a second, seemingly engrossed in the contents of a letter she was reading. Her dark eyes were growing narrower and narrower with every word, the deep lines on her forehead knitting together as she apparently tried to make sense of the script.

'Hmph,' she said at length, folding up the letter and slipping it back into its envelope before booming out at full volume, 'Stevens!'

'Yes, your grace?' muttered the footman, coming to stand alongside her.

'We are to receive another visitor today,' informed the dowager brusquely. 'See to it that the lilac room at the end of Lady Eleanor's corridor is made up immediately.'

As the footman bowed and took his leave of the room, Eleanor said, 'Another visitor, ma'am? May I ask who?'

'Indeed you may, Eleanor. It is a young widow from Hungary, who is keen to participate in the Season here. A protégée of a very old friend of mine, who, I must confess, I have not heard from for quite some time.'

Eleanor raised her brows expectedly. 'A young widow, ma'am? Do you have any idea of her age?'

'One can assume that she is a little older than yourself, Eleanor. However, let us hope she is a little less *hard work*,' replied the dowager, through pursed lips.

Despite her godmother's disparaging comment, Eleanor's spirits lifted a little. It would be fun to have another young lady in the house and it would certainly mean she would not feel outnumbered by James and Mr Lovell. Yes, the news regarding their new guest had cheered her up considerably.

Just at that moment, James entered the breakfast-room. Eleanor had not set eyes on him since the conversation with Felicity yesterday. She had hung around the stables for what seemed like an eternity, not wishing to see Felicity again. When she had returned to the party, many of the guests had already left, the Carmichaels being amongst them – Lady Carmichael having apparently had 'one of her heads'. Fortunately, by the time Eleanor had returned, her godmother had partaken of so much brandy that she had quite lost interest in her goddaughter's whereabouts.

Feigning a great deal of interest in the triangular slice of toast she was buttering, Eleanor mumbled a good morning. She wondered how he was feeling: whether he had had as fitful a night's sleep as she. She didn't have long to wait: in fact, only as long as it took him to sit down and reach for the silver coffee pot.

'Well, Aunt,' he declared blithely, 'I think congratulations are in order. Uncle would have been proud of you. That was one of the best garden parties ever.'

How could he sound so . . . so chirpy? She sneaked a look at him. He looked fine: quite normal in fact in his spotless riding attire. Indeed it appeared as though the conversation with Felicity had not affected him at all.

At her nephew's praise, the dowager's severe expression melted slightly. 'If I do say so myself, James, it did seem to go down rather well thanks in no small part to you playing the perfect host; you had all the young chits positively eating out of your hand.'

James rolled his eyes dramatically. 'It was all I could do to shake some of them off, Aunt.'

'Indeed,' said the dowager, a hint of mischief in her tone, 'well, do not permit Cynthia Carmichael to hear you say such a thing; the woman will never tire in her efforts to marry you off to the ghastly Felicity.'

At the mention of Felicity, Eleanor held her breath for a second and raised her eyes to James. She watched his expression tighten for a moment, before resuming its usual relaxed countenance.

'In that case, my dear Aunt,' he said, 'Cynthia Carmichael will soon be one very exhausted woman.'

A peremptory knock at the door signalled the arrival of Giles. 'Begging your pardon, your grace,' he said, on entering the room and bowing stiffly, 'but there is a *man* at the door with something for Lady Eleanor.'

Eleanor's brow wrinkled as she puzzled over the announcement.

'What *man* and what *something*, Giles?' snapped the dowager impatiently.

'The farmer, Mickey Humphreys, ma'am. With several – er – *dead rabbits.*' He sniffed disapprovingly.

Eleanor's heart sank as she realized that Giles was talking about the prize from the archery competition. With the awful business with Felicity, she had completely forgotten about the competition. Now would be James's ideal opportunity to inform the dowager of what would undoubtedly be classed as Eleanor's 'shockingly unbecoming behaviour' and she would no doubt receive the biggest scolding of her life.

The dowager's eyes widened as she turned her gaze to her goddaughter. 'And what, may I ask, would Mickey Humphreys be doing here with dead rabbits, Eleanor?'

Eleanor flushed guiltily. 'I – er—'

'They are to be distributed between the farmhouses, Aunt,' cut in James. 'Two men were caught poaching in the woods yesterday and when Mickey caught them, Lady Eleanor instructed him to share the bounty between the various farmhouses.'

'Did she indeed?' replied the dowager, suspiciously. 'And why then would Mickey Humphreys be bringing the rabbits here, pray?'

'I – um – have no—' stammered Eleanor, feeling increasingly uncomfortable under her godmother's scrutiny.

'The man has obviously forgotten his instructions,' piped up James. 'Please remind him, Giles, that the rabbits are to be distributed between the houses on the estate.'

'Very well, my lord,' replied Giles, bowing his head and leaving the room.

James rolled his eyes dramatically. 'Damned farmers,' he sniffed. 'Can't remember where they live sometimes, although having seen some of their wives, perhaps that is merely wishful thinking.'

At James's attempt at humour, Eleanor failed to suppress a most unladylike snort of laughter.

'Really, Eleanor,' chided the dowager, 'it does not do for young ladies to snort like a farmyard animal. Indeed, it is most—'

'—*unbecoming*,' chorused Eleanor and James together, before both collapsing into fits of hysterical laughter.

The dowager's pursed lips and stern expression showed that she was not impressed with their uncouth behaviour. 'Hmph,' she chided. 'I do wish, Eleanor, that you would take matters regarding your conduct a little more seriously. How on earth we are to find a man who can cope with you, I have no idea. Now, girl, you are aware, are you not, that we have a number of social occasions to attend next week?'

Eleanor attempted a serious tone. 'Yes, Godmother.'

'And have you, dare I ask, given any thought to what you are to wear to these occasions?'

Eleanor could feel another bubble of laughter slowly working its way up from her stomach. Focusing on her piece of toast, she attempted to think of something serious to quell it, but when a snort of laughter came from James, she could hold it back no longer.

'I'm afraid I have not, Godmother,' she blurted out, tears of laughter now rolling freely down her cheeks. 'I haven't given it a single thought.'

James was now laughing so hard that he had pushed back his chair from the table and was almost doubled up. The dowager, casting despairing looks at them, announced, 'Then it is just as well that one of us has the foresight to think of such matters. You will accompany me to London today, Eleanor, to buy you a new gown. We will leave at eleven of the clock sharp.'

Her announcement resulted in the two of them laughing even harder, until Giles, a most disapproving look on his face at so much activity within one morning, suddenly appeared once again in the doorway. 'Excuse me, my lord,' he announced soberly, 'but a note has been delivered for you. The messenger informed me that it requires your urgent attention.'

Suddenly all laughter ceased as a serious expression spread over James's face. 'Give it here,' he instructed briskly.

Snatching the envelope from the tray Giles was carrying, he hurriedly ripped it open. Eleanor watched his face as all colour visibly drained from his cheeks.

'Excuse me, Aunt, Lady Eleanor,' he said, suddenly thrusting to his feet.

'But I have a matter of some import to attend to.'

And with that he strode purposefully out of the room leaving Eleanor with the distinct, uneasy feeling that the note had had something to do with Felicity Carmichael and her threat.

Eleanor had never been to London before. Indeed, apart from the odd hurried essential purchase, she had never really been shopping before. As their carriage rattled its way along the wide, cobbled streets, she wondered at all the traffic, the cacophony of sounds, the intermingling smells – some more pleasant than others – and the many glass-fronted shops offering everything from pigs' heads to exquisite jewels. She had never seen so many buildings crammed into one space together and gazed wide-eyed at the ancient magnificence of some juxtaposed with the fashionable modernity of others.

'Of course, when the duke was alive we used to move up to a town house in Grosvenor Square for the Season,' declared the dowager looking out of her window, 'but I fear I am getting too old for such upheaval now. Whitlock serves us well enough being only a few miles from the centre.'

Eleanor nodded her agreement. Being a country girl, she didn't think she could have stood it at all if she had been forced to stay in such a place for more than a few hours.

Winding its way into the centre, the coach passed by a dark-haired man on horseback who, from his rear view, put Eleanor rather in mind of James. She had, she was forced to admit, admired his spirit that morning after yesterday's confrontation with Felicity and she had greatly appreciated him not divulging the real reason Mickey Humphreys had turned up with the rabbits. Indeed she would go so far as to say that she had quite enjoyed his company at breakfast. She had never really seen him laugh before. It had affected his features quite pleasantly and she couldn't help but notice he had a rather attractive set of remarkably straight, white teeth.

The dowager, it soon became apparent, was on a mission to replenish Eleanor's wardrobe. Not only did they order three ball gowns, all a little too revealing to suit Eleanor's tastes, but she had little say in the matter, but they also procured day dresses, evening dresses, hats, shoes, bonnets, petticoats and boots. By the time they arrived home, Eleanor was quite exhausted. Milly, on the other hand, was bursting with excitement as she rifled through the packages, marvelling at the delights within.

'Oh, miss, you're going to look mighty fine when we get you in all of this.

I can hardly wait for all them new dresses to come. Why, you're going to look better than a queen, miss.'

Most of the dresses were to be made up and delivered later that week, but in her excitement, for dinner that evening, Milly forced Eleanor into the one new evening dress she had brought back with her. The garment was of dove-coloured silk, with a narrow skirt and a lace-trimmed bodice. She also spent a little longer on her hair, arranging it in a cluster of curls held in place with a new pearl clip. Eleanor admired her reflection in the mirror. She looked – and indeed she felt – very nice indeed.

Her high opinion of herself lasted precisely until she entered the saloon where they gathered before dinner.

'Ah, Eleanor,' said the dowager who was seated in her usual chair at the side of the fire, cradling a large brandy glass. 'Allow me to introduce our new guest, Lady Madeleine Bouvray, from Hungary.'

Lady Madeleine stood up from her chair and turned to face Eleanor. It was all Eleanor could do not to gasp at the woman's perfection. She was shorter than Eleanor with a slim yet curvaceous figure. Her hair was white blonde and dressed high on her head, which accentuated her sharp cheekbones, startling blue eyes and perfect rosebud mouth. She was wearing a beautiful gown of rose-pink sarcanet, which sat well with her flawless alabaster-like skin. Everything about the woman's appearance put Eleanor in mind of a fragile china doll.

She held out a tiny hand to Eleanor. 'Delighted to meet you,' she purred, in an exotic foreign accent.

Eleanor accepted the proffered hand, marvelling at the softness of it. In the presence of this perfect petite creature, she suddenly felt overly tall and gawky. She returned the woman's greeting with a little more enthusiasm than she was actually feeling and, as Lady Madeleine resumed her seat in the armchair opposite that of the dowager, Eleanor made herself comfortable on the sofa between the two. She accepted a glass of orgeat from Stevens then, curious to find out more about her prospective new friend, she said, 'My godmother informs me that you wish to spend the Season in London, Lady Madeleine.'

'Indeed, I do,' purred Madeleine, 'and I am extremely grateful to Lady Ormiston for allowing me the opportunity to do so,' she continued, inclining her head graciously to the dowager.

'I must confess, Madeleine,' announced the dowager, studying the young woman's face through narrowed eyes, 'that I was surprised to hear from Lady

Neilson. It is quite some years now since we were friends here in London. Her husband was the Hungarian ambassador you know, and they had to return to Hungary in quite a hurry if I recall. We corresponded for several years but then lost touch. How is the woman?'

Lady Madeleine broke out into another beguiling smile. 'Oh she is very well, ma'am. And most keen that I pass on her kindest regards. She hopes that you will write to her very soon.'

'Indeed I will,' said the dowager. 'I will give the matter my most urgent attention.'

'She speaks very highly of you, madam,' continued Lady Madeleine. 'She told me you were one of the most charming people she has ever had the good fortune to meet.'

Eleanor bit back a smile. The dowager could be described as many things, but charming was most certainly not amongst them.

'Did she indeed?' said Lady Ormiston, visibly puffing up at the compliment. 'Yes, well, we were very good friends – very good friends indeed. I quite missed her when she had to leave. I shall write to her this very evening.'

'I'm sure she will be delighted, madam,' said the younger woman sincerely.

Eleanor took another sip of her orgeat. 'Well, Lady Madeleine,' she observed, 'I must congratulate you on your excellent English. Where on earth did you learn to speak it so well?'

Lady Madeleine flashed her a grateful smile. 'You are too kind,' she replied graciously. 'My grandmother was English so she—'

She broke off as the door was suddenly thrust open and in sauntered James, looking decidedly melancholy.

'Ah,' said the dowager, her features, as usual, softening at the sight of her adored nephew. 'Madeleine, this is my nephew, James Prestonville, Marquis of Rothwell.'

Lady Madeleine's eyes lit up as James approached her. She rose from her chair. 'Delighted to make your acquaintance, my lord,' she said charmingly, dropping down into a deep curtsy, which permitted him a first-class view of her full bosom.

Eleanor watched with interest, curious to observe the effect Lady Madeleine's exquisite beauty would have on a member of the male species. To her amazement, however, she noted that James, quite atypically, merely offered the woman a cursory bow before plumping down on the sofa next to Eleanor and staring into the crackling fire.

'Lady Madeleine has just arrived this evening from Hungary, James,' declared the dowager, throwing her nephew an imploring glare.

Obviously correctly interpreting the look as an instruction to engage in conversation with Madeleine, James replied flatly, 'Oh, yes. I trust you had a good journey, ma'am?'

Lady Madeleine having resumed her seat, smoothed down her skirts. 'Thank you, sir, it was very good indeed,' she replied, tossing him a dazzling smile.

James merely nodded and smiled fleetingly. What then followed was a rather awkward silence before the dowager announced, 'Well, Madeleine, we are all to attend the Carmichaels' ball on Friday evening and I'm sure James would be delighted to accompany you, would you not, *James*?'

'Hmm?' said James, the sound of his name being spoken obviously breaking his musings.

'I was just informing Lady Madeleine, James,' declared the dowager firmly, 'that you should be delighted to accompany her to the Carmichaels' ball on Friday, would you not?'

There was little doubt that this was not a question, but rather another of the dowager's orders.

'Oh – er – of course,' faltered James. 'I should be delighted, Lady Madeleine.'

The dowager and Lady Madeleine exchanged contented smiles while James went back to his study of the flames. Eleanor threw him a sidelong glance. He looked extremely anxious – the very antithesis of his relaxed state at breakfast that morning. Something had obviously changed since then; something that had had a serious effect on his demeanour; something that had most definitely started with the arrival of the note at breakfast that morning.

# CHAPTER 7

WHATEVER brief notions Eleanor had been harbouring for a friendship with Lady Madeleine, she very quickly discarded, for it soon became very clear that she was not amongst those persons whom Lady Madeleine deemed worthy of her company. Two days ago for example, Eleanor had enquired if Lady Madeleine would care to accompany her in a stroll around the gardens. The woman had declined on the grounds that she was 'feeling a little peaked and was going for a lie down'. An hour later however, Eleanor had bumped into her strolling with James who, despite the presence of the beautiful Hungarian, had remained somewhat subdued over the last few days.

In another incident that very morning the dowager had sent word with Giles asking Lady Madeleine if she wished to accompany herself and Eleanor on a trip into Richmond. The message that came back said that she would have to decline as she had a huge amount of correspondence to catch on. Less than half an hour after their departure though, so Eleanor had been reliably informed by Milly, Lady Madeleine had joined James in the drawing-room where they had spent the entire morning, taking tea and chatting.

'If you're asking me,' said Milly, after she'd passed on the information about Lady Madeleine's morning activities, 'she's a top scholar at flirting, that one.'

'Well, that's as may be, Milly,' Eleanor had replied, 'but it would appear that she has everyone under her spell. Even my godmother appears to have warmed to her. No doubt one can get away with quite a lot when one is as beautiful as Lady Madeleine.'

'Hmph,' Milly had tutted loyally. 'The woman ain't one bit prettier than you, miss.'

Eleanor wasn't the only member of the household to whom Madeleine had taken an instant dislike: the woman made no secret of her growing revulsion of the lecherous Mr Lovell. Indeed that was, so far as Eleanor could see, the only thing which she and the Hungarian had in common. Seemingly undeterred however by Lady Madeleine's snubs and sharp, biting comments, Lovell continued making his lewd remarks whenever the dowager was out of earshot. Meanwhile, his increasing unpopularity did not stop with the females of the house, as even James, in his melancholy state, appeared to be growing tired of the man's irritating, frivolous behaviour.

The previous evening the dowager had taken dinner in her room, leaving the four of them to dine downstairs. Following a rather pathetic, juvenile comment from Mr Lovell regarding two pink moulded blancmanges, Lady Madeleine had piped up: 'In Hungary, we have a saying, Mr Lovell, that the constant need to refer to something signifies that that person is lacking in the certain something to which they are constantly referring.'

Mr Lovell had sneered in his usual way. 'And what do you mean by that exactly, Lady Madeleine?'

'You may read into it what you will, Mr Lovell,' she had replied, caustically. 'Now if you will excuse me, I should like to take a stroll around the gardens. James, will you accompany me?'

'Wh-what?' stammered James, lost in his thoughts once again.

'Please accompany me in a stroll around the gardens,' said Lady Madeleine rising to her feet. 'I have no wish to spend a moment longer in this disgusting man's presence.'

And with that, she flounced out of the room, with James and indeed Lady Eleanor, not too far behind her.

'*Enfin! Enfin!*' Monsieur Aminieux clapped his hands wildly. 'She can do it *enfin*.' Indeed even Eleanor was feeling quite pleased with herself. In addition to her dreaded daily dancing lessons with M. Aminieux, it had taken an additional, and much more enjoyable, two hours each day for the last week with Milly, for her to master the complicated steps of the quadrille. She dared not confess to the dowager or M. Aminieux about her extra tuition in case she got Milly into trouble, but the younger girl appeared to enjoy their sessions just as much as Eleanor, and it was enough for her to take pleasure in seeing her mistress progress so well. Eleanor had, however, made a mental note to give Milly a special treat as a thank you for all her extra hard work.

'Excuse me, ma'am.' Lady Madeleine appeared in the ballroom doorway, looking her usual radiant self in a simple day gown of worked muslin. 'I wondered if I might take the carriage into London this afternoon?'

'Why, of course, you may, my girl,' said Lady Ormiston. 'Stevens,' she boomed, causing them all to jump, 'have the carriage brought out later for Lady Madeleine.'

The timid footman bowed his consent and retreated hastily. Eleanor flashed him a sympathetic look. The man looked as though he was living purely on his wits. Hardly surprising the way the dowager continually bellowed orders at him. Indeed, Eleanor was finding it difficult enough keeping her own nerves in check with the Dowager's constant commands, criticisms and chastizings. Lady Madeleine on the other hand, appeared to have a similar effect on the dowager as her nephew and could do no wrong at all. Perhaps that was because, thought Eleanor, unlike herself, no one could ever accuse Lady Madeleine of being 'unbecoming'.

'Madeleine, have you met Eleanor's dance master, M. Aminieux? He is one of the best in all of London,' said the dowager.

'Pleased to make your acquaintance, sir,' said Lady Madeleine, in her usual charming manner.

'How delightful,' he replied, instantly falling under the woman's bewitching spell. 'May I ask where you are from, madam?'

'I am from Hungary, *monsieur*.'

Monsieur Aminieux clapped his hands together in amazement. 'But this is fantastic,' he enthused. 'Madame Aminieux is from Hungary, too, and she is rarely having the opportunity to speak to her compatriots. I wonder if I might be so bold, *madame*, as to ask if you might accompany me to my house one day? When it is convenient for you, of course.'

At this suggestion, Lady Madeleine visibly balked. Indeed, for one very brief moment, Eleanor thought the woman could not have looked more horrified if someone had asked her to walk barefoot through a pit of large slimy slugs.

'Er, thank you, *monsieur*,' she said, rapidly rearranging her features into their usual perfect order, 'that would be . . . delightful.' She inclined her head. 'Now if you will excuse me,' she continued briskly. 'I have a great many things to do before this afternoon.'

Monsieur Aminieux grinned broadly. 'Of course, *madame*. I will be speaking to Madame Aminieux and we will be sending you the invitation.'

'How very – er – kind,' muttered Lady Madeleine. She shot him a brief smile before disappearing out of the room.

While Eleanor's dancing may have been improving, her embroidery most definitely was not. Later that afternoon, the dowager picked up the little silver silk drawstring reticule Eleanor was still embroidering with tiny pearl daisies and examined it carefully through her lorgnette.

'Good gracious, girl, I had thought,' she sniped, through pursed lips, 'that we were to have this finished in time for you to take to the Carmichaels' ball.'

'Er, yes, we . . . were, Godmother.'

'And when, pray tell, is the ball, Eleanor?'

'The evening of the morrow.'

'And do you really think you can have it finished by then?'

'Oh, of course.'

The dowager cast her an incredulous glance and whisked out of the room.

It was almost time for dinner when Lady Madeleine returned to the castle. Eleanor watched from her bedroom window as the woman alighted from the carriage. She couldn't help but feel a momentary pang of both resentment and jealousy. Of course, being a widow, Lady Madeleine was allowed much more freedom than she and certainly appeared to be making the most of it. Eleanor, on the other hand, had been forced to sit for hours embroidering ghastly daisies on to a ghastly bag with the ghastly dowager. How much longer, she wondered, would she have to stay here and endure this mindless boredom? If the only alternative was marriage, then she feared she could well be enduring mindless boredom for the remainder of her life.

Eleanor was positively dreading Felicity Carmichael's come out ball. As Milly fussed around her, preparing her toilette, it was obvious that the younger girl was a hundred times more excited about the event than her mistress. Indeed the only positive thing Eleanor could think of was that, as the preparations had taken the best part of the day, it had meant that she was able to miss both her dancing lesson and pianoforte practice, both with the dowager's reluctant approval.

Eventually, having put the last diamond comb into her mistress's hair, Milly stood back and gazed at Eleanor. Rather than her usual effusing, she appeared uncharacteristically lost for words and instead simply held her hands over her mouth, staring at her mistress in complete and utter silence.

Eleanor began to panic. What could possibly be so wrong that Milly couldn't tell her? Then it dawned on her: of course, she must look ridiculous. Yes, that was it. She looked utterly ridiculous and the poor girl had not the courage to tell her so. She knew the gown was too low cut. Indeed she had told Lady Ormiston so the day they were at the mantua-maker in London. And she had protested just as strongly at Milly's insistence that she wear a little rouge –

although Milly had, as usual, won. The whole effect must look completely absurd.

'Don't worry, Milly,' she said gently, smiling at the girl. 'I know I look ridiculous. I will inform my godmother immediately that I am not to attend the ball. I will tell her that I am feeling unwell.'

Milly gasped loudly. Then she removed her hands from her mouth and placed them on her hips.

'Are you meaning to say, miss, that you think I've spent all day getting you ready and now you're not wanting to go?'

'No, but I—'

'And what's this about you looking ridiculous? Eeh, I do declare I've never seen you looking more beautiful, miss,' she said, her sparkling blue eyes now brimming with tears. 'Now come over and look in the mirror.'

Eleanor's eyes grew wide as she surveyed her reflection in the mirror. Milly's handiwork to date was nothing to what she had created this evening. Rather than seeing her usual girlish features, the image that was staring back at her was of a beautiful, sophisticated young *woman*.

Her gown, chosen by the dowager, and in which Eleanor had shown absolutely no interest at all until now, was a stunning creation in silver satin with a spider gauze overlay and a skirt, which artfully skimmed her slim hips. Even the very low cut bodice flattered her, showing off her full bosom very well indeed. As usual, Milly had done a superb job with her hair, arranging it in a mass of loose curls, then clipping it to one side so that it tumbled softly over her left shoulder. The trace of rouge she had used merely added a subtle glow to her flawless complexion.

'And don't be forgetting your shoes, miss,' said Milly, holding out a pair of kid slippers in exactly the same shade of silver as her dress. 'Now all we need is your reticule.'

Eleanor cringed. 'Oh no, Milly. I have to take that dreadful thing I have been embroidering myself and I still haven't finished it.'

Milly rolled her eyes. 'Well you'd better hurry up, miss. You're due to leave here in an hour.'

Flying barefoot along the corridors and stairs down to the drawing-room, Eleanor prayed to God that she did not encounter the dowager. The woman had been nagging her for weeks now to have the blasted reticule completed in time for the ball and, despite Lady Ormiston's undisguised scepticism, Eleanor had assured her that it would be. She had no wish now to see the self-satisfied look on the dowager's face, nor to incur the woman's wrath. Seeking out the sewing basket, she retrieved the reticule, a needle and thread and the box of tiny white pearls and hastily began sewing.

The eight chimes of the grandfather clock echoed resoundingly around the enormous entrance hall as Eleanor made her way tentatively down the imposing stone staircase. The sound of her godmother's booming voice competing admirably with the chimes of the clock for superiority, added to her apprehension. As she gingerly descended the stairs, she spotted the dowager, standing in the middle of the hall, talking animatedly to Lady Madeleine. She was wearing a hooped, old-fashioned gown in mauve, which made her appear twice as large as she was. James was standing a little way from the pair, looking distant once again. Dressed all in black he looked, she reluctantly had to admit, quite dashing. It was Lady Madeleine's gown however – or rather the little there was of it – which was the most striking and which caused Eleanor's eyes to widen in astonishment. If she had thought the low cut of her own gown quite shocking, it was nothing compared to that of Lady Madeleine's. Indeed everything about the exotic creation, from the daring cut, both front and back, to the almost sheer, clinging gold fabric, was verging on the outrageous, but with her white-blonde hair arranged in a high creation adorned with two curled feathers, there could be no disputing that Lady Madeleine looked completely stunning. Indeed, her ethereal beauty put Eleanor in mind of a Grecian goddess.

'Ah, Eleanor. At last,' said the dowager briskly, breaking off her conversation as Eleanor walked across the hall towards them. 'Now, where is Mr Lovell?'

All eyes turned to James, who appeared not to have heard the question but who was, instead, gazing intently at Eleanor with the same strange expression on his face she had seen before. Eleanor came to a halt directly in front of him and gulped. His attention was making her feel decidedly uncomfortable. At a loss as to what to do, or where to look, she opted to stare down at her feet. Still she could feel his eyes burning into her. Why was he looking at her so? Why didn't he say something? Why didn't he make one of his usual pathetic jibes? Did he think she looked ridiculous? If he did, she had little doubt he would voice his thoughts; after all, he had made no secret of his low opinion of her so far. Anyway, she remonstrated silently, why did she care what he thought? His worthless opinions did not matter to her one jot. She lifted her head defiantly and met his eyes with her own. The intensity of his dark gaze sent a shiver flashing down her spine and caused her stomach to do something rather strange: something which she could only describe as a rather energetic somersault.

'James!' roared the dowager suddenly, breaking the moment and causing them all to start. 'Where on earth is Mr Lovell?'

James shook himself out of his private musings. 'I – er – believe he is to meet us there, Aunt,' he floundered uncharacteristically.

Lady Ormiston began striding vigorously towards the main door. 'Very well then,' she boomed. 'Now come along, Eleanor, or we shall be late and you know I cannot abide tardiness. It is a most unbecoming characteristic.'

They took their seats in the plush bottle-green carriage and sank into the comfortable velvet squabs: Eleanor and her godmother on one side and James and Lady Madeleine on the other.

'Well, I must say, Eleanor,' announced the dowager as the door of the carriage was closed, 'You are in quite acceptable looks this evening. Indeed I would go as far as to say that you look quite the thing. And if I may say so, I made an excellent choice with that gown. Doesn't make you look like a knitting needle at all. Would you not agree, Lady Madeleine?'

'Oh, indeed, I would, my lady,' purred Madeleine huskily. 'Although I must confess that I thought silver was quite out of vogue this season.'

'Hmph,' snorted the dowager dismissively. 'Things are jumping in and out of vogue so quickly these days, one can hardly keep up with it all. Still, the girl looks a damned sight better than she did a couple of weeks ago. If we're lucky someone will show a bit of interest in her tonight and we might be a step nearer to getting her wed.'

Lady Madeleine regarded Eleanor through narrowed eyes. 'Hmm,' she pondered sceptically. 'If you are *very* lucky, ma'am.'

Eleanor felt the blood rush to her cheeks. Did her godmother really have to refer to her so in front of James and Madeleine? She felt as though she were about to die of a severe case of mortification exacerbated by Lady Madeleine's scrutinizing look and blatantly unconvinced response. The only thing for which she was grateful was that James appeared not to be listening to the conversation at all – yet again completely lost in thought as he gazed meditatively out of the carriage window into the fine spring evening beyond. Unfortunately for Eleanor, however, the other two members of the carriage showed no such signs of becoming distracted.

'What an *interesting* reticule you have with you, Lady Eleanor,' suddenly announced Lady Madeleine. 'And how . . . *quaint* to have decorated it with sheep.'

'They are not sheep,' protested Eleanor stoutly. 'They are daisies.'

'Oh,' replied Lady Madeleine, adopting the same condescending manner one uses when talking to a small child. 'Of course they are, dear.'

'Never mind what they are,' piped up the dowager loudly. 'At least she got the deuced thing finished on time.'

# CHAPTER 8

MAYFAIR, that most fashionable area of London, was the location of the Carmichaels' rented townhouse. By the time she alighted from the carriage however, Eleanor was almost too furious to take any note at all of her surroundings. Lady Madeleine had succeeded in criticizing not only her reticule, but also her gown, her shoes, her hair and even her posture. And she had done so in such a cunning way that it had been impossible for Eleanor to defend herself without appearing churlish and incurring the wrath of her godmother. While Eleanor had sat seething throughout the journey, James on the other hand, had merely sat – staring silently out of the window. He had completely ignored them all during the drive and had not uttered a single word.

Obviously out to impress, the Carmichaels had rented what appeared to be quite the largest townhouse in the whole of London. Set higher than its neighbours, with a majestic set of wide stone stairs leading to the main door, the building gave off a haughty superior air. Every one of its many windows was brightly illuminated and the main door was thrown wide open flooding the street below with a hub-bub of chatter, laughter and music.

As soon as Eleanor set foot in the large black and white tiled entrance hall, it became apparent that the beautiful exterior of the property merely served as a taster for the opulent delights within. Hundreds of candles blazed brightly and the doors to all the rooms leading off the hall had been thrown open allowing arriving guests a first-class view directly into the magnificent ballroom. A large crowd was already gathered in the hall, every one of them dressed in unabashed splendour. Indeed, even Eleanor, who had little time for such profligate frivolity could not help but be amazed at the lavishness of the event. She had never seen so many beautiful gowns or glittering jewels: everywhere she looked her eye caught the shimmer of a diamond tiara, the wink of a sapphire necklace or the twinkle of a ruby ear-ring. Her previous surge of anger quickly dissipated to be replaced by complete and utter astonishment.

'Eleanor! Close your mouth and stop gawping, girl. It is quite unbecoming,' ordered the dowager as they observed the crowd from the threshold. 'Now let us attempt to make our way to the ballroom.'

Intent on her mission not to linger in the hall, the dowager began brandishing her fan in the manner of a sword, rudely sweeping aside anyone in her path. A rather embarrassed Eleanor trotted behind obediently, offering the dowager's stunned victims apologetic smiles on the way. Holding possessively on to James's arm, Madeleine and her escort brought up the rear at a somewhat more leisurely pace: James, obviously having affected a more sociable air, stopping here and there to exchange a few pleasantries and to introduce the beautiful Hungarian to those he deemed worthy of her acquaintance. Eventually they reached the door to the ballroom where Lady Carmichael and Felicity were greeting their guests. From the high flush on Lady Carmichael's cheeks, it appeared that she was in something of a flurry. Felicity on the other hand, appeared quite cool and composed. Eleanor felt the blood freeze in her veins as the girl turned her head to her. She was trussed up in some kind of hideous peach creation with far too much ruching on the bodice to be flattering.

'Ah, Lady Ormiston and Eleanor. How delightful,' gushed Lady Carmichael, bobbing a curtsy. 'I cannot tell you how excited we are that this day has finally arrived. And have you seen how many people are here, Lady Ormiston? I do declare the event is to be the talk of the town for months to come.'

'Indeed,' sniffed the dowager. 'You do seem to have gone to a lot of effort, Cynthia.'

'Well nothing is too much effort for my little pumpkin,' replied Lady Carmichael, looking adoringly at Felicity. 'Let us only hope that it leads to greater things, Lady Ormiston.'

The dowager rolled her eyes.

'Oh my goodness, is that James I see making his way over? How marvellous. We were so hoping he would be able to attend, weren't we, darling?' gushed Lady Carmichael to her daughter.

Grateful for the diversion of Felicity's attention away from herself, Eleanor dared to sneak a look at the girl as all other heads, including Felicity's, turned towards James and Lady Madeleine. An almost palpable ripple of excitement followed the couple as they approached the group. Indeed Lady Madeleine appeared to be the cynosure of all eyes. It was not only her exquisite beauty and daring gown which were causing a stir, but also the fact that she was holding the arm of one of the most sought-after men in the whole of England, providing delicious fodder for the ever-hungry gossips. Observing Felicity's features twist into an ominous mixture of red-hot fury and blatant jealousy as she absorbed the scene, Eleanor felt a rash of prickly goosebumps break out over her body.

Lady Carmichael, too, appeared to be having problems disguising her sentiments. 'Oh,' she sniffed, her tone ripe with disappointment. 'James has a ... *guest*, I see.'

'Indeed, he does,' replied the dowager matter-of-factly. 'Lady Madeleine is from Hungary. She is staying with us for the Season.'

Lady Carmichael whipped open her fan and began fluttering frantically. 'Ah,' she said, breathing an audible sigh of relief. 'Then she will not be staying in London long?'

Before anyone had a chance to reply, James and Madeleine came to a halt before the group.

This time Eleanor watched James's face carefully. She had little doubt that this would be the first occasion he, too, had set eyes on Felicity since the attempted blackmailing incident at the garden party. Would he, she wondered, feel as uncomfortable in the girl's evil presence as she did?

James, however, appeared not in the least perturbed. Indeed he appeared to have exchanged his surly, silent countenance and manner of only a few minutes ago, for one of unadulterated charm – undoubtedly all for the benefit of Felicity. 'Ah, the ladies Carmichael,' he gushed ardently, his face breaking out into a wide, captivating smile. 'May I congratulate you on what appears to be a first-class event.' He bowed graciously. Felicity and her mother dipped a curtsy.

'Thank you, James,' tinkled Lady Carmichael, eyeing Lady Madeleine suspiciously. 'I see that you have brought a guest with you this evening.'

'Indeed I have,' replied James silkily. 'Allow me to introduce you to Lady Madeleine Bouvray. From Hungary no less,' he said, beaming affectionately at his partner.

Not releasing her hold of James's arm for one moment, nor apparently sensing anything in the least odd about his sudden change of behaviour, Lady Madeleine sank into a low curtsy which revealed the shockingly low cut of her dress a little more than propriety would usually allow.

She smiled beatifically at the Carmichaels as she straightened. 'Charmed,' she purred in her exotic accent.

Cynthia Carmichael's eyes widened and her fan fluttering intensified. 'Hmm,' she flustered, inclining her head to the younger woman. 'Er ... all the way from Hungary, Lady Madeleine. How very *interesting* to meet someone from such an – er *interesting* country. Is it not, Felicity dear?'

Felicity's cold, calculating eyes roved malevolently over Lady Madeleine's perfect petite form. She smiled disingenuously. 'Indeed, it is, Mama,' she almost hissed. 'Quite interesting indeed.'

'I believe you are only here for a short visit, Lady Madeleine,' continued Lady Carmichael, now wafting her fan quite wildly. 'Do you have any idea how long you will be staying?'

'Alas, I do not, madam,' replied Lady Madeleine pertly. Then, throwing a knowing look at James, she said, 'Perhaps I might stay for good.'

A look of pure horror swept over Lady Carmichael's face. 'Good gracious,' she declared, before remembering herself and adding quickly, through gritted teeth, 'I mean, how . . . *delightful* that would be.'

'Indeed, it would,' agreed James, throwing Lady Madeleine another winning smile. 'It would be most delightful indeed.'

He suddenly turned his dark eyes to look directly into Felicity's insipid blue ones. 'I do hope this evening lives up to your expectations, madam,' he said coolly.

Eleanor was amazed to see that the girl did not so much as flinch under his contemptuous scrutiny.

'Oh I am sure it will, sir,' she replied with a blatantly false smile. 'There are so many people of consequence here – the Duke and Duchess of Swinton, for example – that one could not fail to enjoy oneself.'

Eleanor gasped loudly at the audacity of the girl. How dare she remind James of her threat? Had she no shame at all? Suddenly she realized that her godmother and Lady Madeleine were both eyeing her suspiciously. She hastily feigned a cough. James and Felicity on the other hand, seemed completely oblivious to those around them, locked in a fierce battle of wits. Eleanor was the only spectator aware of the insidiousness weaved intricately through their apparently innocent exchange. The battle continued as James smiled serenely at his opponent.

'Ah, yes, the Duchess of Swinton. It is some time since I have seen the lady. I trust she is in good health?'

'The finest, sir. As is the duke, of course.'

'Of course,' said James blithely, 'and I am very glad to hear it. I shall look forward to seeing them both later.'

'I'm sure they will *both* be delighted to see *you*, my lord,' replied Felicity.

'Ah, yes,' mused Lady Carmichael. 'The Duchess of Swinton. Now there is a most . . . elegant and . . . decorous lady,' she remarked, casting a disparaging look at Lady Madeleine's audacious gown.

Madeleine, immediately alerted to the unspoken criticism, affected her most saccharine-sweet smile. 'Then I, too, shall look forward to meeting this Duchess of Swinton,' she purred. 'I wish to acquaint myself with all of James's friends.'

Felicity released a contemptuous snort. 'All of them?' she enquired incredulously. 'How very *admirable*.'

Sensing the younger girl's scornful tone, Lady Madeleine cast Felicity a frosty glare before rearranging her features into a much more pleasant countenance.

'James, darling,' she cooed girlishly, gazing up at her escort through her long thick lashes, 'aren't you going to ask me to dance? It can be so dreadfully dull standing around talking all evening.'

'Of course, my dear,' replied James, patting her tiny gloved hand, which appeared to have taken up permanent residence on his arm. 'Please do excuse us, ladies,' he said. 'I'm sure we shall have a chance to continue our conversation later this evening.'

Eleanor's eyes widened as she realized that his last comment was directed most definitively to Felicity – a fact that the younger girl also did not fail to miss.

She bobbed a polite curtsy. 'Oh, I sincerely hope so, sir,' she replied archly. 'Do please now go and enjoy yourselves.'

Realising that his point had been received and understood, James bowed courteously as Lady Madeleine flashed a dazzling, victorious smile and whisked him away through the crowd. Only Eleanor was aware of the menacing glare that followed them as they weaved their elegant way across the floor.

Lady Carmichael watched their retreating backs with a doleful expression on her face. 'My,' she sighed despondently, 'Lady Madeleine and James do seem to be rubbing along well together. You don't think they could make a match of it, do you, Lady Ormiston?'

Eleanor noticed the dowager's lips twitching with suppressed laughter.

'Who knows, Cynthia,' she replied matter-of-factly. 'The girl is quite charming and he seems very taken with her. He could, I think, do worse for himself. Or perhaps you had someone else in mind to shackle him to?'

Lady Carmichael blushed to the roots of her hair. 'Of course not, Lady Ormiston,' she flustered. 'Who on *earth* could I possibly wish to see James wed to?'

*

Now accustomed to her goddaughter's escape tactics, the dowager, much to Eleanor's dismay, appeared to be keeping a very firm eye and indeed, as she dragged her around the room, an equally firm hold, on her charge. Basing her strategy on the garden-party experience, Eleanor realized that the only chance she had of any freedom at all, was to ply the old lady so full of alcohol that she wouldn't give a flying fig where her goddaughter was.

'Would you care for another drink, Godmother?' she enquired innocently, as the dowager downed the last of her champagne. Before she had a chance to reply, Eleanor had snatched the empty glass out of her hands and replaced it with one she had taken earlier from a passing waiter's silver tray.

Lady Ormiston eyed her suspiciously. 'I do hope you are not trying to get me foxed, girl,' she remarked.

Eleanor raised her eyebrows in mock surprise. 'Of course not, Godmother. Why on earth would I wish to do that?'

The dowager, however, much to Eleanor's chagrin, was far too perceptive. 'Because you want to go wandering off on your own, getting up to all kinds of your usual mischief, that's why. Really, Eleanor, it does not do for young ladies to go around unchaperoned at such affairs. Indeed it is most unbecoming.'

'Of course it is, Godmother,' observed Eleanor innocently. 'It would not do at all.'

'Quite,' confirmed the dowager stoutly.

The two of them were sitting on the red velvet gilt chairs, which lined the periphery of the ballroom. She had noticed a number of young men looking in her direction but whenever it looked as though they were about to approach her, she turned her attention to the dowager – a tactic which seemed to serve marvellously in warding off any offers to dance. As a result however, she was feeling decidedly bored, although sitting observing the proceedings was infinitely better than being dragged around having to engage in yet more prosaic chat. She blew out her breath in a huff and slumped down in the chair, crossing her arms over her chest.

'Posture, girl. Posture,' boomed Lady Ormiston.

Eleanor rolled her eyes and suppressed another sigh. Straightening her back, she placed her hands loosely in her lap and crossed her ankles so that she was sitting in exactly the same manner as all the other girls and their chaperons lining the walls. Whilst her posture may have been identical however, there was one enormous difference. Whereas all the other chits were eagerly awaiting an invitation to dance from any eligible and, preferably, wealthy young man, Eleanor was waiting for the dowager to become sufficiently inebriated so she could slip off and escape the tedium.

She slanted a sly glance at the dowager's champagne flute. It was half-empty already. She would take another from the waiter's tray the next time he passed by. That should be more than enough. As she scanned the room for a champagne-carrying servant, she spotted James and Lady Madeleine gliding expertly around the dance floor. The contrast of James's rugged, dark good looks against Lady Madeleine's blonde beauty distinguished them from the majority of the other guests. They looked quite perfect together and, by the admiring looks they were receiving as they swept around the floor, Eleanor was evidently not the only one who thought so. There was one other couple, however, who were equally as striking as James and the Hungarian. Dressed in her trademark white, in a sumptuous gown of diaphanous silk, the Duchess of Swinton and her husband made an equally handsome pair. Eleanor watched with interest the interaction between the two couples. Seemingly oblivious to his fellow dancers, James appeared to have his eyes fixed firmly on a spot directly above Lady Madeleine's head. Each time the couples swung by each other, Eleanor watched as the duchess cast James a hopeful glance attempting, very discreetly, to catch his eye. If he was aware of her intention however, James did an extremely good job of ignoring it. While a shadow of disappointment crept slowly over his wife's beautiful features, the duke's expression was much harder to read. As they waltzed by James and Madeleine once more, Eleanor observed as the duke glanced down at his wife who was staring at James. Ignoring the woman yet again, James and Madeleine swung by in another whirl of shimmering gold. The duke's features hardened slightly. Eleanor couldn't be sure, but there was a very strange look in the man's eyes as they briefly followed James's back. It was something she couldn't quite put her finger on, but it gave her the distinct impression that Felicity Carmichael's threat at the garden party had not been an empty one.

Was she the only one to notice this exchange between the three dancers, she wondered. Was Felicity also observing them from some hidden spot? Watching James's every move? Noticing the stir he and his beautiful guest were creating? She shuddered slightly as she thought of the girl's baleful expression earlier. She hated to admit it, and she was certainly no simpering little goose, but Felicity Carmichael frightened her. James had implied quite strongly that he wished to speak to the girl alone. What had he to say to her, she wondered. Perhaps—

'Excuse me, madam. May I have the pleasure of the next dance? It is another waltz I believe.'

Eleanor's head jerked up sharply. She had been so lost in her thoughts that she had not noticed the young man approaching her. She was not shallow enough to hold a great deal of store by looks, but this man could not, by the largest stretch of anyone's imagination, be referred to as handsome or even remotely good-looking. He was short and podgy with greying skin, with a rather worrying rash around the chin area and greasy fair hair, which looked very much as though it were in need of a decent cut. Damn! She cursed silently. She had not prepared for this at all. She needed to think of an excuse and quickly. But what excuse could she possibly use that would satisfy both the young man and the dowager?

'I'm sorry, sir,' she stammered. 'I – er – that is my feet are a little – er—'

'Ah, Viscount Grayson,' interjected the dowager cheerfully. 'How very splendid. My goddaughter would be delighted to dance with you. Now off you go, Eleanor.'

A wide smile broke out on to Viscount Grayson's face, revealing a set of repulsive, yellowing teeth. He was regarding Eleanor expectantly. She gave him a fleeting smile then immediately averted her eyes to his shoes which, she noticed, were a little scuffed. A bubble of panic began to swell in her stomach. What on earth was she to do? Dancing around her room with Milly was one thing, but dancing in public, in front of hundreds of people, was quite another. The panic bubble began to expand rapidly. Music to the previous dance ended. Ladies were curtsying, their partners bowing. Couples for the next dance were now moving on to the floor and assuming their places. The viscount, she noticed, with a lurch of her stomach, was holding out a podgy, sweaty hand for her to take. Suddenly, an overwhelming urge to pick up her skirts and flee the room washed over her. Then, just at that very moment when she thought things couldn't possibly get any worse, she became aware of a snide, nasally voice: 'Good Lord, man', it said, 'you're taking your life in your hands there. Or should I say your feet.' The statement was followed by a despicable drunken chortle.

Startled out of her panic-ridden stupor, Eleanor turned her head sharply to see Derek Lovell, obviously in his cups, escorting a brazen-looking woman, quite some years older than himself and wearing far too much rouge, on to the dance floor. His lip was curled upward in his unattractive sneer as he swaggered past her drunkenly, uttering something of amusement to his partner, which made her titter unpleasantly.

Eleanor turned to her godmother, hoping she had witnessed Mr Lovell's behaviour, but the dowager, obviously expecting Eleanor to be on the dance floor by now, had engaged in conversation with the matronly looking chaperon sitting to her left.

As Lovell and his partner took their places on the dance floor, they turned back simultaneously, threw Eleanor a satirical look, then burst into a fit of laughter. Eleanor's initial horror at her invitation was completely swept aside by a wave of indignant anger. How dare Derek Lovell insult her so? She could dance. Of course she could. She had danced quite competently in her room with Milly and even M. Aminieux had said she was good. Well, not actually 'good' in so many words, but he had said she was improving. She would not be sniggered and sneered at by anyone. She would show them all. She would dance with this man.

She forced what she hoped was a pleasant smile on to her face.

'Thank you, sir,' she said graciously. 'I should be delighted to dance with you.'

As the obviously elated viscount led her out on to the dance floor, swaying a little too much for Eleanor's liking, she was aware of her legs shaking. For goodness' sake, she chided herself, it's just one stupid dance at one stupid ball. What could possibly go wrong? Viscount Grayson took hold of her and roughly pulled her to him, causing her to gasp. At least a head taller than he his eyes were level with her neck. She flinched slightly as she became aware of his clammy palms upon her and the unpleasant odour of his body. Even M. Aminieux's nauseating cologne was preferable to the viscount's more *natural* approach to personal hygiene. He smelt, in equal measures, of stale sweat and whisky. The orchestra started up and the viscount began swaying on the spot. Eleanor was no expert, but this man, she recognized immediately, was an even worse dancer than herself. Although, not imagining that anyone could be worse than her, she concluded that he was obviously so drunk he had forgotten his steps. Derek Lovell and his painted woman whisked past them, both of them tittering superciliously. The urge she had felt only a few minutes earlier, to pick up her skirts and flee the room returned with renewed vigour. But she couldn't. Not now. It would cause a scene and her godmother would never forgive her. Desperately, she tried to redeem the situation by attempting to lead her partner, but the man was so fat she couldn't shift him one way or the other. They were hovering on the edge of the dance floor, the viscount swaying backwards and forwards, looking like he might empty his accounts at any moment. Eleanor was aware that they were attracting several enquiring looks. Tears prickled her eyes. She felt such a fool. She saw Derek Lovell and his partner waltzing around the room towards them again. If they laughed at her once more, she doubted she would be able to control her temper or her tears.

'Excuse me for cutting in, sir, but may I?'

Relief flooded Eleanor's body. As a muttering, disgruntled viscount swaggered back through the swaying couples in search of another drink, James Prestonville drew Eleanor into his arms. Unlike the short, podgy limbs of the viscount, his were strong and muscular and quite took her by surprise. As he began swinging her masterfully around the floor, she forgot all about the viscount, all about her dance steps, all about Derek Lovell and Felicity Carmichael and every other person in the room. Every one of her senses seemed heightened and focused acutely on James: his strong arms; the broadness of his chest; the closeness of his person. Even the smell of him – clean and fresh and overwhelmingly masculine – was having a rather unsettling effect on her, causing something unfamiliar to stir in the pit of her stomach. The sound of his deep voice, brought her back to reality abruptly.

'You have no need to thank me, madam,' he pronounced bluntly.

Eleanor was a little taken aback by the arrogance of his tone. 'For what exactly, sir?' she enquired.

'Why, for rescuing you, of course,' he replied matter-of-factly.

Indignation pulsed through her at his smugness. 'I can assure you I did not need rescuing, sir,' she replied tartly.

He raised his brows questioningly. 'That, I can assure *you*, is not how it looked to me, madam.'

Unflinching, she met his gaze. 'Then may I suggest your eyesight is failing.'

His lips twitched. 'Are you implying, Lady Eleanor, that you would rather I had not interrupted your *dance* with the viscount?'

Her eyes shined defiance. 'It was rather presumptuous of you, sir.'

He raised a dark dubious eyebrow. 'Was it indeed? Then I take it you were enjoying his company?'

'And why would I not? The man was quite . . . quite . . . *charming*.'

'I see,' he exclaimed, his features hardening slightly. 'Then in that case, my lady, please accept my sincere apologies for spoiling your evening. I do so hope that you will see fit to forgive me,' he added, his voice dripping with sarcasm.

At that moment the music stopped and he abruptly released his hold of her. Despite herself Eleanor felt a stab of disappointment. Observing the usual courtesies, he bowed before her and she dipped a polite curtsy.

'I have no need of a protector, sir,' she declared, as she straightened. 'Indeed, I can assure you I am quite capable of looking after myself.'

James regarded her coolly. 'Oh, of that I have no doubt, Lady Eleanor,' he said, before turning his back to her and strutting purposefully across the dance floor.

Eleanor was pleased with herself. Despite the relief she had felt at not having to spend a second longer in the repulsive viscount's presence, she was not going to add to the already excessive ego of James Prestonville and act like a simpering goose. She had shown him that she was a strong, independent woman, in no need of male intervention. So why then, did she feel so totally deflated?

'Eleanor, what on earth happened to the viscount?' demanded the dowager as Eleanor approached her chair alone.

'He had to retire, Godmother. He was a little *indisposed*.'

'Hmph,' sniffed the dowager. 'I do so hope you didn't discourage him, Eleanor. Whether he was *indisposed* or not is of no import. All men have their little *indiscretions*, girl, as you will soon learn. The point is that the man showed some interest in you. And you could do much worse. Viscount Grayson is an extremely wealthy man. He owns several large estates in both the north and the south of England. Indeed, I would go as far as to say that he is swimming in lard.'

'More like he has eaten too much lard,' muttered Eleanor.

'What was that, girl?'

'Nothing, Godmother,' replied Eleanor innocently.

# CHAPTER 9

HALF an hour and two glasses of champagne later, the dowager was sufficiently befuddled and preoccupied for Eleanor to manage to slip away.
She had no idea where to go only that the atmosphere in the ballroom was
stifling her and she felt in desperate need to escape it.

She decided to explore the house a little. Venturing back into the entrance
hall, she climbed up the impressive branching staircase on to the first-floor
landing. There were several doors leading off the landing, one of which was
ajar. No sounds were coming from the room. Eleanor approached it and
peeped cautiously inside. The room was decorated in green damask and
brightly lit. In the centre was a round table around which were seated four
ladies and six gentlemen – among them Derek Lovell. Several of those present
appeared to have rather large piles of notes and coins in front of them. Derek
Lovell, however, did not and, from the little Eleanor knew about gambling, it
was clear from the man's lack of notes and coins and from his fidgeting that
things were not going his way. He held his head in his hands, his wiry fingers
weaving through his greasy, pale-red hair. As another member of the set,
whom Eleanor took to be the banker, turned over a card, Lovell muttered
something Eleanor was grateful she could not hear, and dropped his head,
despairingly on to the table. Eleanor felt no sympathy for him. He was a
contemptible toad.

Deciding to put as much distance between herself and Lovell as possible,
she made her way back down the stairs, along a corridor and through a small
sitting-room which had its long windows open to the garden. For a town
house in the centre of the city, the garden was surprisingly large, separated on
either side from its neighbours by a tall stone wall. The space immediately
behind the house formed a perfect square with a wall dividing it from the rest
of the garden, through which one could enter via an arch. This area was of
manicured lawn, surrounded by herbaceous borders and scattered with green

wrought-iron garden furniture on which were seated a number of people chatting and drinking and enjoying the still, warm evening air

Eleanor left the house and made her way across the lawn and through the archway framed by sweet smelling jasmine, into the second section of the garden. This led out on to a much larger expanse, so large in fact that due to the dividing wall blocking out most of the light from the house, she could not see all the way down to the bottom of the space but could only make out the outline of a copse. Trees also lined the walls along either side, amongst which were placed a number of ancient-looking stone benches.

Having walked almost to the bottom of the garden from where the sound of the orchestra, could be heard only very faintly, Eleanor sat down on one of the benches, pulled off her slippers and wiggled her bare toes in the cool blades of grass. The refreshing feeling reminded her of home. Propping her elbows on her knees, she rested her head in her hands and gazed at the stars in the clear sky. There was no moon this evening giving the sky a black, velvet-like appearance.

Suddenly a noise, which sounded exactly like a sob caught her attention. It came from the copse, completely in darkness to the right of her. She twisted around but could see nothing in the dark. Someone must be in distress – hurt even. Deciding she should go and investigate, she bent down to pull on her slippers. She had only put on one shoe however, when someone swept directly past her. Eleanor jerked her head upward. The figure was running towards the house, her body shuddering with sobs. Eleanor's eyes widened in surprise. For all she didn't see the woman's face, there was no doubting, from the gown, who she was.

She sat startled for a moment, an uneasy feeling wrapping itself around her body. At the sound of voices coming from the same direction, she froze. She could see the outline of two figures but could not make out their faces.

'Good evening, sir. I trust you are enjoying the ball?'

A shiver flashed through Eleanor as she recognized Felicity's voice. She held her breath, not daring to move a single muscle.

'Good Lord. Where on earth did you—?' spluttered James.

'I was simply waiting for a chance to speak with you, my lord. You did imply earlier that you wished to speak to me, did you not?' replied Felicity, in her usual composed tone.

'Indeed I did, madam,' confirmed James authoritatively. 'I trust that now you have seen fit to inform the Duke of Swinton about my *friendship* with his wife, that this will be the end of your nonsense.'

Felicity adopted a contrite tone. 'Oh believe me, sir, I did not undertake such a task light-heartedly. Indeed, I deliberated for quite some time over exactly which words to use to convey my message. It can be most difficult when one is doing so anonymously. The duchess, I take it from her display a few minutes ago, is quite distressed by the matter. I believe the duke, on the other hand, took the news quite . . . *maturely*. I must admit to thinking that the man would call you out, but he seems to prefer to let things lie. Still, quite what he would do if he were to find out that the two of you had been alone yet again and right under his nose this time—'

'Do not concern yourself, madam,' instructed James, his voice dripping with disgust. 'I can assure you that is the last time the duchess and I shall ever meet alone.'

'Oh what a pity,' declared Felicity drily. 'Particularly when the two of you make such a . . . dashing couple.'

'Your remorse is touching,' pronounced James sardonically. 'However, as you can see, I have no intention at all of giving in to your threats. Perhaps next time you would be better to find a Johnny raw on whom to play your games.'

Felicity gave a hollow laugh. 'Oh no, sir,' she said. 'You underestimate me. I do not give up so easily. The Duke and Duchess of Swinton were only one of my *many* ideas. You would, for example, have little choice but to marry me if I chose to inform Society that you had compromised me. Indeed, all it would take would be for me to tear a little lace here or there on my gown and claim you accosted me, sir.'

James gave a snort of disgust. 'And you think for one moment that anyone would believe you, madam? It is well known that all my mistresses have been diamonds of the first water. Nobody would believe that I would even look at a bracket-faced dowdy such as yourself.'

'Perhaps not,' mused Felicity. 'However, if I was to claim that I was carrying your child. . . .'

James gave an incredulous snort. 'That would be a claim that would be disproved within but a few months, madam.'

'Oh, that would only be the case, sir, if I were *not* with child. If I were, on the other hand—'

'Don't be absurd, woman,' spat James. 'How on earth would you—?'

'Oh, where there is a will there is most definitely a way, sir. Of course, *we* would both know that it wouldn't be your child,' she explained matter-of-factly. 'The two of us and *obviously*, one other person, who would be paid rather a large amount of money to hold their silence.'

James gasped loudly. 'I do believe, madam, that you have quite lost your mind. Can you not go and prey on some other unsuspecting victim?'

Felicity gave a hollow titter. 'It seems you have forgotten, sir, that my greatest desire is to be the new Duchess of Ormiston and mistress of Whitlock Castle. And, I must confess, having seen the jealous looks been awarded Lady Madeleine this evening, I am also desirous of being the centre of such attention and the envied wife of who was England's most coveted bachelor. I think the position should suit me very well indeed. Do you not agree, sir?'

James's tone turned dangerously nasty as he took a step towards the girl, forcing her back against a tree. Eleanor could not make out the expression on his face, which was now only inches away from Felicity's. 'I warn you, madam,' she heard him hiss, 'if you proceed with any of these ridiculous threats, I will personally kill you.'

Felicity gave an insidious laugh, but Eleanor could detect a thread of terror running through it. 'Oh, how very dramatic, sir,' she replied, injecting her tone with a forced lightness. 'Of course, I shall keep you abreast of my plans. When there is anything further to report, I can assure you that you will be the first to know.'

Forgetting herself for a moment, Eleanor's hand shot to her mouth as she saw James raise a clenched fist. His hand hovered in the air for a few tense seconds. Eleanor's eyes widened as she waited for him to do something. Would he really punch the girl, even though it was no more than she deserved? Obviously thinking better of it, James dropped his hand then, taking hold of Felicity's upper arm, he cast her aside roughly.

'Get out of my sight, madam, before I do something I will regret.'

Felicity swung back around to face him. 'Gladly, sir,' she replied innocently, dipping a mocking curtsy. 'But be assured that I shall see you again soon. Very soon, no doubt.'

Then, she tossed back her ringleted head, turned on her heel and began to march confidently back to the house. Just as she was parallel with Eleanor, however, she suddenly stopped in her tracks and turned to face her. Eleanor shrank back further into the shadows, holding her breath. Felicity's eyes lingered on hers for a brief moment, before she continued her route to the house. Eleanor's heart was beating so loudly she was sure even James, who was standing too far away for him to have seen her, could hear it. Thankfully he too had taken his leave although she had not seen in which direction he had disappeared.

Having held her breath for what had seemed like an eternity, Eleanor released it gratefully on a sigh of relief. Completely alone at last, she found that she was shaking – a state which was most definitely not due to the night air. She sat for several minutes more, giving Felicity a generous amount of time to return to the house. She couldn't be sure if the girl had recognized her or not. If she had, Eleanor dared not even think what she would do.

Convincing herself that both Felicity and James had both now sufficiently distanced themselves from the spot, she slipped on her second shoe and stood up. Her back felt quite stiff, as though she had been sitting on the bench for several long hours rather than the ten eventful minutes or so it must actually have been.

She wandered up the garden, keeping to the shadows of the trees.

'Ah!' She almost jumped out of her skin as she became aware of someone following her. Her chest constricted tightly and the hair on the back of her neck immediately stood on end at the thought that it might be Felicity. She stopped and wheeled around quickly. She was relieved to see that it was not Felicity, but a young man who, she realized immediately, had had significantly more glasses of champagne than even the viscount and was far too ripe and ready.

'So here you are,' he leered at Eleanor. 'The best-looking chit in the place and only that fool Grayson had the courage to face that gorgon shielding you,' he slurred. 'Come and dance with me now,' he said, making a lurch for her.

Eleanor stepped adroitly away from him but found herself hemmed between a tree and the wall.

'I think perhaps it would be better if we went inside, sir,' she said, attempting to maintain a sense of calm so as not to agitate the man. If she could just persuade him to move a little, she could make her escape. 'After all, sir,' she continued innocently, 'we can scarce hear the music out here.'

'Pah,' spat the man, waving a drunken arm in dismissal. 'Who cares about music? Indeed who cares about dancing? I have something much more fun in mind, something that does not require music at all.'

He lunged towards her again but this time she had nowhere to move to. He caught hold of her arms and pinned them against the wall. Seeking out her mouth with his he began covering her face in slobbering drunken kisses. His breath, stale with a combination of champagne and tobacco, made her want to vomit. Eleanor screwed up her face and turned her head quickly from side to side. Then, in one smooth, sudden movement, she brought her knee up sharply between the man's legs. He yelped in pain, releasing his hold of her and placing his hands over the affected area. Spotting her opportunity, Eleanor skipped nimbly to the side of him, but he was too quick for her and caught her by the arm, dragging her back to him and pressing her once again up against the wall.

'Oh no you don't,' he sneered drunkenly. 'I'm not finished with you yet. Not by a long shot—'

'Oh, I think perhaps you are, sir,' countered a deep, masculine voice. 'Release your hold of the girl this instant, Smithers. Unless, of course, you wish me to force you to do so.'

The man dropped Eleanor's arm as if it had burnt him. Eleanor thought it a wise choice given the anger that was colouring both James's face and tone.

'Come along, Prestonville, old chap,' simpered the man. 'Just having a bit of fun that's all.'

James did not look in the least amused. 'Then may I suggest you find something else to entertain you, sir. Something preferably away from this house.'

'Of course, old boy. Of course,' muttered Smithers, hastily taking his leave. As the man staggered over the lawn, muttering fiercely to himself, Eleanor remained against the wall shaking.

James approached her slowly. 'Did he hurt you?' he asked, his tone low and soothing.

She managed a weak shake of her head.

Coming to stand directly before her, James reached out and tilted her face upward so that she was looking directly into his eyes. With his other hand, he brushed a stray lock of hair back from her cheek. The feeling of his skin against hers and the intensity of his gaze caused her heart to skip a beat. Then, before she was aware of what was happening, he lowered his head to hers and kissed her.

Eleanor had never been kissed before. She had never even wanted to be kissed before. Indeed, she had never even thought about being kissed before. But, as James pressed his lips to hers and his tongue expertly probed the inside of her welcoming mouth, she felt her insides melting with unadulterated pleasure. In a flash, he pulled away from her, turned on his heel and marched briskly back to the house. Eleanor remained against the wall, every one of her senses reeling.

She had no idea how long she remained in the garden, but when she did eventually manage to regain some sense of equanimity she returned to the house feeling quite weak with exhaustion and the surprising events of the evening.

As she entered the ballroom, she bumped almost immediately into James with Lady Madeleine reattached to his arm. Eleanor's heart froze for a second. What on earth should she say to him? She was vaguely aware that she had come to a sudden halt and was gawping at him and that a deep flush was rapidly creeping upward over her neck and face. James, apart from a deep frown etched on his forehead, appeared quite calm and composed.

'Ah, Lady Eleanor,' he declared, as though he had not set eyes – nor indeed anything else – on her all evening. 'I have sent for the carriage. Lady Madeleine is feeling a little peaked. Please collect my aunt and meet us in the reception hall. We shall be leaving in five minutes.'

Unable to speak, Eleanor merely nodded her compliance. She could think of nothing she wanted more than to go home, crawl into bed and to only come out again when the world around her had calmed down a little. She was not accustomed to such strange happenings as seemed to occur in London. She was used to a quiet life in the country. Indeed she had liked her quiet life in the country very much. People were normal in the country. Here in London, she was beginning to think they were all quite mad.

Returning to where she had left her, she was relieved to see the dowager still on her gilt chair, sipping yet another glass of champagne and chatting merrily to her fellow chaperon and new-found friend. With some coaxing, Eleanor managed to drag her away and lead her into the entrance hall all within her allotted five minutes – exactly as she had been instructed. James and Lady Madeleine were already there. James pacing up and down impatiently.

'Do hurry up, Lady Eleanor,' he shouted brusquely. 'I do not like to be kept waiting.'

Eleanor threw him an infuriated glare. He was obviously in an extremely bad mood. She wondered in what part his encounter with Felicity had added to his bad humour and what part their kiss. Whichever way it was, there was no need to be so rude. She couldn't do anything about the Felicity incident and she had certainly not asked him to kiss her. He was no doubt regretting the whole ridiculous incident. Well, he had no one to blame but himself and she would not be shouted at when she had done nothing wrong. She opened her mouth to protest but then thought better of it. There had been far too much drama for one evening.

All four of them descended the steps of the house. Due to the stream of carriages returning to collect the departing guests, their coachmen had seen fit to turn their carriage around so it faced the direction in which they would be heading. This meant that they had to cross the street to reach it, which they all did, in complete silence. Their coachman was holding open the door on the far side of the vehicle and Lady Madeleine was the first to enter the carriage, followed by the dowager who needed a little help due, apparently, to her *rheumatism*.

Eleanor was the next to climb in and had placed one foot on the bottom step when Madeleine suddenly piped up, 'Oh no, James. I have forgotten my wrap. You couldn't be a darling and go and retrieve it for me.'

From his place behind her, Eleanor heard him release an exasperated sigh. 'Of course,' he muttered coolly.

Interested to see the expression on his face, Eleanor turned back to face him, but as she did so, she slightly lost her balance and several of the loose threads of her reticule caught the door of the conveyance, snapping sharply and sending a shower of hastily sewn on tiny pearls bouncing all over the road.

Eleanor gasped and put a hand over her mouth.

'What is it, girl? What on earth have you done now?' asked the dowager, shifting in her seat in an attempt to gain a better view of her goddaughter's activities.

'Nothing, Godmother,' she replied with forced cheeriness. 'There is a . . . kitten under the carriage. I am just going to coax her out from under it.'

The dowager tutted. 'Really, Eleanor. It does not do for young ladies to be seen cavorting with wild animals. It is quite unbecoming. Now do hurry up before anyone sees you.'

Squatting down, Eleanor began frantically scrabbling around, attempting to retrieve as many pearls as she possibly could. If she hid the bag from her godmother this evening, she could stitch them all on again the morrow and the old lady would be none the wiser.

Picking up the pearls, she felt the ground reverberating slightly. She looked up and saw a team of four jet-black horses, galloping furiously down the street pulling a plain black carriage. They were fair hurtling but the sound of their hoofs was drowned out by the music and chatter emanating from the ball and its departing guests, the front door now wide open as many took their leave. Eleanor looked back towards the house and saw James skipping down the steps, carrying Lady Madeleine's shawl. A crowd of guests had now gathered on the steps, deafeningly bidding each other goodnight. No one but Eleanor appeared to have noticed the conveyance. Quickly, she turned her head back to the galloping horses and then to James. Doing a rapid mental assessment, she realized that if James did not stop at the bottom of the stairs, he would step into the road at exactly the same moment as the carriage hurtled by. She shouted a warning, but he did not hear, nor did he stop. Realizing that there was nothing else for it, Eleanor straightened and lurched herself across the street and into James seconds before the carriage flew past. Having offset his balance, James toppled over and landed with a thud on his back on the road. Eleanor landed directly on top of him. As the dust from the carriage settled over them, James and the other guests realized quickly what had happened.

'Well, Lady Eleanor,' he said, regarding her strangely as she lay atop him, 'I do believe we may now cry quits.'

# CHAPTER 10

ELEANOR was unable to sleep. Every time she closed her eyes a vision of either Felicity Carmichael or James Prestonville flashed through her mind: each of them having a strange, but very different, effect on her senses. She lay staring at the ceiling for a while, contemplating the events of the evening and, in particular, her kiss with James. Why on earth *had* he kissed her? The man had made it quite clear that he thought her completely unsophisticated and nothing more than a source of amusement. Well, if he had kissed her in the hope of proving that even she was not immune to his indisputable charms, he had another thing coming. Eleanor Myers had no desire at all to be added to his already over-large band of doting admirers.

After several more fitful hours spent tossing and turning, she was on the verge of nodding off when she became aware of a noise outside her room. Silently, she moved over to the door and rested her ear against the oak panel. She could distinctly hear a low mumbling sound. But who on earth was standing around in the corridor at this time of the night, she wondered. Squatting down, she pressed her eye against the cool brass of the keyhole. She could see nothing other than the stone wall directly opposite. Growing increasingly curious, she straightened again and, slowly turning the brass handle, cracked the door open a little. It creaked slightly. Gingerly, she poked her head out into the stone corridor and looked both left and right. The moonlight was penetrating the narrow windows of the passage bathing its contents in a silvery hue. There was, however, no sign of any persons at all. Eleanor was puzzled. She had heard nothing to indicate that anyone was beating a hasty retreat from the corridor. Nor, with the exception of her own, had she heard any doors opening or closing. It was as though she had imagined the whole thing. She glanced up and down the passage again. The painted eyes of the many former members of the Ormiston family peered eerily at her from their framed portraits. A shiver of apprehension ran down her spine as an alternative thought flashed through her mind: perhaps she had not imagined the whispering at all. Perhaps what she had heard had been the moans of the infamous Wailing Whitlock Widow. Immediately, she snapped the door shut, ran back to her bed and dived under the coverlet pulling it right over her head. There were no such things as ghosts. It must have been her imagination.

When Eleanor eventually awoke from what little sleep she had managed to grasp, she felt more exhausted than when she retired. Milly was hovering around the room, almost bursting out of her skin, desperate to know every detail of the happenings at the ball.

The minute Eleanor opened her eyes, the girl skipped over to the bed and sank down on the edge of it.

'Oh, miss, how was it?' she asked, her bright blue eyes sparkling with curiosity. 'Did anything exciting happen?'

Quickly gathering her wits, Eleanor mentally ran through the evening's events: she could not tell Milly about Felicity – that would be far too dangerous; she could not tell her about the drunken Smithers – that was far too embarrassing; she could not tell her about the kiss with James – that was even more embarrassing. What on earth then, could she tell her?

Milly was regarding her expectantly. 'Come on, miss,' she urged. 'I'm dying to know how it went. Did you do your dancing? I'll bet they were queueing up to ask you.'

Eleanor pulled a rueful face. 'Well, as a matter of fact, they weren't, Milly.'

The girl's face sank. 'I don't believe that for a minute, miss. Someone must've asked you.'

'Well, two people did,' replied Eleanor.

'Ooh,' exclaimed Milly. 'Were they handsome, miss? Do you want to marry either of them?'

Eleanor giggled as she thought of the contrast between her two dance partners. 'Well, Milly,' she declared truthfully, 'one of them was very handsome indeed, but I can assure you I have no wish to marry either of them.'

To her enormous relief, there was no evidence of any ghostly happenings when Eleanor tentatively opened the door to her bedchamber some thirty minutes later. She had thought about telling Milly what she heard but had decided against it as the girl would most likely think her completely mad. Indeed, with all the hullabaloo of the evening before, she wasn't even sure herself that she wasn't completely mad. Perhaps she had dreamt the entire thing.

She was almost as relieved to find no mortal beings in the breakfast-room when she arrived downstairs. Indeed, by the look of the untouched places, there had not been anyone at all to breakfast that morning. She had certainly not expected to see her godmother. The old lady had drunk so much champagne that she would no doubt be in her bed until well after lunchtime. Eleanor quickly helped herself to a little ham from the silver dish on the sideboard and a spoonful of scrambled egg. If she ate quickly, she might be lucky enough to avoid seeing anyone at all. She did not know if Mr Lovell had returned to the house but if he had, she certainly had no desire to see the odious man. Equally, she had no wish to see James. Indeed, if James were in the same strange mood as he had been in yesterday evening, she would positively go out of her way to avoid him. Her negative feelings also stretched to Lady Madeleine who had been decidedly put out yesterday evening by all the attention Eleanor had received following the carriage incident. The woman had made no attempt at all to disguise her annoyance. While the other guests who had witnessed her prevention of James walking into the path of the hurtling carriage had awarded her with praise and several drunken pats on the back, Lady Madeleine had merely pouted her perfect mouth and stated that she was a little concerned about travelling back in the carriage with Eleanor who was most likely to have picked up fleas from the kitten she had supposedly been coaxing out from under the carriage. Someone had replied that perhaps had she been wearing a little more clothing, then the fleas would not have had so much bare flesh with which to amuse themselves. The comment had merely resulted in more pouting and a jibe at Eleanor for being decidedly indelicate. The dowager who, up until that point, had been amongst those on the praising side, suddenly jumped ship and had agreed with Lady Madeleine that yes, Eleanor was indelicate and that it was actually quite unbecoming.

The person who had reacted most strangely to the incident, however, had been James. Once the two of them were back on their feet and had assured their witnesses that they were unharmed, James had merely stood by watching the proceedings like a complete outsider. He had not even had the courtesy to thank her for her efforts. Back in the carriage, the two of them spent the return journey in exactly the same humour as they had spent the outward one a few hours earlier: Eleanor positively seething – this time at both James and Madeleine – and James, oblivious to all around him, resuming his silent staring out of the window.

Fortunately for Eleanor, she managed to pass the entire day quite peacefully, without encountering the dowager or any of her fellow guests. Lady

Ormiston, Giles had informed her, had taken to her bed with a rather severe attack of her rheumatism. Lady Madeleine also appeared to be spending the day in bed. There was no sign at all of Mr Lovell and James had, early that afternoon, gone off in the carriage somewhere.

She had hoped that the lack of people around the house would mean that she would be the only one taking dinner that evening. Having been deeply engrossed in her book all day, she made a leisurely toilette and wandered down to the dining-room just as the last gong was sounded. Unfortunately, contrary to her expectations, as she pushed open the dining-room door, her heart sank as she set eyes on the dowager and James, already at their places.

'Ah, Eleanor. The last to arrive as usual,' remarked the dowager tartly.

Eleanor rolled her eyes as she slipped into her own chair, opposite that of James who was, she couldn't help but notice, looking somewhat tired, with dark smudges under each of his eyes.

'Good evening, Godmother,' she said sweetly. 'How is your *rheumatism?*'

'Quite dreadful,' she snapped. 'I have felt quite out of frame all day.'

'Oh what a pity,' replied Eleanor innocently. 'I do believe an onion poultice is an excellent cure for rheumatism. Or was that for taking too much wine? Hmm. I do believe I have quite confused the two.'

While Lady Ormiston flashed her a suspicious glare, James was regarding her closely.

'Don't tell me that medicine is another of your *alternative* accomplishments, Lady Eleanor?' he said, raising a questioning eyebrow.

'Indeed it is, sir,' replied Eleanor stoutly, meeting his gaze defiantly.

'And how many more of these *alternative* accomplishments are we still to discover?' enquired James, the corners of his mouth tugging upward.

Eleanor reached for her glass of water. 'Oh, I can assure you there are many more, sir,' she replied matter-of-factly.

The heat of his gaze burned right into her as he said, in a tone of voice that sent a frisson of excitement slithering down her spine, 'Now why, Lady Eleanor, does that not surprise me?'

Attempting to control the deep flush that immediately flooded her cheeks, Eleanor raised the glass of water to her lips. What on earth did he mean by that? Was he referring to—?

'Now, Eleanor,' piped up her godmother, oblivious to the undercurrent running between the pair. 'I have sent a note today to Viscount Grayson, inviting him to call on us. We must encourage the man after he showed so much interest in you yesterday evening. After all he was the only one.'

Eleanor almost choked on her mouthful of water.

'Viscount Grayson, Godmother,' she spluttered. 'But he is— That is I don't— I have no wish to—'

'And if you persist on this ridiculous notion about not wishing to marry, Eleanor,' asserted the dowager, 'then I shall send you back to your stepmama right this instant. The purpose of you being here is to find a man to take you, and Viscount Grayson is quite the catch, is he not, James?'

James had covered his mouth with his white cotton napkin to disguise the fact that he was choking with laughter. With his aunt and Eleanor now regarding him strangely, he could hold it no longer and collapsed into a fit of hysteria.

Eleanor shot him a furious glare. Perhaps it wouldn't be so bad being sent home and facing the wrath of Hester Scones. Could it possibly be any worse than a visit from Viscount Grayson?

She didn't have long to wait to find out.

# CHAPTER 11

'VISCOUNT Grayson, your grace,' announced Giles, as Eleanor, Lady Ormiston, James and Lady Madeleine were sitting in the long, red drawing-room early the following afternoon.

A deep wave of dread immediately crept over Eleanor. The dowager, on the other hand, obviously delighted at the news, beamed broadly.

'Now just a moment, Giles,' she instructed, laying down her tambour-frame and striding over to her goddaughter. 'Really, Eleanor,' she tutted, wrenching the book out of her hands and placing it on the table next to her. 'I did hope you would be wearing your lemon day dress when the man called. It is much more becoming than the lilac you have on. However, there is no time for you to change. Go and sit over by the window, girl, and *smile*. There is nothing more unbecoming than surliness.'

Realizing that any protestation would be completely useless, Eleanor sighed heavily and moved over to the window where she flopped down list-lessly on to the green cushioned seat. The dowager scurried over to the door-way and regarded her through her lorgnette.

'No, no, no,' she bellowed. 'The light is too much. The poor man will have to squint the entire time he is looking at you. No, I think perhaps over by the fireplace would be better. Come now, Eleanor, don't dawdle, girl. The man is waiting to see you. We must not keep him longer than is acceptable.'

Sighing again, Eleanor moved indolently over to the fireplace and slumped down into the wing chair there. From her position at the doorway, the dowager nodded her approval. 'Much better. Much, much better,' she bellowed. 'Now do sit up straight, Eleanor. There's nothing more unbecoming than a young lady with poor posture.'

Straightening herself up, Eleanor blew her breath out in a huff. The dowager however, completely embroiled in her seating arrangements, failed – or more likely ignored – her goddaughter's blatant lack of enthusiasm.

Standing with her hands on her broad hips, she stood on the threshold surveying the room carefully. 'Now,' she pondered verbally, 'where on earth shall *I* sit?'

James and Lady Madeleine who were both by the pianoforte at the far end of the room, had now set aside their books and were watching the proceedings with obvious amusement. James was lounging in a brown leather wing chair, his long legs clad in tight biscuit-coloured breeches, dangling carelessly over the side. Eleanor hoped desperately that the dowager would banish the pair to the library. Her glimmer of hope did not last long.

'You don't mind if we join you, do you, Aunt?' enquired James, his tone rich with amusement. 'It is a long time since I have had a chat with the viscount.'

Eleanor flashed him a baleful glare. He returned it with a beatific smile.

The dowager was now fussily pinning up several stray locks of Eleanor's hair. 'Oh, of course not, James,' she replied enthusiastically. 'We must make the man as welcome as possible. Lord knows he is our only hope at the moment.'

'Indeed, Aunt,' said James, his lips twitching with suppressed laughter. 'Come now, Madeleine. We, too, will need to be seated.'

'Oh my goodness, James. You and Madeleine take the sofa. Yes, definitely the sofa. I will sit in my usual chair and the viscount can sit in the one alongside me, facing Eleanor. Now come along everyone,' she boomed, satisfied with Eleanor's hair and now moving towards her own seat. 'We have kept the man waiting long enough.'

Eleanor rolled her eyes. She felt quite exhausted by the visit already and the man hadn't even set foot in the room yet. She wondered if it could possibly get any worse, but knew instinctively that it could.

'Ah, Viscount Grayson. How delightful of you to come. And so soon,' enthused Lady Ormiston as Giles showed the man into the room. 'Giles, we will require tea and some of Cook's freshly baked raisin cake.' The butler nodded his acquiescence.

As the viscount walked – or rather, waddled – towards them, Eleanor felt her spirits sink right through the floor. The man was even more hideous than she remembered and looked decidedly uncomfortable in tight black pantaloons, which were so obviously straining against his wide girth.

They all stood up to greet him.

'You already know my nephew, I believe,' she continued, gesturing to

James. 'And this is Lady Madeleine Bouvray who is visiting us from Hungary for the Season.'

When the usual courtesies of bowing and curtsying had been observed. The dowager gestured to them all to be seated.

'Do please sit down, Viscount, and tell us how you enjoyed the Carmichaels' ball,' she gushed. 'Eleanor has not stopped talking of you, since the event, have you, my dear?' She threw Eleanor an imploring smile, which was swiftly returned with a dampening glare.

'Indeed she hasn't,' piped up James, cheerfully. 'I believe she described you as the most 'charming' of all her dance partners.'

Eleanor's eyes widened in disbelief as she regarded James: how dare he throw that back in her face?

The viscount opened his mouth to speak revealing his revolting set of teeth. His voice, Eleanor noticed, was much more high-pitched than she recalled. Indeed it was so high-pitched, one could almost describe it as a squeak rather than a voice. Alongside the deep, well-modulated voice of James, it appeared even more ridiculous.

'Really?' said the viscount incredulously. 'Then I hope to have the pleasure of dancing with her again soon.'

He offered Eleanor a broad smile, which revealed the full extent of his lack of oral care making her recoil inwardly.

'Ah, yes,' added Lady Madeleine, wasting no time in spotting another opportunity to embarrass Eleanor. 'She was just telling me how much she hopes you are to attend the Stanningtons' picnic on Saturday, Viscount.'

The viscount flushed with obvious pride and gazed expectantly at Eleanor through his colourless eyes. This really was the outside of enough, she concluded. Whilst James and Madeleine were obviously finding the whole meeting highly amusing, their remarks were visibly encouraging the man to such an extent that Eleanor could hold her tongue not a moment longer.

'Actually, Lady Madeleine,' she asserted strongly, 'I have not yet decided if I am to attend the Stanningtons' picnic.'

The dowager waved a dismissive hand, indicating that Eleanor's statement was not worthy of a second's consideration. 'Don't be ridiculous, girl,' she countered, casting her goddaughter a reprimanding glare. 'Of course you are to attend.' Her admonishing tone melted into one of pure sugar as she then turned to the viscount. 'May I take it that we shall have the pleasure of your company at the Stanningtons' picnic, Viscount?'

'Oh, of course, ma'am,' trilled the viscount a little piece of spittle dangling from the corner of his mouth. 'I shall look forward to it. Very much indeed.'

A muffled snort of laughter came from James's direction, which Eleanor sought vehemently to ignore.

The viscount's visit lasted a total of twenty-eight minutes. Eleanor knew this so precisely because she watched the hands of the gilt timepiece move through every single interminable second of them.

Although the dowager was obviously of the rather strong opinion that she was well on her way to successfully completing her 'project' and satisfactorily marrying Eleanor off to Viscount Grayson, there was, unfortunately, very little reprieve for Eleanor on the learning of her wretched 'accomplishments'. M. Aminieux was therefore, as usual, attending the castle most days to continue her instruction in dance. While she still would not go as far as to say that she enjoyed these lessons, they were certainly becoming much easier thanks, in no small part, to Milly's extra tuition.

As they walked out into the hall after this morning's lesson and bumped straight into Lady Madeleine, the Frenchman could hardly contain his delight. Wearing a pale-blue carriage gown and on her way to the front door, the woman started as the dancing master minced towards her, looking even more colourful than usual in varying shades of yellow, topped off with a red waistcoat.

'Ah, the lovely Lady Madeleine,' he gushed, taking hold of her hand. 'Madame Aminieux is doing the nagging of me. She is anxious to meet you, *madame.*'

A fleeting look of panic washed over Lady Madeleine's face, before being replaced with a charming smile.

'You are too kind, M. Aminieux,' she said, snatching her hand abruptly from his, 'however, I am so busy I do believe I do not have a free evening for the next two weeks at least.'

'Well then,' asserted the dowager, 'why not plan for after that, girl? I must say, Madeleine, that if I had not spoken my own language for several weeks, I would be positively bursting for a good chat.'

'Oh, and of course I am, ma'am,' blustered Lady Madeleine. 'but I really don't know what my plans are to be after that. If I may, M. Aminieux, I will inform you of my arrangements as and when I have made them.'

'Of course, *madame,*' he replied, beaming broadly. 'However do not leave it too long. The Madame Aminieux will be *désolée* if I do not arrange something very soon.'

Lady Madeleine flashed another winning smile and inclined her head before making a dart for the door, which Giles was holding open for her. She disappeared through it like a shot. Eleanor could not recall ever seeing the woman move so quickly.

Having concluded that Viscount Grayson's visit had been a complete success, the dowager talked of very little else. Did Eleanor know, for example, that the Graysons were one of the most respected families in all England? Was she aware that they were one of the largest landowners? Could she believe that the viscount's great-great-great-great-grandfather had personally rescued Queen Elizabeth when she had been attacked by a band of marauders whilst out hawking? Deciding that she could suffer her godmother's enthusings not a second longer, Eleanor managed to escape to the library with a copy of Lord Byron's latest poem *The Corsair* as soon as was feasibly possible. She made herself comfortable in a deep blue damask high-backed chair there, tucking her legs under her. She was there for over an hour, enjoying the poem and the solitude, when her peace was rudely interrupted by the sound of several heavy footsteps making their way briskly along the stone corridor. Having been informed on numerous occasions of the dowager's opinion on Lord Byron's works, she had, in preparation of an unexpected visit from her godmother, left the library door slightly ajar in order that she could hear her approaching and quickly exchange her book for another, should the need arise. She had therefore placed a copy of *One Hundred Essential Etiquette Tips for Young Ladies* on the drum table in front of her for this very purpose. She quickly realized, however, that it wasn't her godmother approaching, but several men, all dressed in black, and all weighed down with hefty bundles of papers tied with pink ribbon. They were marching briskly towards, she assumed, the drawing-room. James was walking behind them, deep in conversation with one of the men, who sported a thick greying beard.

Their conversation was interrupted by the nasally tones of Derek Lovell, hailing James from further down the corridor. He sounded somewhat out of breath. Eleanor recoiled at the sound of his voice. She had not seen him since the Carmichaels' ball. Indeed he appeared rarely to be at the castle, a fact for which she was exceedingly grateful.

'James, wait up, old chap. I couldn't have a quick word, could I?' he puffed, obviously running to catch up with his host.

James came to a halt directly outside the library door allowing Eleanor a perfect view of him. He turned to face Lovell. 'I have a meeting with my solicitors, Lovell,' he pronounced impatiently. 'Can't it wait until later?'

'I'm afraid not, old chap. It's a bit . . . er sensitive,' said Lovell, catching up James and his companion. Eleanor could see all three men now. James rolled his eyes. 'I'll be with you in a moment, Richard,' he said to the bearded man, who nodded his head and walked on after his colleagues.

James placed his hands on his hips in a rather aggressive fashion. 'Now what is it, Lovell?' he snapped irritably.

'You couldn't lend me some money could you, old chap?' asked Lovell.

James sighed heavily and ran a hand through his dark glossy hair. 'I lent you some money yesterday, Lovell, and, if I'm not mistaken, the day before that and the day before that.'

'I know. I know,' replied Lovell, with a forced laugh. 'It's just that things haven't been going very well, if you know what I mean.'

'Oh, I know what you mean, all right,' snapped back James. 'You've been losing hand over fist at the gaming tables is what you mean. Well, I'm sorry, Lovell, but I'm not prepared to fund your gambling any longer. I must refuse your request and would be grateful if you would refrain from asking me again. My answer will not change.'

Lovell's face flushed puce. 'But you can't refuse me,' he spluttered. 'What on earth will I do?'

'That, old chap,' replied James, 'is not my problem. Now I have neither the time nor the inclination to discuss this with you further. I have a rather important meeting which is likely to take quite some time. I bid you good day, sir.'

James inclined his head to him, turned on his heel and proceeded down the corridor. Lovell remained standing as though rooted to the spot, for several long seconds before turning and walking in the opposite direction. The look upon his face as he left was one of red-hot anger.

Ever since Lady Ormiston's garden party, the weather had continued on its glorious way to summer and the balmy days were now extending into equally balmy nights. So much so that the last two evenings, Eleanor had slept with two of her bedroom windows open, enjoying the feeling of the light breeze tickling her warm skin as she lay in the comfortable bed. This particular evening, however, the light breeze had developed into a rather cool wind and Eleanor awoke shivering. There was a full moon reigning proudly over the silvery sky, delivering rays of magical light into her room. Surrounding the imposing moon, she could see a smattering of tiny twinkling stars which immediately put her in mind of her father and the many evenings they had spent together peering through his telescope as he'd pointed out the different constellations. Deciding that she would catch a chill if she did not close the windows soon, she hopped out of bed and padded barefoot over the carpet to the windows, noting from the gilt timepiece on the mantel that it was a little after two o'clock. She secured the catches of the latticed glass panes, but opted to leave the shutters open, in order that, should she have trouble falling asleep again, then she could continue her star gazing.

She had just climbed back into bed, when the sound of shuffling outside her door caught her attention. Her heart missed a beat. Convincing herself that it was probably mice, she closed her eyes tightly again and began furiously counting sheep. A minute or so later, there was a low moaning sound which could definitely not, however vivid one's imagination, be attributed to any kind of rodent.

Eleanor sat bolt upright in the bed, her heart pounding wildly against her ribcage. The sound was ominous and ghostly: exactly the sound one would associate with the Wailing Widow. But it could not be a ghost, she told herself. Ghosts did not exist. As quietly as she could, she climbed out of bed and tiptoed over to the door. Taking in a deep breath, she wasted not a moment in yanking it open and stepping out into the corridor. There was nothing out of the ordinary to be seen, other than a grey-white chiffon scarf, caught on the arm of a suit of armour and blowing a little in the draught of the cold corridor.

# CHAPTER 12

'GOODNESS, miss,' declared Milly as she arranged Eleanor's hair for the Stanningtons' picnic, 'I ain't never seen you looking so miserable. What I wouldn't give to go to some lovely picnic and there's you looking like you've just lost a leg and you've crawled home only to discover some beggar shot your dog.'

Eleanor couldn't resist a smile at Milly's bleak scenario. 'Sorry, Milly,' she said. 'I will try to cheer up.'

The truth was that she couldn't think of a solitary thing about the day looming ominously ahead of her that would cheer her up. She had not the slightest inclination to go to the Stanningtons' picnic. Feigning some sort of debilitating illness had briefly crossed her mind, but it would have been pointless, as nothing short of death itself would prevent the dowager from missing another opportunity to present her to the viscount. Whilst the thought of spending even a minute in the presence of the leering man filled her with dread, there was also one other person Eleanor had no desire at all to see and who would most certainly be attending the event – Felicity Carmichael. Whilst the thought of seeing the viscount was unpleasant enough, the thought of seeing Felicity caused Eleanor's stomach to churn uncontrollably.

After a hesitant start to the day, the sun made a welcoming decision to break through the thin film of wispy cloud that had previously been shielding it. Burning it away effortlessly, the result was a gloriously warm and clement summer day – the perfect day for a picnic. Eleanor was more than a little grateful to Milly who had insisted she wore her jonquil muslin; the girl appeared to have some kind of sixth sense regarding the British weather.

What Eleanor had completely failed to sense, however, was that as well as the viscount and Felicity, there would be yet another of her least favourite people attending the picnic that day. As she made to climb into the carriage, she was amazed to see that Derek Lovell was already seated within, opposite James and Lady Madeleine. She would have thought a picnic would have been far too tame for the man, but then again, she considered, if he had no funds to indulge his gambling, then he would have to temper his amusements. Lady Madeleine, she noted, undoubtedly in an attempt not to have to look at the man, had turned in her seat so that her back was at Lovell and she was looking out of the window.

'Ah,' he exclaimed sarcastically, as Eleanor climbed inside and settled herself on the velvet seat next to him, 'the lovely Lady Eleanor.'

Eleanor flashed him a frosty glare. Neither Madeleine nor James, who was apparently engrossed in a study of his fingernails, paid her any attention at all.

As the carriage made its way down the gravelled drive, it was Lady Madeleine who broke the silence.

'Do you know, James, darling, that I am sure I had a visit from the Whitlock Widow yesterday evening.'

Eleanor's heart stopped for a moment. James though, was less impressed as he shot her a disparaging glare. 'Don't be ridiculous, Madeleine,' he retorted irritably. 'You know I pay no attention to such nonsense.'

'Oh, but it is not nonsense, James,' asserted Madeleine. 'I have a particular gift regarding the spirits. Wherever I go they seek me out.'

'Do they indeed?' sneered Lovell. 'And what do they do when they find you, Lady Madeleine?'

'I do not believe you were included in this conversation, Mr Lovell,' replied Madeleine, flashing him an icy glare. Surprisingly, she then proceeded to turn her attention to Eleanor. 'May I ask if you believe in ghosts, Lady Eleanor?'

An uncontrollable shiver shot down Eleanor's spine as an image of the piece of grey-white chiffon blowing eerily in the draughty corridor the night before, flashed across her mind. She had been more than a little relieved when she had hesitantly opened her bedchamber door that morning to find the offending item had disappeared.

'Er – I confess to not having given the matter a lot of thought, ma'am.'

Madeleine tutted. 'Well, may I suggest you do, Lady Eleanor, particularly when one is residing in a building such as Whitlock. The place is positively crawling with spirits.'

Eleanor had the strange sensation of something crawling over her skin at this last statement.

'I must confess,' continued Madeleine contemplatively, 'that I thought the Widow quite beautiful. One can quite imagine her the day she threw herself from the tower – her long black hair streaming out behind her as she fell to her death in the same white chiffon nightdress she wore on her wedding night. I can think of nothing more romantic.'

For one brief moment, Eleanor thought she was about to pass out until Lovell piped up, 'Well at least the chit had the pleasure of her wedding night. Can you imagine how upset she would have been if she'd been denied that treat? Not that you, of course, Lady Eleanor, will have the slightest idea of the pleasures to which I am referring,' he sniggered superciliously.

'Leave her alone, Lovell,' commanded James, so authoritatively that he quite took them all by surprise.

They travelled in stony silence for some ten minutes, Eleanor pondering the ghostly happenings, James pondering his fingernails, and a slighted Lady Madeleine obviously pondering James's fervent show of protection of Eleanor.

'Oh my goodness!' the Hungarian suddenly cried. 'Stop the carriage immediately!'

All three heads immediately jerked to face her. She was clutching a hand dramatically to her left breast.

'Good God. What is it, Madeleine?' asked James anxiously. 'Have you taken ill?'

Madeleine gazed up at him with her ravishing blue eyes, 'Not ill, no,' she bleated, now wringing her hands in the manner of one deeply troubled, 'but I do not feel very fine, James. In fact, I feel quite ... quite ... *ugly*. I think perhaps we should return to Whitlock so that I may change my gown.'

Eleanor rolled her eyes. If Lady Madeleine did not look fine in her high-waisted gown of soft apricot, then there was little hope for anyone else. The woman was, as usual, playing one of her attention-seeking games.

'Come now, Madeleine,' said James, his tone ripe with impatience, 'you look beautiful, as well you know.'

Her large blue eyes conveniently filled with tears. 'But I do not feel beautiful, James,' she whined. 'And I want to feel beautiful – for you, my darling. It would not do at all for you to turn up at such a grand affair with such an ugly woman.'

'For God's sake, Madeleine,' snapped James, frustration colouring his features. 'I am telling you, you look beautiful. You always look beautiful.'

A little taken aback at James's abrupt response, but obviously having achieved the reaction she was seeking, Madeleine flashed Eleanor a victorious smile and, with a toss of her blonde head, went back to looking out of the window. Eleanor felt a sudden stab of a feeling she had never before experienced but which she had a strong suspicion was that rather disturbing emotion known as jealousy. Indeed, it required a great pull on every one of her resources not to reach across and slap Madeleine's smug face.

For all Lady Ormiston was not one of Eleanor's favourite people, she found herself wishing that the old lady had not travelled ahead of them that morning, but instead had accompanied Eleanor in the carriage. If the dowager had been present, Eleanor had little doubt that they would not have been subjected to Derek Lovell's gutter monologue on his conquests of the fairer sex.

'Do you really think, Mr Lovell,' Lady Madeleine had enquired icily, 'that any one of us here is remotely interested in your alleged conquests?'

'Ooh,' Lovell had countered. 'Do I detect a little jealousy there, Lady Madeleine?' Madeleine had fixed him with an ingenuous smile. 'Alas no, Mr Lovell. You are confusing jealousy with sympathy. I can only hope that the vast amounts of money which you undoubtedly must have paid these poor girls eased their suffering in some way.'

Lovell had given a snort of laughter. 'Oh, I can assure you, Lady Madeleine, that not one of the women was paid for the pleasure.'

'Really?' said Madeleine. 'Then I do hope you returned them safely to the institution from which they came.'

'That's enough, you two,' snapped James, so suddenly and so abruptly that Lovell and Madeleine immediately shut up.

The peace however, lasted only for a few minutes, until James lost himself again in his thoughts and Lovell commenced with yet another, apparently interesting story.

Eleanor was not fooled: She knew the man was doing his utmost to embarrass her and Madeleine. Refusing to give him even the slightest hint of how uncomfortable his detailed descriptions were making her, she adopted a nonchalant air and continued staring out of the window.

When the carriage eventually pulled up at its destination, Eleanor gave a huge sigh of relief. Stannington Hall was an enormous mansion house built by the present earl's father. The drive up to the building opened out into a large, quite unattractive but highly practical gravelled area. Walking around to the rear of the building, the scene was quite different. From here one could see nothing but lightly undulating, emerald-green countryside and a wide flowing river – England at its most perfect. Eleanor felt a sudden pang of homesickness.

It was a little after midday, but judging by the large number of people milling around, it appeared that Eleanor and her party were amongst the last of the guests to arrive. The grounds were dotted with colourful rugs, and people dressed in light summer colours were swarming around, revelling in the heavenly combination of both the beautiful setting and the glorious weather. The dowager was hovering about at the front of the building impatiently awaiting their arrival and, for once, Eleanor felt a little relieved to see her. Her relief lasted only as long as the old lady was silent however. As the first words came booming out of her mouth, Eleanor's spirits immediately reverted back to their previous gloomy state.

'Eleanor, do hurry up, girl. The viscount is here with Lord and Lady Grayson. They are most keen to meet you, although goodness knows where they've wandered off to now. I do declare the Stanningtons' grounds are so large they are the very height of ostentation.'

Before Eleanor had a chance to speak, James cut in. 'You don't mind if I walk around the grounds with you, Aunt, while you seek out the Graysons? I feel the need to stretch my legs a little after the carriage ride.' Then, turning directly to Lovell and Lady Madeleine who were standing alongside him, he said, 'Madeleine why don't you and Lovell go and collect our picnic hamper and find a good spot for us to place the blanket? 1 shall be along to join you shortly.'

At this ill-concealed dismissal, Lady Madeleine pouted petulantly. 'Hmph,' she sniped, with a toss of her head. 'Very well, James, but do not be long. I shall be waiting for you.'

James regarded her darkly for a moment before turning his attention to his aunt. 'Come along then, Aunt,' he said briskly, turning his back to Lovell and Madeleine. 'I thought you were keen to find the Graysons and they may take some finding amongst this crowd.'

The dowager marched purposefully ahead of the two of them, putting Eleanor in mind of an old bloodhound sniffing out a scent. She wondered briefly about voicing this opinion to James, but as he appeared to be in such bad spirits again today, she immediately wiped the idea from her mind. Bad spirits or not however, Eleanor was finding something paradoxically comforting and unsettling walking alongside the man. Comforting, in that his person – tall, strong and overwhelmingly manly – had the effect of making her feel safe and protected. On the other hand, being so close to him again made her think of the Carmichaels' ball and their kiss. Not that she wanted to repeat such a thing ever again. Heaven forbid. Although, she had to admit, it had been rather pleas—

'I feel I must apologize to you, madam,' declared James stoutly, breaking Eleanor's musings.

Oh Lord, she thought immediately. Had he sensed what she was thinking? Was he about to apologize for kissing her? If he did, then what on earth should she say to him? She felt colour rising in her cheeks.

'About what, my lord?' she stammered, not daring to look at him but focusing instead on a section of the lawn several feet in front of her as they carried on walking.

'My friend's behaviour, madam. He can be most *inconsiderate* at times and his conversation in the carriage this morning was not fit for a young lady's ears.'

Eleanor breathed a sigh of relief 'Thank you for the apology, sir,' she said politely, 'however it is quite unnecessary. If anyone should apologize for his unseemly behaviour, it should be Mr Lovell himself.'

James said nothing in response although Eleanor had the distinct feeling he wanted to. They carried on walking in silence with the dowager, still furiously attempting to sniff out the Graysons, some way ahead of them. The heavy silence stretching between them made Eleanor decidedly uncomfortable. She was grateful when someone hailed James and he made his excuses and took his leave of her.

Not only was Eleanor extremely grateful to the person who had rid her of James's rather overwhelming presence, but she was also much indebted to Lord and Lady Stannington both for the extent of their estate and the fact that they had invited so many guests to fill it. Indeed the grounds were so vast and so populated with milling bodies and colourful blankets that not even the dowager was able to locate the Graysons. Under the heat of the unrelenting sun, Lady Ormiston eventually admitted defeat and concluded that they should partake of some refreshment and resume their search a little later. Breathing a sigh of relief, Eleanor had taken no further persuading.

Eventually locating their own party, they found Madeleine and Lovell had opted to picnic on the edge of the crowd in the shade of a group of large oak trees. James was also present, having obviously spent as little time as was socially acceptable with the group of young men who had hailed him earlier. Lady Madeleine was sitting upright on the outspread picnic blanket, her back resting against the trunk of one of the oaks. She was holding a glass of bubbling champagne in her left hand and brushing away a persistent fly with the other. She flashed the dowager a welcoming smile and, as usual, completely ignored Eleanor. Having removed his jacket and rolled up his shirtsleeves, James was lying flat out alongside her with his eyes closed. He made no acknowledgement of their return. Despite his appearance Eleanor was almost sure that he wasn't asleep. In contrast to the relaxed state of James and Madeleine, Derek Lovell appeared quite edgy and not able to settle at all. Eleanor concluded that, without the thrill of cards or dice to amuse him, the man was probably bored stiff. Huffing and puffing and pacing impatiently about like some kind of caged animal, he suddenly announced that he was going for a stroll. No objections to this statement were forthcoming.

'I do declare,' announced James suddenly, bearing out Eleanor's view that he had not been sleeping at all, 'that I think I will spend the entire afternoon lying down here. I have no wish to engage in conversation with anyone today.'

'Now, James,' chided the dowager, rummaging around in the wicker hamper, 'do not be so grumpy. You know fine well that I require your help in finding a husband for Eleanor.'

James suddenly sat upright, bending his knees and hugging them to his chest. 'Ah yes,' he said, with a slight smile. 'And how were the Graysons, Aunt?'

The dowager withdrew a crystal champagne flute from the hamper. 'Alas, we were unable to find them,' she replied mournfully. 'However, I have no doubt they will seek us out at some point.'

'Oh, I have no doubt about that at all,' agreed Lady Madeleine zealously. 'Indeed, I am sure they are most excited that someone has at last shown an interest in the viscount. He is not, after all, the most . . . *outwardly* pleasing man.'

Eleanor felt a sudden surge of rage at the woman's arrogance. 'Looks can be deceiving, Lady Madeleine,' she snapped defensively. 'Indeed some of the most beautiful people can also be the most odious.'

Madeleine smiled beatifically. 'I am sure you are right, my dear,' she said, condescension hanging on every word.

James meanwhile, said absolutely nothing. Instead, his smile disappeared and he shot Eleanor a questioning glance before resuming his horizontal position.

Not only had the Stanningtons provided a marvellous setting for their guests, but they had also seen fit to furnish them all with a hamper packed full of tempting treats. As well as bottles of champagne, there was also a selection of sandwiches, sweetmeats, patties and cake. Eleanor was aware of Lady Madeleine watching her as she tucked into a triangular-shaped salmon sandwich, which she believed was quite the most delicious sandwich she had ever tasted.

'Are you aware, Lady Eleanor,' enquired Madeleine in a supercilious tone, 'that after the age of eighteen, it is most important for a young lady to observe what she eats?'

Eleanor flashed her a beatific smile. 'Oh indeed I am, Lady Madeleine,' she replied reassuringly, 'and I can assure you that I observed this particular sandwich for a full ten minutes before picking it up.'

From his prone position, James gave a snort of laughter. Lady Madeleine meanwhile, evidently not amused, simply shook her head disparagingly.

Much to Madeleine's undisguised disgust, Eleanor had partaken of two more salmon sandwiches and had even forced down a rather large slice of Savoy cake which she had not actually wanted but which she had eaten purely for the pleasure of seeing Madeleine's perfect face contort in contempt. Having amused herself thus, however, she realized that she was a little bored. James, still lying dozing on his back, had made it quite clear that he was in no mood for socializing and the dowager, making the most of the champagne, also appeared to be on the verge of nodding off. With Lady Madeleine preoccupied in the construction of a very long daisy chain, Eleanor felt the need to escape for a little while. The feeling of homesickness, which had enveloped her earlier, continued to linger. Not only did she miss her home and her friends, she realized, but she also missed the feeling of peace, tranquillity and, above all, freedom that she felt there. Here in London, surrounded constantly by people – not one of them normal – she felt, at times, positively claustrophobic.

More than a little mindful of the possibility that she could, quite unwittingly, bump into Felicity Carmichael or the viscount during her stroll, Eleanor determined to take her parasol with her. Both unaccustomed and disinclined to carrying such a frilly feminine article, she did perceive its significant benefit in providing a convenient moving shield from those one had no inclination at all to see. Only Madeleine looked up briefly as she took her leave and, as usual, was so uninterested, that she did not even enquire as to her movements.

Eleanor walked along for several minutes drinking in the beauty of the scene. There were blankets crammed with bodies all the way along the banks of the river and indeed some were so close that she had to actually walk around them. She recognized many of the faces now – amongst them those of the Duke and Duchess of Swinton. Sneaking a discreet look at the couple, she couldn't help but notice that the duchess, although still magnificent in a gown of delicate cream, had an unmistakable touch of sadness about her striking features. Indeed, her face appeared quite wan against the dark contrast of her raven hair and, like James, there were dark shadows under-lining each of her beautiful eyes. Her husband, on the other hand, appeared to be in fine spirits – laughing and joking with the others in their party while his wife sat glumly by his side. Although she knew little of such matters, it appeared to Eleanor that the break-up of James and the duchess's relation-ship had affected both parties very deeply indeed – a fact that left her feel-ing decidedly odd.

She strolled a little further, listening to the chatter of the guests who were all making the most of the beautiful sun-drenched afternoon. As the sound of a high-pitched whiny titter reached her ears, however, she started slightly. It was the unmistakable girlish giggle of Lady Cynthia Carmichael. Eleanor immediately tilted her parasol so that her face was obscured from the party. As she drew level with the group, however, her curiosity got the better of her and she dared to pull it back a little. What she witnessed made her immediately regret her action: Lady Carmichael and her daughter were part of a much larger party who had spread themselves out on several blan-kets. Felicity was sitting on the edge of a blanket, her back to the rest of the group, but facing the river and therefore Eleanor. The girl was wearing a pale lilac dress, which made her pallor appear even greyer than usual. She appeared to be engrossed, much to Eleanor's immediate revulsion, in dissecting a live red and black butterfly, which she was grasping between her podgy fingers. Eleanor recoiled in horror and positioned her parasol once again so that her face wasn't visible. There was no doubt in her mind that Felicity Carmichael was the most evil, hateful girl she had ever had the misfortune to meet.

A fence complete with a stile signified the end of the immaculate gardens immediately surrounding the house and the start of more natural terrain. Delicately negotiating the stile, Eleanor jumped down and continued following the route of the river via a narrow bridle path, which ran alongside it.

As the chatter of the party faded into the distance, she became aware of shouts and laughter of a different nature – those of a group of young boys. Rounding a corner, the group came into view. There were four boys, of varying height ranging in age from around eight to fifteen years. They had mops of thick fair hair, faces crammed with golden freckles and, having stripped off their shirts, were all bare to the waist, displaying lean, brown torsos. Each of them was holding a twig on the end of which was hooked an indignant, wriggling worm. Eleanor observed their playful, teasing behaviour for a few minutes and experienced a momentary pang of envy. Whilst she was well aware, of course, of the advantages of her own class, she also acknowledged that these advantages were not without a price. Confined within the suffocating constraints of a society obsessed with a ridiculously rigid code of conduct, the price for being a member of the privileged classes was a complete and utter loss of freedom. Suddenly, as they became aware of her watching them, a murmur of fear rippled through the boys. They stood stock-still in the water, panic washing over their young, freckled faces.

'We ain't doing nothing wrong, miss,' piped up the oldest of the four. 'We're just larking about that's all.'

'Are you, indeed?' said Eleanor, walking slowly towards them. 'Then I was wrong in thinking you were fishing.'

The boys stood in silence for a moment.

'Well, we were, miss,' replied the boy again, 'but we ain't caught nothing yet and when we did, we were going to put it straight back. Honest.'

Eleanor feigned a serious manner. 'Hmm,' she said, stroking her chin with her free hand, as she now stood on the bank, directly above them. 'You haven't caught anything yet, you say. Then perhaps you had better show me what you were doing.'

A wave of horror spread over the boys' dumbstruck faces.

'Or perhaps,' said Eleanor, closing her parasol, 'you would like me to show you how it's done.'

Staring, open-mouthed, the boys watched in utter amazement as Eleanor put down her parasol, slipped off her kid slippers and tucked her skirts up into her undergarments. She then proceeded to pick her way carefully down the craggy side of the river-bank and waded into the cool, refreshing water.

Realizing that she intended them no harm, it took but a few minutes for the boys to relax in her presence and in a short while all five of them were larking and splashing about in exactly the same manner as they had been before Eleanor's arrival. It was undoubtedly the most fun Eleanor had had since she had been despatched from Nottingham.

Ed, the older boy who had nominated himself as spokesman, suddenly spotted a large trout. All five of them stood deadly still, hardly daring to breathe as they observed the fish. It approached Eleanor. She held her rod quite still watching the worm as it wriggled and writhed. The fish saw it and swam nearer. Still they all held their breath.

All at once, however, a large booming masculine voice broke the silence and caused all five of them to almost jump out of their skin at the unwelcome interruption.

'Lady Eleanor, what on *earth* do you think you are doing?'

Eleanor jerked her head upward and was met by the sight of James standing on the river-bank directly above her, with Lady Madeleine, as usual, glued to his arm. He was wearing the same unfathomable expression on his face that she had witnessed several times before on his catching her in a rather uncompromising situation.

'I'm . . . er. . . .' stammered Eleanor, flushing a deep shade of scarlet.

Madeleine however, was obviously in no mood to hear Eleanor's excuses and was regarding her as though she were not worthy of a minute of their attention.

'Is it not obvious, James?' she scoffed dismissively. 'The girl is engaging in yet more tomboyish behaviour. She is quite simply out of control. How on earth your poor aunt imagines she can find someone to take her, is quite beyond me. Come, let us walk a little longer, my sweet,' she said, tugging on his elbow.

James shrugged her off, rather abruptly. 'You go on walking if you wish, Madeleine. I, however, have a duty to return Lady Eleanor safely to my aunt,' he declared stiffly.

Madeleine flashed Eleanor an accusing glare. 'Very well, then,' she sniped, affecting a hurt expression, 'I *shall* go on alone. But if anything untoward happens to me, it will be *your* fault,' she said, glaring at Eleanor once more.

As Madeleine flounced off down the bridle path in an obvious huff, James continued standing where he was above Eleanor and the boys; his arms now crossed authoritatively across his broad chest; his features set in a grim, serious expression.

'I think it is time, Lady Eleanor,' he said brusquely, 'that you put an end to your fishing expedition and returned to dry land.'

At his severe tone, Eleanor quailed inwardly. She flashed a rueful face at the boys. 'Sorry, boys,' she said, 'but I'm afraid I have to go now.'

Disappointment washed over their young faces before Ed piped up, 'That's a real shame, miss. You're the best fisher, I've ever known – even if you are a girl.' Finishing his speech, the boy blushed a deep shade of scarlet while the others nodded their solemn agreement.

Eleanor gave him a wink to convey her gratitude at the compliment before turning her back to the boys and wading carefully through the water towards James. As she reached the edge, James bent down and extended his arm towards her. She reached out and grasped it and almost started at the pulse of heat which surged through her body as they touched. Still having his shirt-sleeves rolled up, she noticed the fine dark hair which covered his arms and the delineation of his strong muscles as he pulled her, with very little effort, up onto the bank. Once safely delivered, they released their hold of each other and Eleanor found herself standing directly before him, unable to speak. For a moment, he, too, seemed devoid of speech and simply stared at her. A splash from the water below broke the moment as they both became aware once more of their young audience.

James was the first to regain his voice. 'I dread to think what my aunt will say to your appearance, Lady Eleanor,' he said, removing a piece of mossy twig from her hair. 'Although . . .' he continued, in a tone so intimate that it caused her skin to break out in goosepimples, 'I myself, have my own opinion.'

She was aware that he was now staring at her bare legs. Good God, she thought, what on earth must he think of her standing gawping at him so with her gown tucked up in her undergarments. She felt herself flushing a deep shade of crimson and hastily began rearranging her skirts into some semblance of decency. As she bent down to squeeze the water from the hem of her frock, something bright caught the corner of her eye. Something that was glinting ominously in the sunlight as it made its way quickly and silently through the still, warm air. In the split second that it took for her to realize what it was, her instincts kicked in. Without wasting a moment, she straightened and launched the full weight of her body against James. Catching him completely off-guard, he tumbled backwards into a group of large green ferns. Eleanor fell directly on top of him. Their heads turned in unison as the arrow went whistling past them and landed with a thud in the trunk of a nearby tree.

They both regarded the weapon quivering indignantly in the bark, in stunned silence. It was some moments later, both of them lying quite still, before James said, in a matter-of-fact tone, 'Well, Lady Eleanor, it would appear that we are making quite a habit of rescuing one another.'

Having received more compliments and praise from Ed and his pals on how clever she was – especially for a girl – James and Eleanor made their way in silence back along the bridle path towards the manicured grounds of picnic. Eleanor was aware of several enquiring looks as they walked back to their party: the edge of her crumpled gown dripping water around her ankles, and her hair, which Milly had gone to such lengths to arrange, now completely dishevelled and adorned with varying pieces of flora.

The dowager's reaction to her goddaughter's appearance was surprisingly restrained, undoubtedly due to the presence of three other stout persons squeezed onto the blanket. Realizing rapidly that it would not do at all to scold the girl in front of her prospective in-laws, Lady Ormiston had hastily rearranged her initial expression of pure horror, into one of affected concern.

'Ah Eleanor, there you are, my dear,' she had boomed, attempting, rather unsuccessfully, to conceal the disapproval in her tone. 'And looking a little . . . er . . . out of sorts, I see,' she sniffed, holding up her lorgnette and pursing her thin lips. Then, attempting to make light of the situation, 'Obviously you have been involved in some sort of mishap. Now do sit down here with the Graysons, my dear, and tell us all about it.'

Eleanor had never thought she would be so relieved to see Whitlock. Indeed she was so exhausted, she immediately made her excuses and retired to her bedchamber without any supper. For all her fatigue, however, sleep still managed to elude her as her head whirled with the events of the day.

Once news of the 'mishap' had spread, their party had been inundated with a stream of curious, gossip-seeking guests all eager to hear the details of the drama first-hand. The Stanningtons, of course, had been appalled that some rogue poacher had dared to be hunting on their land and had come so close to injuring or, worse still, killing, one of their esteemed guests. Eleanor had wondered, as Lady Stannington had dabbed her eyes so dramatically with her white lace handkerchief, if the couple would have been quite so upset if the guest in question had not been quite so esteemed.

Then there was Lady Madeleine who had appeared on the scene with all the theatre of a newly bereaved widow. Of course, rather than giving Eleanor credit for saving James, Madeleine immediately blamed her by saying that if she had not been larking around like a child in the water, then James would not have been standing on the river-bank in the first place. Eleanor had thought about saying that if blame was being apportioned so, then the whole thing could be perceived as being Lady Madeleine's fault for nagging James so much that he'd been forced to leave his comfortable position on the blanket and go walking in the first place.

Never one to miss out on a drama, Cynthia Carmichael had been one of the first tabbies on the scene, bustling over to them clutching her vinaigrette. She had had, so she informed the dowager, a fit of the vapours upon hearing how close the arrow had come to hitting poor James. Felicity, tagging along behind her, had not spoken a single word, but had regarded James with a strange look that Eleanor had been unable to decipher. The glare she had flashed Eleanor herself, had been much easier to read: it had been one of pure unconcealed disdain.

Another reaction that Eleanor had found difficult to assess was that of the Duke of Swinton. As members of his party had passed by and exchanged a few words with James, the duke and duchess had merely stood a little way back from the group, the duchess looking thoroughly shocked and the duke look-ing, unmistakably . . . disappointed.

Lady Ormiston, despite having had her own fit of the vapours when Madeleine had later informed her of Eleanor's fishing spree, had had little choice but to support her goddaughter's actions in front of the Graysons, particularly as Lord Grayson, the man from whom his son had unquestionably inherited his unfortunate looks, had been most impressed with Eleanor's quick thinking and nimble actions.

'Can't be doing with these simpering little ninnies who do nothing but talk dresses and balls,' he had advocated. 'Like a woman with spirit, so I do.'

A wave of relief had spread over the dowager's face. 'Oh, well, I can assure you, Lord Grayson,' she had replied with alacrity, 'that Lady Eleanor has *plenty* of that.' The young viscount had nodded his approval. 'And not only that but a fine-looking filly too, Papa,' he'd leered.

Eleanor, resentful of being talked of as though she were a horse, had been on the verge of protesting, when she'd caught James staring at her with that same strange expression on his face, which was now becoming familiar. Both Lady Madeleine and Derek Lovell had been fussing around him, chattering away ten to the dozen. For a very brief moment as her eyes met his, every-one else had melted into the background and only the two of them existed.

James had been the first to avert his gaze leaving her wondering if he, like her, was aware of something very strange happening between the two of them.

# CHAPTER 13

THE following morning, it took Eleanor all of five short minutes to realize that Milly was most definitely not herself. Indeed, the girl appeared quite uncharacteristically out of sorts.

'Is something wrong, Milly?' Eleanor asked concernedly, as the girl brushed her hair. She had begun to regale to Milly the events of the picnic, adding in a generous dose of her own distinctive humour. Milly, rather than drinking in every detail as was usually the case, appeared to be paying scant attention.

'No, there's nothing wrong, miss,' Milly replied weakly. 'Nothing to bother yourself with at any rate.'

Eleanor swivelled around on her stool so that she faced the girl. 'But I *want* to bother myself, Milly,' she replied vehemently. 'You are my only friend here and if something is making you miserable, then I want to help. Now, tell me, what is it?'

Milly regarded her for a few seconds, chewing on her bottom lip. 'It's rats, miss,' she replied with more than a hint of embarrassment.

Eleanor wrinkled her forehead. 'Rats?' she repeated incredulously.

'Yes, miss. And lots of 'em,' Milly continued solemnly. 'House was full of them when I went visiting my ma yesterday. Causing some right bother, I can tell you.'

'Well, that I can certainly believe,' agreed Eleanor. 'I've seen first-hand the amount of trouble a plague of rats caused to poor Zach's farm last year. Now tell me, Milly, how does your mother plan to be rid of them?'

Milly emitted a heavy sigh. 'Not much she can do, miss,' she replied resignedly. 'She's put a few traps down but there's so many of them, they don't seem to be making much difference. Reckon she'll just have to wait 'til they get fed up and move on.'

Eleanor looked horrified. 'But we have to do something, Milly. We can't let your family live with rats. I will have a word with the farmer here. What's he called again . . . Mickey Humphreys? I'm sure he'll be able to help us and get his hands on some rat poison.'

'But poison costs money, miss,' objected Milly, 'and my ma ain't—'

'No,' interjected Eleanor authoritatively, 'but I have. And I owe you more than a few packets of rat poison for all the help you've given me with my dancing and for being such a good and loyal friend. I will go and speak to Mickey this very morning and see if he can help us tomorrow. Of course, we will most likely need to get everyone out of the house for the day so that Mickey can do his work and I know exactly what we will do. You said yesterday that you wanted to go to a picnic, and so you shall, Milly. Tomorrow, if Mickey is willing, we shall have a picnic – in Paddy's Meadow. All you will have to do is to get your family to the meadow by noon and I shall arrange everything else. What do you think, Milly? *Milly?*'

Milly was standing staring at her mistress in genuine awe. If only all toffs were as kind and caring as her, she thought, then the world would be in a much better fettle.

After breakfast, Eleanor determined to ride over to the Humphreys' farm to see if Mickey could help with the Maguires' rat problem. She had thought him a decent sort at her godmother's garden party and was almost sure he wouldn't mind lending a hand. Giles had informed her that Lady Ormiston had gone into Richmond and thankfully there was no dancing lesson scheduled for that morning. She had one of the grooms saddle up a chestnut mare and, steadfastly refusing their insistent offer that one of them accompany her, she made her way across the fields and meadows following the directions the grooms had given her to Mickey's farm. It was another beautiful spring morning with the sun already high in the cloudless sky. She trotted gently along the country lanes, marvelling at the abundance of violets, bluebells, buttercups and daisies springing from the hedgerows.

Mickey Humphreys and his plump, pretty wife, Bella, once they had got over their shock at having such a 'top-lofty visitor' had made her most welcome: Bella providing her with a generous slab of delicious freshly baked fruit cake and a dish of sweet tea. Mickey, obviously honoured that Eleanor had thought to turn to him with her problem, was only too delighted to help and promised faithfully to be at the Maguires' house first thing the following morning, complete with rat poison and as many traps as he could muster.

*

Almost two hours later, reluctantly taking her leave of the Humphreys' cosy, welcoming cottage Eleanor felt in no mood to return directly to the large, intimidating, ghostly walls of Whitlock. Instead she decided to make the most of the glorious day, and trotted her horse sedately along a maze of lanes until she was completely free of dwellings, villages and people and surrounded only by a patchwork of gloriously multi-coloured open fields. She had had little chance to ride during her stay at the castle, Lady Ormiston being of the opinion that it was quite unbecoming for young ladies to sit in a saddle and that horses should only be resorted to when there was an unavoidable reason to leave the house and no conveyance of any type available. As Eleanor kicked the horse to a gallop and the two of them flew effortlessly over hedgerows, streams and fences, she forgot all about her problems and was aware of nothing other than the countryside flashing by, the breeze whistling through her hair and the large, powerful beast beneath her. She had no idea how long they had ridden, but when eventually they reached a wide track flanked on either side by fences, she slowed the horse to a trot and found that they were both panting wildly with exhilaration.

The sudden incongruous sound of slow, mocking applause caused Eleanor's heart to miss a beat. Why on earth would anyone be clapping in the middle of the countryside? She had thought that there was no one else around for miles. She swung the horse around to face the direction of the sound and came face-to-face with James and Derek Lovell, both also mounted on horseback.

'Congratulations, Lady Eleanor,' sneered Lovell, still clapping his hands sarcastically, 'a first-class demonstration of yet another of your hidden accomplishments it would appear.'

Eleanor flashed a glance at James who was regarding her rather suspiciously, as if he, too, was of the mind that she had been aware of their presence. Seeking to defend herself, she said haughtily, 'I had no idea that I had an audience, sir.'

'Oh really?' sneered Lovell. 'Then we are not correct in thinking you were hoping to impress us?'

Eleanor felt a wave of indignation flood her body. 'Impress you?' she repeated incredulously. 'And why on earth would I wish to do that, *sir*?'

Lovell tittered derisively. 'Well, for the same reasons I should think, madam, that any lady wishes to impress a gentleman.'

Eleanor tried desperately to quell the colour rising in her cheeks. 'Perhaps,' she replied bluntly, 'if there were any gentlemen here, then your point might have had some credence. Now, if you will excuse me, I must return to the castle. I have a great deal to do today.'

As Lovell made some acerbic comment regarding her pianoforte playing, James remained silent but continued to regard her in that same discomfiting manner he had demonstrated of late.

Seething at the arrogance of the pair, she wheeled her horse around again and, with her head held high, set off at a slow trot back down the lane.

She had only gone a little way when she heard James calling after her. 'Oh, Lady Eleanor,' he shouted, 'I think you will find that the castle is in the opposite direction.'

Eleanor pulled the horse abruptly to a halt, silently cursing herself. She had been in such a rush to distance herself from the pair that she hadn't given a thought as to the correct way back to Whitlock.

Steeling herself for their reaction, she swung the horse around again, to face the two men. Just as she had thought, the pair of them had obviously, to her chagrin, found her actions extremely entertaining. James was doing his best to conceal his amusement although his twitching lips and sparkling eyes betrayed the earnest expression he was affecting. Lovell on the other hand, was laughing so hard he was almost doubled up.

Reluctantly, she trotted the horse back from whence she had just come, pulling it to a stand directly in front of them.

Looking James defiantly in the eyes, she said vehemently, 'I am well aware of that fact, sir. However, I thought I would partake of a little more fresh air and ride out a while longer.'

James affected an understanding countenance and nodded his head gravely. 'I see,' he said drily. 'Then forgive me for interfering, Lady Eleanor. You had, however, given me the impression that you had much to do today and that it was a matter of some import that you returned to the castle immediately.'

Eleanor tossed her head. 'Well, of course I have a great deal to do, sir. However, one should always, I find, make some time in the day for a little recreation.'

This remark caused another snort of laughter from Derek Lovell. Eleanor shot him a baleful glare.

'Oh, I could not agree more, Lady Eleanor,' said James solemnly, 'as I am sure will my aunt. She is, I take it, fully aware that you are galloping wildly around the countryside without the accompaniment of a groom?'

Eleanor's heart sank. Damn the man, she thought. Damn him to hell. He would know, fine well, what the dowager's opinion on such conduct would be.

His lips were twitching furiously as she regarded him once more.

'My godmother was not present when I left the house this morning, sir. I was therefore unable to inform her of my plans.'

'I see,' said James gravely, 'then I think it best perhaps that you allow us to accompany you back to the castle. There are, as you are no doubt aware, Lady Eleanor, numerous unmentionable mishaps which could befall a young lady out riding alone.'

It wasn't only Eleanor who resented this unwelcome invitation but, by the sudden sobering of Lovell, he too had no wish at all for her to join them. 'Oh, come on, old chap,' he expostulated, all signs of previous hilarity rapidly evaporating, 'let her go on. The last thing we need is some chit tagging along behind us.'

Eleanor was about to protest at this disparaging remark when James forestalled her. 'On the contrary, Lovell,' he countered, 'I think I can safely say, from what we have just witnessed, that Lady Eleanor is a match for any man in the saddle. What would you say to a race back to Whitlock, Lady Eleanor?'

Eleanor cast a look at Lovell. He was looking as though he could quite happily murder her for invading on his time with his friend. Moving her gaze to James, she found him regarding her expectantly, with raised brows and eyes glinting mischievously, almost daring her to accept. Well, thought Eleanor stoutly, she had never refused a challenge in all her nineteen years and six months and she was certainly not about to start now.

'Very well, then,' she replied blithely, 'I accept your challenge, sir.'

James smiled knowingly. 'I did not, for a single moment, doubt that you would not, Lady Eleanor.'

The three of them lined up their steeds on the edge of the meadow through which Eleanor had just ridden and on James's count of three, kicked their mounts to a gallop. It was James who immediately took the lead with Eleanor just behind him as they cleared the first meadow and both soared over the stone wall separating it from the next. Eleanor was aware of Lovell shouting something from behind her and she tossed a look over her shoulder just in time to see him draw his horse to a halt in front of the wall – evidently the beast had refused to jump which meant Lovell was out of the race, leaving just her and James. James was still slightly ahead. A vision of his smug arrogant face and the comments she would no doubt have to endure should he win, stoked Eleanor's determination. She pressed her heels harder into the mare's flanks, spurring it on and bent low over its head, the wind streaming through her hair. Half way up the next meadow, a mass of bobbing buttercups,

Eleanor's horse nudged in front of James's: she had taken the lead. So intent was she on her race that this time she failed to see the glint of the arrowhead. Her horse, however, did not. As the weapon soared just across the beast's eye-line, it reared, tossing Eleanor to the ground with a deathly thud.

Drifting in and out of consciousness, Eleanor was only vaguely aware of the consternation caused by James and Lovell returning to the castle carrying her limp, lifeless body. She heard the dowager loudly demanding an explanation of the two men; Lady Madeleine declaring that 'some people will do anything to gain attention'; and James replying, 'Well, if anyone should know of that, Madeleine, it will most certainly be you'. She was aware of strong arms carrying her upstairs and laying her gently in her bed and of cold hands expertly lifting her eyelids and taking her pulse. During all of this activity, a strange medley of images flitted in and out of her mind: of Felicity Carmichael laughing callously as she dissected an enormous red and black butterfly; of a plague of rats taking over the castle; of Derek Lovell sitting before a huge pile of bills at a gaming table, and of the dowager chiding her for her unbecoming behaviour.

She even dreamt of James Prestonville. A dream so vivid that she had thought she could even smell the faint aroma of his cologne and feel the touch of his lips gently upon hers.

It was late into the evening when she awoke. Milly was sitting in the armchair at her bedside, concern etched all over her young, freckled face.

'Lord, miss,' she exclaimed, her voice ripe with relief, 'you ain't half given us all a scare. Thought you were dead so we did when the master first brought you in. We've had the doctor here and everything.'

Eleanor smiled weakly. 'It'll take more than a fall from a horse to get rid of me, Milly.'

'And we're thanking God for it,' smiled Milly, taking hold of Eleanor's hand and squeezing it affectionately. 'I've never known such a to-do,' she carried on breathlessly, leaving her hold of Eleanor's hand to stand up and begin furiously plumping up the pile of pillows behind her mistress's head. 'Never seen the master looking so worried. Been in and out of here all day so he has.'

'What?' said Eleanor wrinkling her brow.

'The master, miss,' repeated Milly, still energetically plumping. 'Been in and out more times than a poss-stick in a wash tub. Even stayed and kept an eye on you while I nipped downstairs to grab a bite to eat.'

Eleanor's heart missed beat. 'Did he indeed?' she said, raising her hand to her lips.

Much to everyone's relief, Eleanor had awoken with rather a large appetite and Milly had wasted no time in bringing her up a tray from the kitchen containing a bowl of beef stew, a large hunk of fresh bread, a slice of apple pie and a jug of fresh cream. Having devoured the stew and the bread, Eleanor was tucking heartily into the apple pie and entertaining Milly with those of her dreams she dared repeat.

'And I even dreamt,' she said with a giggle, as she held a spoonful of pie smothered in fresh cream to her mouth, 'that I heard my godmother saying she had invited the ghastly viscount and his family over for tea on Thursday.'

Milly regarded her solemnly. 'Oh that weren't no dream, miss,' she said gravely. 'The three of them Graysons are coming for tea and, if I'm not mistaken, miss, it's more than the pleasure of their company they'll be offering.'

Eleanor put down her spoon. Her appetite had suddenly completely disappeared.

As the rest of the house was retiring, Eleanor, having slept most of the day and eaten rather late into the evening, felt no inclination at all to return to sleep. Milly had maintained that it was only right and proper that she stayed in the room with Eleanor that night and would have no problem at all sleeping in the armchair. Eleanor, however, had maintained that there was absolutely no need for such a fuss and had insisted that Milly return to her own room under the threat of Eleanor refusing to divulge a single detail of any of the events she attended, if Milly did not obey. Instead, she had asked that the girl bring her up the poem by Byron which she had hidden from her godmother in the library. By the light of a single candle she was still engrossed in the text well after midnight. It was a little after two o'clock when she suddenly heard a sound which simultaneously caused her stomach to lurch and her heart to jam in her throat – the unmistakable ghostly moaning of the Wailing Whitlock Widow.

This time Eleanor felt no compulsion at all to rush to her bedroom door; in fact she felt as though her body were made of lead and she could not move even if she had wanted to. She lay stock-still waiting for the sound to pass but, to her utter horror, it seemed to linger for several minutes right outside her bedchamber door. And then something happened which caused her body to freeze in complete and utter terror. She watched, her eyes almost popping out of her head, as the brass knob slowly turned and the door creaked gradually open. Her heart was now pounding so wildly that she thought it would burst out of her ribcage. She opened her mouth to scream, but no sound was forthcoming. Instead, her eyes stared unblinking at the doorway. She gasped loudly as a stream of dirty white chiffon floated partway into the room followed by more gruesome moaning. In a flash it disappeared and the door clicked shut, leaving Eleanor trembling from head to foot.

# CHAPTER 14

ELEANOR had not slept a wink during the night but, in her attempt to think of anything other than the Wailing Widow, she had remembered very early on that today was the day of the picnic she had promised Milly and her family, and that due to her fall yesterday, she had done absolutely nothing regarding the food.

She could hear the faint stirrings of the servants going about their various duties preparing the enormous castle for yet another day. Feeling restless and anxious to be out of her room, she jumped out of bed and padded over to the windows. Pushing open the shutters, she found that the morning held all the promise of another beautiful day. Gazing out across the lawn and the surrounding lush countryside, she pushed aside all memories of the terrifying scene she had witnessed several sleepless hours ago and discovered that, apart from a rather large sore bump on her head, she actually felt quite the thing.

She quickly pulled on a plain, unfashionable brown day gown she had brought from Nottingham, the same gown that, upon seeing it for the first time, had inspired the dowager to enquire sarcastically if Eleanor had inclinations towards becoming a monk. For the task she was intending this morning, however, the gown would suit perfectly well.

It was the first time Eleanor had visited the kitchens of the castle. Located deep in the bowels of the building she found them to be cavernous and, despite the early hour, already abuzz with energetic activity. Hovering tentatively in the large arched doorway, she observed a whole host of bustling scullery maids and kitchen maids going about their arduous tasks under the watchful eye of the formidable cook, Mrs Green, who was standing at a long wooden table vigorously pummelling a large mound of dough into pliable submission.

Eleanor started slightly as Mrs Green suddenly raised her head and spotted her.

'Well I never,' she declared ceasing her kneading. 'What on earth are you doing down here and at this hour, Lady Eleanor?'

Eleanor felt extremely self-conscious as all other activity stopped abruptly and she felt a dozen or so pairs of eyes regarding her incredulously.

'Please do forgive the intrusion, Mrs Green,' she said, tentatively approaching the older woman, 'but I have promised Milly and her family a picnic today and I had a bit of an – er accident yesterday and well, I didn't arrange for any food so I was wondering if you would mind if I baked a few things.'

'Baked a few things?' repeated Mrs Green in amazement. 'You, miss?'

'Only a few pies. . . .' replied Eleanor expectantly.

A look of pure disbelief spread over Mrs Green's ruddy countenance. 'Lord, miss,' she declared, shaking her head, 'there's us all thinking you're on your death bed and here you are at this ungodly hour down in my kitchen wanting to bake a few things.'

'I promise not to be any trouble,' said Eleanor, 'and I have done it before. Mrs Bentley – that's Zach the farmer's wife. In Nottingham. Where I live. Well, I've often helped her with the baking but I've never actually done any all by myself and I'm sure my efforts will come nowhere near your own. I mean, that mutton pie we had several days ago was the best I had tasted in my entire life.'

Mrs Green now flushed with pride. 'Well, I must say,' she flustered, tucking a stray lock of hair into her cap, 'Mr Green do say I make the best mutton pie in the whole of the county.'

'Oh, and I agree with him,' enthused Eleanor, truthfully.

'Well then,' said Mrs Green, bustling over to a hook on the wall on which hung a gleaming white apron, 'we'd best get a move on if you're to bake enough to fill that Maguire clan. And seeing as how we were all so worried about you yesterday, I might just share with you a couple of secrets about my pastry. . . .'

An hour or so later and Eleanor stood wiping her floury hands on her apron admiring the fruits of her labours. Indeed, the large rectangular table was almost straining under the weight of pies, cakes and scones. Yes, she thought, with a stab of pride, this was going to be the best picnic ever.

Fortunately for Eleanor, she had managed to avoid her godmother all morning, despite returning to her chamber to change out of her 'monastery dress' and into one of lawned muslin.

'Please tell Lady Ormiston that I am feeling quite well today, Giles,' Eleanor informed the butler, as she stood tying her bonnet strings in the hall, 'and that I shall be spending the day in the fresh air.'

The man, with a rather perplexed, disapproving expression on his face, had nodded his compliance.

Being an only child, Eleanor couldn't help but feel a stab of envy whenever she saw a large, loving family together. There was something about a large family that made her feel safe and secure. She loved her father very much indeed but she was aware that, should anything happen to him, she would be quite alone in the world and, as independent and as self-sufficient as she was, that thought sometimes frightened her. With a large family however, one need never have such concerns: there was always a younger brother to fight, or an older sister with whom to gossip. Eleanor had often wondered how many siblings she would have had and what they would have been like, if her mother had not died so young.

In the brilliant sunlight Paddy's Meadow looked quite glorious. As she made her way there now, the gig crammed with baskets of food wrapped, thanks to cook and the kitchen maids, in clean red and white gingham cloths, she could see what seemed to be all thirteen of the Maguire children, including Milly, running wildly around the meadow, laughing and squealing.

Eleanor smiled to herself. It was good to see Milly happy again. They really had developed a deep genuine fondness for each other in the short time she had been at Whitlock. Indeed she really didn't know how she would have survived there so long without Milly's friendship. The girl was the only person she had met in London so far who seemed anywhere near normal. Of course sometimes, unfortunately she had to pull rank over the girl, like this morning for instance when Milly had awoken quite late and was appalled to find her mistress already up and about.

'Oh, miss,' she had exclaimed. 'Don't know what sort of a lady's-maid I am, letting you get yourself up and all. You should be resting, miss, not gallivaning around.'

'Milly,' Eleanor had replied, 'I am perfectly fine as you can see and if you insist on fussing about me, I shall dismiss you from your post instantly. Now I don't want to hear another word on the subject.'

\*

137

As she pulled the gig to a halt, some of the children, including Milly ran up to help her. Eleanor was amazed to see that three of the brothers were the same boys with whom she had enjoyed her fishing experience at the Stanningtons' picnic. Ed, it appeared, had, due to Eleanor's demonstration of her rather unconventional talents that day, elevated her to some kind of goddess-like status, gazing at her in wide-eyed awe and practically tripping over himself in his energetic efforts to help her with the unloading.

The matriarch of the brood, Mrs Maguire, was a woman in her mid-forties who, in spite of the lines on her tired, haggard face, was still remarkably handsome with the same startling blue eyes and blonde hair of all of her offspring, although her hair was now dull and flecked with grey. The woman was obviously very shy and very much in awe of Eleanor, not daring to meet her eyes when she addressed her and thanking her over and over again for all she was doing for them.

'Mrs Maguire,' said Eleanor firmly, after the woman had told her how grateful she was for what seemed like the twenty-fifth time, 'let me assure you that this is nothing compared to what Milly has done for me. Without your daughter, I would not have a single friend in London, nor would I be able to dance and, let me tell you, Mrs Maguire, that that, in my godmother's books, is as bad as going to a ball wearing nothing but one's undergarments.'

At Eleanor's forthright, down-to-earth tone, Mrs Maguire had stared at her in utter amazement before collapsing into a fit of giggles – an activity, which, if the worry lines on her forehead were anything to go by, the woman probably did not engage in very often.

'See, Ma,' said Milly, beaming proudly at her mistress, 'I told you she were a one, didn't I?'

'Aye, you did,' said Mrs Maguire, still laughing. 'And I'll not disagree with you there, girl.'

Eleanor, with Ed's eager help, organized various games for them all to play. She had had the foresight to bring along several bats and balls and they played rounders; their own version of the new game known as cricket; as well as several others which they ingeniously devised especially for the occasion. Then, having built up hearty appetites, they tucked into the feast Eleanor had brought along. As well as the pies, cakes and scones she had baked that morning, there were thick slices of ham and roast beef, a selection of cheeses, plump tomatoes, fresh fruit and jellies.

'Ooh,' said Ed, lying back on one of the blankets and rubbing his stomach, 'I don't believe I've eaten so much in all my life, miss.'

This appeared to be the general sentiment of the group who then decided that a little repose would be a good idea. The younger Maguires then proceeded to fall asleep with various limbs draped carelessly over their nearest sibling. The older ones chatted amongst themselves, revelling in the heat of the afternoon and the chance to have a rare day off from their never-ending chores. How hard these people worked, thought Eleanor, and how much they appreciated the simple things in life unlike those of her own class, many of whom had never done a day's work in their lives but who instead searched endlessly for some kind of inner fulfilment in the form of empty, frivolous amusements.

When the younger children woke up, Ed decided that they should split into two teams and play another game of rounders. Various items of clothing were placed around the meadow marking out the six bases. Eleanor was the third person to take her turn with the bat. She took up her position waiting for Ed to throw the ball to her. As it flew threw the air towards her, she pulled the bat back as far as she could and, with all her strength, belted the ball far out into the field.

'OW!' came an almighty screech.

All the Maguires and Eleanor stared wide-eyed as James Prestonville slowly approached them from the bottom of the meadow. He was wearing brown riding breeches and a white shirt which, due to the heat of the day, was unbuttoned at the neck with the sleeves rolled up to his elbow. Leading his horse, he held the reins in one hand and with his other, rubbed a spot on the left side of his head. Observing the dark, foreboding way in which he was regarding her, Eleanor quailed inwardly. She was sorry that the ball had hit him, of course, but, damn him, why did he have to be out riding today anyway? He was now about to spoil what had so far been a perfect afternoon.

The full complement of Maguire eyes were also staring at James, but slowly, one by one, as he approached her, they turned around to regard Eleanor. For the first time in a very long while, Eleanor could imagine, every single one of the Maguires was completely silent.

Almost as if he were unaware of his audience however, James strode purposefully towards Eleanor, never taking his eyes off her for a moment. As he came to a halt directly before her, she found that her heart was pounding loudly.

His face was stony as he regarded her with the same strange, unfathomable expression she was now used to seeing. He slid a hand into his breeches pocket and retrieved the ball, which he held out to her. Eleanor gulped and, at a complete loss as to what to say, she took it from him and muttered her thanks.

'I am glad to see that you have recovered from your accident yesterday, Lady Eleanor,' he said, in the same intimate tone he had used at the ball, just before he had kissed her.

Eleanor felt a strange longing in the pit of her stomach and was aware of a flush rising in her cheeks. 'Thank you, sir,' she said. 'I am feeling quite well today.'

James nodded his head. Aware that the entire Maguire clan was continuing to regard them warily, they then stood looking at one other for a few brief seconds, which seemed to Eleanor more like several hours.

It was five-year-old Tom, the youngest of the Maguires, who eventually broke the silence. 'Here, sir,' piped up the tot, 'will you be in my team?'

James raised his eyebrows in surprise and turned around to face Tom who was completely oblivious to the reprimanding looks of his older siblings, all of whom were in complete and utter awe of Master James. 'We could do with a good bowler, sir,' continued the child innocently. 'We're losing and our Ed is rubbish so he is.'

'Is that a fact?' said James. There was a brief hiatus when nobody dared move, then James suddenly strode over to a tree to which he tethered his horse. 'Well then,' he said, as he returned to the group, 'if you're losing, young man, then we had better see what we can do to rectify that situation. Now who is up next?'

Eleanor could not recall seeing James look so relaxed. Apart from the times when he was busy laughing at her unbecoming and unsophisticated antics, she had noted that he had a concerned look about him: tired and troubled – like a man with a great many worries on his young shoulders. But then was it any wonder, she thought, with the combination of the 'title' business dragging on; Felicity's threats haunting him, and the uncertainty of the Duke of Swinton's actions following the discovery of his wife's affair. James Prestonville did indeed have a great many troubles at the moment.

With the organized games finished, James was lying on his back on one of the rugs, a thick blade of grass sticking out of his mouth.

'Will you not have a piece of this apple pie, Master James?' offered Ed. 'Tastes much better than grass, sir. Indeed, I'd go as far as to say that it's the best apple pie I've ever tasted.'

'Thank you, Ed,' replied James, pushing himself up to a seated position. 'I must admit that I am rather partial to apple pie.'

Ed handed a piece of the pie over to James. Swallowing his first mouthful, James's eyes lit with pleasure.

'Well I have to agree with you, Ed,' he said. 'That is quite the most delicious apple pie. My compliments, Mrs Maguire.'

'Oh, it's not mine, sir,' chuckled Mrs Maguire, who was sitting on the blanket alongside him. 'Lady Eleanor baked it – fresh this morning – and with her own fair hands. She ain't half a one that girl.'

'Yes,' said James pensively, watching Eleanor run around the field with Tom on her shoulders. 'She is a one indeed.'

Some hours later, as evening – and the younger Maguires – began to fall, the group was disbanded and everyone headed home.

'I do hope all the rats have gone when you get back, Mrs Maguire,' said Eleanor, as they bid their farewells.

'Oh, whether they have or not, miss,' replied the older woman, 'I've had a wonderful day. We can't thank you enough, miss, really we can't.'

Then, with tears in her eyes, she pulled Eleanor to her and embraced her tightly. Eleanor returned the gesture, recalling the first day she had met Milly when she, too, had spontaneously flung her arms around her.

Eleanor had instructed Milly to take the gig back to the Maguires' house in order that she could transport the younger children, who were now fit to drop, and the remainder of the food. This meant, she had noted rather nervously after she had waved them all off, that only she and James were to return to the castle. They walked along the country lanes in silence, James leading his horse by the reins. The air was still warm, scented with the sweet smell of pollen and the sound of evening birdsong. Being alone with him again, Eleanor found she had quite lost control of her senses. Her eyes were insisting on straying disobediently to the strong, masculine hand that was clutching the horse's rein. The thought of the same hand touching her body was resulting in that strange stirring in the pit of her stomach.

'Well, Lady Eleanor,' said James, definitively breaking the pregnant silence and Eleanor's outrageous musings, 'of the two picnics we have attended recently, I can honestly say that this one wins hands down. It has been a marvellous day.'

Hastily trying to push her lascivious thoughts aside and say something, which would not betray her, Eleanor found herself failing miserably.

'Well, at least I did not end up atop of you this time, sir,' she said, blushing to the roots of her hair as soon as she had blurted out the words and another shocking image flashed through her mind.

James regarded her strangely for a moment. Then he said smoothly, 'Indeed, Lady Eleanor. However, I did not say it was a perfect day.'

No other words were spoken as they made their way back to the castle, Eleanor burning with embarrassment and James seemingly reverting back to his distant, withdrawn state. Upon reaching Whitlock, James handed his horse over to one of the grooms and they made their way up the steps into the hall, where Giles greeted them.

'Her grace is in the drawing-room, sir,' the man informed solemnly, as James handed him his riding gloves. 'She requested that both you and Lady Eleanor join her the moment you arrive. Although she was not aware, of course,' he sniffed, as his eyes travelled disapprovingly over Eleanor's bedraggled appearance, 'that you had been out together.'

'And nor could she have been, Giles,' replied James brusquely. 'For Lady Eleanor and I stumbled upon one another quite by chance this afternoon. Now, Lady Eleanor, may I suggest we obey my aunt's command and go to her at once?'

Eleanor grimaced. She knew she was undoubtedly going to be told off for leaving the house so soon after her fall and for being absent most of the day. She had no wish to make matters worse by appearing before her godmother looking like a scarecrow. 'I really think that perhaps I should go upstairs and make myself presentable, James,' she explained.

James turned his attention back to the butler. 'You did say, Giles, that my aunt wished to see us *the moment* we arrived back, did you not?'

'Yes, sir,' said Giles.

'Then come along, Lady Eleanor,' said James, strutting off in the direction of the drawing-room.

Eleanor emitted a heavy sigh, which drew another critical look from Giles. Well, she thought, she might as well get it over with. After all, it couldn't possibly be any worse than she was imagining it to be.

It was worse.

Not only was her godmother waiting to pounce on her for her 'irresponsible conduct' but so too was Hester Myers. Upon seeing her father also present in the room however, Eleanor's heart leapt with joy. He was standing in front of the fireside chair, opposite that of the dowager, shaking hands with James.

'Papa!' she cried.

As James stepped aside to greet the new Lady Myers who was seated on the red sofa in front of the fireplace, her father opened his arms to her and she ran to him, throwing herself enthusiastically into his warm embrace. 'Oh Papa,' she said, burying her head in his chest, 'this is the most wonderful surprise. What on earth are you doing here and how long are you staying?'

Lord Myers laughed at his daughter's effusive greeting. Releasing his hold of her, he took a step back and, taking both of her hands in his, gazed down on her affectionately.

'We have been to visit Hester's Great Aunt Sylvie in Bath and thought we should make a slight detour here to see you on our return journey. We shall be staying for three nights. If,' he added hastily, shifting his gaze to the dowager, 'that meets with Lady Ormiston's approval.'

'Of course,' said the Dowager. 'I will have one of the maids make up a room for you at once.'

'Oh, how wonderful, Papa,' said Eleanor, gazing lovingly into his green eyes. 'I have had the most marvellous day and now you are here, it is quite perfect.'

'Well, I must say, I am very glad indeed that you have had a good day, Eleanor,' sniped the dowager from her chair. 'I, on the other hand, have spent the entire time worrying in case another accident had befallen you. Would you mind, pray, telling us, where you have been all day?'

Leaving hold of her father's hands, Eleanor turned to face her godmother. 'At a picnic, ma'am,' she said sheepishly.

The dowager's face adopted an incredulous expression. 'A *picnic?*' she repeated, holding up her lorgnette and examining Eleanor in the manner which always made the girl think back to the time when she was thirteen, 'and what kind of *picnic*, results in a young lady arriving home in such a *dishevelled* state of dress?'

'Erm, well,' stammered Eleanor, feeling Hester Myers's eyes boring coldly into her, 'it wasn't a picnic like the – er – Stanningtons, ma'am. It was more of a fun occasion. One where we were playing . . . games.'

'Good God,' exclaimed Lady Ormiston, casting her eyes skyward. Then she raised her voice several octaves and bellowed, 'Stevens!' so loudly, that she caused Hester Myers to jump several inches from her sofa.

As the quivering servant appeared, as if by magic, at her side, the dowager, boomed, 'A tray of large brandies – at once, man.'

As Stevens scurried off obediently to collect the drinks, Hester Myers eyed her stepdaughter in a manner from which one would assume, that Eleanor had a very unpleasant smell emanating from her. 'Well, I must say, Lady Ormiston,' said Hester eventually, 'I had hoped for some improvement in the girl's conduct. However, I can see that absolutely none has been made. It would appear that she is still far too unruly and wilful. Indeed,' she continued, a little hysterically as she produced a lace handkerchief from the silk purse she was clutching on her lap and began to dab her forehead with it, 'I am rapidly coming around to the idea that we will never find a man to take her at all.'

The dowager whipped a glass of brandy from the tray Stevens was now proffering and took a very large gulp of it. 'Now, now, Hester, my dear,' she replied briskly, 'there is no need for us to despair quite so soon. Indeed there is a young gentleman who appears, for reasons known only to himself, to have quite a *tendre* for the girl. I have been led to believe that he will be making an offer for her in the next few days.'

While Eleanor's heart sank directly to the ground, a strange choking sound came from James who was taking a sip of brandy.

'An – an offer?' he spluttered incredulously. 'The Viscount Grayson making an *offer* for *Lady Eleanor*?'

Eleanor, rapidly tiring of being spoken of as though she were not present, felt a very large stab of indignation. 'Are you implying, sir,' she demanded coolly, 'that it is quite inconceivable that someone should wish to marry *me*?'

James regarded her for a moment with a very odd look in his eyes. Before he could reply however, Hester Myers cut in.

'Well, I must say, Eleanor,' she declared, 'that the news is somewhat surprising. Particularly in view of the fact that you display none of the characteristics present in . . . in . . . *normal* young ladies. I have no idea what kind of man would wish to shackle himself to an oddity who is so . . . so—'

'Rambunctious,' interjected the dowager stoutly, nodding her head as though in complete agreement with every word Hester Myers was saying.

Lady Myers flashed the dowager a grateful smile. 'Exactly, Lady Ormiston,' she agreed convivially. 'I for one, cannot believe that the man is quite right in the head.'

At such blatant insults, Eleanor felt her temper rapidly rising. 'Yes, well,' she spluttered indignantly, placing her hands on her slim hips, 'I can assure you that Viscount Grayson is quite, quite normal. In fact, I would go as far to say that he is quite the most normal man I have ever met. And he is most . . .

most . . . *charming*. I can assure you that he most certainly does not think me anything of an oddity. Indeed,' she continued, crossing her arms victoriously over her chest, 'I do believe the man is quite in love with me.'

Hester Myers gave a snort of incredulous laughter. 'In love with *you?*' she sneered. 'How on earth can he be—'

'Well the proof of the pudding is in the eating, is it not, *Stepmama?*' said Eleanor defiantly. 'If the viscount does offer for me, then we shall soon see who is right, will we not?'

And with her parting comment, she whisked briskly out of the room with her head held high, leaving a stunned audience gaping after her open-mouthed and James Prestonville taking another very large gulp of brandy.

In her bedchamber Eleanor changed her dress for dinner and, having calmed down somewhat, proceeded down the stairs to seek out her father. She found him, thankfully alone, in the rose garden. She linked her arm through his and joined him in his early evening stroll.

'So,' said Lord Myers, after he had told his daughter all the news from home, 'it looks like perhaps you will be a married woman soon. Indeed, I got the impression earlier that you are quite keen on this viscount and hopeful of an offer from him.'

Eleanor gave a derisory snort. '*That*, dear Father,' she said, hugging his arm tightly to her, 'was for the benefit of the others in the room. Viscount Grayson does not interest me in the slightest. The man quite repulses me and I can assure you that if he were to make an offer I would turn it down in an instant, regardless of what my godmother thinks of the man.'

'I see,' said her father; then, after a brief silence, 'And there is no other man whom you would like to marry?'

'None at all, Father,' said Eleanor firmly. 'I have no intention of marrying anyone.'

Lord Myers nodded his head. 'I see,' he said thoughtfully.

They wandered around the gardens for another half an hour, enjoying the last of the day's sunlight. When they returned to the castle a little before dinner, they found Hester Myers already seated in the saloon, looking as dour as ever, cradling a small glass of sherry. She cast Eleanor a disapproving look as the girl entered the room, giggling at a joke her father had just told her.

'What is for dinner this evening, Stevens?' asked Eleanor, still smiling broadly as she accepted a glass of ratafia from the man's silver tray.

145

'I'm not sure, ma'am,' mumbled the servant apologetically. 'Although I do believe cook mentioned something about ham and pea soup.'

Eleanor stifled a giggle as she caught her stepmother's eye. 'Ham and pea soup, eh?' she said. 'How very very tempting.'

# CHAPTER 15

A LTHOUGH a great many things were conspiring to do so, Eleanor did not allow a single one of them to detract from the pleasure of having her father's company for a few days. Not even the fact that Lady Madeleine appeared to have worked her charm on Hester and that the two of them were seemingly in cahoots to make as many disparaging remarks as possible to Eleanor each day.

'My,' Hester had exclaimed upon first being introduced to Madeleine, 'what a charming and accomplished young woman. I should not be surprised if every man who has the pleasure of meeting her, should not wish for *her* hand in marriage.' Her last statement had, quite pointedly, been directed to her stepdaughter.

Eleanor had ignored the spiteful pair and, for once, had been rather grateful for the brief, infrequent appearances of Mr Lovell, whose presence incensed Lady Madeleine to such a point that Eleanor was temporarily forgotten and all insults directed at him. James's behaviour too, had the potential to be extremely distracting. There was no doubt, as he stomped around the castle, slamming doors and barking orders at the terrified servants, that he was not in the best of humours. He had apparently spent the last day in prolonged meetings with the solicitors over the 'title' business which, from his behaviour, Eleanor could only assume had not gone as well as he had hoped.

Perhaps the largest distraction, however, which Eleanor was doing her absolute utmost to ignore, was the visit by the Graysons later that day. The dowager, as was now to be expected, was in quite a flurry and appeared to have worked up the poor servants into a veritable frenzy. Everywhere Eleanor looked that morning, she found one of the staff frantically washing, polishing, scrubbing, plumping or brushing. Large vases overflowing with fresh flowers had been placed on every available gleaming surface and, by the delicious smells of baking wafting around the corridors, the kitchen staff were working just as hard as their colleagues upstairs.

'Good Lord, Aunt,' snapped James impatiently, as he entered the drawing-room and almost tripped over the young maid who was on all fours vigorously polishing the wooden skirting board, 'is there really any need for all of this? One would think that it was the King himself who was coming to tea.'

'Now, James,' replied the dowager briskly, 'you know as well as I that this visit could be far more important than one from the King. We must do all we can to further Eleanor's chances of an offer. God only knows, it could be the only one we ever receive.'

'That's as may be, Aunt,' challenged James, as he cast a look at Eleanor, curled up in a chair by the window reading and pretending not to notice that she was, once again, being spoken of as though she were not in the room. 'However perhaps Lady Eleanor does not wish for an offer. Perhaps, as she has informed us on several occasions, she still has no wish to marry.'

'Nonsense!' boomed the dowager, causing both Eleanor and James to start. 'I will not hear another word on the subject, James. Of course the girl wishes to marry and she should be extremely grateful that we have found someone of such consequence as the viscount who is willing to take her. I can think of a hundred chits who would welcome an offer from such a charming man. What we must all now do, is our very best to encourage the man, without, of course, allowing him even a glimpse of our desperation. Now come, Eleanor,' she bellowed suddenly, 'it is time for you to prepare yourself. I have already given Milly strict instructions on what she is to do with you and what you are to wear.'

Unable to ignore her godmother a moment longer, Eleanor sat upright and turned around to face the older woman. 'But they are not due for another two hours, Godmother, and anyway, what is wrong with the gown I am wear—'

'Your yellow gown is much more becoming, Eleanor. Please go upstairs and change into it immediately. The Graysons have been known, on one or two occasions, to arrive a few minutes . . . *prematurely*,' she sniffed disapprovingly, 'and it would not do at all for them to arrive when you are half-dressed. Now hurry along, girl, and *do* put a smile on your face.'

Milly followed the dowager's detailed instructions to the very letter, dressing Eleanor in her new yellow muslin day dress and arranging her hair in a fashionable braided chignon.

'Aren't you excited, miss?' she asked, as she stuck in the final hairpin.

'If you want the truth, Milly,' replied Eleanor soberly, 'I would rather chew off my own toe than marry Viscount Grayson.'

Then, just when Eleanor had thought her spirits couldn't possibly drop any lower, the Graysons arrived, all dressed up in their finery as though they were indeed on some kind of very serious undertaking: Lady Grayson in puce-coloured silk, dripping with jewels; Lord Grayson in fine military attire and the viscount in another ridiculously tight pair of black breeches.

The dowager, as usual, had spent an inordinate amount of time planning the seating arrangements and had ensured everyone was in their allotted place well in advance of the visitors' arrival. The dowager herself was seated in her usual chair to the right of the fireplace; Lord Myers in the chair to the left of the fireplace; Hester Myers in a matching chair alongside that of her husband; and Lady Madeleine on a chair next to the dowager with James on a gilt chair alongside her. Eleanor had been placed on a matching gilt chair in between the sofa and Hester.

Once she had reluctantly exchanged the usual courtesies with the Graysons and the guests had taken their seats, Eleanor slumped back in her chair, having absolutely no inclination at all to partake in the tedious ensuing conversation. The dowager, Hester and Lady Madeleine however, were all doing their utmost to impress the Graysons, all obviously hoping the viscount would offer for Eleanor for their own selfish reasons. Chattering away ten-to-the-dozen, the three women could not have been more nauseatingly charming if their lives had depended upon it. They tittered politely at the viscount's rather feeble attempts at humour; cooed obsequiously over Lady Grayson's rather ostentatious jewels and agreed wholeheartedly with absolutely everything Lord Grayson advocated. Eleanor had had to stifle a giggle when the man had been effusive on Byron's work. Hester had nodded her head understandingly as if in complete agreement, while Eleanor knew for a fact that the last time *she* had mentioned Byron, Hester Myers had dismissed the man as 'a crippled little rake' and his works as 'nothing but licentious rubbish'.

James and her father on the other hand, had entered into the conversation very little. While her father appeared to be listening intently, no doubt forming his own opinions on the personalities involved, James seemed, once again, to have drifted off into that far-away space which he seemed to inhabit frequently of late.

The inane chatter seemed, to Eleanor, to be interminable. Indeed the only positive thing to come out of the situation was the delicious spread, which cook had provided for the occasion and which was beautifully laid out on the large round ormolu table in front of the fire. Taking solace in the food,

Eleanor reached for her third macaroon. No sooner had she done so, however, than she felt the reprimanding glares of her godmother and Hester burn right through her. Not wishing to give the pair yet another excuse to reproach what they would undoubtedly class as her 'unbecoming behaviour', she hastily withdrew her empty hand and sank back in her seat miserably. The entire visit seemed to Eleanor to have lasted three weeks but was actually little short of an hour. James, too, was obviously finding it difficult to conceal his boredom. After muttering something about needing to stretch out a twinge in his back, he had vacated his seat and taken up a position looking out of the window. Eleanor was just wondering if she closed her eyes, how long it would take her to fall asleep, when she suddenly heard the words which made her blood run cold: 'I wonder, sir,' squeaked the viscount, directly addressing Eleanor's father, 'if I might have a word with you in priv—'

The knowing smiles which had begun to appear on the dowager's and Lady Grayson's faces, swiftly changed into a look of horror as James suddenly cried, 'Good God, Lord Grayson. I do believe someone is running off with your carriage.'

In a flash, every one of the party was at the window just in time to see the burgundy crested coach disappearing down the gravelled drive of the castle and out of the large wrought-iron gates.

'Good Lord,' exclaimed the dowager incredulously. 'Why I have never known—'

'This is no time for talking, Aunt,' interjected James authoritatively. 'Come, Lord Grayson, Viscount. We must try and catch the culprits. If we waste a moment, they might get away.'

Muttering their agreement, the viscount and his father followed James out of the drawing-room and a few minutes later the rest of the party observed as the three of them, now mounted on horses, galloped furiously down the drive after the stolen coach.

'How very odd,' exclaimed the dowager, wrinkling her forehead.

'Yes,' replied Lord Myers pensively. 'How very odd indeed.'

A short half-hour later, James and the men returned to the castle with the stolen carriage. It had been found, so they informed the rest of the party, abandoned at the side of the road, half a mile or so from the castle, with no harm done to it and no sign at all of the perpetrators. The incident had caused quite a stir and there was a great deal of speculation flying around as to how on earth the thieves could have got into the grounds and indeed the carriage, without being seen by anyone. James himself had personally gone down to the stables to reprimand the staff for their apparent negligence. Eleanor, however, had no interest at all in how or why the thieves had stolen the carriage. Indeed, had she met the culprits she would have gladly rewarded them for their impeccable timing.

Eleanor's eyes filled up with tears when Milly handed her the carved box. 'It's a present, miss,' she said proudly. 'From all of us – for the picnic like. Our Ed made it – it was his idea.'

'Oh, Milly,' said Eleanor, throwing her arms around the younger girl, 'there is no need at all for any of you to go to any trouble on my behalf. The picnic was the least I could do.'

'Well, not according to our Ed, miss. He thinks you're a right one and he'll not be wrong. Never seen the young ones as happy as that day they went home and all those pesky rats had gone. Not a trace of them anywhere. Like a little palace it was.'

'Yes, Mickey did us all proud,' agreed Eleanor. 'I took some cheese and some ham over there yesterday when I went to pay him for his trouble, and some biscuits for the children.'

'Oh, miss,' exclaimed Milly with a warm smile. 'You ain't half a one.'

Eleanor returned the smile with one of her own. 'Tell me, Milly,' she said, her voice lilting with amusement, 'is being "half a one" better than being a full one?'

Milly looked at her, puzzled. 'Cor, miss,' she said, scratching her fair head. 'Now you're asking.'

As devastated as she was to see her father leave, Eleanor put on a brave face. She had wanted desperately to ask if she could travel home with him, but she had known, beyond a shadow of a doubt, what Hester's reply would have been. Instead, she had bitten her lip and not shed a single tear until she was in the privacy of her own rooms.

Regardless of how she was feeling, the tiresome unrelenting round of social events continued. That evening they were all invited to Lady Illingsworth's musical soirée. Eleanor had no inclination at all to attend the gathering not even being convinced that, as Milly had put it: 'It'll be better than moping round the house.' Her godmother though, was in no mood for excuses and so, dressed in another of her new evening gowns – a flattering, high-waisted garment of purple-blue satin, Eleanor arrived at the large mansion house in Grosvenor Square, accompanied by the dowager, James, Lady Madeleine and, unfortunately, the odious Derek Lovell. Lord and Lady Illingsworth were two of the most enormous people Eleanor had ever set eyes upon and, obviously having a rather high opinion of their own importance, they were both dressed in attire which was more regal than that worn by the King and Queen themselves. Once they had exchanged greetings, the party made their way into the rather vulgar music-room, which was crammed with an astonishing array of ornaments, all no doubt intended to demonstrate the family's evident great wealth. As the other members of her party greeted their hosts, Eleanor's eyes travelled around the room, which was already milling with bodies. She recognized almost all of them; it appeared that the same boring souls turned up at every event, with their dreary topics of conversation and predictable witticisms. She really was feeling so out of spirits that she couldn't even pretend to be interested. Scanning the crowd, she noted the presence of the Duke and Duchess of Swinton talking to Lord and Lady Stannington. Moving her gaze further her eyes suddenly met a pair of insipid blue ones, glaring at her menacingly – Felicity Carmichael. Eleanor's heart skipped a beat and she quickly averted her gaze. Thankfully, the girl and her mother were on the other side of the room, deep in conversation with Lady Lydia Armstrong – a renowned gossip. Eleanor hoped desperately that there would be no time for the pair to wind their way over to her party before the performances began. Thankfully there wasn't and, as the performances were announced, it was with a sigh of relief that Eleanor took her seat on one of the blue gilt chairs, which had been laid out before the pianoforte. She was sandwiched between her godmother and James and discreetly sneaked a sideways glance at him. He, too, she noticed, was looking decidedly melancholy, giving the distinct appearance that he would rather be anywhere else other than the Illingsworths' or, more likely, anywhere else other than in the presence of Felicity Carmichael. The same dark, angry expression he had borne for the last few days, was still very much in evidence. Lady Madeleine meanwhile, was, as usual, completely oblivious to anyone's needs but her own.

'James, darling,' she purred, just as they had taken their seats – Eleanor on James's right and Lady Madeleine on his left – 'I feel a little thirsty. Would you be a dear and bring me a glass of champagne?'

James refused to look at her. 'The performance is about to start, Madeleine,' he replied impatiently.

'Oh, but I am so thirsty, I think I shall *die* if I do not have my champagne,' she continued pleadingly.

'For God's sake, Madeleine,' snapped back James, 'I am not going to get you any champagne. Now kindly be quiet!'

Madeleine gasped loudly at James's outburst, which had been so loud, it had caused two rows of inquisitive, scandal-seeking heads to swing around abruptly and gaze at them.

Not wishing to create even more of a spectacle of herself, Lady Madeleine stuck out her bottom lip petulantly and folded her arms across her chest. Eleanor stifled a giggle. Perhaps, she thought, the Illingsworths' musical soirée may not be so boring after all.

Eleanor's optimism for the evening though, proved extremely short-lived. She had endured a painful piece by Haydn played by a gentleman so old and frail she was afraid he might collapse at any point, and an Italian piece played and sung by a spotty young girl with a squeaky voice who was obviously so nervous, she was perspiring profusely. So jaded was she that at one stage she lost the fight with her eyelids and had nodded off only to wake by James nudging her in the ribs sharply.

She was more than a little grateful when the interval was called and they made their way to the supper-room – the gargantuan, extravagant feast laid out before them providing a rather hefty clue as to how the Illingsworths had acquired their bulk.

'Good evening, Lady Ormiston,' said a high-pitched male voice, just as Eleanor was helping herself to a lobster patty.

'Ah, Viscount Grayson,' said the dowager, turning to face the young man. 'How very splendid. Eleanor was so hoping you would be here this evening, weren't you, my dear?' she said, shooting her goddaughter an imploring glare.

Eleanor steeled herself to turn around and face the man attempting, rather unsuccessfully to remove the frown from her face. 'Good evening, Viscount,' she said, her tone completely neutral as she dipped a curtsy.

'Lady Eleanor,' replied the man, almost salivating as he greedily drank in the low cut of her dress. 'May I ask if you are enjoying the performances this evening?'

Eleanor looked at him blankly. How on earth could anyone be enjoying them? 'I must confess, sir,' she replied truthfully, 'that I have never before spent an evening quite like it.'

A snort of laughter, transformed quickly into a cough, came from behind her. She turned abruptly around to see James standing there. He and the viscount exchanged bows and pleasantries.

'I trust, sir,' squeaked the viscount, 'that you have had no more trouble with thieves at Whitlock following the incident with our carriage?'

James adopted a very serious countenance. 'Indeed we have not, sir,' he replied solemnly. 'It would appear that the incident with your carriage, sir was quite . . . *unique*.'

Just at that moment, the butler appeared and held out a silver platter to James. 'Excuse me, my lord,' he said gravely, 'but an urgent note has just been delivered for you.'

'For me?' asked James, furrowing his brow. 'Who on earth—?'

He retrieved the envelope from the tray and tore it open. Unfolding the piece of white paper inside, he read the contents, the furrows on his forehead deepening as he did so.

'I'm afraid,' he said, refolding the paper and slipping it back into the envelope and then into his breeches' pocket, 'that you will have to excuse me. I have a little *personal matter* to attend to.'

The dowager rolled her eyes. 'Hmph,' she sniffed light-heartedly, 'I think the less we ladies know of your *personal matters*, James, the better, don't you?'

James appeared not to have heard his aunt's question. A decidedly puzzled and worried expression had spread over his countenance. Without uttering another word, he turned his back on the group and strode purposefully out of the supper-room in the direction of the entrance hall.

While the dowager was busily muttering something about young men today, Eleanor took the opportunity to observe the other guests in the room. She saw Felicity Carmichael and her mother, both with plates piled high with food, chatting to old Lord Kenilworth; the Duke and Duchess of Swinton were standing with a crowd of six or seven other people from which loud spontaneous bursts of laughter continued to emanate. Lord Illingsworth appeared to have cornered a very pretty young lady, whom Eleanor recognized as Penelope Hartly and who looked as though she were desperate to escape the man's overpowering attentions; Lady Illingsworth, meanwhile, appeared to be having a similar effect on a handsome, but rather short young man, who looked as though he were about to be suffocated by the woman's enormous bosom levelled exactly with his head.

'Where is James?' demanded Lady Madeleine tartly, when she returned from speaking to Lydia Armstrong. 'Do not tell me he has gone into the card-room with that hideous man, Lovell?'

'Indeed, he has not, Madeleine,' replied the Dowager defensively. 'He had a little business to attend. He will be back shortly.'

'Hmm,' seethed Madeleine, crossing her arms over her chest. 'He is not at all attentive to me this evening. In fact he has been so grumpy, he has quite put me in a bad humour. I would wager, Viscount,' she continued, peering seductively at the man through a fan of thick, dark lashes, 'that you would not treat a lady so.'

While Madeleine began flirting unashamedly with the viscount, and the dowager was exchanging pleasantries with another matronly figure, an uneasy feeling was slowly creeping over Eleanor regarding James and the note. It was a feeling so strong that she felt compelled to follow him and make sure he was safe. Whilst no one was paying her any attention, she put down her plate with the untouched lobster patty and walked nonchalantly towards the door of the room, following the route James had just taken.

There was no sign of him when she arrived in the main entrance hall and, of course, she had no idea where he had intended to go. She decided therefore, to explore the ground floor of the house first. She turned a corner and made her way down a brightly lit corridor in which it appeared their hosts had attempted to cram as many family portraits, side tables and artefacts as they possibly could.

Suddenly, from around the corner, she heard the approaching sound of footsteps and the swishing of silk skirts. Her heart began to pound loudly. She had no idea who it was, but she had a strong feeling that, if she did, she would not wish to encounter them. The door to her left was slightly ajar. Quickly, she pushed it open and slipped inside. The room was ostentatiously decorated in gold brocade. Standing in the middle of it, she quickly assessed the best place to hide. In a dimly lit corner was a large armoire with a narrow space between it and the wall. Eleanor squeezed into the space at exactly the same time as the swishing skirts entered the room.

The skirts did not sit down, but began swishing furiously around the room, giving the impression that their owner was pacing up and down the black and white marble floor. Eleanor stood stock-still, hardly daring to breathe or to sneak a peep at the woman. She did not have long to wait, however, before her identity was revealed, as Eleanor was aware of more footsteps, these much heavier than a female's, and a second person entering the room.

'Good evening, sir,' said Felicity Carmichael.

'*You!*' declared James, his voice dripping with surprise.

'But of course,' replied Felicity, matter-of-factly. 'Don't tell me you were actually under the misapprehension that your little duchess would dare to meet with you again?'

James said nothing.

'I feel I should point out, sir,' continued Felicity imperiously, 'that I do not care to be kept waiting.'

'I beg your pardon, ma'am,' came back James's voice, rich with sarcasm, 'however I am afraid that nature does not take your desires into account.'

Eleanor stifled a gasp. What on earth did Felicity Carmichael want with James now? Surely the woman hadn't come up with yet more ridiculous threats. She inclined her head a little so that she peeped out from the side of the armoire. She could see Felicity, as bold as brass in an unflattering amber gown, bustling over to the door.

'Hmph,' she replied haughtily to James, 'then in future may I recommend it does,' she said, turning the key in the lock of the door.

James, standing in the middle of the room, in exactly the same spot Eleanor had occupied but a few short seconds ago, turned to watch her. 'What on earth are you doing locking the door?' he asked, puzzled, running a hand through his thick dark hair.

Felicity straightened and tossed back her tightly ringleted head. 'Why, I wish, of course, that we should not be disturbed, sir,' she replied, depositing the key down the deep cleft between her full breasts. 'What I have to say must be said in private.'

'Oh, really?' replied James sardonically, placing his hands on his hips. 'I think perhaps what you actually mean, madam, is that you do not wish for anyone else to overhear your fantastic blackmailing attempts.'

'There is no need to be facetious, sir,' replied Felicity, sauntering over to a sofa by the window along which was arranged a row of neatly placed cushions. Eleanor watched as the girl randomly scattered the cushions about both the sofa and the floor. Then, turning again to James, she said, 'Please do forgive me, sir, if I sit down. It is not recommended that a woman in my condition stands for long periods of time.'

An incredulous expression spread over James's face. 'A woman in your condit—' he sneered. 'What on earth are you—?'

Felicity lowered herself on to the sofa and smoothed down her skirts. 'It would appear, sir,' she said evenly, 'that you have quite forgotten our conversation at my come out ball. The conversation in which I informed you of my second plan.'

'Ah, yes,' said James musingly, thrusting his hands into this breeches pockets and regarding the ceiling as though deep in thought. 'Your second plan. The plan where you claim to be carrying *my* child?'

Felicity flashed him a congratulatory smile. 'The very same, sir,' she said charmingly. 'And this evening I merely wished to inform you that I am now some way down the line with that plan and that within a few weeks we shall be in a position to announce our betrothal.'

James gave an incredulous snort of laughter.

Felicity ignored him and, still smoothing down her skirts, continued cheerfully with her speech. 'I have given the matter careful consideration, sir, and I am of the opinion that events have occurred in such a well-timed fashion, that we shall be well placed to make our announcement at the masquerade ball at Almack's at the end of the month – just after the unmasking at midnight would be so romantic I thought.'

James gave another hollow laugh. 'If you think for one moment, madam,' he said icily, regarding Felicity through narrowed eyes, 'that anyone will believe you, then you are gravely mistaken. And even if they did and there was the remotest chance that you did get me down the aisle, I would not lay a finger on you and within a few months you would be exposed for the fraud that you are. Unless, of course,' he said, slapping a hand to his forehead in the manner of one to whom a remarkable idea had just occurred, 'you intend to say, after a reasonable amount of time, that you have simply lost the child. Well, I can assure you, madam, that by that time there would be so much suspicious gossip flying around about you that no one would believe that story either.'

Felicity smiled serenly. 'Oh, I am in complete agreement with you, sir,' she said innocently. 'Which is why I actually *am* now with child and, when it is born, everyone will believe it is yours – arrived a little earlier than expected of course,' she added with an affected laugh.

James's mouth twisted into a contemptuous sneer. 'If you expect me to believe *that*, madam,' he scoffed, 'then you must think I have windmills in my head.'

'Oh, I can assure you, I do not think that at all, sir,' said Felicity archly. 'I would not wish for a husband who was not exceedingly clever.'

'To be honest, madam,' said James menacingly, 'I do not give a fig for your requirements of a husband. Now if you will excuse me, I have nothing more to say on this absurd matter.'

Turning his back to Felicity, Eleanor watched as he marched resolutely to the door and turned the brass knob.

Realizing that it was still locked, he swung around to face the girl again. 'I should be grateful, madam,' he said acidly, 'if you would unlock the door at once.'

'Ah, yes. The door,' mused Felicity, rising from her chair and sashaying over to James nonchalantly. Stopping directly in front of him, she raised a podgy white finger to her thin lips, giving the impression of one in deep consideration of a problem. 'Do you know, sir, I believe I have quite forgotten where I put the key.'

James drew his hands from his pockets. Eleanor noticed that they were clenched tightly into fists. 'Oh, I can tell you exactly where you put it,' he sneered derisively. 'Although wild horses would not drag me there to retrieve it myself.' He flashed a hateful glare at Felicity's bosom.

Felicity smiled beatifically before adjusting the top of her gown so that it was askew and pulling several clips from her hair, causing sections of tight ringlets to hang disorderly. James watched in amazement as she then marched directly up to the door and began banging frantically upon it. 'Help! Help!' she shouted vociferously.

James turned to watch her, his mouth gaping open in bewilderment. 'What on earth are you—?' he began to ask, furrowing his brow.

Felicity stopped banging for a moment and tossed him a disarming smile over her shoulder. 'Oh, don't worry, sir. You will soon see,' she informed him, before turning back to the door and resuming her banging and shouting.

A minute or so later, some scuffling could be heard outside the room and in a flash the door was whisked open and the Duke of Swinton appeared in the doorway, followed closely by Lydia Armstrong and Lady Illingsworth, who was clasping a large bunch of keys in her hand.

The two ladies gasped loudly at the shock of finding Felicity alone with James. The conclusion to which they immediately jumped, taking in both Felicity and the room's disordered appearances, was written all over their rouged faces. It was the Duke of Swinton, however, who spoke first.

'Miss Carmichael,' he asked, in a tone which gave little doubt that he was of the same opinion as the two tabbies, 'what on earth has happened to you? I trust that this man has not been forcing his attentions upon you?'

James's expression grew dark. 'I can assure, sir,' he spat defiantly, 'that nothing at all has happened to her.'

The two women threw James a disbelieving look. The Duke of Swinton narrowed his eyes. 'Well, it most certainly does not look like that to me, *sir*,' he said. 'The girl looks quite *distressed*.'

All eyes turned to Felicity who was pressing a hand to her forehead. 'Oh, forgive me, sir,' she fluttered to the duke. 'I didn't know . . . that is . . . I didn't understand when he said that he wanted to. . . . Oh,' she rasped suddenly, 'I have been such a silly innocent. Why, I do believe I feel quite faint. Would you assist me, sir, in seeking out my mama? I think it best, given what has . . . *occurred*,' she continued, flashing an accusing glance at James, 'that I return home immediately.'

All three new occupants were now eyeing James very suspiciously. Lydia Armstrong had produced a lace handkerchief, which she was holding to her mouth.

'Hmm,' said the duke, scratching his head as if wondering how to proceed with matters, 'I think that a very wise idea indeed, madam.'

Felicity flashed a grateful smile, which encompassed all three of her rescuers, before waltzing victoriously out of the room on the Duke of Swinton's arm.

Lady Illingsworth and Lady Armstrong continued staring at an astonished James for what seemed like an eternity, before both wheeling around and taking their leave. It seemed, to Eleanor, another eternity before James then took his and she could slip out of her hiding place and sink down gratefully into one of the room's armchairs attempting to make some sense of the incredible scene she had just witnessed.

# CHAPTER 16

WHEN Eleanor eventually returned to the supper-room, she found James standing beside Lady Madeleine, his face dark with fury. Madeleine, however, appeared not to have noticed anything untoward and, having obviously decided to follow her plan of making James jealous, was currently engrossed in informing him what a fascinating character she thought the viscount to be. Eleanor was only grateful that the man in question, her godmother and indeed Felicity Carmichael were nowhere to be seen. What was very much in evidence, however, was the fact that the gossipmongers were already busily at their work. Lady Armstrong and Lady Illingsworth, one at either side of the room, had each gathered around them a gaggle of middle-aged matrons and, from the gasps and glances which were emanating from the two groups, were obviously freely embellishing the details of the scene they had just witnessed. The Duke of Swinton, a grave expression on his face, had taken his wife to a corner of the room and was currently deep in conversation with her. An expression of pure horror was slowly creeping over the duchess's perfect features as her eyes flitted back and forth from her husband to James. Eleanor watched James's expression grow harder still as he absorbed the happenings.

Unaware of the atmosphere in the room, Lady Madeleine suddenly whipped open her fan and began fluttering it vigorously.

'Why I do declare, James,' she announced, 'that I am feeling somewhat flushed. I think perhaps a little air is in order. Will you join me in a stroll around the garden, my darling? Or would you perhaps,' she continued, gazing up at him with her startling blue eyes, 'prefer that I ask the viscount?'

James glanced down at her and released a heavy sigh. 'There is no need for that, Madeleine,' he said with some asperity. 'Indeed, I feel in great need of some fresh air myself.'

Completely oblivious to the brusqueness of his tone, Madeleine's beautiful face glowed with her victory.

'Oh, how splendid,' she replied, flashing Eleanor another of her triumphant smiles. 'I wish only to dress my hair a little, my dear,' she purred, placing her tiny hand on James's arm, 'then I shall meet you beside the fountain.' She shot him a knowing look before whisking away in a whirl of emerald satin, leaving him and Eleanor alone. Eleanor suddenly felt awkward. She had no idea what she should say or do next. She was conscious that James was aware of the questioning looks being thrown in his direction and of the gossip which was now almost palpably wafting around the room with every flutter of the ladies' fans. Eleanor felt herself in something of a quandary. She could stop all this immediately if she came out and told them what she had witnessed. But would anyone believe her? Would they assume that she was only trying to protect James because she herself had designs on him? Felicity, of course, would most definitely deny everything. Perhaps then, she should just inform James that she knew of the girl's scheming, but how on earth would he react? Would he think she was meddling? Following him around? Stalking him even?

She was suddenly aware that James was speaking to her. 'Would you care to accompany Lady Madeleine and myself in a stroll around the garden, Lady Eleanor?' he asked. 'If you don't mind me saying so, you are looking somewhat peaked.'

For a moment, Eleanor's mind ground to a complete halt. She opened her mouth hoping desperately that some semblance of intelligent sounding words would emanate from it. It didn't.

James tugged at the sleeves of his coat. 'Come along then,' he said impatiently, already striding off to the French windows, which were standing open at the back of the room. 'I am feeling quite stifled by the atmosphere in this room.'

Aware that all eyes were following him and at a complete loss as to what else to do, Eleanor trotted after him meekly. Quite what Madeleine's reaction to her tagging along would be, she did not even want to imagine.

To her surprise, James had obviously managed to curb his impatience somewhat and was waiting for her just outside the doors. They walked together in silence along the gravelled path that ran alongside the house.

'I say, Prestonville, old boy, you couldn't come and settle a wager for us could you?'

Eleanor and James stopped abruptly and turned around in the direction of the voice. Sitting at a picnic table on the lawn at the back of the house was the man Eleanor recognized as Smithers from the Carmichaels' ball – the odious drunken oaf who had attempted to kiss her.

'Come on, Prestonville,' they all jeered. 'It won't take you a minute.'

James closed his eyes for a moment, as if counting to ten. 'Excuse me for a moment, Lady Eleanor,' he said through clenched teeth.

Eleanor gave him a brief nod, before he strode off towards the men. Having no desire to be within a mile of the hideous Smithers, she carried on following the path around the enormous house. As she turned a corner, however, she found that none of the lanterns on that side of the house appeared to be lit and she could barely see where she was walking. She could hear the fountain though and knew that she only had a little way to walk before she would be in a much better illuminated area of the garden. She had only taken a few steps, however, when she found that the ground was no longer beneath her and that she had stepped into thin air. She was aware of falling and of a terrifying thought flashing through her mind that these could be the last living moments that she would ever experience. But then, quite suddenly, she felt two big strong arms catch her as easily as if she weighed nothing more than a feather. It took a moment for her to realize that she was still alive and another for her to realize that she hadn't dreamt the whole thing. Looking up, she found herself gazing into the round face of a man who looked exactly like the Illingsworths' butler.

'Lord, miss,' said the man who looked equally as nonplussed as Eleanor, 'you's lucky I were 'ere. Dread to think what state you'd be in otherwise.'

Eleanor glanced down at the floor below her and the pickaxe, which was embedded, point upwards, in a piece of wood lying directly below the trap door.

She shivered involuntarily. 'Yes,' she whispered, 'I dread to think too.'

Lady Ormiston, not even attempting to conceal her dwindling impatience with Eleanor's calamitous exploits, had appeared much more concerned with the narrowly avoided embarrassment to their hosts rather than the narrowly avoided skewering of her goddaughter.

Once the incident had been made public, the guests, eager to assimilate the exact details of the scene to pass on to those unfortunates who were not present and who had therefore missed out on the potentially gory drama, had flocked outside and gathered around the trap door. The air was thick with the powerful, heavy smell of intermingling toilettes and there was much ooh-ing and ah-ing as the audience set eyes on the ill-appointed pickaxe.

The dowager, making good use of both elbows, had cleared a path through the throng and marched directly towards Eleanor who had been carried outside by her rescuer and placed on a wooden bench at the side of the house, a little way from the crowd.

Upon arriving at her destination, Lady Ormiston had pulled out her fan and begun waving it profusely in front of her flustered face. 'My dear girl,' she had chided, 'you really *must* learn to look where you are going. Why, I dare not even *think* of the embarrassment you would have caused Lord and Lady Illingsworth if something . . . *dreadful* had happened to you.'

Eleanor, weak with relief, had wanted to reply that causing embarrassment to their hosts was really the very last thing on her mind. But she was so over-come with the thought of the fate that would have befallen her had it not been for the serendipitous presence of her rescuer in the cellar, that she had been robbed of her ability to speak for some thirty minutes afterwards. Mr Stanley Mortimer, the hero of the hour, and the butler's younger brother, had, very providentially for Eleanor, spotted the open door several short minutes in advance of the incident, and had 'nipped down' to make sure all was in order. Having made a rapid search of the cellar, Mr Mortimer had informed that he had found nothing at all to arouse suspicion other than the position of the pickaxe, which was generally kept in a garden shed.

Milly, however, had her own view on the incident. 'If I didn't know better, miss,' she'd remarked solemnly, as she'd prepared Eleanor for bed later that evening, 'I'd think someone were trying to do away with you.'

Eleanor had shivered involuntarily at Milly's theory and had immediately dismissed it as absurd. The girl however, remained impervious to her mistress's blithe disregard of the matter.

'That's as may be, miss,' she had replied, 'but it ain't normal all these so-called accidents happening every time you go out.'

Milly's words had continued to play on Eleanor's mind and at two o'clock, in the dead of the night, she found herself giving the girl's theory serious consideration. What she failed to comprehend about the matter was that she was just an ordinary girl of no significance whatsoever and, as far as she was aware, there was no one who would benefit from her death. If that were the case, then why on earth would anyone want to kill her?

She was still deliberating the matter a half an hour later, when she heard someone quietly padding along the stone floor of the corridor. She froze for a second, fearing she was about to receive another visit from the Wailing Widow, but it didn't take her long to realize that the footsteps were of a decid-edly more mortal nature. Jumping quietly out of bed, she ran to the door and crouched down, pressing her eye to the keyhole just in time to see a man, wearing a navy-blue brocade dressing gown, march straight by, heading towards the far end of the corridor. Eleanor's stomach lurched, causing her to fall back on to the floor. There was only one reason James Prestonville would be visiting Lady Madeleine's room at this hour of the morning and that reason made her feel decidedly nauseous.

By breakfast time, Eleanor had experienced not the slightest hint of sleep and had succeeded in working herself up into the foulest of humours. Arriving downstairs, she found, to her chagrin, James and Lady Madeleine already seated at the breakfast table. Had they dared to come down together, she wondered? Surely even Madeleine wouldn't be that brazen. Beneath lowered lashes, Eleanor studied them both carefully as she slipped into her seat. The discrepancy between their two appearances could not have been greater: while Madeleine looked as fresh as a daisy in an apple-green morning dress, James's countenance was one of pure exhaustion. Eleanor had sympathized with his plight the evening before, but now she found herself quite devoid of any compassion at all for the man. He was obviously, she mused, not sufficiently concerned about Felicity Carmichael's threats to be distracted from other *recreational pursuits*. In no mood for pleasantries, she merely grunted in reply to the pair's greetings and shook out her napkin.

In response to Eleanor's grunt, Madeleine lifted her eyes from the plate of food in front in her and surveyed her critically. 'My, my,' she declared, 'it does appear that Lady Eleanor is quite out of sorts today. I would have thought that having been the centre of attention *again* yesterday evening, my dear, you would have been feeling quite the thing this morning.'

Eleanor's hackles, in no state at all to be toyed with, rose instinctively. She fixed Lady Madeleine with an icy glare, adding no more warmth to her tone. 'Are you implying, madam,' she enquired, 'that I would risk killing myself in order to gain the attention of a roomful of boring, arrogant people in whom I do not even feign to have the slightest interest?'

Madeleine focused her eyes on her plate and the slice of ham, which she was delicately dissecting into miniscule pieces. 'I am merely saying, Lady Eleanor,' she replied smoothly, 'that you do appear to thrive on having everyone fuss about you so.'

James suddenly slammed down his knife and fork, causing Eleanor to jump and Madeleine to jerk her head up sharply. 'For God's sake, Madeleine,' he snapped, 'what on earth are you talking about now?'

Madeleine gazed at him with wide-eyed innocence. 'I was simply saying,

James—' she began.

'Yes, well, don't,' interjected James sourly. 'I have no wish at all to hear your ridiculous theories. It's enough that the girl can't be let out on her own without some disaster or other happening to her, than you—'

'I beg your pardon, *sir*,' expostulated Eleanor, gazing at him defiantly, 'but none of those *disasters* were actually of *my* doing.'

'So you say,' muttered Madeleine under her breath, refocusing on her ham.

Eleanor felt red-hot rage beginning to pulse through her body. 'Indeed, I do say, madam,' she replied stoutly. 'Although quite what any of it has to do with you is completely beyond—'

'For God's sake,' cried James, his voice now several octaves higher and reverberating with annoyance, 'will the two of you just be quiet? I have a thumping headache and the last thing I need is for two bickering women to be—'

Eleanor refused to be put down so rudely. 'Oh, so you have a thumping headache, do you, *sir*?' she cut in tartly. 'I wonder what could possibly be the cause of *that*?' She glared accusingly at Lady Madeleine.

Sensing Eleanor's implication, Madeleine raised her brows at the younger girl. 'I hope you are not implying, Lady Eleanor, that *I* am the cause of James's headache.'

Eleanor stuck her chin defiantly in the air. 'Well, *perhaps*, madam,' she began disapprovingly, 'if you didn't accept gentlemen callers to your rooms in the middle of the night, then—'

Madeleine's eyes grew wide in her head. 'How dare you,' she remonstrated, a slight flush appearing on her cheeks.

'Oh, I dare,' retorted Eleanor, 'because it is the tru—'

'That is enough!' cried James loudly.

Madeleine now tilted her chin upward defiantly. 'It wasn't *I*, sir,' she protested haughtily, 'who began making wild accusations about—'

'Be quiet, Madeleine,' he bellowed. 'I am far too tired to suffer any of your opinions today.'

By the flabbergasted expression which spread over Madeleine's face, it was obvious the woman was quite taken aback by James's rudeness. Eleanor, on the other hand, found she was unable to control her tongue.

'Oh, I see,' she declared mockingly. 'So it is *tiredness* that is to blame for your bad humour, sir. Well, in that case, might I suggest, that perhaps if you stayed in your own bed of an evening, then you might save us all the unpleasantness of having to breakfast with you while you are in such a ghastly frame of mind.'

James regarded her incredulously. 'And might *I* suggest, Lady Eleanor, that you take a little air after breakfast to clear your head, for I confess I have not the slightest idea to what you are referring.'

'Hmph,' huffed Eleanor sardonically, folding her arms defiantly over her chest. Mirroring her action, James did the same. There then followed a brief hiatus where each furiously regarded the other. Then James suddenly thrust to his feet, threw down his napkin and strode from the room muttering something which Eleanor could only vaguely make out but which most definitely included the words, 'damned mad women'.

# CHAPTER 17

TWO things happened over the next few days for which Eleanor was extremely grateful. Firstly, she received a note from Viscount Grayson conveying his deepest regrets to her that he had been required to visit his estate in the north regarding a matter of some import, and was unlikely to return for quite some time. While Eleanor had spent several elated minutes jumping up and down with joy at the news, the dowager had been extremely irked and proceeded to spend several hours speculating aloud on what matter could possibly be of more import than taking a wife. Having eventually tired even herself of that topic, she had then digressed to the now well-worn subject of her exasperation at the thieves who had stolen the viscount's carriage at the very moment he had been about to offer for Eleanor. If it wasn't for them, they could be making wedding preparations and Eleanor could be off their hands in a matter of weeks.

Her godmother's rantings, however, did not last long, as the second note-worthy event that occurred was that the old lady contracted an exceedingly unpleasant case of influenza and took to her bed. The welcome consequence of this occurrence was that Eleanor was, at last, allowed some respite from the Season's hectic social whirl and, consequently, from all the gossip of the staged seduction scene which would undoubtedly by now, have been embell-ished with large, generous doses of fictional detail and scandalous conjecture – exactly, of course, how Felicity Carmichael had planned it.

James, too, although quite capable of attending events without the company of his aunt, appeared to have temporarily stepped off the social merry-go-round. While Eleanor did wonder if the gossips might take this as an admission of his guilt in all that they were surmising, she thought it overall the wisest course of action. Lady Madeleine who, as far as Eleanor was aware, was still completely oblivious to the events, was of a different frame of mind altogether and her constant moaning and whinging at having to stay at home was becoming increasingly tedious.

The atmosphere in the castle since the Illingsworths' soirée and the ensuing row at breakfast the following morning was overflowing with tension as relationships between the various members of the household became increasingly strained. Eleanor and Madeleine spoke to each other only when necessary, or when one of them spotted an opportunity to snipe at the other; Eleanor had no wish at all to speak to James who was so grumpy he had everyone within a twenty-yard radius of him walking on wafer-thin egg-shells; Eleanor was avoiding the odious Derek Lovell at all costs; Madeleine's relationship with James appeared to consist of nothing but arguments and bickering while her relationship with Derek Lovell had reached an all time low, with the woman now refusing to even be in the same room as the man. With only a few more weeks of the Season remaining, Eleanor longed to return to some normality and found her thoughts turning, with increasing regularity, to her home.

The end of the Season was not sufficiently in sight, however, for the dowager to allow Eleanor a reprieve from her dancing lessons. A viscount's wife would, after all, she pointed out, be expected to be an accomplished dancer. This thought did very little to inspire her goddaughter.

Eleanor, spotting an ideal opportunity to make a little mischief however, said to her dance master on this particular day, 'May I ask, M. Aminieux, if Lady Madeleine has yet arranged a date to meet your good wife?'

He adopted a rather hurt expression. 'Alas, *non*, *mademoiselle*,' he replied wistfully. 'I am thinking that the Lady Madeleine is an extremely busy lady, *non?*'

Eleanor smiled understandingly. 'Oh indeed, she is, *monsieur*,' she agreed with alacrity, 'however, I believe that, because of my godmother's illness and James being otherwise occupied with business matters, Lady Madeleine will most certainly have at least one evening free this week.'

His face broke out into a wide smile. 'Then in that case, *mademoiselle*,' he enthused, 'I will be writing a note to her this instant.'

'Oh, we can do better than that, M. Aminieux,' said Eleanor. 'We shall go and find her at once and arrange it.'

'*Quelle bonne idée, mademoiselle*,' he agreed, following Eleanor down the corridor, which led to the drawing-room.

'Lady Madeleine,' announced Eleanor, as she entered the room to find the older woman sitting in a window seat reading, 'I have had the most wonderful idea.'

Madeleine eyed her suspiciously.

'Look whom I have brought to see you,' she announced, beckoning M. Aminieux to step inside. She noticed with glee how Lady Madeleine's jaw dropped several inches. 'I was just telling M. Aminieux, Lady Madeleine, that I am quite sure you will have one or two evenings free this week when you could meet his wife.'

Madeleine's face grew dark with the combination of disdain and panic.

'Ah, Madame Aminieux is *so* looking forward to it, *madame*,' informed the dancing master, wringing his hands together anxiously.

'How delightful,' smiled Eleanor sweetly. 'I know that Lady Madeleine is very much looking forward to it too, *monsieur*. Now, if I'm not mistaken, Lady Madeleine, I do believe you are free on Thursday evening – the evening of Lady Thorpe's ball which James has declined to attend.'

'Indeed,' spat Madeleine. 'However, I have – er—'

'How wonderful,' cut in Eleanor. 'Thursday it is then, *monsieur*,' she said, shuffling the man out of the room. 'Shall we say, six o'clock?'

The following day the dowager, complaining that lying in bed was quite driving her to distraction, demanded that she be brought downstairs. The move of her bath chair together with the immense weight of the woman, developed into a somewhat complicated operation involving every one of the poor, long-suffering footmen and two of the strongest gardeners. It took a little over an hour before Lady Ormiston was safely deposited in the drawing-room and less than five minutes following her arrival, before she began bellowing out orders.

'Stevens,' she boomed, 'I shall require a tray of tea, some of cook's fruit cake and the company of my nephew. Inform the young man that I wish him to join me immediately.'

The servant, who had been looking noticeably more relaxed during the dowager's illness, had not taken long to resume his pinched downtrodden expression. He nodded his acquiescence and retreated from the room.

Eleanor, picking up her book and rising from the sofa, made to follow him. She had no desire at all to even see James, let alone take tea with him. In fact, she had been doing her utmost to avoid him for several days now. During the few brief encounters she had unavoidably had with him, it was obvious that his mood continued to be as dark as ever.

No sooner had she risen to her feet however, than the Dowager said, 'And where do you think you are going, girl?'

'To the garden, Godmother,' replied Eleanor.

'Indeed you are not,' stated Lady Ormiston firmly. 'I wish us all to take tea together in order that you and James may bring me up to date with the latest happenings both here in the castle and outside it.'

Eleanor's spirits sank. 'I'm afraid that I am not really the person to ask, ma'am,' she replied. 'I have hardly left the house myself since you were taken ill.'

'In that case,' retorted the dowager, 'I think it most imperative that you stay. I am sure the viscount would not wish for a wife who was not fully up to date with all the latest *on dits*.'

Eleanor suppressed a heavy sigh. Her godmother had obviously made up her mind and she knew, from experience, that there was little point even attempting an excuse. She reluctantly resumed her seat and put down her book.

Just at that moment, James joined them and, after planting a kiss on his aunt's cheek, dropped into the chair opposite her.

'So,' said the dowager, as Stevens deposited a heavy silver tea tray on the table, 'please do tell me all the latest happenings, James. The only thing you talked of when you visited me in my chambers was the blasted weather.'

'Indeed,' said James, crossing one long leg over the other. 'However, I can assure you, Aunt, that the weather is a good deal more interesting than some of the people with whom we are acquainted.'

'I won't disagree with you there,' said the dowager, accepting the cup of tea, which Stevens was now offering her. 'But it is so awfully tedious being stuck in one's room. One would die for even the tiniest bit of gossip.'

'Unfortunately, Aunt,' said James, taking his cup from the footman, 'I am not aware of—'

He broke off as Giles appeared in the doorway.

'Lady Carmichael and Miss Felicity Carmichael, your grace,' he announced.

Eleanor felt all colour drain from her face. James too, looked several shades paler than he had a few moments before.

'Oh well,' sighed the dowager, raising her cup to her lips, 'if there is one thing Cynthia Carmichael is good for, it's gossip-mongering. Now *she* will most definitely know what is going on. You young people appear to be quite, quite useless at such things. Show the pair of them in, Giles,' she instructed, with a dismissive wave of her hand.

A short minute later, both Lady Carmichael and Felicity bustled into the room. The older of the two women was clutching a large bunch of pink and white roses, which she began frantically waving at the dowager causing several stray petals and a number of leaves to fall into the old woman's lap.

'Oh my goodness, Lady Ormiston,' she gushed, 'we have been so *dreadfully* worried about you. We thought we simply *must* come and see how you are.'

The dowager picked a pink petal out of the cup of tea she was holding and held it away from her with a disdainful look on her face. 'Well, as you can see, Cynthia,' she said coolly, 'I am on my way to recovery.'

Stevens, pre-empting yet another order, removed the dripping petal from the dowager's fingers and, correctly interpreting her nod of the head at the bigger bunch, removed them from Lady Carmichael's grasp and vacated the room presumably in search of a vase.

Lady Ormiston waved a hand at the sofa, which the Carmichaels assumed was their invitation to be seated.

'I must confess, we have been quite at sixes and sevens ourselves,' flustered Lady Carmichael, as she sank on to the sofa next to Eleanor and began untying her bonnet strings. 'Felicity, too, has been quite out of frame and we have no idea at all what the problem is, do we, my dear?'

All eyes focused on Felicity who, sitting beside her mother, was adopting a rather forlorn expression.

'Indeed, we do not, Mama,' replied the girl serenely.

'I won't go into details in front of a gentleman, of course,' continued Lady Carmichael, throwing a coy glance at James as she tugged her bonnet from her head, 'however the doctors believe that it is a matter regarding the *female* disposition.'

'Really,' said the dowager prosaically, as she brushed the remaining foliage from her lap with her free hand. 'How *very* interesting.'

'Do you know, Lady Ormiston,' declared Lady Carmichael, 'that those are the *very* words Dr Gosport used to describe her condition last week. The man is quite obviously flummoxed by it and the poor girl has been so out of sorts that we have been quite out of circulation since the Illingsworths' soirée.'

The dowager eyed Felicity suspiciously as the girl accepted her cup of tea from Stevens. 'In that case,' she said, 'what on earth is she doing gallivanting about here?'

'Oh she was *most* anxious, Lady Ormiston, that we come and see you. In fact, she quite *insisted* upon it,' pronounced Lady Carmichael. 'Such a thoughtful child.'

Felicity gave a bashful smile, which encompassed them all. Good God, thought Eleanor, the girl looked the very epitome of innocence, but there was something about what Lady Carmichael was saying that was transmitting warning signals to Eleanor's brain. What on earth had Felicity told her mother about the incident at the Illingsworths' and was the girl purposefully keeping the woman out of circulation so she wouldn't be aware of the gossip which would undoubtedly be flying around? She sneaked a glance at James. He was observing Felicity with cool, narrowed eyes. Was he, too, Eleanor wondered, trying to piece together the next stage of Felicity's plan?

As Lady Carmichael, having completed her imparting of all the small tit-bits of gossip she had brought with her, and moved on to discussing that well-worn topic involving meteorological observances, Felicity suddenly clasped a hand to her left breast and declared, 'Oh Mama, I do believe I feel quite faint. I am most definitely in need of a little air.'

The dowager, holding out her cup for Stevens to refill, said briskly, 'Then go and stand over by the window, girl.'

Felicity regarded her hostess with wide eyes. 'Oh no, Lady Ormiston,' she replied magnanimously. 'I couldn't possibly. It is most likely that the draught would only serve to exacerbate your cold. I think perhaps it best if I take a stroll around the garden.'

'Oh, of course, my dear,' agreed Lady Carmichael. 'But you cannot possibly go alone when you are so out of sorts. I am sure James would not mind accompanying you in the slightest. Would you be willing to help out a damsel in her hour of distress, James?' asked Lady Carmichael expectantly.

All heads turned towards James. The look on his face had now turned to one of utter disbelief.

Lady Carmichael raised her brows quizzically. 'James?' she repeated.

Before James had a chance to say anything, however, Felicity rose to her feet. 'I fear I must go this very instant, sir,' she declared, walking slowly around the back of the sofa and gripping it tightly in the manner of one about to fall over. 'I should not wish at all to embarrass Lady Ormiston by having a faint-ing fit in her drawing-room.'

'Oh, is she not all that is consideration,' gushed Lady Carmichael raising her free hand to her chest. 'Now, James, dear, if you would be so kind?' she said, tilting her head as she observed him with a hopeful expression.

Still failing to acknowledge the request, James continued to sit quite still with his tea cup in one hand, gazing balefully at Felicity. For a moment Eleanor held her breath. Would he, she wondered, dare to expose the girl here, in front of her own mother and the dowager? The problem was, of course, that as the only proof was that which had been fabricated by Felicity, would anyone at all believe James? Just as she finished her musing, James leaned forward and placed his cup on the table, then he rose from his chair and marched from the room. A fluttering Felicity followed him.

Lady Carmichael emitted a loud sigh of relief. 'Well,' she exclaimed, with a knowing smile, 'I'm not one to jump to conclusions, as you know, Lady Ormiston, but, I believe James appeared to quite leap at the chance to be alone with Felicity. Perhaps,' she continued, lowering her voice and casting a wary glance at Stevens who was busy clearing away James and Felicity's cups, 'it will present him with the ideal opportunity to discuss his, *intentions* towards her.'

'And what *intentions* do you assume those to be, Cynthia?' asked the dowager drily.

'Oh, well, of course, I have no idea, I'm sure,' retorted Lady Carmichael, with a slight flush.

Eleanor was feeling decidedly uncomfortable about the situation. She could make a rather accurate assumption regarding James's intentions towards Felicity Carmichael. What was making her so uneasy was the thought that the girl might sufficiently rile him to the point that he would carry out these intentions. She had to follow them, but what excuse could she possibly give? Her mind was racing frantically. And then she hit upon it.

She leaned forward and put down her tea cup. Then, smoothing down the front of her skirts, she declared soberly, 'I hope you don't mind me saying so, Lady Carmichael, but I am quite concerned for Felicity – she was looking decidedly wan. May I suggest that I take out a vinaigrette, or perhaps a little hartshorn to revive her should she have a fit of the vapours? Men, I find, are generally of little use in such situations. Indeed, I believe they are positively embarrassed by them. To have such an attack in front of a gentleman can, so I have heard, quite turn his affections from a lady.'

Lady Carmichael's eyes widened in horror and she immediately reached for her reticule. 'Good Lord, Lady Eleanor,' she declared, rummaging in her bag, 'I do believe you are quite right. Men are indeed quite useless creatures when it comes to such *sensitive feminine* matters. Here,' she said, producing a vinaigrette and holding it out to Eleanor, 'I'm sure Felicity will be most indebted to you for helping her out of a potentially delicate situation.'

'Oh, I assure you it is the *least* I can do, Lady Carmichael,' replied Eleanor, as she rose from her seat, snatched the vinaigrette from the older woman's grasp and flew out of the room quicker than if it had been on fire. Not stopping for a second, she ran as fast as she could down across the great entrance hall, down the steps of the castle and out on to the lawn which was busy with gardeners mowing and trimming. She spotted James and Felicity heading towards the walled orchard to the right of the castle, James striding purposefully ahead, his hands clasped behind his back. Felicity was puffing along behind him, vainly attempting to keep up – all signs of her previous fainting symptoms apparently having vanished. As the pair disappeared around the corner and into the orchard, Eleanor ran as fast as she could following the route they had just taken, receiving several quizzical looks from the gardeners in the process as she flew by in a blur of sprigged muslin.

Reaching the orchard, she ceased running and leaned back against the wall, catching her breath. She could hear their voices. Slowly, she edged to the archway which formed the entrance and peeped around it. She saw a pink-faced, obviously out-of-breath Felicity seated on an old stone bench. An angry-looking James was pacing up and down in front of her, still with his hands behind his back.

'So, madam,' he said, 'now that we are alone, we can be frank with each other. I am assuming that this nonsense about being unwell is all part of your devious plan?'

Felicity tilted up her head to him and flashed a beguiling smile. 'Congratulations, sir,' she said brightly. 'You assume correctly.'

'Hmm,' said James thoughtfully, continuing his pacing. 'And just for my own benefit, madam, I will summarize, if I may, what I believe to be your plan.'

'Oh, please do, sir,' said Felicity with alacrity. 'I believe that will serve us both quite well.'

James flashed her a scornful glare. 'Very well, then,' he continued, still pacing. 'My reading of the situation is this: now that I have apparently been caught seducing you – against your will *of course* – you are now feigning an illness which covers all the symptoms one normally associates with being with child. When it is discovered, at some point quite soon, that you actually *are* with child, everyone will naturally assume that I am the father, although,' he added in a conspiratorial tone, '*we* both know that I am not, and, in order to avoid the most outrageous scandal which would most certainly occur, I will be forced to marry you and raise the child as if it were my own.'

Felicity clapped her hands together in mocking applause. 'Goodness,' she exclaimed breathlessly, 'although I do say so myself, it does all sound rather

174

marvellous when you put it like that. I do believe I am positively bursting with excitement at the mere thought of the whole plan coming together so well.'

James ignored her, continuing his pacing. 'Can I assume then, madam, that, as Lady Carmichael is still speaking to me, your mother is unaware of the incident you staged?'

Felicity attempted a tinkling laugh. 'Oh, she is aware that something occurred, sir,' she explained. 'I simply told her that, having requested my company and tricked me into being alone with you, you could control your feelings for me no longer and became a little amorous. A fact which, as you can imagine, sir, given how anxious my mother is that we make a match of it, did not displease her in the slightest.'

'Hmm,' pondered James. 'And I assume that when the doctors discover that you are actually with child, you will tell your mother that it was conceived during that incident?'

Felicity nodded her round head. 'Oh yes. But, of course, as she thinks me quite an innocent,' she added demurely, 'I shall have to explain that I had no idea what was happening to me.'

'Well, I have to hand it to you, Miss Carmichael,' pronounced James, suddenly stopping his pacing and coming to a halt directly in front of her, 'it does indeed appear to be a first-class plan. I take it that the true father of the child is unaware that you have conceived?'

'Oh, of course,' chirped Felicity. 'He has served his purpose famously and has, I can assure you, been very well rewarded for his efforts. I believe the man to have received more from our little *arrangement* than he would earn in five years from his work on the farm.'

James's upper lip curled into a sneer. 'Your generosity knows no bounds, madam,' he said, his tone dripping with disgust.

Felicity regarded him beatifically. 'Thank you, sir,' she replied graciously. 'I do think it so important that the future Duchess of Ormiston is in possession of certain *admirable* qualities. Do you not agree?'

'Oh indeed I do, madam,' he hissed. 'It is a great pity however, that you are not in possession of a single one of the qualities which *I* consider to be admirable,' and with that parting comment, he turned on his heel and stormed out of the orchard.

Eleanor held her breath and pressed her body tight to the wall as he strode past her. Her effort was wasted however: James Prestonville appeared completely absorbed in his thoughts and, by the murderous expression on his face, there was very little doubt what those thoughts were.

Eleanor waited a few short minutes before following James's route back to the castle. She would inform Lady Carmichael that she had been unable to find her daughter for, in that moment, she had no desire at all to speak to Felicity Carmichael ever again.

# CHAPTER 18

THE loud hoot of an owl directly outside her bedchamber window caused Eleanor to awake with a start. Anxious that the bird sounded so close it might, at any moment take it into its head to fly inside the room, she ran to the window and quietly closed it. She remained standing there for several minutes more, observing the bird as it swooped majestically downward, menacingly surveying its prey with haunting orange eyes.

Sleep rapidly overtaking her, she was on the verge of returning to her bed when she became aware of a sound in the corridor, exactly the same sound she had heard several nights previously: the now familiar sound of James Prestonville, Marquis of Rothwell, *en route* yet again to his lover's room.

Beset by a painful combination of anger and jealousy, all notions of sleep immediately deserted her as she found herself lying awake for several long hours, tossing and turning as she attempted to push all thoughts of what might be happening in the room at the end of the corridor, out of her frantic mind.

In a flash, however, every trace of every thought completely deserted her as, without any warning at all, her bedroom door suddenly burst wide open. Eleanor immediately jerked upright and felt the hairs on her neck stand on end at the sight before her. The Wailing Whitlock Widow in her gown of dirty white chiffon, drifted into the room, moaning and wailing, her dark hair hanging wildly over her face and shoulders. Eleanor watched the vision astounded; her mouth gaping open; her mind a complete blank. The spirit appeared oblivious to her spectator, drifting agitatedly around the room, presumably continuing the eternal search for her husband. Failing yet again, she came to a standstill in front of the fireplace and, raising her head and her arms upward, she emitted a pitiful, high-pitched wail, which cut through Eleanor like a cold steel blade and caused her to screw her eyes shut and clamp both hands over her ears. Several seconds later, she opened her eyes hesitantly to find all trace of the woman gone and the door to the room now closed.

Terror turned to relief as she sagged against her pillows, her heart racing madly. She could not recall ever being so terrified. Indeed, the Widow had almost scared her half to death. *Death.* At this last thought, Eleanor was alerted once again to Milly's remarks following her accident at the soirée. Was that the intention? Was the ghost another ploy to kill her? Was somebody trying to scare her to death? Or did their intentions go beyond scaring her? With her mind now whirling, rapidly catching up with the racing of her heart, she reflected on the events of the last few weeks: the incident with the carriage following the Carmichaels' ball; the near-miss with the arrow at the Stanningtons' garden party; the weapon which had caused the fall from her horse; and the open trap door and pickaxe at the Illingsworths'. She sat bolt upright yet again as a stab of realization shot straight through her. How could she have been so dim? Milly was absolutely right: someone was out to kill her and she could think of only one person who could hate her that much – Felicity Carmichael.

Felicity Carmichael was aware that Eleanor had overheard two of her conversations with James: two conversations in which the girl had clearly outlined her ruthless plans to become the new Duchess of Ormiston; two conversations which, if Eleanor chose to disclose the contents, had the potential to seriously hinder Felicity's callous ambitions. It was obvious: Felicity Carmichael wanted her dead.

Having reached her shocking conclusion, Eleanor then proceeded to ponder what she should do about it. She could, of course, tell James that she knew of Felicity's scheming and the two of them together could make public the girl's wicked plans. But, she mused, if Felicity really was with child, then their chances of being believed were minimal, particularly given that the staged seduction scene had been witnessed by two of the most notorious gossips, and one of the most respected gentlemen in Society. No, if they publicized Felicity's scheme without any proof, then Society would undoubtedly assume that James, having ruined the girl, was simply trying to talk his way out of marrying her. Besides, she pondered further, if she did tell James at this stage, he was in such bad humour that the likelihood was he would simply brand her as a neurotic female and her theory as complete and utter nonsense. What she really needed, she concluded, was some concrete evidence of Felicity's scheming; something that would prove, beyond a shadow of a doubt, the extent of the girl's evil plans. An idea suddenly hit her. She knew exactly how to do it and just who to help her.

\*

The area in front of the Maguires' house was, as usual, filled with a crowd of laughing, screaming children, making Eleanor once again feel the stab of envy at the joy of having a large family around. Directly in front of the house, the garden was long and rectangular, surrounded by a low wooden fence, with a narrow dirt path splitting it exactly in half. To the left-hand side of the path was a well-tended vegetable patch currently sporting strawberry plants, cabbages, potatoes and carrots. To the right was a lawned area, scattered with bald brown patches where the playing children had worn it away.

Smiling at the scene, Eleanor creaked open the gate and, closing it behind her, made her way up to the house, nimbly avoiding the curious, excited, welcoming children who insisted on stepping into her path.

The door to the cottage was open and Eleanor stuck her head inside and called out a greeting. In a flash, Mrs Maguire appeared at the door, wiping her floury hands on her apron.

'Oh, miss,' she exclaimed, her eyes growing wide in her head and a broad smile breaking out on her face. 'It's a pleasure to see you.'

'And you too, Mrs Maguire,' replied Eleanor. 'I was wondering perhaps if I might have a word with Ed?'

'He's working at the farm, miss,' informed Mrs Maguire, indicating with her head across the surrounding field to Mickey Humphrey's farm. 'Come in and have a dish of tea, while I send one of the young ones over to fetch him.'

'Oh there's really no need, Mrs Maguire,' protested Eleanor. 'I can easily ride over there, myself. But I certainly wouldn't say no to a dish of tea before I go.'

Mrs Maguire smiled and beckoned to Eleanor to step inside. The house, now completely free of rats, was cosy, clean and welcoming and full of the children's laughter flowing in from outside and the smell of fresh bread. Perhaps, mused Eleanor as she chatted easily with Mrs Maguire over a cup of tea, it wouldn't be so bad being married with a home of one's own after all – a happy home filled with love and children: a home exactly like the Maguires'.

Having taken her leave, almost two hours later, Eleanor rode over to Mickey Humphrey's farm. She found Ed working alone in one of the fields in front of the farm buildings. He was, as usual, more than delighted to see her and fussed attentively around her, aiding her dismount from her horse. She tethered the animal to the fence which surrounded the field and sank down on to the grass next to the section of the fence Ed was busy repairing.

'I'm glad I've caught you alone, Ed,' she said. 'I have quite a . . . sensitive matter to discuss with you.'

Ed looked slightly taken aback. 'I ain't done nothing wrong, have I, miss?' he said, running a brown hand through his golden blond hair.

'No, of course not,' said Eleanor stoutly. 'Quite the contrary in fact. Mr Humphreys informs me you are doing a marvellous job here.'

Ed flushed at the praise. 'I'm doing my best, miss,' he said shyly.

'Of that I have no doubt, Ed,' continued Eleanor. 'But what I was wanting to speak to you about has nothing to do with your work. I was rather hoping that you could help me with something. Tell me, Ed, do you know of a young lady by the name of Felicity Carmichael. . . ?'

Early the next morning Eleanor was just leaving the stable block mounted upon the chestnut mare when she spotted James, dressed in riding attire striding across the courtyard towards her. She had been relieved that neither he nor Madeleine had been at breakfast. She was finding it increasingly difficult to look at either of them without a series of shocking images flooding her mind regarding their furtive night-time activities. She only wondered why he bothered to feign such blatant impatience with the woman during daylight hours.

He nodded his head as she approached him, 'Lady Eleanor,' he said brusquely in greeting. His expression was grave and he looked exhausted. Hardly surprising with all his nocturnal exploits, she concluded with a pang of resentment.

Not finding it within herself to smile at the man, she merely nodded her head in acknowledgement of his greeting and trotted straight by him. She had not even reached the bottom of the gravelled drive however, when she perceived that her horse was limping. Drawing the beast to a halt, she vaulted down from the saddle and secured the reins on the wrought-iron gate. Lifting the animal's right hind leg, she found, just as she had suspected, a rather sizeable pebble caught in its shoe. She had removed many such offending objects at home and could remove this one quite easily – if only she had a knife with her. She did not though and concluded that she would have to return to the stables in order not to cause the poor animal any further suffering. She therefore unfastened the reins from the gate, gently turned the horse around and led it slowly back up the drive to the stable block.

She had only just reached the courtyard, when there was a blood-curdling scream. Acting completely upon instinct, she immediately dropped the horse's reins and flew to the stable block from whence the sound had come. Three of the grooms, who had been busy swilling down the yard, dropped their brushes and buckets and darted into the building just in front of her. The first thing that met their eyes as they entered was James Prestonville standing with his back pressed to the wooden wall. The second thing they noticed was a pitchfork, standing proud in the ground only inches from James's booted feet.

Eleanor felt her eyes growing wide in her head. This was undeniably yet another 'accident' and one which, from the look on James's face, had given him an almighty fright.

They all observed the scene in silence for what seemed like an age, but was actually a little short of a minute. It was Jack, one of the young grooms who broke the silence and spoke first. 'Lord, sir,' he said, removing his cloth cap and scratching his head, 'what happened?'

James swallowed before replying. 'I really have no idea, Jack,' he said wearily. 'I had no sooner stepped out of Samson's stall, when this pitchfork fell from the hayloft above and gave me a nasty fright.'

'Must've been rats, sir,' said Jack, now rubbing a hand over his chin. 'Knocked the thing down from the hayloft. You've been lucky mind. Had a right near miss, so you have.'

James released a deep sigh and raised his eyes to the loft, which ran around three sides of the wooden roof. 'You are not wrong there, Jack,' he agreed shakily. 'Indeed, it would appear that I have had quite a number of near misses over the last few weeks. I seem to have more lives than a cat.'

The men chuckled politely, assuming that James was trying to make light of the situation. The man's expression though could not have been more serious. Eleanor's heart began to thump loudly. Was James, like her, beginning to think that there was more – much, much more – to these 'accidents' than they had originally thought? It hadn't even occurred to her in the dead of night when he was cavorting with Lady Madeleine, and she was thinking over the incidents of the last few weeks, that *he* could possibly be the intended victim. It would make more sense: James was a person of much more consequence than herself. She quickly thought back over all the incidents to which he was referring. He had been with her at every single one of them. Indeed, even at the soirée, had he not been distracted by the odious Smithers, then he, too, could have fallen down the open trap door. In fact, if he hadn't invited her to join him and Madeleine, then the accident would have befallen only him. Her mind began racing wildly once again. Was Felicity trying to kill James?

She had no doubt the girl was capable of it. But why would she want him dead when he formed the major part of her ambitions? It didn't make sense. Without James, it would be impossible for Felicity to become the new Duchess of Ormiston. Perhaps then, Felicity was trying to kill her and someone else was trying to kill James, but it seemed too ludicrous that there were two would-be murderers on the loose. What on earth then was going on? She held her breath as Jack nimbly climbed the wooden ladder to the loft.

'Ain't nothing to be seen up here, sir,' he shouted down from the top of the ladder. 'Reckon it's been propped up badly and the rats have knocked it down.'

By the look upon James's face, Eleanor could see that Jack's theory was miles away from his own.

'Stevens!' boomed the dowager from her fireside chair. 'Tell Lady Madeleine that I wish her to join me for tea this afternoon. I have not set eyes on the girl for several days now.'

'As you wish, your grace,' muttered Stevens, before leaving the room.

Eleanor carried on with her embroidery. She was attempting an image of a swan, but each day she worked on it, it seemed to be adopting an appearance more akin to a salt-cellar. At the dowager's remark she suddenly realized that she, too, had not set eyes on Madeleine for some time – a fact which had obviously not perturbed her in the slightest.

'Begging your pardon, your grace,' said Stevens, returning to the room some minutes later and bowing to the dowager, 'but Lady Madeleine says to inform you that she is somewhat indisposed today.'

The dowager lifted her lorgnette to study Stevens's obsequious face.

'In-dis-posed?' she repeated slowly. 'What on earth does she mean by that, man?'

'I believe she has a headache, ma'am.'

'A *headache*?' snapped the Dowager. 'But she is to meet Madame Aminieux this evening.'

'Apparently she has already sent word to the woman's husband, ma'am, informing him of her indisposition,' explained Stevens, his voice noticeably quivering.

'I see,' said the dowager, lowering her lorgnette and pursing her lips in the manner of one most displeased with the news they have just heard.

Eleanor was not in the least surprised. Lady Madeleine obviously thought that meeting a mere dancing master, even a renowned and popular a figure as

M. Aminieux, was quite beneath her. She only wondered, as she stabbed viciously at the linen with her needle, if the woman's headache would be so bad as to turn away her lover this evening. She would wager all she owned that it would not.

The days were growing decidedly hotter and subsequently so were the nights. Eleanor found herself tossing and turning for several hours yet again before admitting defeat and slipping out from under the covers. She pulled her armchair up to the window and, hugging her knees to her chest, gazed up at the clear night sky. The owl, which had awoken her a few nights previously, once again dominated the scene, swooping daringly low in its unwavering hunt for sustenance. She watched its graceful form suddenly dive behind a gorse bush and a few seconds later, reappear with something that resembled a mouse dangling precariously from its beak.

Her attention was then diverted by the sound of footsteps in the corridor once more. Jealousy and anger began coursing through her veins. She had to admit that James did an admirable job of disguising his lust for Madeleine during daylight hours. If one didn't know better, it could easily be assumed that he found the woman intolerable. Despite herself, she padded over to the keyhole and crouched down to it just as the familiar blue brocade robe marched past – and something painful twisted in her stomach.

'James, darling,' bleated Lady Madeleine, as she was spreading the tiniest scrape of butter on to a slice of toast at breakfast the next morning, 'I do so wish to go to Lady Armitage's party this evening. Please can we go, my sweet?'

James sighed heavily as he reached for the silver coffee pot. 'I have already told you a dozen times, Madeleine,' he said wearily, 'I am in no mood for parties. Besides, I thought you were ill.'

She jerked her head upward, momentarily ceasing her buttering. '*Ill?*' she repeated, wrinkling her smooth forehead. 'Why should I be ill?'

'That was your excuse for not seeing the Aminieuxs yesterday evening,' declared James, tipping the pot upward to fill his cup.

Madeleine rolled her eyes and made to continue her buttering. 'Really, James, I think it is quite rude of the man to ask me. How on earth does anyone expect me to see a *dancing master*, for goodness' sake? Now, darling,' she continued silkily, 'please can we go to the party this evening? It will be such fun and I have purchased the most delightful gown to wear for the occasion.'

'I am sure the gown will suffice perfectly well for another occasion, Madeleine,' stated James, his tone ripe with impatience as he raised his cup to his lips.

Madeleine put down her butter knife and regarded him through lowered lashes. 'No it will not,' she replied in a tear-stained voice. 'The gown is only suitable for an occasion such as that planned for this evening. If I do not wear it tonight, then I may have no other need of it this Season and I could not possibly wear it next year as the thing will be quite out of mode.' A lone, single tear rolled down her velvety-smooth cheek.

Derek Lovell, making a rare appearance at the breakfast-table, shot her a sardonic glance. 'My, my,' he remarked sarcastically, loading up his fork with a large portion of scrambled egg, 'such a pressing problem. I really do not profess to understand how admirably you women cope with matters of such consequence.'

Madeleine's tearful eyes suddenly adopted an icy glaze. 'Given that your dealings with women are undoubtedly extremely limited, Mr Lovell,' she replied derisively, 'may I suggest that you keep your worthless opinions to yourself.'

A sneer formed on Lovell's thin lips. 'You can suggest whatever you like, Lady Madeleine,' he replied, holding the forkful of egg before his mouth, 'however, no *woman* will ever tell me what to do.'

'Oh, really?' said Madeleine, raising her shaped brows. 'You do surprise me, sir. I would have thought that women were forever telling you what to do. Something along the lines of *get away from me*, was what springs immediately to mind.'

Suddenly thrusting to his feet, James flung down his napkin and made to leave the table. 'For God's sake,' he declared, as he walked towards the door, 'if you two cannot be civil to one another, then may I suggest you stay out of each other's way or, at the very least, out of mine. I am sick of all the constant bickering in this house.' In a flash he was out of the room with the door slamming loudly shut behind him.

# CHAPTER 19

L ADY Ormiston had been ordered to her bed again. Eleanor had had to bite back a smile when Giles had told her, using exactly those words. Eleanor could not imagine anyone, let alone the sparrow-like, decrepit Dr Gosport, ordering the dowager to do anything at all. However, taken to her bed she had, with a severe case of laryngitis, which, the doctor warned, if she even tried to speak, had the potential to seriously damage her vocal chords forever. Dr Gosport had left specific instructions that she was to receive plenty of rest and to remain completely silent until her throat was recovered. Eleanor couldn't be sure, but she was almost certain she had seen a brief look of both elation and relief flicker over Stevens's normally anxious features, when James had gathered the servants together to inform them of his aunt's predicament.

It was such a gloriously hot day that Eleanor had forbidden Milly to do any work at all other than to arrange a picnic hamper from the kitchens. Once the hamper had been procured, Eleanor had it carried out to the gig in which she had then driven herself and Milly over to the Maguires' cottage. Milly had been thrilled when she had realized where they were going and Mrs Maguire had been equally as thrilled when the two of them arrived. Having shared the delicious contents of the picnic hamper with the children, the three of them had then spent the afternoon merrily chatting away in the garden while the children played around them.

As day turned to evening, Eleanor said her goodbyes and began her return journey to Whitlock. She had refused to let Milly accompany her, insisting instead that the girl stay at the cottage and spend the evening with her family. As she drove the gig home alone, she marvelled at how the happy atmosphere of the Maguires' cottage always had an uplifting effect on her spirits, making her forget temporarily all her wretched problems. As she neared Whitlock, however, and the formidable castle came into view, she felt a shiver of apprehension slide down her spine as the realization that somebody wanted her dead slowly crept through her veins. She would take dinner in her room this evening, she decided. She had no desire at all to spend a moment longer than she had to in the presence of the other moody, petulant, arrogant, suffocating guests.

Handing the conveyance over to Jack at the stable block, she exchanged some light-hearted chatter with the boy, before making her way to the main door of the castle and, after informing Giles of her wish to eat in her room, went directly up to her chamber. Yet again, it was another beautiful June evening, the sky, a brilliant shade of pink, casting deep shadows into the room. Having lain on her bed reading for an hour or so, there was a knock at her door and Stevens appeared with her supper tray of baked carp and new potatoes. The tray was placed on her writing bureau and Eleanor had just removed the silver lid when she heard an almighty bang followed by the unmistakeable sound of shattering glass. In a flash, she was out of her chair and at the window from where she observed Jack and two other grooms sprinting towards the castle from the stable block. All three men appeared to be gazing up at the floor below hers as they ran.

Eleanor's stomach began to lurch uncontrollably. Something, she sensed, was terribly wrong. Flying to the door, she flung it wildly open; tore along to the end of the corridor and bounded down the narrow flight of stone stairs, which connected the floors. She marched vigorously along the corridor towards an open door on her right from which she could hear a voice emanating. Reaching the door, she rushed into the room and came to an immediate halt at the side of a peacock-blue *chaise-longue*, on which was seated an obviously dumbstruck James Prestonville, wearing nothing but a dressing-gown. Despite herself, Eleanor's eyes were immediately drawn to his strong muscular legs covered in fine dark hair, which were clearly visible to just above the knee. She gulped and quickly assembled her thoughts into some sort of order. This was clearly not the time to be indulging in daydreams about what other delights the robe might be concealing.

Davies, James's valet, a extremely tall, thin man with a completely bald, shiny head was standing over by a window, pulling out the few remaining shards of glass which were still obstinately clinging to the wooden frame. The remainder of the glass was scattered all over the Persian carpet below.

Desperately attempting to control the colour rising in her cheeks, Eleanor adopted a business-like tone. 'What has happened, Davies?' she demanded, regarding the scene from the side of the *chaise*.

James did not even look at her. Davies turned around briefly before returning to the glass. 'It was a shot, miss,' he replied disbelievingly. 'Someone shot at Master James, right through this window.'

Eleanor's mouth dropped open. 'Sh-shot?' she repeated, wrinkling her brow. 'Somebody has *shot* at him? But-but . . . how . . . who?'

The valet continued with his task. 'Can't say, miss,' he replied earnestly. 'Didn't see nothing and I was straight over here looking and all. If I ever get my hands on them they'll be—'

'But-but . . . I don't understand,' said Eleanor. 'How would anyone dare—?'

'Oh they dare, miss. Got a neck for anything these days, they have. You wouldn't want to know, miss, the tales I've been hearing about what them highwaymen are getting up to – and with innocent folk too – folk just going about their own business. Just like the master there. There I was, miss, getting him ready for Lady Armitage's party and—'

'But I thought he did not wish to go to Lady Armitage's party,' cut in Eleanor, aware that she was speaking about James as if he were not present. 'He stated quite emphatically yesterday that he had no desire at all to—'

'Changed his mind, miss,' informed the valet, matter-of-factly.

'I see,' replied Eleanor flatly, feeling slightly sickened at the thought of the tricks Madeleine might have employed in order to bring about James's change of mind. 'Well, I will leave you to your clearing up, Davies,' she said.

The valet nodded his thanks. As she was leaving the room, a thought suddenly struck her.

'Davies,' she said, 'this may sound like a rather strange question, but is that his own dressing-robe Master James is wearing?'

'Of course, miss,' replied the valet turning to her with a puzzled expression. 'Who else's would he be wearing?'

Not surprisingly, Eleanor's eyes had not closed for an instant that night as she pondered the puzzling state of affairs. She arose early deciding that a ride before breakfast would perhaps help clear her head. She was just descending the steps of the castle *en route* to the stables, when she was aware of two men on horseback clattering up the drive. They came to a halt before her just as she reached the bottom step.

'Begging your pardon there, miss,' said the older of the two men, thick grey whiskers peeping out from under his grubby hat, 'but we're looking for a Mr Lovell.' His accent had a thick northern twang to it and it was obvious, despite their aspiring appearances, these were no gentlemen.

'Mr Lovell?' repeated Eleanor, at once on her guard. 'I have not seen him this morning. I believe he has not yet returned.'

'Not back yet?' repeated the second man. 'Well, we can guess what he's been up to all night, miss.' They both sniggered before the second man said, 'Perhaps you'd be good enough to pass on a message to him, miss?'

'Of course,' replied Eleanor warily.

'Tell him that wherever he goes, Dick and Sam'll track him down. Tell him we're looking for payment in full this time, miss and if we don't get it. . . .'

The man made a gesture with his index finger across the width of his throat, which made Eleanor's eyes widen in horror.

'Oh,' she spluttered. 'Very well then. I will . . . er . . . pass that message on.'

'You do that, miss,' replied the man. 'And tell him we'll be back same time tomorrow and whether he's at home or not, we'll be wanting our money.'

Eleanor nodded numbly as the two men wheeled their horses around and thundered off back down the drive, laughing loudly. Then she turned and made her way back up the castle steps. Her desire to ride out alone in the countryside had suddenly completely deserted her.

She entered the breakfast room to find James and Lady Madeleine already there. James was looking as white as a sheet and wholly fatigued. Madeleine, on the other hand, appeared to be in full flow, exaggerating the recent drama to her full advantage. Eleanor slipped into her chair while the Hungarian dramatically continued her tale, suddenly dropping her knife and raising the back of her hand to her forehead.

'Oh my word,' she declared theatrically, 'Whenever I think of that bullet only inches away from you, James, it makes me feel positively weak.'

James tossed her a fleeting, derogatory glance as he raised his coffee cup to his lips. 'The thought does not exactly fill me with joy, Madeleine,' he retorted sourly.

Madeleine tossed her head of blonde curls before picking up her knife and resuming the dissection of a kipper. 'But that man should be punished for it at once,' she pronounced. 'We must pay a visit to the Bow Street Runners as soon as we have finished breakfast.'

James replaced his cup into its saucer and lifted his napkin to his mouth. 'Don't be ridiculous, Madeleine,' he chided dismissively, as he dabbed at his lips. 'We have no idea who was responsible.'

Madeleine lifted her head to regard him with her startling blue eyes. 'Oh but of course we do, my darling,' she countered. 'Who else could it *possibly* have been?'

Curiosity overcame Eleanor as she pulled a slice of rather cold toast from the silver rack before her. 'May I ask to whom you are referring?' she enquired smoothly.

Madeleine flashed her a contemptuous glare. 'The Duke of Swinton, of course.'

Eleanor dropped the piece of toast on to her plate. 'The Duke of Swinton?' she repeated dubiously.

Madeleine regarded her with an incredulous glare. 'Why of course the Duke of Swinton,' she affirmed fervently. 'There can be no one else who would wish ill of my James.'

Madeleine put down her knife again and reached out to place a tiny hand on James's forearm, which was now resting on the table. Eleanor felt a pang of the now familiar jealousy and jerked her eyes away to seek out the dish of butter.

'Perhaps not, Lady Madeleine,' she replied coolly. 'However I think the Bow Street Runners would require some proof before they are in a position to accuse anyone.'

'Phoo,' scoffed Madeleine, removing her hand from James's arm and flourishing a dismissive wave. 'If they want proof then I shall go out and find some.'

Now that, Madeleine, mused Eleanor, is a most excellent idea.

Quite what drove Eleanor to Derek Lovell's bedchamber in her first search for clues, she could not honestly say other than she had always been in possession of that rather elusive, intangible quality known as 'women's intuition'. In this case, the reliability of that quality proved as dependable as ever as, in the brief minute or so it took for her to peep her head around the man's empty bedchamber door, a very crucial piece of what she now realized was an extremely large jigsaw puzzle, slotted magically into place. In order to find the next piece, she decided, it would be quite remiss of her to pass on to Mr Lovell the message left by Dick and Sam for she was now suddenly consumed with a overwhelming desire to meet the two men again and the sooner, she concluded, the better.

Thankfully for all concerned, the dowager's rooms were situated in the east wing of the castle and from her sickbed the old woman had apparently heard nothing of the shooting. James had ordered vehemently that this state of affairs should not be altered as the old lady was quite ill and in need of her rest. The servants were therefore sworn not to talk about the matter above stairs. Downstairs, in their own domain, it was doubtful the talk would be of very little else, with particular emphasis on who on earth had been holding the gun.

Indeed it was that matter which was on everyone's mind, particularly when it was revealed that the Duke of Swinton – the most popular candidate – had retired to Bath with his wife, several days before the incident.

Despite this removal of the man from most people's list of – in some cases, quite outlandish – suspects, Lady Madeleine refused to be swayed. 'It is not unheard of, James,' she observed over dinner that evening, 'for gentlemen to pay a lackey to carry out their dirty work.'

Eleanor had fervently countered this suggestion. 'I hardly think, Lady Madeleine,' she had declared, 'that a man who has been awarded a medal for bravery in the Battle of Vittoria would stoop so low as to pay a lackey to dispose of his wife's lover.'

Madeleine had tossed her yet another disparaging glare while James had toyed silently with his food for several minutes more, before making his excuses and retiring to his chambers.

After dinner, Eleanor paid a visit to her godmother's room. Despite visiting her three times a day, in order to read, or attempt to cheer her up with progress on her accomplishments, she continued to find it a rather incongruous sight to have the dowager lying there looking her usual robust self, albeit a little paler, with no sound at all emanating from her. Indeed, she found the experience a little unnerving, expecting the woman at any time to open her mouth and roar for poor Stevens.

Having read her another chapter of Mrs Edgeworth's *Castle Rackrent*, Eleanor made the dowager comfortable and was just on the verge of leaving the room when she asked blithely, 'Oh, I was just wondering, Godmother, if you have yet received a reply from Lady Neilson in Hungary?'

The dowager shook her head vigorously. It was exactly the response Eleanor had expected.

The following morning, Eleanor was dressed and outside the gates of the castle at exactly the same time as she had vacated it the previous day. Just as she had hoped, the two men whom she was awaiting, came cantering into view a few minutes after her arrival. She kicked her horse to a gallop and thundered towards them, meeting them just on the edge of the castle grounds.

'Good morning, Mr Dick. Mr Sam,' she said graciously, attempting not to show the men any hint of the nerves she was feeling.

The men both doffed their scruffy hats to her. 'Morning, miss,' replied the older man. 'I'm taking it you've seen Mr Lovell and he's got the money ready for us?'

Eleanor pulled a rueful face. 'I am afraid I did not have the – er – *pleasure* of meeting Mr Lovell at all yesterday,' she explained solemnly. 'The man's social life is quite . . . *active* and he is rarely at home.'

The two men sneered knowingly. Eleanor ignored them, but carried on with the speech she had been rehearsing in her head for several hours now. 'I have, however,' she continued, in quite a haughty tone, 'another mission for the two of you if you would be interested, one which would pay very well indeed, but, should you wish to accept the task, you must both assure me of your complete confidence.'

A lop-sided smirk appeared on the younger man's face. 'Oh, you can have as much confidence as you like, miss,' he confirmed, 'so long as the price is right.'

The other man nodded his agreement.

'Very well then,' said Eleanor authoritatively. 'What I shall require you both to do is this. . . .'

Eleanor, James and Lady Madeleine were all seated in the drawing-room later that afternoon when Giles appeared carrying his silver tray on which lay a note. 'This has been delivered for Lady Ormiston, ma'am,' he informed Eleanor gravely, 'but her grace has requested that it should be passed to you for reply.'

'Oh really?' replied Eleanor, sitting up straight and wrinkling her forehead. 'Bring it here please, Giles.'

Taking the envelope from the tray, she dismissed the man with a nod, before proceeding to read the note. A large smile spread across her countenance as she did so. 'Oh how charming,' she pronounced, as she read. 'We have all been invited to a ball at Carlton House.'

James merely grunted and did not raise his eyes from the book he was reading. Lady Madeleine's reaction, however, was one of complete and utter joy. 'Carlton House?' she repeated incredulously, setting aside her embroidery tambour. 'How wonderful. Who on earth has invited us?'

'Oh my word,' declared Eleanor, clutching a hand to her chest. 'None other than the Countess Lieven.'

'Countess Lieven?' squealed a delighted Lady Madeleine, her eyes shining with excitement. 'We simply must go, James but . . . oh my goodness . . . what on *earth* shall I wear? I shall have to have a new gown,' she gushed. 'I must go to London tomorrow and visit the very best mantua-maker there is in Bruton Street. When is the ball, Lady Eleanor?'

'Next Thursday,' replied Eleanor smoothly, before adding nonchalantly,

'Oh, I think perhaps you will be required to wear Hungarian dress, Lady Madeleine. The ball, it appears, is in honour of the Hungarian ambassador and his family.'

As the smile suddenly faded from Lady Madeleine's face, the woman turned a very curious shade of green.

# CHAPTER 20

'MILLY?' said Eleanor the following morning, as the girl was busying herself tidying up the items on the dressing-table. 'Do you know if your mother has any rat poison left in the cottage?'

Milly gasped in horror and swung around to face Eleanor. 'Oh no, miss,' she exclaimed, 'don't be telling me them pesky rats have moved in here now.'

Eleanor, seated on the blue sofa in her dressing-room, couldn't resist a smile at Milly's aghast expression. 'No, Milly,' she explained calmly. 'It's nothing like that. I just need a little for an . . . experiment. Actually, Milly, I'm going to need your help too – and Ed's.'

'What on earth are you doing, girl?' enquired Derek Lovell brusquely as, later that afternoon, he came across Milly on all fours, on the stone floor of the corridor with her blonde head stuck under an old Tudor church pew.

'Rats, sir,' she declared solemnly, from her position.

'*Rats?*' he repeated in a disgusted tone.

'That's right, sir,' affirmed Milly. 'Miss Eleanor swears blind she saw the biggest rat of them all creeping about last night. Looked everywhere on her floor, I have, and everything is pointing to them nesting here. Going to have to search all the rooms, I am, otherwise Miss Eleanor ain't going to get no sleep, sir, 'til she knows they're gone.'

Lovell pulled a repulsed expression. 'How very *interesting*,' he replied. 'And what exactly are you planning on doing with them when you find them? I do hope we're not going to have traps going off at all hours of the day and night.'

'Oh no, sir,' replied Milly, matter-of-factly, 'I'm not messing about with traps. Going to kill the beggers with poison. That'll get rid of them once and for all. Nice and quick and no mess, like.'

Lovell raised his brows. 'Really?' he said musingly. 'Nice and quick and no mess. Hmm. Well, get on with your work, girl. I'm sure Lady Eleanor will be needing you soon to help with her hair, or something of equally great import. Oh, and if you absolutely *must* go into my room, don't steal anything,' and with that, he turned on his heel and marched along the corridor towards the stairs.

Milly pulled her head out from under the bench and stuck her tongue out at the man's arrogant retreating back.

'Oh, Milly, well done,' declared Eleanor, slipping out from her hiding place behind a large suit of armour, just as Lovell disappeared around the corner. 'You did so well.'

Milly straightened up. 'I wasn't half bad, was I, miss?' she said, glowing at the compliment. 'Maybe I should be one of them actresses in them theatres. Might even nab myself a rich lord or something.'

Eleanor raised her hand to her mouth in mock horror. 'I can just imagine my godmother's reaction if I told her *that* was what you were planning, Milly.'

They both giggled before Eleanor said, 'Now come on. We'd better be quick in case he or his valet come back up. Give me the box of poison, Milly, and I'll go and put it in his room.'

Milly handed her the box. 'I'll whistle if anyone comes, miss,' she said, evidently relishing her importance in their secret mission.

Eleanor nodded her agreement and, cracking open the door to Derek Lovell's bedchamber, quickly slipped inside. The room was so obviously that of a man, with none of the delicate touches normally evident in a female's room. Eleanor placed the box of rat poison on the window seat. There was very little left in the bottom of the box, which would, she hoped give Lovell the impression that Milly, having probably opened a new packet, had simply forgotten to take the almost empty one with her. Having successfully accomplished her mission, she slipped out of the room.

Later that evening, Eleanor, James and Lady Madeleine had convened in the saloon just before dinner when in swaggered Derek Lovell.

'Good God, Lovell,' declared James, his long legs stretched out before him as he slouched in the armchair normally occupied by his aunt, 'don't tell me you are joining us for dinner this evening?'

Lovell came to a halt in front of the fireplace and bowed a greeting to them all. Lady Madeleine, seated in the chair opposite James, speared the unexpected dinner guest with a contemptuous glare before moving on to study the rings on her fingers.

'Didn't think it was right that I'd deprived you of my company for so long,

Prestonville, old chap,' informed Lovell. 'Not a problem is it?'

James didn't reply, but instead addressed himself to the footman who was standing in attendance at the back of the room. 'Stevens,' he said, 'set another place for Mr Lovell. He will be joining us for dinner.'

'Aren't we the lucky ones,' muttered Lady Madeleine sardonically, still toying with her jewelled fingers. James flashed her a reprimanding glare.

Stevens bowed his head and was about to take his leave of the room when Eleanor added, 'Oh, and Stevens, I would be most grateful if you could then go down to the kitchens and arrange a mustard plaster to be taken up to Lady Ormiston. She requested it earlier, but, I must confess, it quite slipped my mind.'

'Yes, ma'am,' said the servant solemnly with a stiff bow. He exited the room immediately, leaving Lovell looking a little disgruntled.

'Hmph,' he huffed, surveying the almost empty glass James was cradling in both hands. 'Suppose I'd better help myself to a drink in that case.'

'Yes, I suppose you had,' replied James coolly.

Lovell took a few steps towards the drinks tray and then came to an abrupt stop at the side of James's chair. 'Looks like you could do with a little more, Prestonville,' he said, holding out his hand to take James's glass.

James handed the item over to him without saying a word and, still in his slouched position, plunged both hands into his breeches' pockets.

'Thought I might go into London later,' prattled Lovell, his back to the rest of them as, amidst much clinking of glass, he poured the liquor.

'Really?' declared Madeleine ironically. 'Now that *would* make a change, Mr Lovell.'

Lovell emitted another of his irksome sniggers as he turned, carrying two brandy glasses. He held out the one in his right hand to James before turning his attention to Lady Madeleine. 'Why, Lady Madeleine,' he declared with a twisted sneer as James accepted the glass from him, 'do I detect a hint of sarcasm? Or are you perhaps a little put out that I have not done you the plea-sure of asking you to accompany me?'

Madeleine gave a snort of contempt. 'If you think that I would consider such an invitation for even a second, then you are more of an imbecile than I thought you, Mr Lovell, and *that* would be quite a feat for any man.'

'That is enough, you two,' snapped James, resuming the cradling of his glass. 'If anyone wishes to argue, then please refrain from doing so until I am no longer present.'

Madeleine pursed her lips and, sticking her chin in the air, turned her head away from Lovell and towards the fireplace in the manner of one extremely piqued.

This resulted in another grating titter from Lovell, who proceeded to seat himself at the far end of the sofa to Eleanor. 'Cheers then, Prestonville,' he exclaimed, raising his glass in a toast. 'Here's to an argument-free dinner.'

James mirrored the gesture, but before he had a chance to raise the glass to his lips, in a motion so quick and so nimble that it caused them all to start, Eleanor suddenly leapt from the sofa, whisked across the room and snatched the brandy glass from James's hand.

'What the—' began James, jerking into an upright position.

At that very moment, before any of the startled observers of the incident had time to utter another word, the door to the saloon suddenly burst open and in entered Giles followed immediately by M. Aminieux and a colourful, plump lady, dressed in clashing shades of pink and orange.

Giles looked even more put out than usual. 'Begging your pardon, sir,' he began curtly, 'but—'

'That's quite all right, Giles,' cut in Eleanor, now standing in front of the fireplace and still holding the glass she had taken from James. 'I instructed Monsieur and Madame Aminieux that they were to follow you to the room and not wait to be announced.' She turned her head to Madeleine and affected an innocent smile. 'We did so not wish to spoil your surprise, Lady Madeleine. After all, we all know how upset you were at having to miss the Aminieuxs on Thursday and how much you are so looking forward to conversing in your own language.' Madeleine looked completely dumbstruck as Eleanor then turned her attention back to the butler. 'Thank you for adhering to my instructions, Giles,' she continued. 'We shall call if we require you again.'

As a perplexed Giles left the room, closing the door behind him, Lady Madeleine, it appeared, was not the only person to be struck speechless – James and Derek Lovell both looked equally as flabbergasted as they gazed at the colourful, beaming visitors standing just inside the doorway.

'Please do come in, monsieur, madame,' invited Eleanor, gesturing to the two to be seated on the sofa, alongside Lovell. 'I can see that Lady Madeleine is positively bursting to speak with you.'

'Hogy vagy,' gushed Madame Aminieux, holding out her plump arms as she walked towards Lady Madeleine's chair. Madeleine shrank back in horror as the woman then proceeded to bend down and embrace her in a hug.

'Ah,' sighed M. Aminieux, clutching both hands to his rounded chest, 'she has been looking forward to this for so long. It is terrible that there are so few people from Hungary here. She is never having the chance to be speaking her own language.'

'Oh, indeed that is a pity, M. Aminieux,' agreed Eleanor. 'And what a treat for us all to witness Lady Madeleine speaking her mother tongue.'

Madame Aminieux released her hold of a breathless Lady Madeleine. 'Ah, milyen csinos végre találkozni veled,' she sighed,

Madeleine said nothing but turned her eyes imploringly to Lovell.

'I do believe, Lady Madeleine, that you are quite in shock,' remarked Eleanor concernedly. 'Perhaps a sip of this brandy which Mr Lovell very kindly poured for James earlier will help soothe your nerves.' She handed the glass to Madeleine who, casting another terrified look at Lovell, reluctantly accepted it from her.

Lovell suddenly thrust energetically to his feet. 'I do believe Lady Eleanor,' he declared, walking over to Madeleine and swiping the glass from her tiny hand, 'that Lady Madeleine is not in the habit of drinking brandy. Perhaps you would prefer a sherry, ma'am?' he suggested.

A wave of relief washed over Madeleine's face. 'Er yes, thank you, Mr Lovell,' stammered Madeleine. 'That would be most kind.'

'Oh, indeed it would, Mr Lovell,' replied Eleanor, retrieving the glass in one swoop from Mr Lovell as he passed by her. 'However, it would be a great pity to waste this measure – unless of course there is perhaps another reason why Lady Madeleine does not wish to consume the brandy?' She fixed Madeleine with a quizzical look.

The Hungarian shifted uncomfortably in her seat. 'I have no idea—' she began.

'Oh, well, in that case, Lady Madeleine,' broke in Eleanor smoothly, 'please do allow me to demonstrate.' She turned her head to the door, before calling, 'Ed!' No sooner was the summons out of her mouth, than the door opened again and in marched Ed Maguire, carrying a small wire cage in which was a large black rat.

Lady Madeleine wrinkled up her face in disgust and Madame Aminieux immediately produced a handkerchief, which she pressed over her nose and mouth.

Eleanor greeted the boy and his companion with her most charming of smiles. 'Good evening, Ed,' she said genially. 'Would you care to carry out your instructions?' she said, handing the boy the brandy glass.

Ed nodded his acquiescence and placed the cage on the table around which the group were seated, Mr Lovell having now resumed his position alongside the Aminieuxs on the sofa. They all watched in stunned silence as the boy proceeded to open the cage door, retrieve a small bowl from inside, fill the bowl with the brandy, replace the bowl in the cage and close the door once more. He nodded to Eleanor to indicate the completion of his instructions before crouching down at the side of the table and observing the animal as it sniffed about its alcoholic offering.

It was Derek Lovell who broke the bewildered silence, by first nervously clearing his throat and then remarking in a voice that was noticeably quivering, 'Lady Eleanor, you appear to have gone quite queer in your attic. I think perhaps we should escort her to her room, James,' he continued, with a hollow laugh. 'Perhaps a little rest may restore her spirits.'

James fixed him with cold, narrowed eyes for a few seconds before stating, 'I must agree, Lovell, that Lady Eleanor is indeed acting rather strangely; however, she is perfectly correct in pointing out that none of us have yet had the pleasure of hearing Lady Madeleine converse in her mother tongue.' He turned his cool gaze to Madeleine. 'I wonder if you would now be so kind as to oblige us all, Lady Madeleine.'

Lady Madeleine shifted uneasily. 'Well, I am not really fluent in Hungarian,' she floundered. 'That is, I mean I have never—'

'Never even been to Hungary, madam?' interjected Eleanor, with raised brows.

Monsieur Aminieux gasped loudly, while Madame Aminieux assumed the countenance of one on the verge of disappointed tears. James's already raised eyebrows meanwhile, moved even higher up his forehead while Derek Lovell looked as though he were about to murder Eleanor.

'Indeed,' continued Eleanor, 'I have a couple of people here who will tell us exactly where you have been. Do come in, gentlemen,' she shouted.

The door opened once more and in came Dick and Sam grinning broadly. They hovered about on the threshold, twisting their hats in their hands. Upon setting eyes on the pair, Derek Lovell's previous wrathful countenance miraculously transformed into one of pure terror.

'What the devil!' he declared, staring open-mouthed at the two beaming men.

Eleanor smiled serenely. 'I believe you are already acquainted with Richard and Samuel, Mr Lovell. I thought it was the least I could do to invite them to join us this evening. My memory does fail me quite terribly at times and it rather slipped my mind to advise you of their visit yesterday in which these two rather patient moneylenders were kind enough to inform me of the horrifying scale of your gambling debts – debts which you have accumulated over several years in your home town of Newcastle.'

'Newcastle?' repeated James. 'But I thought you said you'd only just—'

'Arrived back from overseas,' cut in Eleanor. 'I can reliably inform you, sir, that Mr Lovell has not spent any time overseas recently. Indeed he has had little time for travel given how occupied he has been both with the fervent accumulation of his debts and . . . one other thing. Hmm . . . what was it again? Oh yes . . . his recent marriage.'

James's brows now disappeared under his fringe. 'Marriage?' he repeated, gazing perplexedly at Lovell. 'But you never mentioned you were—'

'That is because, sir,' clarified Eleanor, 'you were not supposed to know. Indeed, it would have completely ruined the happy couple's plans if you had by chance discovered that Lady Madeleine here was the wife of your old friend.'

This time James was at a complete loss for words as his mouth hung open.

Everyone's attention, however, then turned to the noise emanating from the rat's cage. They all watched in horror as the animal convulsed violently for a few short seconds before dropping down, obviously dead. A stunned, appalled silence ensued before Eleanor, attempting to regain her composure, turned to James stating, 'That sir, was the fate intended for yourself this evening. Courtesy of the rat poison added to your drink by your good friend, Mr Lovell.'

'Phwoah!' scoffed Lovell, leaping to his feet. 'That is complete and utter nonsense. Do you honestly think I'd be stupid enough to murder James right here in front of an audience?'

'Oh, indeed I do not, sir,' declared Eleanor. 'Even you are too clever to make such an obvious *faux-pas*, Mr Lovell. In fact, that is why you not only poisoned James's drink, but why you also added poison to the decanter. This means, of course, that your own drink – which I note you have not yet touched – is also poisoned. A fact which you hoped would have eliminated you from suspicion once James was dead.'

'Poppycock!' cried Lovell.

'Is it, sir?' enquired Eleanor beatifically. 'Then perhaps you would like to take a sip in front of us all now.'

Lovell marched directly to the pot plant behind James's chair and tipped the contents of his glass into it. 'I believe you are all about in your head, Lady Eleanor,' he declared stiffly. 'Why—'

'Oh do be quiet, you idiot,' snapped Madeleine, in a northern accent so broad and so different to the exotic parlance in which they were all so used to hearing her. 'You can't talk your way out of this one, Lovell. I told you we should have got rid of her as well,' she said, indicating her head to Eleanor. 'Far too clever by half that one. Even dressing me up as that damned stupid ghost didn't scare her away. I told you the poison idea was far too risky, but would you listen? Oh no! And now we're both in trouble. Can't believe I was stupid enough to marry such a fool.'

'Oh you were stupid enough all right,' sneered Lovell, his eyes flashing with white-hot hatred as he stared down at Madeleine. 'Stupid enough and greedy enough. Why all I had to say were the words "Duchess" and "Castle" and you couldn't get out of your father's shop and on your back quick enough.'

Madeleine now thrust to her feet and strutted furiously over to her husband, bearing an expression of unadulterated loathing. 'Why you slimy—'

'That is enough,' boomed James, rising from his chair and forcing husband and wife apart. 'I cannot believe what I am hearing here. But one thing I can't understand, Lovell, is why. Why did you want to kill me?'

'Because that blasted inheritance should be mine,' declared Lovell loudly, beginning to pace up and down the room. 'Only it was looking like I wasn't going to get a penny of it whereas with you out of the way, I'd have stood a much better chance. A fact, which Maddy here found far too tempting to resist.'

James screwed up his face. 'But how on earth can you have any claim on the Ormiston inheritance?'

Lovell came to a halt directly in front of James. 'Because, you idiot, I'm the son of your late uncle. Bit of a rebel was my father by all accounts. Took up with my mother – a lowly serving girl – and ended up marrying her, just to spite his own father after the pair of them had an almighty row and he was thrown out of the house. Trouble was, after a few months, the novelty wore off and he went crawling back home. Of course, once he was back ensconced in the family mansion, my mother was seen as nothing more than a nuisance – something to be disposed of when no longer needed. He thought he could pay her off with a tidy sum – which she took, of course – and thought that was the end of the matter. But my mother was much cleverer than that. Not only had she managed to get herself with child, but she'd also ensured that the only bit of paper which proved the marriage had ever taken place was in her own safekeeping: she'd managed to tear the page from the church register. So then, when she found out – because she made it her business to – that my father had got engaged to an Ormiston and was intending taking on the name to continue the line – she got in touch.'

James shook his head as if trying to clear it. 'Blackmail?' he murmured.

Lovell nodded. 'Oh, yes,' he declared proudly. 'She knew that if the Ormistons found out he was already married and with a brat on the way, they would have called off the wedding in a second.'

'So he paid her more money to keep her quiet?'

'Oh yes – lots more. Problem was, when the old goat died, the money dried up, didn't it? Of course my mother didn't tell me any of this until the day she died which was only a few weeks after the old man. Well, I didn't want to be left high and dry so I spoke to a lawyer. Told him the story and he said I might have a claim but best to play my cards close to my chest. Problem was, Mother didn't tell me where she'd hidden the page from the register. Then with that cursed case dragging on and on and me with hardly a penny to my name – well, just enough to keep her in her posh frocks,' he said, throwing a disparaging glare at Madeleine, 'I had to do something: I had to get rid of *you*.'

James stood quite still – a look of pure astonishment on his face. Then, after several minutes of attempting to assimilate the information, he said, 'But how did you come up with the connection with Hungary? How on earth could you have known about that?'

Lovell gave another of his sneers. 'Oh that one was easy. Cast your mind back to university – an education paid for by your uncle, I hasten to add – and that guest speaker we had once, that old Hungarian chap. He sought you out with a letter from the ambassador to pass on to your aunt.'

James nodded his head slowly as he regarded Lovell through narrowed eyes. 'Well, I don't know what to say,' he declared at length, turning to eye the dead rat. 'You appear to have gone to an exceptional amount of trouble, Lovell, to see me out of the way.'

'And I would have as well,' declared Lovell, 'if *she* hadn't kept getting in the way.' He indicated his head to Eleanor.

James fixed her with a rather strange gaze before declaring, 'You have indeed been in the way – quite a lot in fact, Lady Eleanor. However, I am now of the opinion that we should place the matter in the hands of the Bow Street Runners.'

Unable to draw her eyes away from his, Eleanor replied, 'I agree, sir. They are waiting outside.'

# CHAPTER 21

TWO days following the incident, Eleanor was still quite exhausted. The entire household – including herself – had been subjected to hours of rigorous questioning by the Bow Street Runners who arrested Lovell and Lady Madeleine (previously Maddy Burke – ruthless, ambitious daughter of one Mr Raymond Burke, proprietor of a small drapers in Newcastle) on the charge of attempted murder. The pair were currently being held in gaol awaiting trial.

Once word had spread via the proverbial grapevine, the inevitable stream of visitors had made their way to the castle eager to hear all the enthralling details firsthand. Lady Ormiston, still unable to speak, had steadfastly refused to be omitted from all the excitement and had insisted, despite Dr Gosport's specific orders, on being brought down to the drawing-room every day in order that she might stay abreast of the latest happenings.

This particular day, she was especially glad that she had made such an effort as, included amongst her morning visitors, was one Viscount Grayson, newly returned from his business in the north. Suitably impressed by the news of Eleanor's detective work and its successful conclusion, he proceeded to solicit the old lady's permission to request her goddaughter's hand in marriage. Without hesitating for even a second, the dowager nodded her enthusiastic affirmation and made certain animated gestures and several unnerving groans, which the viscount correctly interpreted as meaning he was to go and seek out his beloved and put the question to her that very instant.

Feeling in desperate need of some solitude following the recent, rather taxing, events, Eleanor was seated on a wooden garden bench in the orchard, engrossed in her book of poems and revelling in the glorious June sunshine when the heavenly tranquillity was suddenly broken by a deep masculine voice.

'Good morning, Lady Eleanor.'

She tilted her head upward and, shielding her eyes from the sun with her hand, found herself looking directly at James Prestonville. Startled by not only the mere sight of him, but also how devastatingly handsome he looked in a simple white shirt and beige breeches, it was all she could do to murmur a simple, rather unenthusiastic 'Oh' in response to his greeting, as she vainly attempted to quell the butterflies which had suddenly begun an energetic quadrille in the pit of her stomach.

She was more than a little aware that she had barely spoken to James since the confrontation with Lovell and Madeleine. She was also rather acutely aware that each time the two of them had happened to be in the same room, James was forming a disconcerting habit of fixing her with that familiar unfathomable look which, without fail, succeeded in sweeping all rational thought from her mind. Now, as he stood before her, his eyes burning into hers, she was filled with an overwhelming desire to throw her arms around his neck, press herself to him and lose herself in his kiss. All at once, she realized that the sensuous lips she was now gazing at longingly were moving and emitting sounds: he was speaking to her and she had absolutely no idea what he had said.

'Lady Eleanor?' he repeated, regarding her quizzically.

'Wh-what?' stammered Eleanor, feeling colour flooding her cheeks.

'Would you mind if I joined you?' His voice was so smooth it made her tingle.

'Er, no,' she managed to reply, averting her eyes from his face and focusing them instead on the open book on her lap.

He lowered himself on to the bench beside her, closer than was necessary, she noticed, as the pleasant scent of his subtle cologne gently tickled her nostrils.

'I believe I have not yet had the opportunity to thank you for all your efforts, Lady Eleanor,' he declared silkily.

'Oh,' muttered Eleanor, desperately trying to steer her mind on to something which did not involve being in his arms. She closed her book and began fidgeting with the edge of its brown leather spine. 'That's quite all right,' she murmured, chiding herself for sounding so pathetic.

'*All right?*' repeated James incredulously. 'But you saved my life. On several occasions, I believe.'

Eleanor said nothing, but continued her fidgeting, conscious that his upper arm encased in the white cotton of his shirt, was now touching the bare skin of her own. The heat of him seemed to burn into her, flooding her body with a deep sense of longing.

James did not seem affected in the least, as he continued with his speech. 'I have been wondering, Lady Eleanor,' he said, 'how on earth you knew what was going on.'

'Well, actually, I didn't,' she confessed, grateful that her ability to speak was at least making some effort to return. 'That is, I thought at first that some-one was trying to kill *me*, but that made no sense. I mean, I'm just an ordinary girl and—'

'Oh I can assure you, Lady Eleanor,' he cut in softly, 'that you are far from ordinary.'

She was aware that he had shifted his body slightly and was now gazing at her face. Not daring to look at him, she felt her cheeks flush an even deeper shade of crimson and kept her eyes focused on her book. She cleared her throat before continuing.

'Well, after the – er – incident with the pitchfork, I realized that it wasn't me they were trying to kill, but rather that it was you. And then, when I discovered it wasn't you who was creeping along to Madeleine's room every night but—'

He cut in again, his tone disbelieving this time. 'You thought *I* was paying a visit to Madeleine's rooms every evening? So that's what you were talking about that morning when you referred to me not spending the night in my own bed?'

Eleanor nodded her head. 'I must confess, sir, that did leave me feeling a little. . . .'

'A little what?' prompted James softly, still gazing down at her.

She flustered. Should she admit to him how she had actually felt? How she had been so hurt and jealous that she had not been able to sleep a wink? She decided it was best not to; after all, she had no idea of his feelings for her and the last thing she wanted to do in front of James Prestonville – a man who had women throwing themselves at him from every angle – was to make a cake of herself. She squirmed a little in her seat aware that it was now not only his arm which was touching her, but also his muscular thigh which was pressing enticingly against hers, causing her heart to race rather alarmingly. She swallowed and did not remove her eyes for even a second from the brown leather book cover. 'A little – er – *puzzled*, sir,' she said at length.

His disappointment was palpable. 'Oh,' he muttered mournfully.

'But then,' continued Eleanor softly, 'when I noticed that your dressing robe was crimson and was not the blue one I had seen in the corridor at all hours, then I looked in Mr Lovell's room and discovered that it was indeed he who was paying nightly visits to Madeleine.'

Still she dared not look at him, but was aware that he was nodding.

'And then, of course,' she carried on, 'that immediately made me suspicious, given that we were all of the opinion that the pair could not abide one another.'

He nodded again.

Eleanor continued her explanation. 'And there was also Madeleine's rather strong reluctance to make the acquaintance of Madame Aminieux. At first I attributed this to her being too high in the instep; however, when my godmother informed me that she had still not received a reply from her friend in Hungary – Lady Neilson who had introduced Madeleine – my suspicions were heightened further.'

'Hmm,' mused James. 'I suppose then, that when the invitation arrived from Countess Lieven, this added to your theory?'

'Oh, we received no invitation from Countess Lieven, sir,' she clarified adroitly. 'I sent that invitation – to test the theory myself.'

James emitted a snort of laughter. '*You* sent that invitation?' he asked.

Eleanor nodded and carried on, 'Of course, having established that Madeleine was terrified of meeting any of her compatriots, I realized then that something was seriously afoot.'

'And then you met the moneylenders?'

'And thank goodness I did, sir. When they arrived and informed me that Lovell had run up enormous gambling debts in his home town, it was obvious that he, too, had been lying through his teeth. Thankfully for me, Dick and Sam make it their business to find out all they can about their clients. They were therefore able to fill in the missing details, although, I have to confess, that none of us was exactly aware of how Lovell was connected with the Ormistons. The man himself generously provided us with those details on his last evening in the castle.'

'Indeed he did,' said James wistfully.

'I then had to establish that it was indeed Lovell and Madeleine who were trying to kill you so I set up the trap with the rat poison.'

'But how did you know it would work?' queried James.

'I didn't,' admitted Eleanor, 'but I knew by the rather large risk they had taken with the pitchfork, and the shooting, that they were becoming desperate. I thought that when Milly planted the idea that it was a quick, no-nonsense death, they would be unable to resist.'

'And you were right,' said James, shaking his head incredulously. 'I do declare, Lady Eleanor, that you are quite the most astonishing woman I have ever met.'

Unable to resist for a second longer, Eleanor diffidently turned her head towards him and fixed her eyes once again on his full, moist lips.

Her heart began racing wildly as he slowly lowered his head to hers. 'I will take that as a compliment, sir,' she whispered.

'Oh, believe me, it was,' he replied, with a seductive smile.

Eleanor closed her eyes, desperate for the touch of his lips upon hers. Aching for him to wrap his arms around her and—

'Good morning, my lord. Lady Eleanor.'

They could not have jumped apart more abruptly if they had been struck by a flash of lightening.

'I am so glad to have found you, Lady Eleanor,' squeaked Viscount Grayson, as he brought his podgy form to a halt directly in front of them. 'I was wondering if I could have a word with you in . . . private,' he added, raising his brows expectantly at James.

'Oh,' muttered Eleanor, fervently resenting not only the man's disastrous timing, but his mere disagreeable presence. 'Well, Lord Prestonville and I were just – er—'

'We can continue later, Lady Eleanor,' asserted James, rising to his feet. 'Good morning to you, madam,' he said, inclining his head to her. Doing likewise to the viscount, he then marched purposefully towards the arch which led out into the main gardens, leaving Eleanor alone with Viscount Grayson and a profound sense of dread.

'There's a young . . . *gentleman* waiting in the library to see you, my lady,' sniffed Giles disapprovingly, as Eleanor entered the castle some twenty minutes later. From his derisory tone, it was obvious that the visitor did not meet with the butler's exacting standards. Indeed, despite her own recent rise in status to something akin to a heroine, it remained very much in evidence that Eleanor, too, still had some way to go before Giles would consider bestowing his approval upon her person.

'Oh, I wonder who it is,' replied Eleanor, handing her book to him. 'Have they a card, Giles?'

Giles regarded her for a moment as though she were a complete nodcock. 'No, madam,' he replied vehemently. 'They most *definitely* have no card.'

Concluding that the only way in which she was going to discover the identity of this mysterious visitor was to go to the library herself, she made her way along the corridor and, upon reaching her destination, hesitantly pushed open the door. She was both relieved and delighted to find herself looking straight into the golden, freckled face of Ed Maguire, seated in one of the brown leather wing chairs. He stood up as soon as she entered.

'Ed!' exclaimed Eleanor, walking over to give him a hug. 'How lovely to see you.

The young man, as usual in Eleanor's presence, blushed to the roots of his hair. 'I'm sorry I've been so long in getting that information you wanted, miss,' he blustered, as he tentatively returned her warm embrace. 'But that Miss Carmichael is a bit of a canny one and it's taken me an age to find out what she's been up to.'

Eleanor released her hold of him and gestured to him to resume his seat as she sank down in the chair opposite him. 'Does this mean you have something to tell me, Ed?' she asked hopefully.

'Aye, miss,' he replied, 'although to tell the truth, I'm not sure you're going to believe it.'

Eleanor raised her brows to him. 'Oh, don't worry about that, Ed,' she declared. 'I can assure you that where Felicity Carmichael is concerned, nothing would surprise me.'

'We-ll,' began Ed hesitantly, 'it turns out it's not a farmworker you're wanting to talk to, miss, but a young man by the name of Horace Edgeware who works at Tunbridges' stables.'

'And this is the man Felicity has been . . . seeing?'

'Yes, ma'am,' replied Ed. 'Seems that her mother, Lady Carmichael, bought a new horse from there six months ago and took Felicity along with her to choose it. While they were there, Horace, and his sweetheart, young Betsy Mills, were having a heart to heart about getting married and Betsy was all crying and everything, miss, 'cos she said on their wages, they'd never be able to afford to wed.'

Eleanor nodded encouragingly as Ed took a breath.

'So, miss,' he continued solemnly, 'it turns out that Felicity had overheard the conversation and saw Betsy in a right state and everything, so the next day she went back to the stables – without her ma – and said she had one of them there propositions to put to Horace.'

Eleanor widened her eyes. She could guess the rest. 'So Felicity offered money to Horace to. . . .'

Ed flushed an even deeper shade of crimson and nodded vigorously. 'Aye, miss. Paid him well, by all accounts.'

Eleanor shook her head disbelievingly. 'Hmm,' she mused. 'Well, I suppose some good has come out of it – at least now Horace and Betsy can afford to be married.'

'Oh no, miss,' explained Ed, earnestly. 'Betsy happened to come across Horace and Felicity one day. Barged right in, and there they were . . . you know, miss,' flustered Ed, burning with embarrassment.

'Oh, I can imagine, Ed,' said Eleanor, pulling a disgusted face.

'Anyway, when she found them . . . you know . . . Horace was all apologies like and tried to explain, but that Felicity told him to shut up otherwise she'd make sure he never got another job within fifty miles of here. Betsy was in a right state, of course, miss, crying and everything, and that Felicity, she just laughed at her. Laughed right in her face and called her all sorts of names.'

'Good God,' exclaimed Eleanor disgustedly.

'So now, miss, Betsy wants nothing to do with Horace, and Horace is fair fuming with that Felicity. Wishes he'd never set eyes on her – never mind anything else.'

'Hmm,' mused Eleanor. 'Now that I can fully understand, Ed. Do you think though that Horace would be willing to speak to me about it?'

Ed nodded affirmatively. 'Know for a fact he would, miss. He's a good lad. Just thought he was doing the right thing at the time.'

Eleanor nodded. 'Oh, I'm sure he did. Would you take me to see him, Ed?'

'Oh, aye, miss,' beamed the boy proudly. 'I'd love to.'

The prestigious masquerade ball at Almack's was to be held that evening. The dowager had written instructions that James was to escort Eleanor – an arrangement which, she had to confess, had left her feeling both nervous and excited. Her feelings were subsequently equally divided when Giles delivered a note from James later that afternoon explaining that he had been detained in London and would therefore meet her at the venue itself at eight o'clock. The fact that she had not seen him since he had left her with the viscount in the orchard that morning, had done nothing to quell the irksome thought which had been preying heavily on her mind all day: had he been on the verge of kissing her again before they were so rudely interrupted?

The fact that James was to meet Eleanor at Almack's, had provided a welcome solution to another problem she had been puzzling over. She could now, without any interrogation from James, instruct the driver to take a detour via the Maguires' cottage to collect two more guests for the ball. The man had said nothing, but the surprise on his face was obvious, when a young lady and a young gentleman – both dressed in traditional Spanish mode – joined Eleanor in the carriage.

The dowager had left Eleanor under no illusion that to be invited to attend any event at the exclusive Almack's was a great honour – its esteemed patronesses being renowned for adhering to the most idiosyncratic of rules when selecting those suitable for receiving one of their highly sought after vouchers. The very cream of Society and most of the *haut ton* were therefore already milling around when Eleanor alighted from the carriage with her two masked guests and found James waiting for them in the entrance hall.

As she approached him, she was aware of his eyes growing wide under his mask as they travelled over her costume. She was dressed as a fourteenth-century lady, in a cream velvet gown that, in the candlelight adopted a delicate rose sheen. The front of the dress plunged in a low, revealing V which was adorned with sapphires and rubies. The same jewels also glittered from the belt hung loosely around her slim waist and the golden snood encasing her thick glossy hair. James himself was not in costume, but was sporting the all black evening wear which accentuated his dark, masculine looks.

'I hope you don't mind, James,' said Eleanor, still aware of his eyes on her body and suddenly feeling quite shy again in his presence, 'but I have brought along my cousins, Maribeth and Neville. They have been visiting on the coast and made a detour especially to see me on their way home to Cambridge. As the voucher did say we may each bring a guest, I did not think it would signify.'

James inclined his head to the two masked guests. Neville returned the gesture, whilst Maribeth sank into a deep curtsy.

Obviously in no mood for pleasant chit-chat, having greeted the unexpected guests thus, James wasted no time in making his impatience at being kept waiting, quite clear.

'Let us make our way inside,' he instructed authoritatively. 'There is quite a crowd gathering already and I am in little mood for yet more interrogation regarding Lovell and Madeleine. I would suggest you fix your mask, Lady Eleanor, before we enter the ballroom.'

Good lord, thought Eleanor, as she clipped the jewelled mask to her hair with the help of Maribeth, one could never tell what sort of mood this man was going to be in. He had been so tender with her that morning and now he was positively bossing her around again. The thought did briefly pass through her mind that he was so vexatingly unpredictable that perhaps she should just let Felicity marry him and be done with it.

Upon entering the ballroom however and setting eyes on Felicity and her mother, both dressed in Tudor-style dresses which served only to accentuate their rotund forms, she knew that she could not. James had stopped to talk briefly to an acquaintance just as they approached the Carmichaels and it was Eleanor and her two cousins who reached the pair first.

'Oh, Eleanor,' exclaimed Lady Carmichael, obviously, by her flushed face, in a high state of excitement, 'how are you, my dear, after that *dreadful* business?'

'Oh, quite well, I can assure you, Lady Carmichael,' replied Eleanor blithely.

'You must give me all the details,' instructed Lady Carmichael. 'Felicity and I did pay a visit to Lady Ormiston, but unfortunately both you and James were not present and it was rather difficult to glean any information from the dowager. We did though have the honour of seeing Viscount Grayson there. What a pity he is unable to be here this evening.'

'Indeed it is a great pity,' agreed Eleanor archly. 'However, please do allow me to introduce my cousins, Lady Carmichael – Maribeth and Neville.'

'Oh,' said Lady Carmichael, casting the pair a cursory glance. 'Pleased to make your acquaintance, I'm sure. It is always a pleasure to meet anyone related to the Ormiston family, is it not, Felicity dear?'

'Indeed it is, Mama,' agreed Felicity, inclining her head to the two guests.

'Oh,' squealed Lady Carmichael as James joined the group. 'And here at last is James. Oh my goodness, James,' she gushed, grabbing hold of his hand and squeezing it so tightly that it caused him to grimace. 'How dreadfully exciting it all is. I can scarcely wait for twelve o'clock. I do declare I am positively bursting with anticipation.'

James flashed her a dampening look and pulled his hand roughly from hers. 'May I suggest you curb your excitement, ma'am? I hardly think the unmasking worthy of so much eager anticipation,' he declared quellingly, shaking the hand he had just removed from her over-enthusiastic clasp.

'Oh, you know it is not the unmasking to which I am referring, silly,' giggled Lady Carmichael, giving him a playful tap on the arm with her closed fan.

James fixed Felicity with a menacing glare. 'I can think of nothing else that is planned to occur this evening, madam, which could possibly cause you so much excitement.'

'Oh you are amusing, James,' twittered the older woman, now whipping open her fan and fluttering furiously. 'Is he not amusement itself, Felicity?'

'Indeed, he is, mama,' agreed Felicity, with a demure smile.

As Lady Carmichael then attempted, rather unsuccessfully to glean the latest details of the Lovell/Madeleine saga from James, Eleanor suddenly felt extremely nervous. She wondered at Felicity who was so composed, when tonight was to be the culmination of all her weeks of planning and plotting. What if Eleanor's own plan, designed to counter Felicity's, failed to work? What if Felicity announced, as she so obviously planned to, that she and James were betrothed, right here in front of the entire *ton*? If James then reneged on his word, and Felicity was indeed with child, then it was likely to cause the biggest scandal since Caroline Lamb and Lord Byron and James would undoubtedly be forced to leave the country. A shiver of fear washed over her as she had the most painful thought – if James left the country she might never see him again. There was only one way to make sure that didn't happen and that was to make sure her plan worked.

The ball, although undoubtedly grand in its exalted venue, with hoards of opulently clad, esteemed guests, held very little interest for Eleanor. Apart from the masks and the costumes, it differed little from the other tedious engagements she had been forced to endure during her stay in London. Indeed, were she not so anxious about the events planned to occur at midnight, then she would unquestionably, have found the whole event incredibly boring. The only redeeming feature about the entire evening was the fact that Viscount Grayson had been unable to attend – a fact for which she was extremely grateful.

She wandered disconsolately into the supper-room where there was yet another disgusting display of indulgence and greed – the tables groaning under the weight of the food and the floor no doubt groaning under the weight of some of the grotesque guests indulging in it. Her heart froze for a second as her eyes were drawn to the Duchess of Swinton, looking stunning in a rather daring white chiffon toga, her hair dressed in the Roman fashion and adorned with tiny white pearls. There was no sign of the duke. Standing by one of the floor-to-ceiling windows, she observed the duchess as she put down her plate and made to leave the room – just at the very same moment James chose to enter it. The two of them exchanged a look that spoke volumes; a look that speared Eleanor through the heart like a cold blade of steel and left her in no doubt at all that James Prestonville was still in love with the Duchess of Swinton.

Eleanor spent the remainder of the interminable evening wishing she were somewhere else – anywhere else in fact. In no mood for dancing, she spent much of the time wandering aimlessly around the house and gardens. Shortly before midnight, however, she pulled herself together. Just because James loved another woman, did not mean she could walk away and leave him to the mercy of Felicity Carmichael. She realized that she loved him too much for that – even if her feelings were not reciprocated. She had never been in love before and due to the immense pain it was causing her, she vowed to herself that evening that she would never be so negligent as to allow the wretched thing to creep up on her again. For now though, she needed to be strong – for James.

At one minute before midnight, Felicity Carmichael was looking decidedly pleased with herself – almost as pleased as her mother who was sporting a smile as wide as the Thames and shifting nervously from foot to foot as she gazed proudly at her daughter. James was nowhere to be seen and Eleanor noticed Felicity's eyes anxiously darting around the room in an attempt to locate him.

People began counting down the seconds in time to the chimes. 'Ten – nine – eight—'

'Oh, excuse me, Miss Carmichael,' apologized a gentleman, dressed in the Spanish fashion, who had bumped into Felicity.

Felicity flashed him a reprimanding glare.

'I take it you don't recognize me then, miss,' said the man.

Felicity looked decidedly irritated. 'Indeed, I do not, sir. I have never set eyes on you before this evening,' she snapped, her eyes still darting around the room, searching out James.

As the crowd counted down to midnight 'two – one – hurrah!' and everyone whisked off their masks, so too did the young man standing in front of Felicity.

'Oh, I believe you have, ma'am,' he replied with a bow.

Felicity Carmichael looked as though her eyes were about to pop out of her ugly head. 'You,' she hissed venomously. 'What in hell's name are you doing here?'

'Felicity, dear. Language,' chided Lady Carmichael who was standing alongside her daughter. 'Now, where on earth is James, pumpkin. You really should be—'

'Be quiet, mother!' snapped Felicity loudly.

Shock washed over Lady Carmichael's face. She opened her mouth to reply, but seeing the hatred flashing in her daughter's eyes, obviously thought better of it and swiftly closed it again.

Felicity meanwhile, turned her attention back to the man in front of her. 'I told you to keep away from me,' she snarled, 'and I paid you *very* well to do so.'

Horace Edgeware nodded his head. 'Aye, you did that, ma'am,' he agreed. 'But you can have it back – every last cursed penny of it.'

Aware of the enquiring glances which were being cast their way, Lady Carmichael attempted a rather wavering smile at the spectators whilst in a lowered voice, muttered to daughter, 'Felicity, what on earth is this man talk—?'

'Be quiet!' snapped Felicity, paying no heed to her increasing audience. 'This man was just leaving.'

'Oh, no I wasn't,' declared Horace stoutly. 'Not until I've made sure you're not about creating more havoc. You've ruined my life and Betsy's and I'm sure as eggs not going to sit by and watch you ruin someone else's.'

Felicity stamped her furious foot. 'You idiot!' she screamed, tears of furious anger now rolling down her plump face. 'You are nothing! Nothing! You and your pathetic, snivelling girl! I, on the other hand, could have been something – a great lady in a great house. I had it all planned. Every last bit of it . . . and now you – you—'

'Aye, miss,' sniffed Horace, shaking his head in mock sympathy, 'well you know what they say about the best laid plans.'

'Get out of my sight!' roared Felicity. 'Or I'll . . . I'll—'

'You'll what, miss?' cut in Horace calmly. 'Tell all these top-lofty folk here about how you paid me to lie with you? About how you wanted a babe so you could fob the poor child off as someone else's? Someone with a big fancy title and a big fancy house? Well, let me tell you something, *Miss Carmichael*, if you really are with child then it's mine all right and I'll fight you for it. Oh, I know I might not have a fancy title and a fancy house, but I have plenty of love to give it and *that* is something an evil little witch like you will never have.'

Quivering with frustration and anger and now conscious of the large, astounded crowd which had gathered around the pair, a tearful, snivelling Felicity, picked up her skirts and, holding her chin high, made her way through the crowd and towards the door. At exactly the same moment, Lady Carmichael collapsed in a heap on the floor in a very justifiable fit of the vapours.

'I thought you said that that man was your cousin, Lady Eleanor,' remarked a puzzled, and visibly relieved James as, having sought her out, he then proceeded to steer her out on to the terrace at the back of the house, away from all the drama inside.

'I did,' replied Eleanor, 'but only because I couldn't think of any other way to get him and Milly in here.'

'I see,' said James, as they reached a corner of the stone balustrade. 'And why exactly did you want to get him in here?'

'To stop Felicity blackmailing you, of course,' replied Eleanor matter-of-factly. She had her back to the balustrade and was aware that James was standing very close to her. She suddenly felt quite shy again.

He regarded her with a bemused smile. 'But how did you know she was?'

She raised her eyes to him and said sheepishly, 'I overheard her – on several occasions, sir. But I did not dare say anything to you because you have been rather . . . grumpy of late and besides, I didn't know what good it would do, you knowing that I knew.'

James shook his head, regarding her in amazement. 'I don't know how I can ever repay you for what you have done, Lady Eleanor. You really are an astonishing woman.'

This time she dared not look at his face but focused instead on the broadness of his chest which was level with her eyes. 'I believe you have bestowed that label upon me already, sir, in the orchard at Whitlock,' she almost whispered.

'Ah, yes,' said James softly, moving closer still. He raised a hand and trailed a finger down her soft cheek, causing Eleanor to tremble. 'And what was it we were talking about there,' he asked tenderly, 'before we were so rudely interrupted?'

His face was now so close to hers that his breath feathered across her skin, causing her heart to race uncontrollably.

'I believe I have quite forgotten, sir,' murmured Eleanor, closing her eyes and parting her lips in anticipation of his kiss.

'Then perhaps I should remind you,' whispered James.

The first time he had kissed her he had, quite literally taken her breath away. This time he took not only her breath but every single one of her senses. He started hesitantly at first, as if almost unsure of how she would react – his lips gently brushing against hers, teasing her, making her yearn for more. As he began probing the inside of her mouth with his tongue, deepening the kiss, she pressed her body unashamedly to his and emitted a small groan of pure pleasure.

'Marry me, Eleanor,' he murmured, as his lips briefly left hers. He gave her no chance to reply as he kissed her again, harder this time, wiping every other thought from her mind. She felt herself drowning in his lips, his arms, his words. Suddenly however, an image flashed through her mind – an image of the look she had seen him exchange earlier that evening with the Duchess of Swinton. The effect could not have been more explosive if someone had thrown a bucket of ice-cold water over her.

'No,' she said, pushing him away from her. 'I am sorry but I cannot marry you, sir,' and with that she picked up her skirts and marched back to the house, fighting back the tears burning her eyes.

Milly and Horace chattered all the way home in the carriage about the magnificence of the ball, the success of their plan and the reaction in the room once Felicity had left. Eleanor, however, heard not a word of it. She could think of nothing other than James and his proposal. She now knew that she loved the wretched man to complete and utter distraction but he had made no declaration of love for her. Obviously, he was only asking her to marry him because he felt obliged; because that was the only way he could think of repaying her for saving his life. Having witnessed his brief encounter with the duchess that evening, it was more than obvious where his true feelings lay.

# CHAPTER 22

FOR all it was only two months since Eleanor had left Merryoaks, it felt so very much longer. As soon as the house came into view – its golden bricks glowing welcomingly in the sunshine, surrounded by trees laden down with heavy pink cherry blossom, she knew immediately that she had made the right choice in coming home and declining the dowager's offer to accompany them all to Brighton. As well as having tired of all the endless, meaningless socializing, she could not bear the pain it would have caused her to set eyes upon James again.

Grateful that the house appeared unchanged, the same could not be said regarding her feelings for her objectionable stepmama. Much to Eleanor's disappointment, it was Hester who provided her 'welcome', storming into the entrance hall as she arrived and informing her that her father had had to go into town on some urgent business and would be back within the hour.

Having imparted that information, the woman then launched into a rather predictable diatribe, which Eleanor was both expecting and prepared for.

'Really, Eleanor,' she began, before the girl had even had time to remove her bonnet, 'words cannot express my disappointment. I had hoped that in London someone would take you. I mean, one hears of so many poor second sons who encounter such difficulties in finding a wife. Surely one of those would have been grateful for you.'

'I am not a horse looking for a new owner, madam,' replied Eleanor curtly, handing her bonnet to the butler.

Hester ignored her and began pacing frustratedly up and down the marble floor of the hall. 'But what of this viscount?' she enquired. 'You were most certain he was going to propose.'

'As indeed he did,' informed Eleanor, tugging an arm out of her pelisse. 'And I refused him.'

Hester stopped pacing and dramatically grabbed the back of a chair as if to steady herself 'Refused him?' she repeated incredulously. 'But how could you possibly. . . ? I mean why did you. . . ? Do you not know, girl, that beggars cannot be choosers?'

'I am not a beggar,' replied Eleanor stoutly, now handing her pelisse to the servant and dismissing him with a fleeting smile.

'Oh, I beg to differ,' countered Hester resuming her pacing. 'For if you cannot find a husband in London then where on earth do you think you are going to find one? They do not grow on trees, you know.'

Eleanor regarded her coolly. 'Then perhaps I shall never have one,' she declared blithely. 'I shall live out my days here with you and Papa.'

Hester stopped pacing and came to a halt directly in front of Eleanor, her face only inches away from the girl's. 'The only way you will do that, Eleanor,' she declared vehemently, 'is over my dead body.'

Eleanor smiled sweetly. 'I am quite sure that could be arranged, madam,' she pronounced, before picking up her skirts and heading towards the staircase.

Eleanor spent most of the next two days in her room. For all the weather was still glorious, she was in little mood for company and, particularly, Hester's incessant condemnations. Indeed she was feeling so low that even the pleasure of seeing her father again had failed to shake her melancholy.

This morning, she had positioned her armchair in front of the open latticed window and was attempting – rather unsuccessfully – to lose herself in a copy of Miss Austen's Mansfield Park. Annoyingly, unable to hold her concentration for more than a minute, she inevitably found herself staring into space as yet another image of James Prestonville invaded her thoughts. She had not seen the man since the evening of his proposal. He had not come home that night and she had done all she could not to think about where he was or who he was with. It had been bad enough imagining him with Lady Madeleine and that had been before she realized how much she loved him. To now imagine him with the Duchess of Swinton was more than she could bear.

A timid knock at the door intruded on her ruminations. 'Are you all right, my dear?' enquired her father concernedly.

She smiled to herself. At least here was someone who genuinely cared for her. 'Yes, Father,' she replied, with forced brightness. 'Come in.'

He entered the room, smiling warily. 'I've brought you a cup of tea,' he said, walking over to her and placing the cup and saucer on the pie-crust table in front of her.

217

'Thank you,' she replied, with a grateful smile. 'That's very kind.'

'Well, then,' he began rather awkwardly, sinking on to the small cushioned footstool at the opposite side of the table. 'You don't need to tell me what has caused this melancholy, but you do need to assure me that you really are all right.'

Unable to help herself, tears began silently streaming down Eleanor's face. 'I'm fine, Father, really I am.'

'You certainly have a strange way of showing it,' declared Lord Myers, shaking his head despairingly. 'I dread to think of the state you would be in if something *was* wrong.'

Eleanor flashed him a watery smile. 'I'm sorry. I don't mean to worry you.'

'Well, you do, my girl. A great deal,' he informed her, with mock severity. 'Oh, I know I don't understand much about matters of the heart – not in the same way your mother did – but I can see that someone or something has upset you and I would wager, knowing our ways, that it is most likely a man.'

Eleanor wiped away the tear that was midway down her cheek and pulled a rueful face. 'You are right, as ever, Father,' she confirmed, with a sniff. 'It is a man. But in a couple of days I shall be right as ninepence. I shall put him to the back of my mind and carry on exactly as I was before. As if I had never even met him.'

Lord Myers nodded his head in sympathetic agreement. 'Put him out of your head, eh? Well, yes, that's probably for the best. No doubt, like the rest of us, he's more bother than he's worth.'

'Indeed, he is,' she replied resolutely.

'And then you can spend the rest of your days here with Hester and me,' said Lord Myers, innocently. 'Won't that be delightful for you?'

'Indeed, it will,' replied Eleanor vehemently, pushing all thoughts of her own home, filled with love and children out of her mind.

'Very well then,' asserted Lord Myers, rising to his feet. 'You wipe this wretched man from your mind and we shall all carry on as though he doesn't exist. Agreed?' He held out a hand to her.

She reached out and shook the proffered hand with a hesitant smile. 'Agreed,' she said, wishing desperately that that were only possible.

Three days later and Eleanor's spirits had not lifted in the slightest, despite her father's valiant efforts to cheer her up.

'Any further forward with our little agreement?' he asked at breakfast that morning.

Eleanor shook her head. 'I'm afraid not, Father,' she said, pulling an apologetic face.

'I see,' said Lord Myers pensively, just as his new wife, burst – with uncharacteristic fervour – into the breakfast-room.

'Do I not have the most marvellous news, Husband,' she declared dramatically, marching across the room and claiming the seat opposite Lord Myers.

He raised his eyebrows. 'Really, my dear?' he replied flatly. 'And what would that be?'

'I have just heard that Kitty Osbourne's brother is to visit – Mr Jeremiah Osbourne. Is that not the best news ever?'

Lord Myers looked puzzled. 'I am sure Kitty is thrilled by it, my dear. But what pray has Mr Jeremiah Osbourne to do with us?'

Lady Myers rolled her eyes. 'Is it not obvious? He can marry Eleanor, of course,' she declared, matter-of-factly.

This time Lord Myers's eyes grew wide in his head. 'But if the man is of a similar age to Kitty, my dear, then he must be nearing sixty.'

'Nonsense,' scoffed Hester, waving a dismissive hand. 'He is only eight and fifty and quite respectable so I have heard. I believe he has fifteen thousand a year.'

Lord Myers looked unconvinced. 'Regardless, my dear,' he countered softly, 'I do think that eight and fifty is a little old for a girl of not yet twenty.'

'Poppycock,' declared Hester stoutly. 'The girl needs a mature man; someone experienced who can control her wilful ways. Mr Jeremiah Osbourne will be perfect. I have invited him to tea this very afternoon.'

Eleanor knew not at what hour Miss Kitty Osbourne and Mr Jeremiah Osbourne were expected at Merryoaks for tea. She had paid scant attention to Hester's twittering, having not the slightest interest in anything the spiteful woman said. At a little before three, however, while Eleanor was sitting in her room, making yet another futile attempt to read, Lord Myers sought out his daughter and informed her that he had a horse in dire need of exercise and would appreciate it greatly if Eleanor would take it out for a short ride. Aware that he could have asked any one of the grooms to perform such a task and that the request was therefore a thinly disguised ploy designed to get her out of the house and into the fresh air, she could not find it in her heart to refuse. Her father made no disguise of how worried he was about her and she had no desire to cause him even greater concern. She had therefore managed a fleeting smile and, having changed into her riding attire, had gone to the stables to collect the horse.

She followed her usual route along the banks of the river, having neither the strength nor the inclination to do anything other than hold the animal at a brisk trot. When she reached her favourite spot – a small circular clearing which awarded magnificent views of the surrounding countryside, she dismounted and tethered the horse to a tree before lying down on the carpet of emerald green grass, scattered with buttercups and daisies and staring up at the clear blue sky. Immediately a vision of James, lying on the grass in Paddy's Meadow with a blade of grass sticking out of his mouth, flashed through her mind. Was she to be plagued by thoughts of the man forever – it certainly felt like it when everything around her reminded her of him.

'Not fishing today I see, Lady Eleanor,' suddenly came a deep voice from behind her. Startled, she jerked up into a sitting position and swung her head around to see James walking towards her.

Her eyes grew wide in her head. 'You!' she exclaimed. 'But how . . . I mean . . . how on earth did you—?'

'Your father told me this was where you would stop.'

She screwed up her face, unable to believe what she was seeing or hearing. 'My father?' she stammered. 'But how did you—?'

James came to halt and sat down alongside her on the grass. 'It seems that your father is a very perceptive man, Lady Eleanor,' he declared, as he appeared to admire the view of the countryside.

'Perceptive?' queried Eleanor, regarding him quizzically.

'Indeed,' he continued, matter-of-factly, still not looking at her. 'Far cleverer than I for example, for he guessed immediately that it was I who organized the robbery of the Graysons' coach the day the viscount was supposed to propose to you.'

Eleanor's mouth dropped open. 'The coach? But I don't understand.'

'Don't you?' said James, suddenly turning his head to her and locking his dark eyes on to hers. 'I organized a distraction, Lady Eleanor, because I did not wish you to marry Viscount Grayson.'

She gasped loudly. 'But I never had any intention of marrying Viscount Grayson,' she declared candidly.

'And how, exactly, did you expect me to know that?' he asked bluntly. 'Every time anyone said anything the least bit derogatory about the man, you had an annoying habit of defending him.'

Eleanor emitted an embarrassed chuckle. 'Did I really?' she said. 'Well, I can assure you, sir, that if that was the case, it was more to protect my own pride, rather than the viscount's.'

James did not smile but continued to regard her gravely. 'So,' he continued, lowering his voice to a level of intimacy which sent her already racing heart beating even faster, 'I hear you have declined that man's offer too.'

She immediately averted her eyes from his and focused them instead on her riding boots. 'Indeed I have,' she muttered.

'So am I right in assuming you are still determined that you will never marry?' he asked softly.

She continued looking at her boots. 'I will never marry a man who does not love me, sir,' she declared, fervently.

'Then why on earth didn't you accept my proposal, Eleanor?' he asked in an incredulous tone.

She turned to look at him once more. 'Because it was made only out of obligation, sir. You felt that you had to propose to me because I had saved your life.'

James shook his head disbelievingly. 'I am extremely grateful, Eleanor, that you saved me not only from death, but from a fate much worse than death – marriage to Felicity Carmichael. But if you really believe that that is the reason I asked you to marry me, Eleanor, then you are—'

She averted her eyes back to her shoes. 'And because I know that you are still in love with the Duchess of Swinton,' she pronounced softly.

'The Duchess of Swinton?' he echoed in amazement. 'What on earth are you talking about?'

'I saw the way you looked at her at the masquerade ball,' confessed Eleanor.

He nodded his head. 'I see.'

Still staring at her feet, Eleanor stopped breathing for a moment, terrified of what he was going to say next. Terrified that the slight glimmer of hope she had felt at seeing him here was suddenly going to be extinguished forever by the information he chose to reveal with his next words.

There was a brief hiatus before he said, 'I trust you know that that liaison is now at an end?'

Eleanor nodded her head.

'I was forced to end it even though I had developed a deep . . . affection for the woman and she for me.'

'I see,' said Eleanor tersely, still refusing to look at him.

'Oh, I know it is wrong, ma'am,' said James, noting her disapproval, 'but hers was not a love match: it was a marriage of convenience. She is deeply unhappy with her husband.'

Eleanor tossed back her head haughtily. 'How very magnanimous of you, sir to cheer the woman up.'

'That is not what I meant, Eleanor,' he said smoothly. 'And talking of looks, for God's sake, haven't you noticed the way I look at *you*? I can barely take my eyes off you. I was very fond of the duchess but I was never in love with her. Not the way I love you.'

She jerked her head round to look at him. 'You love *me*? But you never said. I mean how can you—?'

'Oh, I can quite easily,' said James, moving closer to her. 'And I do. I love you to distraction, Eleanor Myers. I have been going out of my mind these last few days not knowing what to do. I thought you had not changed your mind – that you never wanted to marry and I had no wish to make another cake of myself in front of you again. You cannot even begin to imagine the relief I felt when I received your father's note.' He lifted his hand to her face, tilting it towards him. 'I can assure you, Eleanor,' he whispered, as he lowered his head to hers, 'that there are a great many women out there like the Duchess of Swinton, but you – you are something incredibly special.' He planted a tender kiss on her forehead. 'So beautiful.' He planted another on her cheek. 'So funny.' Another just brushed her lips. 'And so—'

'—unbecoming,' they both chorused together before breaking out into fits of laughter.

# CHAPTER 23

THE wedding of Lady Eleanor Jane Myers to James, newly appointed Duke of Ormiston, took place on a perfect July day by special licence in the same parish church in which the bride had been baptized some nineteen years and eight months earlier.

With the exception perhaps of the groom, the bride's father was the proudest man in the land as he escorted his beautiful, radiant daughter up the aisle followed by a beaming Milly Maguire looking pretty as a picture in her bridesmaid dress of exactly the same colour as the damask roses which filled the church.

'Of course I always knew that she would make such a good match,' Eleanor overheard her stepmama saying as she walked down the steps of the church on the arm of her new husband. 'Nothing but the best would do for her, I made sure of that.'

As bride and groom were reluctantly forced apart by their guests, all eager to pass on their congratulations, it was Hester's old Uncle Arthur who was the first to embrace her.

'I must admit, my girl,' he confessed cheerfully, 'I did have my doubts when Hester came up with that plan for me to feel your leg that evening – just before you went away, lass. Although she did make me an offer I couldn't refuse,' he concluded with a wink.

Eleanor gazed wide-eyed at him, as the meaning of what he had just said, sank in. 'You don't mean to tell me, Uncle Arthur,' she questioned, 'that Hester *bribed* you to feel my leg that evening?'

'Sworn to secrecy, I was,' replied the old man, tapping the side of his nose with a wrinkled finger, 'but let's just say, the bottles of whisky didn't half hit the spot. Hope it didn't get you into too much bother, girl.'

Eleanor looked at James, her new husband, chatting merrily with Zach, the farmer, and felt her heart swell with love. 'No, Uncle Arthur,' she replied, slipping her arm through his. 'No bother at all.'